I0762926

CLASSIC Princess Fairy Tales

HANS CHRISTIAN
ANDERSEN

TRANSLATED BY J. H. STICKNEY
ILLUSTRATED BY J.R. WEGUELIN

Copyright © 2026 by Harper Muse

All rights reserved. No portion of this book may be reproduced, stored in a retrieval system, or transmitted in any form or by any means—electronic, mechanical, photocopy, recording, scanning, or other—except for brief quotations in critical reviews or articles, without the prior written permission of the publisher.

Published by Harper Muse, an imprint of HarperCollins Focus LLC, 501 Nelson Place, Nashville, TN 37214, USA.

This book is a work of fiction. The characters, incidents, and dialogue are drawn from the author's imagination and are not to be construed as real. Any resemblance to actual events or persons, living or dead, is entirely coincidental.

ISBN 978-1-4003-5572-3 (HC)
Without limiting the exclusive rights of any author, contributor or the publisher of this publication, any unauthorized use of this publication to train generative artificial intelligence (AI) technologies is expressly prohibited. HarperCollins also exercise their rights under Article 4(3) of the Digital Single Market Directive 2019/790 and expressly reserve this publication from the text and data mining exception.

HarperCollins Publishers, Macken House, 39/40 Mayor Street Upper, Dublin 1, D01 C9W8, Ireland (https://www.harpercollins.com)

Printed in Vietnam

26 27 28 29 30 31 32 33 34 35 36 37 38 / RRD / 16 15 14 13 12 11 10 9 8 7 6 5 4 3 2 1

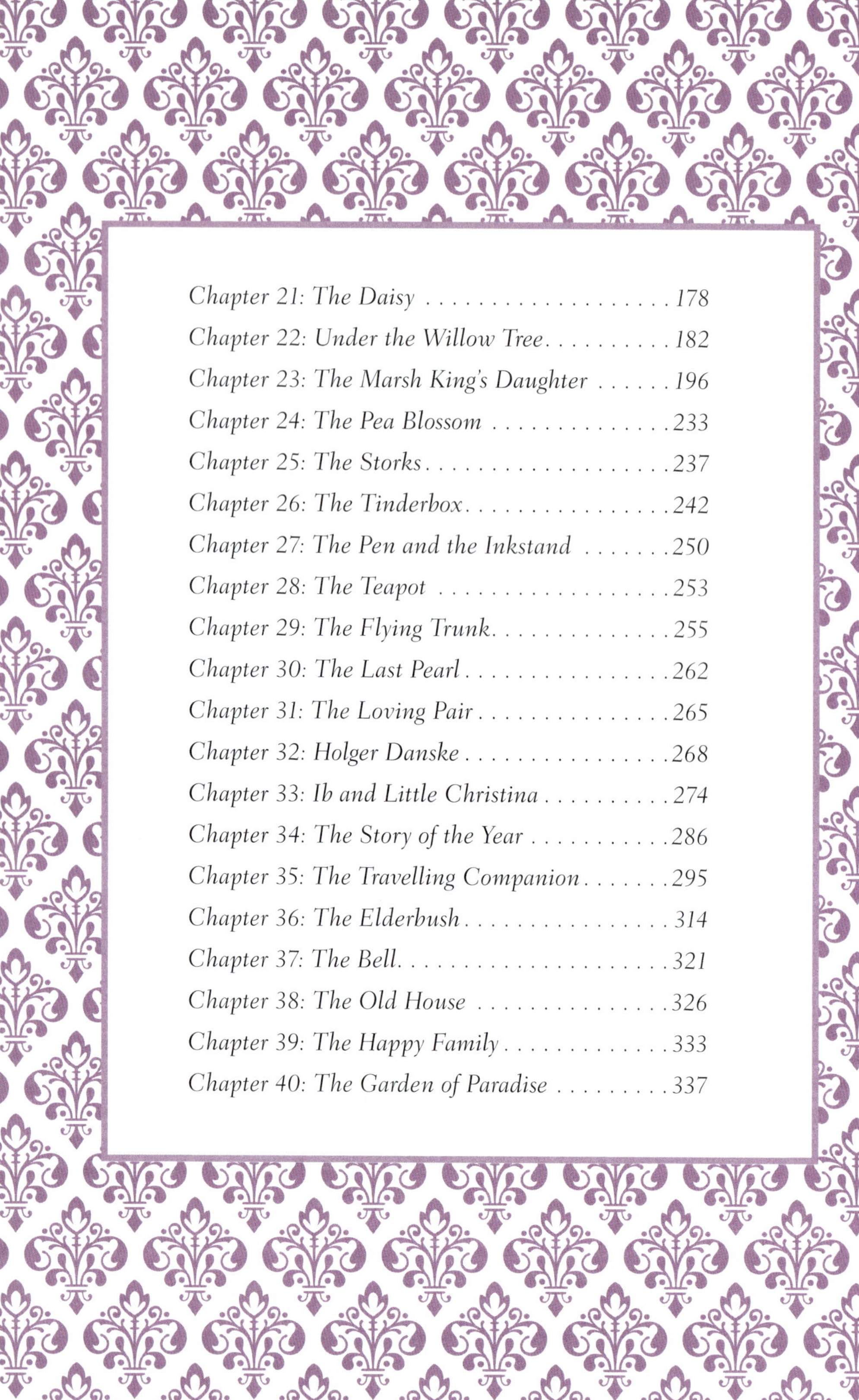

These tales are presented as Hans Christian Andersen first wrote them in the nineteenth century. While originally written for children, many are darker and more morally complex than the happier versions found in modern retellings. We encourage you to read and enjoy them with that context in mind.

Introduction

The Hans Andersen Fairy Tales will be read in schools and homes as long as there are children who love to read. As a storyteller for children the author has no rival in power to enlist the imagination and carry it along natural, healthful lines. The power of his tales to charm and elevate runs like a living thread through whatever he writes. These stories in which they are presented here have met the tests and held an undiminishing popularity among the best children's books. They are recognized as standards, and as juvenile writings come to be more carefully standardized, their place in permanent literature will grow wider and more secure. A few children's authors will be ranked among the Immortals, and Hans Andersen is one of them.

Denmark and Finland supplied the natural background for the quaint fancies and growing genius of their gifted son, who was storyteller, playwright, and poet in one. Love of nature, love of country, fellow-feeling with life in everything, and a wonderful gift for investing everything with life wrought together to produce in him a character whose spell is in all his writings. "The Story of My Life" is perhaps the most thrilling of all of them. Recognized in courts of kings and castles of nobles, he recited his little stories with the same simplicity by which he had made them familiar in cottages of the peasantry, and endeared himself alike to all who listened. These attributes, while they do not account for his genius, help us to unravel the charm of it. The simplest of the stories meet Ruskin's requirement for a child's story—they are sweet and sad.

From most writers who have contributed largely to children's literature only a few selected gems are likely to gain permanence. With Andersen the case is different. While there are such gems, the greater value lies in taking these stories as a type of literature and living in it a while, through the power of cumulative reading. It is not too much to say that there is a temper and spirit in Andersen which is all his own—a simple philosophy which continuous reading is sure to impart. For this reason these are good books for a child to own; an occasional rereading will inspire in him a healthy, normal taste in reading. Many of the stories are of value to read to very young children. They guide an exuberant imagination along natural channels.

The text of the present edition is a reprint of an earlier one which was based upon a sentence-by-sentence comparison of the four or five translations current in Europe and America. It has been widely commended as enjoyable reading, while faithful to the letter and spirit of the Danish original. This book is also full of lovely illustrations that bring Andersen's world to life. Look closely at the pictures as you read. You'll see the icy beauty of the Snow Queen's palace, the ocean where the Little Mermaid swims, and the soft feathers of a swan taking flight. These drawings show how Andersen imagined his magical tales.

Get ready to go on an adventure. Picture the magical places, feel the emotions, and step into a world where anything is possible. Whether you read these stories by yourself or with a loved one, you're about to enjoy tales that have inspired people for years.

Excitement, magic, and wonder are waiting for you in every story.

J. H. Stickney

Little Tiny or Thumbelina

There was once a woman who wished very much to have a little child, but she could not obtain her wish. At last she went to a fairy, and said, "I should so very much like to have a little child; can you tell me where I can find one?"

"Oh, that can be easily managed," said the fairy. "Here is a barleycorn of a different kind to those which grow in the farmer's fields, and which the chickens eat; put it into a flowerpot, and see what will happen."

"Thank you," said the woman, and she gave the fairy twelve shillings, which was the price of the barleycorn. Then she went home and planted it, and immediately there grew up a large handsome flower, something like a tulip in appearance, but with its leaves tightly closed as if it were still a bud. "It is a beautiful flower," said the woman, and she kissed the red and golden-colored leaves, and while she did so the flower opened, and she could see that it was a real tulip. Within the flower, upon the green velvet stamens, sat a very delicate and graceful little maiden. She was scarcely half as long as a thumb, and they gave her the name of "Thumbelina," or Tiny, because she was so small. A walnut shell, elegantly polished, served her for a cradle; her bed was formed of blue violet leaves, with a roseleaf for a counterpane. Here she slept at night, but during the day she amused herself on a table, where the woman had placed a plateful of water. Round this plate were wreaths of flowers with their stems in the water, and upon it floated a large tulip leaf, which served Tiny for a boat. Here the little maiden sat and rowed herself from side to side, with two oars made of white horsehair. It really was a very pretty sight. Tiny could, also, sing so softly and sweetly that nothing like her singing had ever before been heard. One night, while she lay in her pretty bed, a large, ugly, wet toad crept through a broken pane of glass in the window, and leaped right upon the table where Tiny lay sleeping under her rose leaf quilt.

"What a pretty little wife this would make for my son," said the toad, and she took up the walnut shell in which little Tiny lay asleep, and jumped through the window with it into the garden.

In the swampy margin of a broad stream in the garden lived the toad, with her son. He was uglier even than his mother, and when he saw the pretty little maiden in her elegant bed, he could only cry, "Croak, croak, croak."

"Don't speak so loud, or she will wake," said the toad, "and then she might run away, for she is as light as swan's down. We will place her on one of the waterlily leaves out in the stream; it will be like an island to her, she is so light and small, and then she cannot escape; and, while she is away, we will make haste and prepare the stateroom under the marsh, in which you are to live when you are married."

Far out in the stream grew a number of waterlilies, with broad green leaves, which seemed to float on the top of the water. The largest of these leaves appeared farther off than the rest, and the old toad swam out to it with the walnut shell, in which little Tiny lay still asleep. The tiny little creature woke very early in the morning, and began to cry bitterly when she found where she was, for she could see nothing but water on every side of the large green leaf, and no way of reaching the land. Meanwhile the old toad was very busy under the marsh, decking her room with rushes and wild yellow flowers, to make it look pretty for her new daughter-in-law. Then she swam out with her ugly son to the leaf on which she had placed poor little Tiny. She wanted to fetch the pretty bed, that she might put it in the bridal chamber to be ready for her. The old toad bowed low to her in the water, and said, "Here is my son, he will be your husband, and you will live happily in the marsh by the stream."

"Croak, croak, croak," was all her son could say for himself; so the toad took up the elegant little bed, and swam away with it, leaving Tiny all alone on the green leaf, where she sat and wept. She could not bear to think of living with the old toad, and having her ugly son for a husband. The little fishes, who swam about in the water beneath, had seen the toad, and heard what she said, so they lifted their heads above the water to look at the little maiden. As soon as they caught sight of her, they saw she was very pretty, and it made them very sorry to think that she must go and live with the ugly toads. "No, it must never be!" so they assembled together in the water, round the green stalk which held the leaf on which the little maiden stood, and gnawed it away at the root with their teeth. Then the leaf floated down the stream, carrying Tiny far away out of reach of land.

Tiny sailed past many towns, and the little birds in the bushes saw her, and sang, "What a lovely little creature;" so the leaf swam away with her farther and farther, till it brought her to other lands. A graceful little white butterfly constantly fluttered round her, and at last alighted on the leaf. Tiny pleased him, and she was glad of it, for now the toad could not possibly reach her, and the country through which she sailed was beautiful, and the sun shone upon the water, till it glittered like liquid gold. She took off her girdle and tied one end of it round the butterfly, and the other end of the ribbon she fastened to the leaf, which now glided on much faster than ever, taking little Tiny with it as she stood. Presently a large cockchafer flew by; the moment he caught sight of her, he seized her round her delicate waist with his claws, and flew with her into a tree. The green leaf floated away on the brook, and the butterfly flew with it, for he was fastened to it, and could not get away.

Oh, how frightened little Tiny felt when the cockchafer flew with her to the tree! But especially was she sorry for the beautiful white butterfly which she had fastened to the leaf, for if he could not free himself he would die of hunger. But the cockchafer did not trouble himself at all about the matter. He seated himself by her side on a large green leaf, gave her some honey from the flowers to eat, and told her she was very pretty, though not in the least like a cockchafer. After a time, all the cockchafers turned up their feelers, and said, "She has only two legs! how ugly that looks." "She has no feelers," said another. "Her waist is quite slim. Pooh! she is like a human being."

"Oh! she is ugly," said all the lady cockchafers, although Tiny was very pretty. Then the cockchafer who had run away with her, believed all the others when they said she was ugly, and would have nothing more to say to her, and told her she might go where she liked. Then he flew down with her from the tree, and placed her on a daisy, and she wept at the thought that she was so ugly that even the cockchafers would have nothing to say to her. And all the while she was really the loveliest creature that one could imagine, and as tender and delicate as a beautiful roseleaf. During the whole summer poor little Tiny lived quite alone in the wide forest. She wove herself a bed with blades of grass, and hung it up under a broad leaf, to protect herself from the rain. She sucked the honey from the flowers for food, and drank the dew from their leaves every morning. So passed away the summer and the autumn, and then came the winter—the long, cold winter. All the birds who had sung to her so sweetly were flown away, and the trees and the flowers had withered. The large clover leaf under the shelter of which she had lived, was now rolled together and shrivelled up, nothing remained but a yellow withered stalk. She felt dreadfully cold, for her clothes were torn, and she was herself so frail and delicate, that poor little Tiny was nearly frozen to death. It began to snow too; and the snowflakes, as they fell upon her, were like a whole shovelful falling upon one of us, for we are tall, but she was only an inch high. Then she wrapped herself up in a dry leaf, but it cracked in the middle and could not keep her warm, and she shivered with cold. Near the wood in which she had been living lay a cornfield, but the corn had been cut a long time; nothing remained but the bare dry stubble standing up out of the frozen ground. It was to her like struggling through a large wood. Oh! how she shivered with the cold. She came at last to the door of a fieldmouse, who had a little den under the corn-stubble. There dwelt the fieldmouse in warmth and comfort, with a whole roomful of corn, a kitchen, and a beautiful dining room. Poor little Tiny stood before the door just like a little beggar-girl, and begged for a small piece of barleycorn, for she had been without a morsel to eat for two days.

"You poor little creature," said the fieldmouse, who was really a good old fieldmouse, "come into my warm room and dine with me." She was very pleased with Tiny, so she said, "You are quite welcome to stay with me all the winter, if you like; but you must keep my rooms clean and neat, and tell me stories, for I shall like to hear them very much." And Tiny did all the fieldmouse asked her, and found herself very comfortable.

"We shall have a visitor soon," said the fieldmouse one day; "my neighbor pays me a visit once a week. He is better off than I am; he has large rooms, and wears a beautiful black velvet coat. If you could only have him for a husband, you would be well provided for indeed. But he is blind, so you must tell him some of your prettiest stories."

But Tiny did not feel at all interested about this neighbor, for he was a mole. However, he came and paid his visit dressed in his black velvet coat.

"He is very rich and learned, and his house is twenty times larger than mine," said the fieldmouse.

He was rich and learned, no doubt, but he always spoke slightingly of the sun and the pretty flowers, because he had never seen them. Tiny was obliged to sing to him, "Ladybird, ladybird, fly away home," and many other pretty songs. And the mole fell in love with her because she had such a sweet voice; but he said nothing yet, for he was very cautious. A short time before, the mole had dug a long passage under the earth, which led from the dwelling of the fieldmouse to his own, and here she had permission to walk with Tiny whenever she liked. But he warned them not to be alarmed at the sight of a dead bird which lay in the passage. It was a perfect bird, with a beak and feathers, and could not have been dead long, and was lying just where the mole had made his passage. The mole took a piece of phosphorescent wood in his mouth, and it glittered like fire in the dark; then he went before them to light them through the long, dark passage. When they came to the spot where lay the dead bird, the mole pushed his broad nose through the ceiling, the earth gave way, so that there was a large hole, and the daylight shone into the passage. In the middle of the floor lay a dead swallow, his beautiful wings pulled close to his sides, his feet and his head drawn up under his feathers; the poor bird had evidently died of the cold. It made little Tiny very sad to see it, she did so love the little birds; all the summer they had sung and twittered for her so beautifully. But the mole pushed it aside with his crooked legs, and said, "He will sing no more now. How miserable it must be to be born a little bird! I am thankful that none of my children will ever be birds, for they can do nothing but cry, 'Tweet, tweet,' and always die of hunger in the winter."

"Yes, you may well say that, as a clever man!" exclaimed the field-mouse, "What is the use of his twittering, for when winter comes he must either starve or be frozen to death. Still birds are very high bred."

Tiny said nothing; but when the two others had turned their backs on the bird, she stooped down and stroked aside the soft feathers which covered the head, and kissed the closed eyelids. "Perhaps this was the one who sang to me so sweetly in the summer," she said; "and how much pleasure it gave me, you dear, pretty bird."

The mole now stopped up the hole through which the daylight shone, and then accompanied the lady home. But during the night Tiny could not sleep; so she got out of bed and wove a large, beautiful carpet of hay; then she carried it to the dead bird, and spread it over him; with some down from the flowers which she had found in the fieldmouse's room. It was as soft as wool, and she spread some of it on each side of the bird, so that he might lie warmly in the cold earth. "Farewell, you pretty little bird," said she, "farewell; thank you for your delightful singing during the summer, when all the trees were green, and the warm sun shone upon us." Then she laid her head on the bird's breast, but she was alarmed immediately, for it seemed as if something inside the bird went "thump, thump." It was the bird's heart; he was not really dead, only benumbed with the cold, and the warmth had restored him to life. In autumn, all the swallows fly away into warm countries, but if one happens to linger, the cold seizes it, it becomes frozen, and falls down as if dead; it remains where it fell, and the cold snow covers it. Tiny trembled very much; she was quite frightened, for the bird was large, a great deal larger than herself—she was only an inch high. But she took courage, laid the wool more thickly over the poor swallow, and then took a leaf which she had used for her own counterpane, and laid it over the head of the poor bird. The next morning she again stole out to see him. He was alive but very weak; he could only open his eyes for a moment to look at Tiny, who stood by holding a piece of decayed wood in her hand, for she had no other lantern. "Thank you, pretty little maiden," said the sick swallow; "I have been so nicely warmed, that I shall soon regain my strength, and be able to fly about again in the warm sunshine."

"Oh," said she, "it is cold out of doors now; it snows and freezes. Stay in your warm bed; I will take care of you."

Then she brought the swallow some water in a flower leaf, and after he had drank, he told her that he had wounded one of his wings in a thornbush, and could not fly as fast as the others, who were soon far away on their journey to warm countries. Then at last he had fallen to the earth, and could remember no more, nor how he came to be where she had found him. The whole winter the swallow remained underground, and Tiny nursed him with care and love. Neither the mole nor the fieldmouse knew anything about it, for they did not like swallows. Very soon the springtime came, and the sun warmed the earth. Then the swallow bade farewell to Tiny, and she opened the hole in the ceiling which the mole had made. The sun shone in upon them so beautifully, that the swallow asked her if she would go with him; she could sit on his back, he said, and he would fly away with her into the green woods. But Tiny knew it would make the fieldmouse very grieved if she left her in that manner, so she said, "No, I cannot."

"Farewell, then, farewell, you good, pretty little maiden," said the swallow; and he flew out into the sunshine.

Tiny looked after him, and the tears rose in her eyes. She was very fond of the poor swallow.

"Tweet, tweet," sang the bird, as he flew out into the green woods, and Tiny felt very sad. She was not allowed to go out into the warm sunshine. The corn which had been sown in the field over the house of the fieldmouse had grown up high into the air, and formed a thick wood to Tiny, who was only an inch in height.

"You are going to be married, Tiny," said the fieldmouse. "My neighbor has asked for you. What good fortune for a poor child like you. Now we will prepare your wedding clothes. They must be both woollen and linen. Nothing must be wanting when you are the mole's wife."

Tiny had to turn the spindle, and the fieldmouse hired four spiders, who were to weave day and night. Every evening the mole visited her, and was continually speaking of the time when the summer would be over. Then he would keep his wedding day with Tiny; but now the heat of the sun was so great that it burned the earth, and made it quite hard, like a stone. As soon as the summer was over, the wedding should take place. But Tiny was not at all pleased; for she did not like the tiresome mole.

Every morning when the sun rose, and every evening when it went down, she would creep out at the door, and as the wind blew aside the ears of corn, so that she could see the blue sky, she thought how beautiful and bright it seemed out there, and wished so much to see her dear swallow again. But he never returned; for by this time he had flown far away into the lovely green forest.

When autumn arrived, Tiny had her outfit quite ready; and the fieldmouse said to her, "In four weeks the wedding must take place."

Then Tiny wept, and said she would not marry the disagreeable mole.

"Nonsense," replied the fieldmouse. "Now don't be obstinate, or I shall bite you with my white teeth. He is a very handsome mole; the queen herself does not wear more beautiful velvets and furs. His kitchen and cellars are quite full. You ought to be very thankful for such good fortune."

So the wedding day was fixed, on which the mole was to fetch Tiny away to live with him, deep under the earth, and never again to see the warm sun, because he did not like it. The poor child was very unhappy at the thought of saying farewell to the beautiful sun, and as the fieldmouse had given her permission to stand at the door, she went to look at it once more.

"Farewell bright sun," she cried, stretching out her arm towards it; and then she walked a short distance from the house; for the corn had been cut, and only the dry stubble remained in the fields. "Farewell, farewell," she repeated, twining her arm round a little red flower that grew just by her side. "Greet the little swallow from me, if you should see him again."

"Tweet, tweet," sounded over her head suddenly. She looked up, and there was the swallow himself flying close by. As soon as he spied Tiny, he was delighted; and then she told him how unwilling she felt to marry the ugly mole, and to live always beneath the earth, and never to see the bright sun anymore. And as she told him she wept.

"Cold winter is coming," said the swallow, "and I am going to fly away into warmer countries. Will you go with me? You can sit on my back, and fasten yourself on with your sash. Then we can fly away from the ugly mole and his gloomy rooms—far away, over the mountains, into warmer countries, where the sun shines more brightly—than here; where it is always summer, and the flowers bloom in greater beauty.

Fly now with me, dear little Tiny; you saved my life when I lay frozen in that dark passage."

"Yes, I will go with you," said Tiny; and she seated herself on the bird's back, with her feet on his outstretched wings, and tied her girdle to one of his strongest feathers.

Then the swallow rose in the air, and flew over forest and over sea, high above the highest mountains, covered with eternal snow. Tiny would have been frozen in the cold air, but she crept under the bird's warm feathers, keeping her little head uncovered, so that she might admire the beautiful lands over which they passed. At length they reached the warm countries, where the sun shines brightly, and the sky seems so much higher above the earth. Here, on the hedges, and by the wayside, grew purple, green, and white grapes; lemons and oranges hung from trees in the woods; and the air was fragrant with myrtles and orange blossoms. Beautiful children ran along the country lanes, playing with large gay butterflies; and as the swallow flew farther and farther, every place appeared still more lovely.

At last they came to a blue lake, and by the side of it, shaded by trees of the deepest green, stood a palace of dazzling white marble, built in the olden times. Vines clustered round its lofty pillars, and at the top were many swallows' nests, and one of these was the home of the swallow who carried Tiny.

"This is my house," said the swallow; "but it would not do for you to live there—you would not be comfortable. You must choose for yourself one of those lovely flowers, and I will put you down upon it, and then you shall have everything that you can wish to make you happy."

"That will be delightful," she said, and clapped her little hands for joy.

A large marble pillar lay on the ground, which, in falling, had been broken into three pieces. Between these pieces grew the most beautiful large white flowers; so the swallow flew down with Tiny, and placed her on one of the broad leaves. But how surprised she was to see in the middle of the flower, a tiny little man, as white and transparent as if he had been made of crystal! He had a gold crown on his head, and delicate wings at his shoulders, and was not much larger than Tiny herself. He was the angel of the flower; for a tiny man and a tiny woman dwell in every flower; and this was the king of them all.

"Oh, how beautiful he is!" whispered Tiny to the swallow.

The little prince was at first quite frightened at the bird, who was like a giant, compared to such a delicate little creature as himself; but when he saw Tiny, he was delighted, and thought her the prettiest little maiden he had ever seen. He took the gold crown from his head, and placed it on hers, and asked her name, and if she would be his wife, and queen over all the flowers.

This certainly was a very different sort of husband to the son of a toad, or the mole, with his black velvet and fur; so she said, "Yes," to the handsome prince. Then all the flowers opened, and out of each came a little lady or a tiny lord, all so pretty it was quite a pleasure to look at them. Each of them brought Tiny a present; but the best gift was a pair of beautiful wings, which had belonged to a large white fly and they fastened them to Tiny's shoulders, so that she might fly from flower to flower. Then there was much rejoicing, and the little swallow who sat above them, in his nest, was asked to sing a wedding song, which he did as well as he could; but in his heart he felt sad for he was very fond of Tiny, and would have liked never to part from her again.

"You must not be called Tiny anymore," said the spirit of the flowers to her. "It is an ugly name, and you are so very pretty. We will call you Maia."

"Farewell, farewell," said the swallow, with a heavy heart as he left the warm countries to fly back into Denmark. There he had a nest over the window of a house in which dwelt the writer of fairy tales. The swallow sang, "Tweet, tweet," and from his song came the whole story.

The Little Mermaid

Far out in the ocean, where the water is as blue as the prettiest cornflower, and as clear as crystal, it is very, very deep; so deep, indeed, that no cable could fathom it: many church steeples, piled one upon another, would not reach from the ground beneath to the surface of the water above. There dwell the Sea King and his subjects. We must not imagine that there is nothing at the bottom of the sea but bare yellow sand. No, indeed; the most singular flowers and plants grow there; the leaves and stems of which are so pliant, that the slightest agitation of the water causes them to stir as if they had life. Fishes, both large and small, glide between the branches, as birds fly among the trees here upon land. In the deepest spot of all, stands the castle of the Sea King. Its walls are built of coral, and the long, gothic windows are of the clearest amber. The roof is formed of shells, that open and close as the water flows over them. Their appearance is very beautiful, for in each lies a glittering pearl, which would be fit for the diadem of a queen.

The Sea King had been a widower for many years, and his aged mother kept house for him. She was a very wise woman, and exceedingly proud of her high birth; on that account she wore twelve oysters on her tail; while others, also of high rank, were only allowed to wear six. She was, however, deserving of very great praise, especially for her care of the little sea-princesses, her granddaughters. They were six beautiful children; but the youngest was the prettiest of them all; her skin was as clear and delicate as a roseleaf, and her eyes as blue as the deepest sea; but, like all the others, she had no feet, and her body ended in a fish's tail. All day long they played in the great halls of the castle, or among the living flowers that grew out of the walls. The large amber windows were open, and the fish swam in, just as the swallows fly into our houses when we open the windows, excepting that the fishes swam up to the princesses, ate out of their hands, and allowed themselves to be stroked. Outside the castle there was a beautiful garden, in which grew bright red and dark blue flowers, and blossoms like flames of fire; the fruit glittered like gold, and the leaves and stems waved to and fro continually. The earth itself was the finest sand, but blue as the flame of burning sulphur. Over everything lay a peculiar blue radiance, as if it were surrounded by the air from above, through which the blue sky shone, instead of the dark depths of the sea. In calm weather the sun could be seen, looking like a purple flower, with the light streaming from the calyx. Each of the young princesses had a little plot of ground in the garden, where she might dig and plant as she pleased. One arranged her flowerbed into the form of a whale; another thought it better to make hers like the figure of a little mermaid; but that of the youngest was round like the sun, and contained flowers as red as his rays at sunset.

She was a strange child, quiet and thoughtful; and while her sisters would be delighted with the wonderful things which they obtained from the wrecks of vessels, she cared for nothing but her pretty red flowers, like the sun, excepting a beautiful marble statue. It was the representation of a handsome boy, carved out of pure white stone, which had fallen to the bottom of the sea from a wreck. She planted by the statue a rose-colored weeping willow. It grew splendidly, and very soon hung its fresh branches over the statue, almost down to the blue sands. The shadow had a violet tint, and waved to and fro like the branches; it seemed as if the crown of the tree and the root were at play, and trying to kiss each other. Nothing gave her so much pleasure as to hear about the world above the sea. She made her old grandmother tell her all she knew of the ships and of the towns, the people and the animals. To her it seemed most wonderful and beautiful to hear that the flowers of the land should have fragrance, and not those below the sea; that the trees of the forest should be green; and that the fishes among the trees could sing so sweetly, that it was quite a pleasure to hear them. Her grandmother called the little birds fishes, or she would not have understood her; for she had never seen birds.

"When you have reached your fifteenth year," said the grandmother, "you will have permission to rise up out of the sea, to sit on the rocks in the moonlight, while the great ships are sailing by; and then you will see both forests and towns."

In the following year, one of the sisters would be fifteen: but as each was a year younger than the other, the youngest would have to wait five years before her turn came to rise up from the bottom of the ocean, and see the earth as we do. However, each promised to tell the others what she saw on her first visit, and what she thought the most beautiful; for their grandmother could not tell them enough; there were so many things on which they wanted information. None of them longed so much for her turn to come as the youngest, she who had the longest time to wait, and who was so quiet and thoughtful. Many nights she stood by the open window, looking up through the dark blue water, and watching the fish as they splashed about with their fins and tails. She could see the moon and stars shining faintly; but through the water they looked larger than they do to our eyes. When something like a black cloud passed between her and them, she knew that it was either a whale swimming over her head, or a ship full of human beings, who never imagined that a pretty little mermaid was standing beneath them, holding out her white hands towards the keel of their ship.

As soon as the eldest was fifteen, she was allowed to rise to the surface of the ocean. When she came back, she had hundreds of things to talk about; but the most beautiful, she said, was to lie in the moonlight, on a sandbank, in the quiet sea, near the coast, and to gaze on a large town nearby, where the lights were twinkling like hundreds of stars; to listen to the sounds of the music, the noise of carriages, and the voices of human beings, and then to hear the merry bells peal out from the church steeples; and because she could not go near to all those wonderful things, she longed for them more than ever. Oh, did not the youngest sister listen eagerly to all these descriptions? and afterwards, when she stood at the open window looking up through the dark blue water, she thought of the great city, with all its bustle and noise, and even fancied she could hear the sound of the church bells, down in the depths of the sea.

In another year the second sister received permission to rise to the surface of the water, and to swim about where she pleased. She rose just as the sun was setting, and this, she said, was the most beautiful sight of all. The whole sky looked like gold, while violet and rose-colored clouds, which she could not describe, floated over her; and, still more rapidly than the clouds, flew a large flock of wild swans towards the setting sun, looking like a long white veil across the sea. She also swam towards the sun; but it sunk into the waves, and the rosy tints faded from the clouds and from the sea.

The third sister's turn followed; she was the boldest of them all, and she swam up a broad river that emptied itself into the sea. On the banks she saw green hills covered with beautiful vines; palaces and castles peeped out from amid the proud trees of the forest; she heard the birds singing, and the rays of the sun were so powerful that she was obliged often to dive down under the water to cool her burning face. In a narrow creek she found a whole troop of little human children, quite naked, and sporting about in the water; she wanted to play with them, but they fled in a great fright; and then a little black animal came to the water; it was a dog, but she did not know that, for she had never before seen one. This animal barked at her so terribly that she became frightened, and rushed back to the open sea. But she said she should never forget the beautiful forest, the green hills, and the pretty little children who could swim in the water, although they had not fish's tails.

The fourth sister was more timid; she remained in the midst of the sea, but she said it was quite as beautiful there as nearer the land. She could see for so many miles around her, and the sky above looked like a bell of glass. She had seen the ships, but at such a great distance that they looked like seagulls. The dolphins sported in the waves, and the great whales spouted water from their nostrils till it seemed as if a hundred fountains were playing in every direction.

The fifth sister's birthday occurred in the winter; so when her turn came, she saw what the others had not seen the first time they went up. The sea looked quite green, and large icebergs were floating about, each like a pearl, she said, but larger and loftier than the churches built by men. They were of the most singular shapes, and glittered like diamonds. She had seated herself upon one of the largest, and let the wind play with her long hair, and she remarked that all the ships sailed by rapidly, and steered as far away as they could from the iceberg, as if they were afraid of it. Towards evening, as the sun went down, dark clouds covered the sky, the thunder rolled and the lightning flashed, and the red light glowed on the icebergs as they rocked and tossed on the heaving sea. On all the ships the sails were reefed with fear and trembling, while she sat calmly on the floating iceberg, watching the blue lightning, as it darted its forked flashes into the sea.

When first the sisters had permission to rise to the surface, they were each delighted with the new and beautiful sights they saw; but now, as grown-up girls, they could go when they pleased, and they had become indifferent about it. They wished themselves back again in the water, and after a month had passed they said it was much more beautiful down below, and pleasanter to be at home.

Yet often, in the evening hours, the five sisters would twine their arms round each other, and rise to the surface, in a row. They had more beautiful voices than any human being could have; and before the approach of a storm, and when they expected a ship would be lost, they swam before the vessel, and sang sweetly of the delights to be found in the depths of the sea, and begging the sailors not to fear if they sank to the bottom. But the sailors could not understand the song, they took it for the howling of the storm. And these things were never to be beautiful for them; for if the ship sank, the men were drowned, and their dead bodies alone reached the palace of the Sea King.

When the sisters rose, arm-in-arm, through the water in this way, their youngest sister would stand quite alone, looking after them, ready to cry, only that the mermaids have no tears, and therefore they suffer more. "Oh, were I but fifteen years old," said she: "I know that I shall love the world up there, and all the people who live in it."

At last she reached her fifteenth year. "Well, now, you are grown up," said the old dowager, her grandmother; "so you must let me adorn you like your other sisters;" and she placed a wreath of white lilies in her hair, and every flower leaf was half a pearl. Then the old lady ordered eight great oysters to attach themselves to the tail of the princess to show her high rank.

"But they hurt me so," said the little mermaid.

"Pride must suffer pain," replied the old lady. Oh, how gladly she would have shaken off all this grandeur, and laid aside the heavy wreath! The red flowers in her own garden would have suited her much better, but she could not help herself: so she said, "Farewell," and rose as lightly as a bubble to the surface of the water. The sun had just set as she raised her head above the waves; but the clouds were tinted with crimson and gold, and through the glimmering twilight beamed the evening star in all its beauty. The sea was calm, and the air mild and fresh. A large ship, with three masts, lay becalmed on the water, with only one sail set; for not a breeze stiffed, and the sailors sat idle on deck or amongst the rigging. There was music and song on board; and, as darkness came on, a hundred colored lanterns were lighted, as if the flags of all nations waved in the air. The little mermaid swam close to the cabin windows; and now and then, as the waves lifted her up, she could look in through clear glass windowpanes, and see a number of well-dressed people within. Among them was a young prince, the most beautiful of all, with large black eyes; he was sixteen years of age, and his birthday was being kept with much rejoicing. The sailors were dancing on deck, but when the prince came out of the cabin, more than a hundred rockets rose in the air, making it as bright as day. The little mermaid was so startled that she dived under water; and when she again stretched out her head, it appeared as if all the stars of heaven were falling around her, she had never seen such fireworks before. Great suns spurted fire about, splendid fireflies flew into the blue air, and everything was reflected in the clear, calm sea beneath. The ship itself was so brightly illuminated that all the people, and even the smallest rope, could be distinctly and plainly seen. And how handsome the young prince looked, as he pressed the hands of all present and smiled at them, while the music resounded through the clear night air.

It was very late; yet the little mermaid could not take her eyes from the ship, or from the beautiful prince. The colored lanterns had been extinguished, no more rockets rose in the air, and the cannon had ceased firing; but the sea became restless, and a moaning, grumbling sound could be heard beneath the waves: still the little mermaid remained by the cabin window, rocking up and down on the water, which enabled her to look in. After a while, the sails were quickly unfurled, and the noble ship continued her passage; but soon the waves rose higher, heavy clouds darkened the sky, and lightning appeared in the distance. A dreadful storm was approaching; once more the sails were reefed, and the great ship pursued her flying course over the raging sea. The waves rose mountains high, as if they would have overtopped the mast; but the ship dived like a swan between them, and then rose again on their lofty, foaming crests. To the little mermaid this appeared pleasant sport; not so to the sailors. At length the ship groaned and creaked; the thick planks gave way under the lashing of the sea as it broke over the deck; the mainmast snapped asunder like a reed; the ship lay over on her side; and the water rushed in. The little mermaid now perceived that the crew were in danger; even she herself was obliged to be careful to avoid the beams and planks of the wreck which lay scattered on the water. At one moment it was so pitch dark that she could not see a single object, but a flash of lightning revealed the whole scene; she could see everyone who had been on board excepting the prince; when the ship parted, she had seen him sink into the deep waves, and she was glad, for she thought he would now be with her; and then she remembered that human beings could not live in the water, so that when he got down to her father's palace he would be quite dead. But he must not die. So she swam about among the beams and planks which strewed the surface of the sea, forgetting that they could crush her to pieces. Then she dived deeply under the dark waters, rising and falling with the waves, till at length she managed to reach the young prince, who was fast losing the power of swimming in that stormy sea. His limbs were failing him, his beautiful eyes were closed, and he would have died had not the little mermaid come to his assistance. She held his head above the water, and let the waves drift them where they would.

In the morning the storm had ceased; but of the ship not a single fragment could be seen. The sun rose up red and glowing from the water, and its beams brought back the hue of health to the prince's cheeks; but his eyes remained closed. The mermaid kissed his high, smooth forehead, and stroked back his wet hair; he seemed to her like the marble statue in her little garden, and she kissed him again, and wished that he might live. Presently they came in sight of land; she saw lofty blue mountains, on which the white snow rested as if a flock of swans were lying upon them. Near the coast were beautiful green forests, and close by stood a large building, whether a church or a convent she could not tell. Orange and citron trees grew in the garden, and before the door stood lofty palms. The sea here formed a little bay, in which the water was quite still, but very deep; so she swam with the handsome prince to the beach, which was covered with fine, white sand, and there she laid him in the warm sunshine, taking care to raise his head higher than his body. Then bells sounded in the large white building, and a number of young girls came into the garden. The little mermaid swam out farther from the shore and placed herself between some high rocks that rose out of the water; then she covered her head and neck with the foam of the sea so that her little face might not be seen, and watched to see what would become of the poor prince. She did not wait long before she saw a young girl approach the spot where he lay. She seemed frightened at first, but only for a moment; then she fetched a number of people, and the mermaid saw that the prince came to life again, and smiled upon those who stood round him. But to her he sent no smile; he knew not that she had saved him. This made her very unhappy, and when he was led away into the great building, she dived down sorrowfully into the water, and returned to her father's castle. She had always been silent and thoughtful, and now she was more so than ever. Her sisters asked her what she had seen during her first visit to the surface of the water; but she would tell them nothing. Many an evening and morning did she rise to the place where she had left the prince. She saw the fruits in the garden ripen till they were gathered, the snow on the tops of the mountains melt away; but she never saw the prince, and therefore she returned home, always more sorrowful than before. It was her only comfort to sit in her own little garden, and fling her arm round the beautiful marble statue which was like the prince; but she gave up tending her flowers, and they grew in wild confusion over the paths, twining their long leaves and stems round the branches of the trees, so that the whole place became dark and gloomy. At length she could bear it no longer, and told one of her sisters all about it. Then the others heard the secret, and very soon it became known to two mermaids whose intimate friend happened to know who the prince was. She had also seen the festival on board ship, and she told them where the prince came from, and where his palace stood.

"Come, little sister," said the other princesses; then they entwined their arms and rose up in a long row to the surface of the water, close by the spot where they knew the prince's palace stood. It was built of bright yellow shining stone, with long flights of marble steps, one of which reached quite down to the sea. Splendid gilded cupolas rose over the roof, and between the pillars that surrounded the whole building stood lifelike statues of marble. Through the clear crystal of the lofty windows could be seen noble rooms, with costly silk curtains and hangings of tapestry;

while the walls were covered with beautiful paintings which were a pleasure to look at. In the centre of the largest saloon a fountain threw its sparkling jets high up into the glass cupola of the ceiling, through which the sun shone down upon the water and upon the beautiful plants growing round the basin of the fountain. Now that she knew where he lived, she spent many an evening and many a night on the water near the palace. She would swim much nearer the shore than any of the others ventured to do; indeed once she went quite up the narrow channel under the marble balcony, which threw a broad shadow on the water. Here she would sit and watch the young prince, who thought himself quite alone in the bright moonlight. She saw him many times of an evening sailing in a pleasant boat, with music playing and flags waving. She peeped out from among the green rushes, and if the wind caught her long silvery-white veil, those who saw it believed it to be a swan, spreading out its wings. On many a night, too, when the fishermen, with their torches, were out at sea, she heard them relate so many good things about the doings of the young prince, that she was glad she had saved his life when he had been tossed about half-dead on the waves. And she remembered that his head had rested on her bosom, and how heartily she had kissed him; but he knew nothing of all this, and could not even dream of her. She grew more and more fond of human beings, and wished more and more to be able to wander about with those whose world seemed to be so much larger than her own. They could fly over the sea in ships, and mount the high hills which were far above the clouds; and the lands they possessed, their woods and their fields, stretched far away beyond the reach of her sight. There was so much that she wished to know, and her sisters were unable to answer all her questions. Then she applied to her old grandmother, who knew all about the upper world, which she very rightly called the lands above the sea.

"If human beings are not drowned," asked the little mermaid, "can they live forever? Do they never die as we do here in the sea?"

"Yes," replied the old lady, "they must also die, and their term of life is even shorter than ours. We sometimes live to three hundred years, but when we cease to exist here we only become the foam on the surface of the water, and we have not even a grave down here of those we love. We have not immortal souls, we shall never live again; but, like the green seaweed, when once it has been cut off, we can never flourish more.

Human beings, on the contrary, have a soul which lives forever, lives after the body has been turned to dust. It rises up through the clear, pure air beyond the glittering stars. As we rise out of the water, and behold all the land of the earth, so do they rise to unknown and glorious regions which we shall never see."

"Why have not we an immortal soul?" asked the little mermaid mournfully; "I would give gladly all the hundreds of years that I have to live, to be a human being only for one day, and to have the hope of knowing the happiness of that glorious world above the stars."

"You must not think of that," said the old woman; "we feel ourselves to be much happier and much better off than human beings."

"So I shall die," said the little mermaid, "and as the foam of the sea I shall be driven about never again to hear the music of the waves, or to see the pretty flowers nor the red sun. Is there anything I can do to win an immortal soul?"

"No," said the old woman, "unless a man were to love you so much that you were more to him than his father or mother; and if all his thoughts and all his love were fixed upon you, and the priest placed his right hand in yours, and he promised to be true to you here and hereafter, then his soul would glide into your body and you would obtain a share in the future happiness of mankind. He would give a soul to you and retain his own as well; but this can never happen. Your fish's tail, which amongst us is considered so beautiful, is thought on earth to be quite ugly; they do not know any better, and they think it necessary to have two stout props, which they call legs, in order to be handsome."

Then the little mermaid sighed, and looked sorrowfully at her fish's tail. "Let us be happy," said the old lady, "and dart and spring about during the three hundred years that we have to live, which is really quite long enough; after that we can rest ourselves all the better. This evening we are going to have a court ball."

It is one of those splendid sights which we can never see on earth. The walls and the ceiling of the large ballroom were of thick, but transparent crystal. Many hundreds of colossal shells, some of a deep red, others of a grass green, stood on each side in rows, with blue fire in them, which lighted up the whole saloon, and shone through the walls, so that the sea was also illuminated. Innumerable fishes, great and small, swam past the crystal walls; on some of them the scales glowed with a purple brilliancy, and on others they shone like silver and gold. Through the halls flowed a broad stream, and in it danced the mermen and the mermaids to the music of their own sweet singing. No one on earth has such a lovely voice as theirs. The little mermaid sang more sweetly than them all. The whole court applauded her with hands and tails; and for a moment her heart felt quite gay, for she knew she had the loveliest voice of any on earth or in the sea. But she soon thought again of the world above her, for she could not forget the charming prince, nor her sorrow that she had not an immortal soul like his; therefore she crept away silently out of her father's palace, and while everything within was gladness and song, she sat in her own little garden sorrowful and alone. Then she heard the bugle sounding through the water, and thought, "He is certainly sailing above, he on whom my wishes depend, and in whose hands I should like to place the happiness of my life. I will venture all for him, and to win an immortal soul, while my sisters are dancing in my father's palace, I will go to the sea witch, of whom I have always been so much afraid, but she can give me counsel and help."

And then the little mermaid went out from her garden, and took the road to the foaming whirlpools, behind which the sorceress lived. She had never been that way before: neither flowers nor grass grew there; nothing but bare, gray, sandy ground stretched out to the whirlpool, where the water, like foaming millwheels, whirled round everything that it seized, and cast it into the fathomless deep. Through the midst of these crushing whirlpools the little mermaid was obliged to pass, to reach the dominions of the sea witch; and also for a long distance the only road lay right across a quantity of warm, bubbling mire, called by the witch her turfmoor. Beyond this stood her house, in the centre of a strange forest, in which all the trees and flowers were polypi, half animals and half plants; they looked like serpents with a hundred heads growing out of the ground. The branches were long slimy arms, with fingers like flexible worms, moving limb after limb from the root to the top. All that could be reached in the sea they seized upon, and held fast, so that it never escaped from their clutches. The little mermaid was so alarmed at what she saw, that she stood still, and her heart beat with fear, and she was very nearly turning back; but she thought of the prince, and of the human soul for which she longed, and her courage returned. She fastened her long flowing hair round her head, so that the polypi might not seize hold of it. She laid her hands together across her bosom, and then she darted forward as a fish shoots through the water, between the supple arms and fingers of the ugly polypi, which were stretched out on each side of her. She saw that each held in its grasp something it had seized with its numerous little arms, as if they were iron bands. The white skeletons of human beings who had perished at sea, and had sunk down into the deep waters, skeletons of land animals, oars, rudders, and chests of ships were lying tightly grasped by their clinging arms; even a little mermaid, whom they had caught and strangled; and this seemed the most shocking of all to the little princess.

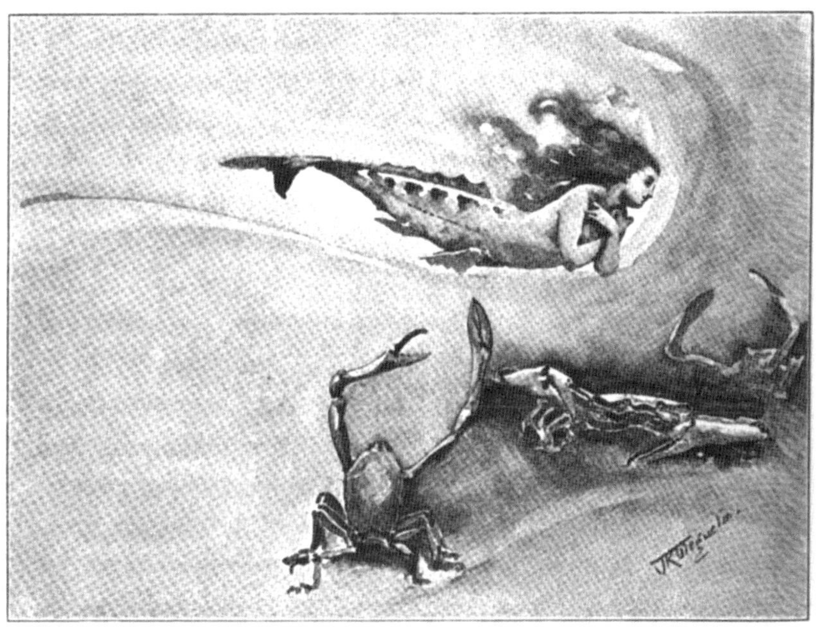

She now came to a space of marshy ground in the wood, where large, fat water snakes were rolling in the mire, and showing their ugly, drab-colored bodies. In the midst of this spot stood a house, built with the bones of shipwrecked human beings. There sat the sea witch, allowing a toad to eat from her mouth, just as people sometimes feed a canary with a piece of sugar. She called the ugly water snakes her little chickens, and allowed them to crawl all over her bosom.

"I know what you want," said the sea witch; "it is very stupid of you, but you shall have your way, and it will bring you to sorrow, my pretty princess. You want to get rid of your fish's tail, and to have two supports instead of it, like human beings on earth, so that the young prince may fall in love with you, and that you may have an immortal soul." And then the witch laughed so loud and disgustingly, that the toad and the snakes fell to the ground, and lay there wriggling about. "You are but just in time," said the witch; "for after sunrise tomorrow I should not be able to help you till the end of another year. I will prepare a draught for you, with which you must swim to land tomorrow before sunrise, and sit down on the shore and drink it. Your tail will then disappear, and shrink up into what mankind calls legs, and you will feel great pain, as if a sword were passing through you. But all who see you will say that you are the prettiest little human being they ever saw. You will still have the same floating gracefulness of movement, and no dancer will ever tread so lightly; but at every step you take it will feel as if you were treading upon sharp knives, and that the blood must flow. If you will bear all this, I will help you."

"Yes, I will," said the little princess in a trembling voice, as she thought of the prince and the immortal soul.

"But think again," said the witch; "for when once your shape has become like a human being, you can no more be a mermaid. You will never return through the water to your sisters, or to your father's palace again; and if you do not win the love of the prince, so that he is willing to forget his father and mother for your sake, and to love you with his whole soul, and allow the priest to join your hands that you may be man and wife, then you will never have an immortal soul. The first morning after he marries another your heart will break, and you will become foam on the crest of the waves."

"I will do it," said the little mermaid, and she became pale as death.

"But I must be paid also," said the witch, "and it is not a trifle that I ask. You have the sweetest voice of any who dwell here in the depths of the sea, and you believe that you will be able to charm the prince with it also, but this voice you must give to me; the best thing you possess will I have for the price of my draught. My own blood must be mixed with it, that it may be as sharp as a two-edged sword."

"But if you take away my voice," said the little mermaid, "what is left for me?"

"Your beautiful form, your graceful walk, and your expressive eyes; surely with these you can enchain a man's heart. Well, have you lost your courage? Put out your little tongue that I may cut it off as my payment; then you shall have the powerful draught."

"It shall be," said the little mermaid.

Then the witch placed her cauldron on the fire, to prepare the magic draught.

"Cleanliness is a good thing," said she, scouring the vessel with snakes, which she had tied together in a large knot; then she pricked herself in the breast, and let the black blood drop into it. The steam that rose formed itself into such horrible shapes that no one could look at them without fear. Every moment the witch threw something else into the vessel, and when it began to boil, the sound was like the weeping of a crocodile. When at last the magic draught was ready, it looked like the clearest water. "There it is for you," said the witch. Then she cut off the mermaid's tongue, so that she became dumb, and would never again speak or sing. "If the polypi should seize hold of you as you return through the wood," said the witch, "throw over them a few drops of the potion, and their fingers will be torn into a thousand pieces." But the little mermaid had no occasion to do this, for the polypi sprang back in terror when they caught sight of the glittering draught, which shone in her hand like a twinkling star.

So she passed quickly through the wood and the marsh, and between the rushing whirlpools. She saw that in her father's palace the torches in the ballroom were extinguished, and all within asleep; but she did not venture to go in to them, for now she was dumb and going to leave them forever, she felt as if her heart would break. She stole into the garden, took a flower from the flowerbeds of each of her sisters, kissed her hand a thousand times towards the palace, and then rose up through the dark blue waters. The sun had not risen when she came in sight of the prince's palace, and approached the beautiful marble steps, but the moon shone clear and bright. Then the little mermaid drank the magic draught, and it seemed as if a two-edged sword went through her delicate body: she fell into a swoon, and lay like one dead. When the sun arose and shone over the sea, she recovered, and felt a sharp pain; but just before her stood the handsome young prince. He fixed his coal-black eyes upon her so earnestly that she cast down her own, and then became aware that her fish's tail was gone, and that she had as pretty a pair of white legs and tiny feet as any little maiden could have; but she had no clothes, so she wrapped herself in her long, thick hair. The prince asked her who she was, and where she came from, and she looked at him mildly and sorrowfully with her deep blue eyes; but she could not speak.

Every step she took was as the witch had said it would be, she felt as if treading upon the points of needles or sharp knives; but she bore it willingly, and stepped as lightly by the prince's side as a soap bubble, so that he and all who saw her wondered at her graceful-swaying movements. She was very soon arrayed in costly robes of silk and muslin, and was the most beautiful creature in the palace; but she was dumb, and could neither speak nor sing.

Beautiful female slaves, dressed in silk and gold, stepped forward and sang before the prince and his royal parents: one sang better than all the others, and the prince clapped his hands and smiled at her. This was great sorrow to the little mermaid; she knew how much more sweetly she herself could sing once, and she thought, "Oh if he could only know that! I have given away my voice forever, to be with him."

The slaves next performed some pretty fairy-like dances, to the sound of beautiful music. Then the little mermaid raised her lovely white arms, stood on the tips of her toes, and glided over the floor, and danced as no one yet had been able to dance. At each moment her beauty became more revealed, and her expressive eyes appealed more directly to the heart than the songs of the slaves. Everyone was enchanted, especially the prince, who called her his little foundling; and she danced again quite readily, to please him, though each time her foot touched the floor it seemed as if she trod on sharp knives.

The prince said she should remain with him always, and she received permission to sleep at his door, on a velvet cushion. He had a page's dress made for her, that she might accompany him on horseback. They rode together through the sweet-scented woods, where the green boughs touched their shoulders, and the little birds sang among the fresh leaves. She climbed with the prince to the tops of high mountains; and although her tender feet bled so that even her steps were marked, she only laughed, and followed him till they could see the clouds beneath them looking like a flock of birds travelling to distant lands. While at the prince's palace, and when all the household were asleep, she would go and sit on the broad marble steps; for it eased her burning feet to bathe them in the cold seawater; and then she thought of all those below in the deep.

Once during the night her sisters came up arm-in-arm, singing sorrowfully, as they floated on the water. She beckoned to them, and then they recognized her, and told her how she had grieved them. After that, they came to the same place every night; and once she saw in the distance her old grandmother, who had not been to the surface of the sea for many years, and the old Sea King, her father, with his crown on his head. They stretched out their hands towards her, but they did not venture so near the land as her sisters did.

As the days passed, she loved the prince more fondly, and he loved her as he would love a little child, but it never came into his head to make her his wife; yet, unless he married her, she could not receive an immortal soul; and, on the morning after his marriage with another, she would dissolve into the foam of the sea.

"Do you not love me the best of them all?" the eyes of the little mermaid seemed to say, when he took her in his arms, and kissed her fair forehead.

"Yes, you are dear to me," said the prince; "for you have the best heart, and you are the most devoted to me; you are like a young maiden whom I once saw, but whom I shall never meet again. I was in a ship that was wrecked, and the waves cast me ashore near a holy temple, where several young maidens performed the service. The youngest of them found me on the shore, and saved my life. I saw her but twice, and she is the only one in the world whom I could love; but you are like her, and you have almost driven her image out of my mind. She belongs to the holy temple, and my good fortune has sent you to me instead of her; and we will never part."

"Ah, he knows not that it was I who saved his life," thought the little mermaid. "I carried him over the sea to the wood where the temple stands: I sat beneath the foam, and watched till the human beings came to help him. I saw the pretty maiden that he loves better than he loves me;" and the mermaid sighed deeply, but she could not shed tears. "He says the maiden belongs to the holy temple, therefore she will never return to the world. They will meet no more: while I am by his side, and see him every day. I will take care of him, and love him, and give up my life for his sake."

Very soon it was said that the prince must marry, and that the beautiful daughter of a neighboring king would be his wife, for a fine ship was being fitted out. Although the prince gave out that he merely intended to pay a visit to the king, it was generally supposed that he really went to see his daughter. A great company were to go with him. The little mermaid smiled, and shook her head. She knew the prince's thoughts better than any of the others.

"I must travel," he had said to her; "I must see this beautiful princess; my parents desire it; but they will not oblige me to bring her home as my bride. I cannot love her; she is not like the beautiful maiden in the temple, whom you resemble. If I were forced to choose a bride, I would rather choose you, my dumb foundling, with those expressive eyes." And then he kissed her rosy mouth, played with her long waving hair, and laid his head on her heart, while she dreamed of human happiness and an immortal soul. "You are not afraid of the sea, my dumb child," said he, as they stood on the deck of the noble ship which was to carry them to the country of the neighboring king. And then he told her of storm and of calm, of strange fishes in the deep beneath them, and of what the divers had seen there; and she smiled at his descriptions, for she knew better than anyone what wonders were at the bottom of the sea.

In the moonlight, when all on board were asleep, excepting the man at the helm, who was steering, she sat on the deck, gazing down through the clear water. She thought she could distinguish her father's castle, and upon it her aged grandmother, with the silver crown on her head, looking through the rushing tide at the keel of the vessel. Then her sisters came up on the waves, and gazed at her mournfully, wringing their white hands. She beckoned to them, and smiled, and wanted to tell them how happy and well off she was; but the cabin boy approached, and when her sisters dived down he thought it was only the foam of the sea which he saw.

The next morning the ship sailed into the harbor of a beautiful town belonging to the king whom the prince was going to visit. The church bells were ringing, and from the high towers sounded a flourish of trumpets; and soldiers, with flying colors and glittering bayonets, lined the rocks through which they passed. Every day was a festival; balls and entertainments followed one another.

But the princess had not yet appeared. People said that she was being brought up and educated in a religious house, where she was learning every royal virtue. At last she came. Then the little mermaid, who was very anxious to see whether she was really beautiful, was obliged to acknowledge that she had never seen a more perfect vision of beauty. Her skin was delicately fair, and beneath her long dark eyelashes her laughing blue eyes shone with truth and purity.

"It was you," said the prince, "who saved my life when I lay dead on the beach," and he folded his blushing bride in his arms. "Oh, I am too happy," said he to the little mermaid; "my fondest hopes are all fulfilled. You will rejoice at my happiness; for your devotion to me is great and sincere."

The little mermaid kissed his hand, and felt as if her heart were already broken. His wedding morning would bring death to her, and she would change into the foam of the sea. All the church bells rung, and the heralds rode about the town proclaiming the betrothal. Perfumed oil was burning in costly silver lamps on every altar. The priests waved the censers, while the bride and bridegroom joined their hands and received the blessing of the bishop. The little mermaid, dressed in silk and gold, held up the bride's train; but her ears heard nothing of the festive music, and her eyes saw not the holy ceremony; she thought of the night of death which was coming to her, and of all she had lost in the world. On the same evening the bride and bridegroom went on board ship; cannons were roaring, flags waving, and in the centre of the ship a costly tent of purple and gold had been erected. It contained elegant couches, for the reception of the bridal pair during the night. The ship, with swelling sails and a favorable wind, glided away smoothly and lightly over the calm sea. When it grew dark a number of colored lamps were lit, and the sailors danced merrily on the deck. The little mermaid could not help thinking of her first rising out of the sea, when she had seen similar festivities and joys; and she joined in the dance, poised herself in the air as a swallow when he pursues his prey, and all present cheered her with wonder. She had never danced so elegantly before. Her tender feet felt as if cut with sharp knives, but she cared not for it; a sharper pang had pierced through her heart. She knew this was the last evening she should ever see the prince, for whom she had forsaken her kindred and her home; she had given up her beautiful voice, and suffered unheard-of pain daily for him, while he knew nothing of it. This was the last evening that she would breathe the same air with him, or gaze on the starry sky and the deep sea; an eternal night, without a thought or a dream, awaited her: she had no soul and now she could never win one. All was joy and gayety on board ship till long after midnight; she laughed and danced with the rest, while the thoughts of death were in her heart. The prince kissed his beautiful bride, while she played with his raven hair, till they went arm-in-arm to rest in the splendid tent. Then all became still on board the ship; the helmsman, alone awake, stood at the helm. The little mermaid leaned her white arms on the edge of the vessel, and looked towards the east for the first blush of morning, for that first ray of dawn that would bring her death. She saw her sisters rising out of the flood: they were as pale as herself; but their long, beautiful hair waved no more in the wind, and had been cut off.

"We have given our hair to the witch," said they, "to obtain help for you, that you may not die tonight. She has given us a knife: here it is, see it is very sharp. Before the sun rises you must plunge it into the heart of the prince; when the warm blood falls upon your feet they will grow together again, and form into a fish's tail, and you will be once more a mermaid, and return to us to live out your three hundred years before you die and change into the salt sea foam. Haste, then; he or you must die before sunrise. Our old grandmother moans so for you, that her white hair is falling off from sorrow, as ours fell under the witch's scissors. Kill the prince and come back; hasten: do you not see the first red streaks in the sky? In a few minutes the sun will rise, and you must die." And then they sighed deeply and mournfully, and sank down beneath the waves.

The little mermaid drew back the crimson curtain of the tent, and beheld the fair bride with her head resting on the prince's breast. She bent down and kissed his fair brow, then looked at the sky on which the rosy dawn grew brighter and brighter; then she glanced at the sharp knife, and again fixed her eyes on the prince, who whispered the name of his bride in his dreams. She was in his thoughts, and the knife trembled in the hand of the little mermaid: then she flung it far away from her into the waves; the water turned red where it fell, and the drops that spurted up looked like blood. She cast one more lingering, half-fainting glance at the prince, and then threw herself from the ship into the sea, and thought her body was dissolving into foam. The sun rose above the waves, and his warm rays fell on the cold foam of the little mermaid, who did not feel as if she were dying. She saw the bright sun, and all around her floated hundreds of transparent beautiful beings; she could see through them the white sails of the ship, and the red clouds in the sky; their speech was melodious, but too ethereal to be heard by mortal ears, as they were also unseen by mortal eyes. The little mermaid perceived that she had a body like theirs, and that she continued to rise higher and higher out of the foam. "Where am I?" asked she, and her voice sounded ethereal, as the voice of those who were with her; no earthly music could imitate it.

"Among the daughters of the air," answered one of them. "A mermaid has not an immortal soul, nor can she obtain one unless she wins the love of a human being. On the power of another hangs her eternal destiny. But the daughters of the air, although they do not possess an immortal soul, can, by their good deeds, procure one for themselves. We fly to warm countries, and cool the sultry air that destroys mankind with the pestilence. We carry the perfume of the flowers to spread health and restoration. After we have striven for three hundred years to all the good in our power, we receive an immortal soul and take part in the happiness of mankind. You, poor little mermaid, have tried with your whole heart to do as we are doing; you have suffered and endured and raised yourself to the spirit-world by your good deeds; and now, by striving for three hundred years in the same way, you may obtain an immortal soul."

The little mermaid lifted her glorified eyes towards the sun, and felt them, for the first time, filling with tears. On the ship, in which she had left the prince, there were life and noise; she saw him and his beautiful bride searching for her; sorrowfully they gazed at the pearly foam, as if they knew she had thrown herself into the waves. Unseen she kissed the forehead of his bride, and fanned the prince, and then mounted with the other children of the air to a rosy cloud that floated through the aether.

"After three hundred years, thus shall we float into the kingdom of heaven," said she. "And we may even get there sooner," whispered one of her companions. "Unseen we can enter the houses of men, where there are children, and for every day on which we find a good child, who is the joy of his parents and deserves their love, our time of probation is shortened. The child does not know, when we fly through the room, that we smile with joy at his good conduct, for we can count one year less of our three hundred years. But when we see a naughty or a wicked child, we shed tears of sorrow, and for every tear a day is added to our time of trial!"

The Ugly Duckling

It was lovely summer weather in the country, and the golden corn, the green oats, and the haystacks piled up in the meadows looked beautiful. The stork walking about on his long red legs chattered in the Egyptian language, which he had learnt from his mother. The cornfields and meadows were surrounded by large forests, in the midst of which were deep pools. It was, indeed, delightful to walk about in the country. In a sunny spot stood a pleasant old farmhouse close by a deep river, and from the house down to the water side grew great burdock leaves, so high, that under the tallest of them a little child could stand upright. The spot was as wild as the centre of a thick wood. In this snug retreat sat a duck on her nest, watching for her young brood to hatch; she was beginning to get tired of her task, for the little ones were a long time coming out of their shells, and she seldom had any visitors. The other ducks liked much better to swim about in the river than to climb the slippery banks, and sit under a burdock leaf, to have a gossip with her. At length one shell cracked, and then another, and from each egg came a living creature that lifted its head and cried, "Peep, peep." "Quack, quack," said the mother, and then they all quacked as well as they could, and looked about them on every side at the large green leaves. Their mother allowed them to look as much as they liked, because green is good for the eyes.

"How large the world is," said the young ducks, when they found how much more room they now had than while they were inside the eggshell.

"Do you imagine this is the whole world?" asked the mother. "Wait till you have seen the garden; it stretches far beyond that to the parson's field, but I have never ventured to such a distance. Are you all out?" she continued, rising. "No, I declare, the largest egg lies there still. I wonder how long this is to last, I am quite tired of it;" and she seated herself again on the nest.

"Well, how are you getting on?" asked an old duck, who paid her a visit.

"One egg is not hatched yet," said the duck, "it will not break. But just look at all the others, are they not the prettiest little ducklings you ever saw? They are the image of their father, who is so unkind, he never comes to see."

"Let me see the egg that will not break," said the duck; "I have no doubt it is a turkey's egg. I was persuaded to hatch some once, and after all my care and trouble with the young ones, they were afraid of the water. I quacked and clucked, but all to no purpose. I could not get them to venture in. Let me look at the egg. Yes, that is a turkey's egg; take my advice, leave it where it is and teach the other children to swim."

"I think I will sit on it a little while longer," said the duck; "as I have sat so long already, a few days will be nothing."

"Please yourself," said the old duck, and she went away.

At last the large egg broke, and a young one crept forth crying, "Peep, peep." It was very large and ugly. The duck stared at it and exclaimed, "It is very large and not at all like the others. I wonder if it really is a turkey. We shall soon find it out, however, when we go to the water. It must go in, if I have to push it myself."

On the next day the weather was delightful, and the sun shone brightly on the green burdock leaves, so the mother duck took her young brood down to the water, and jumped in with a splash. "Quack, quack," cried she, and one after another the little ducklings jumped in. The water closed over their heads, but they came up again in an instant, and swam about quite prettily with their legs paddling under them as easily as possible, and the ugly duckling was also in the water swimming with them.

"Oh," said the mother, "that is not a turkey; how well he uses his legs, and how upright he holds himself! He is my own child, and he is not so very ugly after all if you look at him properly. Quack, quack! come with me now, I will take you into grand society, and introduce you to the farmyard, but you must keep close to me or you may be trodden upon; and, above all, beware of the cat."

When they reached the farmyard, there was a great disturbance, two families were fighting for an eel's head, which, after all, was carried off by the cat. "See, children, that is the way of the world," said the mother duck, whetting her beak, for she would have liked the eel's head herself. "Come, now, use your legs, and let me see how well you can behave. You must bow your heads prettily to that old duck yonder; she is the highest born of them all, and has Spanish blood, therefore, she is well off. Don't you see she has a red flag tied to her leg, which is something very grand, and a great honor for a duck; it shows that everyone is anxious not to lose her, as she can be recognized both by man and beast. Come, now, don't turn your toes, a well-bred duckling spreads his feet wide apart, just like his father and mother, in this way; now bend your neck, and say 'quack.'"

The ducklings did as they were bid, but the other duck stared, and said, "Look, here comes another brood, as if there were not enough of us already! and what a queer looking object one of them is; we don't want him here," and then one flew out and bit him in the neck.

"Let him alone," said the mother; "he is not doing any harm."

"Yes, but he is so big and ugly," said the spiteful duck, "and therefore he must be turned out."

"The others are very pretty children," said the old duck, with the rag on her leg, "all but that one; I wish his mother could improve him a little."

"That is impossible, your grace," replied the mother; "he is not pretty; but he has a very good disposition, and swims as well or even better than the others. I think he will grow up pretty, and perhaps be smaller; he has remained too long in the egg, and therefore his figure is not properly formed;" and then she stroked his neck and smoothed the feathers, saying, "It is a drake, and therefore not of so much consequence. I think he will grow up strong, and able to take care of himself."

"The other ducklings are graceful enough," said the old duck. "Now make yourself at home, and if you can find an eel's head, you can bring it to me."

And so they made themselves comfortable; but the poor duckling, who had crept out of his shell last of all, and looked so ugly, was bitten and pushed and made fun of, not only by the ducks, but by all the poultry. "He is too big," they all said, and the turkey cock, who had been born into the world with spurs, and fancied himself really an emperor, puffed himself out like a vessel in full sail, and flew at the duckling, and became quite red in the head with passion, so that the poor little thing did not know where to go, and was quite miserable because he was so ugly and laughed at by the whole farmyard.

So it went on from day to day till it got worse and worse. The poor duckling was driven about by everyone; even his brothers and sisters were unkind to him, and would say, "Ah, you ugly creature, I wish the cat would get you," and his mother said she wished he had never been born. The ducks pecked him, the chickens beat him, and the girl who fed the poultry kicked him with her feet. So at last he ran away, frightening the little birds in the hedge as he flew over the palings.

"They are afraid of me because I am ugly," he said. So he closed his eyes, and flew still farther, until he came out on a large moor, inhabited by wild ducks. Here he remained the whole night, feeling very tired and sorrowful.

In the morning, when the wild ducks rose in the air, they stared at their new comrade. "What sort of a duck are you?" they all said, coming round him.

He bowed to them, and was as polite as he could be, but he did not reply to their question. "You are exceedingly ugly," said the wild ducks, "but that will not matter if you do not want to marry one of our family."

Poor thing! he had no thoughts of marriage; all he wanted was permission to lie among the rushes, and drink some of the water on the moor. After he had been on the moor two days, there came two wild geese, or rather goslings, for they had not been out of the egg long, and were very saucy. "Listen, friend," said one of them to the duckling, "you are so ugly, that we like you very well. Will you go with us, and become a bird of passage? Not far from here is another moor, in which there are some pretty wild geese, all unmarried. It is a chance for you to get a wife; you may be lucky, ugly as you are."

"Pop, pop," sounded in the air, and the two wild geese fell dead among the rushes, and the water was tinged with blood. "Pop, pop," echoed far and wide in the distance, and whole flocks of wild geese rose up from the rushes. The sound continued from every direction, for the sportsmen surrounded the moor, and some were even seated on branches of trees, overlooking the rushes. The blue smoke from the guns rose like clouds over the dark trees, and as it floated away across the water, a number of sporting dogs bounded in among the rushes, which bent beneath them wherever they went. How they terrified the poor duckling! He turned away his head to hide it under his wing, and at the same moment a large terrible dog passed quite near him. His jaws were open, his tongue hung from his mouth, and his eyes glared fearfully. He thrust his nose close to the duckling, showing his sharp teeth, and then, "splash, splash," he went into the water without touching him, "Oh," sighed the duckling, "how thankful I am for being so ugly; even a dog will not bite me." And so he lay quite still, while the shot rattled through the rushes, and gun after gun was fired over him.

It was late in the day before all became quiet, but even then the poor young thing did not dare to move. He waited quietly for several hours, and then, after looking carefully around him, hastened away from the moor as fast as he could. He ran over field and meadow till a storm arose, and he could hardly struggle against it. Towards evening, he reached a poor little cottage that seemed ready to fall, and only remained standing because it could not decide on which side to fall first. The storm continued so violent, that the duckling could go no farther; he sat down by the cottage, and then he noticed that the door was not quite closed in consequence of one of the hinges having given way. There was therefore a narrow opening near the bottom large enough for him to slip through, which he did very quietly, and got a shelter for the night. A woman, a tomcat, and a hen lived in this cottage. The tomcat, whom the mistress called, "My little son," was a great favorite; he could raise his back, and purr, and could even throw out sparks from his fur if it were stroked the wrong way. The hen had very short legs, so she was called "Chickie short legs." She laid good eggs, and her mistress loved her as if she had been her own child. In the morning, the strange visitor was discovered, and the tomcat began to purr, and the hen to cluck.

"What is that noise about?" said the old woman, looking round the room, but her sight was not very good; therefore, when she saw the duckling she thought it must be a fat duck, that had strayed from home. "Oh what a prize!" she exclaimed. "I hope it is not a drake, for then I shall have some duck's eggs. I must wait and see." So the duckling was allowed to remain on trial for three weeks, but there were no eggs.

Now the tomcat was the master of the house, and the hen was mistress, and they always said, "We and the world," for they believed themselves to be half the world, and the better half too. The duckling thought that others might hold a different opinion on the subject, but the hen would not listen to such doubts. "Can you lay eggs?" she asked. "No." "Then have the goodness to hold your tongue." "Can you raise your back, or purr, or throw out sparks?" said the tomcat. "No." "Then you have no right to express an opinion when sensible people are speaking." So the duckling sat in a corner, feeling very low spirited, till the sunshine and the fresh air came into the room through the open door, and then he began to feel such a great longing for a swim on the water, that he could not help telling the hen.

"What an absurd idea," said the hen. "You have nothing else to do, therefore you have foolish fancies. If you could purr or lay eggs, they would pass away."

"But it is so delightful to swim about on the water," said the duckling, "and so refreshing to feel it close over your head, while you dive down to the bottom."

"Delightful, indeed!" said the hen, "why you must be crazy! Ask the cat, he is the cleverest animal I know, ask him how he would like to swim about on the water, or to dive under it, for I will not speak of my own opinion; ask our mistress, the old woman—there is no one in the world more clever than she is. Do you think she would like to swim, or to let the water close over her head?"

"You don't understand me," said the duckling.

"We don't understand you. Who can understand you, I wonder? Do you consider yourself more clever than the cat, or the old woman? I will say nothing of myself. Don't imagine such nonsense, child, and thank your good fortune that you have been received here. Are you not in a warm room, and in society from which you may learn something. But you are a chatterer, and your company is not very agreeable. Believe me, I speak only for your own good. I may tell you unpleasant truths, but that is a proof of my friendship. I advise you, therefore, to lay eggs, and learn to purr as quickly as possible."

"I believe I must go out into the world again," said the duckling.

"Yes, do," said the hen. So the duckling left the cottage, and soon found water on which it could swim and dive, but was avoided by all other animals, because of its ugly appearance. Autumn came, and the leaves in the forest turned to orange and gold. Then, as winter approached, the wind caught them as they fell and whirled them in the cold air. The clouds, heavy with hail and snowflakes, hung low in the sky, and the raven stood on the ferns crying, "Croak, croak." It made one shiver with cold to look at him. All this was very sad for the poor little duckling.

One evening, just as the sun set amid radiant clouds, there came a large flock of beautiful birds out of the bushes. The duckling had never seen any like them before. They were swans, and they curved their graceful necks, while their soft plumage shown with dazzling whiteness. They uttered a singular cry, as they spread their glorious wings and flew away from those cold regions to warmer countries across the sea. As they mounted higher and higher in the air, the ugly little duckling felt quite a strange sensation as he watched them. He whirled himself in the water like a wheel, stretched out his neck towards them, and uttered a cry so strange that it frightened himself. Could he ever forget those beautiful, happy birds; and when at last they were out of his sight, he dived under the water, and rose again almost beside himself with excitement. He knew not the names of these birds, nor where they had flown, but he felt towards them as he had never felt for any other bird in the world. He was not envious of these beautiful creatures, but wished to be as lovely as they. Poor ugly creature, how gladly he would have lived even with the ducks had they only given him encouragement. The winter grew colder and colder; he was obliged to swim about on the water to keep it from freezing, but every night the space on which he swam became smaller and smaller. At length it froze so hard that the ice in the water crackled as he moved, and the duckling had to paddle with his legs as well as he could, to keep the space from closing up. He became exhausted at last, and lay still and helpless, frozen fast in the ice.

Early in the morning, a peasant, who was passing by, saw what had happened. He broke the ice in pieces with his wooden shoe, and carried the duckling home to his wife. The warmth revived the poor little creature; but when the children wanted to play with him, the duckling thought they would do him some harm; so he started up in terror, fluttered into the milk-pan, and splashed the milk about the room. Then the woman clapped her hands, which frightened him still more. He flew first into the butter-cask, then into the meal-tub, and out again. What a condition he was in! The woman screamed, and struck at him with the tongs; the children laughed and screamed, and tumbled over each other, in their efforts to catch him; but luckily he escaped. The door stood open; the poor creature could just manage to slip out among the bushes, and lie down quite exhausted in the newly fallen snow.

It would be very sad, were I to relate all the misery and privations which the poor little duckling endured during the hard winter; but when it had passed, he found himself lying one morning in a moor, amongst the rushes. He felt the warm sun shining, and heard the lark singing, and saw that all around was beautiful spring. Then the young bird felt that his wings were strong, as he flapped them against his sides, and rose high into the air. They bore him onwards, until he found himself in a large garden, before he well knew how it had happened. The apple trees were in full blossom, and the fragrant elders bent their long green branches down to the stream which wound round a smooth lawn. Everything looked beautiful, in the freshness of early spring. From a thicket close by came three beautiful white swans, rustling their feathers, and swimming lightly over the smooth water. The duckling remembered the lovely birds, and felt more strangely unhappy than ever.

"I will fly to those royal birds," he exclaimed, "and they will kill me, because I am so ugly, and dare to approach them; but it does not matter: better be killed by them than pecked by the ducks, beaten by the hens, pushed about by the maiden who feeds the poultry, or starved with hunger in the winter."

Then he flew to the water, and swam towards the beautiful swans. The moment they espied the stranger, they rushed to meet him with outstretched wings.

"Kill me," said the poor bird; and he bent his head down to the surface of the water, and awaited death.

But what did he see in the clear stream below? His own image; no longer a dark, gray bird, ugly and disagreeable to look at, but a graceful and beautiful swan. To be born in a duck's nest, in a farmyard, is of no consequence to a bird, if it is hatched from a swan's egg. He now felt glad at having suffered sorrow and trouble, because it enabled him to enjoy so much better all the pleasure and happiness around him; for the great swans swam round the newcomer, and stroked his neck with their beaks, as a welcome.

Into the garden presently came some little children, and threw bread and cake into the water.

"See," cried the youngest, "there is a new one;" and the rest were delighted, and ran to their father and mother, dancing and clapping their hands, and shouting joyously, "There is another swan come; a new one has arrived."

Then they threw more bread and cake into the water, and said, "The new one is the most beautiful of all; he is so young and pretty." And the old swans bowed their heads before him.

Then he felt quite ashamed, and hid his head under his wing; for he did not know what to do, he was so happy, and yet not at all proud. He had been persecuted and despised for his ugliness, and now he heard them say he was the most beautiful of all the birds. Even the elder tree bent down its bows into the water before him, and the sun shone warm and bright. Then he rustled his feathers, curved his slender neck, and cried joyfully, from the depths of his heart, "I never dreamed of such happiness as this, while I was an ugly duckling."

The Emperor's New Clothes

Many, many years ago lived an emperor, who thought so much of new clothes that he spent all his money in order to obtain them; his only ambition was to be always well dressed. He did not care for his soldiers, and the theatre did not amuse him; the only thing, in fact, he thought anything of was to drive out and show a new suit of clothes. He had a coat for every hour of the day; and as one would say of a king "He is in his cabinet," so one could say of him, "The emperor is in his dressing room."

The great city where he resided was very gay; every day many strangers from all parts of the globe arrived. One day two swindlers came to this city; they made people believe that they were weavers, and declared they could manufacture the finest cloth to be imagined. Their colours and patterns, they said, were not only exceptionally beautiful, but the clothes made of their material possessed the wonderful quality of being invisible to any man who was unfit for his office or unpardonably stupid.

"That must be wonderful cloth," thought the emperor. "If I were to be dressed in a suit made of this cloth I should be able to find out which men in my empire were unfit for their places, and I could distinguish the clever from the stupid. I must have this cloth woven for me without delay." And he gave a large sum of money to the swindlers, in advance, that they should set to work without any loss of time. They set up two looms, and pretended to be very hard at work, but they did nothing whatever on the looms. They asked for the finest silk and the most precious gold cloth; all they got they did away with, and worked at the empty looms till late at night.

"I should very much like to know how they are getting on with the cloth," thought the emperor. But he felt rather uneasy when he remembered that he who was not fit for his office could not see it. Personally, he was of the opinion that he had nothing to fear, yet he thought it advisable to send somebody else first to see how matters stood. Everybody in the town knew what a remarkable quality the stuff possessed, and all were anxious to see how bad or stupid their neighbours were.

"I shall send my honest old minister to the weavers," thought the emperor. "He can judge best how the stuff looks, for he is intelligent, and nobody understands his office better than he."

The good old minister went into the room where the swindlers sat before the empty looms. "Heaven preserve us!" he thought, and opened his eyes wide, "I cannot see anything at all," but he did not say so. Both swindlers requested him to come near, and asked him if he did not admire the exquisite pattern and the beautiful colours, pointing to the empty looms. The poor old minister tried his very best, but he could see nothing, for there was nothing to be seen. "Oh dear," he thought, "can I be so stupid? I should never have thought so, and nobody must know it! Is it possible that I am not fit for my office? No, no, I cannot say that I was unable to see the cloth."

"Now, have you got nothing to say?" said one of the swindlers, while he pretended to be busily weaving.

"Oh, it is very pretty, exceedingly beautiful," replied the old minister looking through his glasses. "What a beautiful pattern, what brilliant colours! I shall tell the emperor that I like the cloth very much."

"We are pleased to hear that," said the two weavers, and described to him the colours and explained the curious pattern. The old minister listened attentively, that he might relate to the emperor what they said; and so he did.

Now the swindlers asked for more money, silk and gold cloth, which they required for weaving. They kept everything for themselves, and not a thread came near the loom, but they continued, as hitherto, to work at the empty looms.

Soon afterwards the emperor sent another honest courtier to the weavers to see how they were getting on, and if the cloth was nearly finished. Like the old minister, he looked and looked but could see nothing, as there was nothing to be seen.

"Is it not a beautiful piece of cloth?" asked the two swindlers, showing and explaining the magnificent pattern, which, however, did not exist.

"I am not stupid," said the man. "It is therefore my good appointment for which I am not fit. It is very strange, but I must not let anyone know it;" and he praised the cloth, which he did not see, and expressed his joy at the beautiful colours and the fine pattern. "It is very excellent," he said to the emperor.

Everybody in the whole town talked about the precious cloth. At last the emperor wished to see it himself, while it was still on the loom. With a number of courtiers, including the two who had already been there, he went to the two clever swindlers, who now worked as hard as they could, but without using any thread.

"Is it not magnificent?" said the two old statesmen who had been there before. "Your Majesty must admire the colours and the pattern." And then they pointed to the empty looms, for they imagined the others could see the cloth.

"What is this?" thought the emperor, "I do not see anything at all. That is terrible! Am I stupid? Am I unfit to be emperor? That would indeed be the most dreadful thing that could happen to me."

"Really," he said, turning to the weavers, "your cloth has our most gracious approval;" and nodding contentedly he looked at the empty loom, for he did not like to say that he saw nothing. All his attendants, who were with him, looked and looked, and although they could not see anything more than the others, they said, like the emperor, "It is very beautiful." And all advised him to wear the new magnificent clothes at a great procession which was soon to take place. "It is magnificent, beautiful, excellent," one heard them say; everybody seemed to be delighted, and the emperor appointed the two swindlers "Imperial Court weavers."

The whole night previous to the day on which the procession was to take place, the swindlers pretended to work, and burned more than sixteen candles. People should see that they were busy to finish the emperor's new suit. They pretended to take the cloth from the loom, and worked about in the air with big scissors, and sewed with needles without thread, and said at last: "The emperor's new suit is ready now."

The emperor and all his barons then came to the hall; the swindlers held their arms up as if they held something in their hands and said: "These are the trousers!" "This is the coat!" and "Here is the cloak!" and so on. "They are all as light as a cobweb, and one must feel as if one had nothing at all upon the body; but that is just the beauty of them."

"Indeed!" said all the courtiers; but they could not see anything, for there was nothing to be seen.

"Does it please your Majesty now to graciously undress," said the swindlers, "that we may assist your Majesty in putting on the new suit before the large looking glass?"

The emperor undressed, and the swindlers pretended to put the new suit upon him, one piece after another; and the emperor looked at himself in the glass from every side.

"How well they look! How well they fit!" said all. "What a beautiful pattern! What fine colours! That is a magnificent suit of clothes!"

The master of the ceremonies announced that the bearers of the canopy, which was to be carried in the procession, were ready.

"I am ready," said the emperor. "Does not my suit fit me marvellously?" Then he turned once more to the looking glass, that people should think he admired his garments.

The chamberlains, who were to carry the train, stretched their hands to the ground as if they lifted up a train, and pretended to hold something in their hands; they did not like people to know that they could not see anything.

The emperor marched in the procession under the beautiful canopy, and all who saw him in the street and out of the windows exclaimed: "Indeed, the emperor's new suit is incomparable! What a long train he has! How well it fits him!" Nobody wished to let others know he saw nothing, for then he would have been unfit for his office or too stupid. Never emperor's clothes were more admired.

"But he has nothing on at all," said a little child at last. "Good heavens! listen to the voice of an innocent child," said the father, and one whispered to the other what the child had said. "But he has nothing on at all," cried at last the whole people. That made a deep impression upon the emperor, for it seemed to him that they were right; but he thought to himself, "Now I must bear up to the end." And the chamberlains walked with still greater dignity, as if they carried the train which did not exist.

The Swineherd

Once upon a time lived a poor prince; his kingdom was very small, but it was large enough to enable him to marry, and marry he would. It was rather bold of him that he went and asked the emperor's daughter: "Will you marry me?" but he ventured to do so, for his name was known far and wide, and there were hundreds of princesses who would have gladly accepted him, but would she do so? Now we shall see.

On the grave of the prince's father grew a rose tree, the most beautiful of its kind. It bloomed only once in five years, and then it had only one single rose upon it, but what a rose! It had such a sweet scent that one instantly forgot all sorrow and grief when one smelt it. He had also a nightingale, which could sing as if every sweet melody was in its throat. This rose and the nightingale he wished to give to the princess; and therefore both were put into big silver cases and sent to her.

The emperor ordered them to be carried into the great hall where the princess was just playing "Visitors are coming" with her ladies-in-waiting; when she saw the large cases with the presents therein, she clapped her hands for joy.

"I wish it were a little pussy cat," she said. But then the rose tree with the beautiful rose was unpacked.

"Oh, how nicely it is made," exclaimed the ladies.

"It is more than nice," said the emperor, "it is charming."

The princess touched it and nearly began to cry.

"For shame, pa," she said, "it is not artificial, it is natural!"

"For shame, it is natural," repeated all her ladies.

"Let us first see what the other case contains before we are angry," said the emperor; then the nightingale was taken out, and it sang so beautifully that no one could possibly say anything unkind about it.

"Superbe, charmant," said the ladies of the court, for they all prattled French, one worse than the other.

"How much the bird reminds me of the musical box of the late lamented empress," said an old courtier, "it has exactly the same tone, the same execution."

"You are right," said the emperor, and began to cry like a little child.

"I hope it is not natural," said the princess.

"Yes, certainly it is natural," replied those who had brought the presents.

"Then let it fly," said the princess, and refused to see the prince.

But the prince was not discouraged. He painted his face, put on common clothes, pulled his cap over his forehead, and came back.

"Good day, emperor," he said, "could you not give me some employment at the court?"

"There are so many," replied the emperor, "who apply for places, that for the present I have no vacancy, but I will remember you. But wait a moment; it just comes into my mind, I require somebody to look after my pigs, for I have a great many."

Thus the prince was appointed imperial swineherd, and as such he lived in a wretchedly small room near the pigsty; there he worked all day long, and when it was night he had made a pretty little pot. There were little bells round the rim, and when the water began to boil in it, the bells began to play the old tune:

"A jolly old sow once lived in a sty,
Three little piggies had she."

But what was more wonderful was that, when one put a finger into the steam rising from the pot, one could at once smell what meals they were preparing on every fire in the whole town. That was indeed much more remarkable than the rose. When the princess with her ladies passed by and heard the tune, she stopped and looked quite pleased, for she also could play it—in fact, it was the only tune she could play, and she played it with one finger.

"That is the tune I know," she exclaimed. "He must be a well-educated swineherd. Go and ask him how much the instrument is."

One of the ladies had to go and ask; but she put on pattens.

"What will you take for your pot?" asked the lady.

"I will have ten kisses from the princess," said the swineherd.

"God forbid," said the lady.

"Well, I cannot sell it for less," replied the swineherd.

"What did he say?" said the princess.

"I really cannot tell you," replied the lady.

"You can whisper it into my ear."

"It is very naughty," said the princess, and walked off.

But when she had gone a little distance, the bells rang again so sweetly:

"A jolly old sow once lived in a sty,
Three little piggies had she."

"Ask him," said the princess, "if he will be satisfied with ten kisses from one of my ladies."

"No, thank you," said the swineherd: "ten kisses from the princess, or I keep my pot."

"That is tiresome," said the princess. "But you must stand before me, so that nobody can see it."

The ladies placed themselves in front of her and spread out their dresses, and she gave the swineherd ten kisses and received the pot.

That was a pleasure! Day and night the water in the pot was boiling; there was not a single fire in the whole town of which they did not know what was preparing on it, the chamberlain's as well as the shoemaker's. The ladies danced and clapped their hands for joy.

"We know who will eat soup and pancakes; we know who will eat porridge and cutlets; oh, how interesting!"

"Very interesting, indeed," said the mistress of the household. "But you must not betray me, for I am the emperor's daughter."

"Of course not," they all said.

The swineherd—that is to say, the prince—but they did not know otherwise than that he was a real swineherd—did not waste a single day without doing something; he made a rattle, which, when turned quickly round, played all the waltzes, galops, and polkas known since the creation of the world.

"But that is superbe," said the princess passing by. "I have never heard a more beautiful composition. Go down and ask him what the instrument costs; but I shall not kiss him again."

"He will have a hundred kisses from the princess," said the lady, who had gone down to ask him.

"I believe he is mad," said the princess, and walked off, but soon she stopped. "One must encourage art," she said. "I am the emperor's daughter! Tell him I will give him ten kisses, as I did the other day; the remainder one of my ladies can give him.

"But we do not like to kiss him," said the ladies.

"That is nonsense," said the princess; "if I can kiss him, you can also do it. Remember that I give you food and employment." And the lady had to go down once more.

"A hundred kisses from the princess," said the swineherd, "or everybody keeps his own."

"Place yourselves before me," said the princess then. They did as they were bidden, and the princess kissed him.

"I wonder what that crowd near the pigsty means!" said the emperor, who had just come out on his balcony. He rubbed his eyes and put his spectacles on.

"The ladies of the court are up to some mischief, I think. I shall have to go down and see." He pulled up his shoes, for they were down at the heels, and he was very quick about it. When he had come down into the courtyard he walked quite softly, and the ladies were so busily engaged in counting the kisses, that all should be fair, that they did not notice the emperor. He raised himself on tiptoe.

"What does this mean?" he said, when he saw that his daughter was kissing the swineherd, and then hit their heads with his shoe just as the swineherd received the sixty-eighth kiss.

"Go out of my sight," said the emperor, for he was very angry; and both the princess and the swineherd were banished from the empire. There she stood and cried, the swineherd scolded her, and the rain came down in torrents.

"Alas, unfortunate creature that I am!" said the princess, "I wish I had accepted the prince. Oh, how wretched I am!"

The swineherd went behind a tree, wiped his face, threw off his poor attire, and stepped forth in his princely garments; he looked so beautiful that the princess could not help bowing to him.

"I have now learnt to despise you," he said. "You refused an honest prince; you did not appreciate the rose and the nightingale; but you did not mind kissing a swineherd for his toys; you have no one but yourself to blame!"

And then he returned into his kingdom and left her behind. She could now sing at her leisure:

"A jolly old sow once lived in a sty,
Three little piggies has she."

The Princess and the Peas

Once upon a time there was a prince who wanted to marry a princess; but she would have to be a real princess. He travelled all over the world to find one, but nowhere could he get what he wanted. There were princesses enough, but it was difficult to find out whether they were real ones. There was always something about them that was not as it should be. So he came home again and was sad, for he would have liked very much to have a real princess.

One evening a terrible storm came on; there was thunder and lightning, and the rain poured down in torrents. Suddenly a knocking was heard at the city gate, and the old king went to open it.

It was a princess standing out there in front of the gate. But, good gracious! what a sight the rain and the wind had made her look. The water ran down from her hair and clothes; it ran down into the toes of her shoes and out again at the heels. And yet she said that she was a real princess.

"Well, we'll soon find that out," thought the old queen. But she said nothing, went into the bedroom, took all the bedding off the bedstead, and laid a pea on the bottom; then she took twenty mattresses and laid them on the pea, and then twenty eiderdown beds on top of the mattresses.

On this the princess had to lie all night. In the morning she was asked how she had slept.

"Oh, very badly!" said she. "I have scarcely closed my eyes all night. Heaven only knows what was in the bed, but I was lying on something hard, so that I am black and blue all over my body. It's horrible!"

Now they knew that she was a real princess because she had felt the pea right through the twenty mattresses and the twenty eiderdown beds.

Nobody but a real princess could be as sensitive as that.

So the prince took her for his wife, for now he knew that he had a real princess; and the pea was put in the museum, where it may still be seen, if no one has stolen it.

There, that is a true story.

The Shoes of Fortune

A Beginning

Every author has some peculiarity in his descriptions or in his style of writing. Those who do not like him, magnify it, shrug up their shoulders, and exclaim: There he is again! I, for my part, know very well how I can bring about this movement and this exclamation. It would happen immediately if I were to begin here, as I intended to do, with: "Rome has its Corso, Naples its Toledo." "Ah, that Andersen; there he is again!" they would cry. Yet I must, to please my fancy, continue quite quietly, and add: "But Copenhagen has its East Street."

Here, then, we will stay for the present. In one of the houses not far from the new market a party was invited; a very large party, in order, as is often the case, to get a return invitation from the others. One half of the company was already seated at the card table, the other half awaited the result of the stereotype preliminary observation of the lady of the house:

"Now let us see what we can do to amuse ourselves."

They had got just so far, and the conversation began to crystallize, as it could but do with the scanty stream which the commonplace world supplied. Amongst other things they spoke of the Middle Ages: some praised that period as far more interesting, far more poetical than our own too sober present; indeed Councilor Knap defended this opinion so warmly, that the hostess declared immediately on his side, and both exerted themselves with unwearied eloquence. The Councilor boldly declared the time of King Hans to be the noblest and the happiest period (1482–1513).

While the conversation turned on this subject and was only for a moment interrupted by the arrival of a journal that contained nothing worth reading, we will just step out into the antechamber, where cloaks, mackintoshes, sticks, umbrellas, and shoes were deposited. Here sat two female figures, a young and an old one. One might have thought at first they were servants come to accompany their mistresses home, but on looking nearer, one soon saw they could scarcely be mere servants—their forms were too noble for that, their skin too fine, the cut of their dress too striking. Two fairies were they; the younger, it is true, was not Dame Fortune herself, but one of the waiting-maids of her handmaidens who carry about the lesser good things that she distributes; the other looked extremely gloomy— t was Care. She always attends to her own serious business herself, as then she is sure of having it done properly.

They were telling each other, with a confidential interchange of ideas, where they had been during the day. The messenger of Fortune had only executed a few unimportant commissions, such as saving a new bonnet from a shower of rain, and so forth, but what she had yet to perform was something quite unusual.

"I must tell you," said she, "that today is my birthday, and in honor of it, a pair of walking-shoes or galoshes has been entrusted to me, which I am to carry to mankind. These shoes possess the property of instantly transporting him who has them on to the place or the period in which he most wishes to be; every wish, as regards time or place, or state of being, will be immediately fulfilled, and so at last man will be happy, here below."

"Do you seriously believe it?" replied Care, in a severe tone of reproach. "No, he will be very unhappy, and will assuredly bless the moment when he feels that he has freed himself from the fatal shoes."

"Stupid nonsense!" said the other angrily. "I will put them here by the door. Someone will make a mistake for certain and take the wrong ones—he will be a happy man."

Such was their conversation.

What Happened to the Councilor

It was late; Councilor Knap, deeply occupied with the times of King Hans, intended to go home, and malicious Fate managed matters so that his feet, instead of finding their way to his own galoshes, slipped into those of Fortune. Thus caparisoned the good man walked out of the well-lighted rooms into East Street. By the magic power of the shoes, he was carried back to the times of King Hans; on which account his foot very naturally sank in the mud and puddles of the street, there having been in those days no pavement in Copenhagen.

"Well! This is too bad! How dirty it is here!" sighed the Councilor. "As to a pavement, I can find no traces of one, and all the lamps, it seems, have gone to sleep."

The moon was not yet very high; it was besides rather foggy, so that in the darkness all objects seemed mingled in chaotic confusion. At the next corner hung a votive lamp before a Madonna, but the light it gave was little better than none at all; indeed, he did not observe it before he was exactly under it, and his eyes fell upon the bright colors of the pictures which represented the well-known group of the Virgin and the infant Jesus.

"That is probably a wax-work show," thought he, "and the people delay taking down their sign in hopes of a late visitor or two."

A few persons in the costume of the time of King Hans passed quickly by him.

"How strange they look! The good folks come probably from a masquerade!"

Suddenly was heard the sound of drums and fifes; the bright blaze of a fire shot up from time to time, and its ruddy gleams seemed to contend with the bluish light of the torches. The Councilor stood still and watched a most strange procession pass by. First came a dozen drummers, who understood well how to handle their instruments; then came halberdiers, and some armed with crossbows. The principal person in the procession was a priest. Astonished at what he saw, the Councilor asked what the meaning of all this parade was, and who that man was.

"That's the Bishop of Zealand," was the answer.

"Good heavens! What has taken possession of the Bishop?" sighed the Councilor, shaking his head. It certainly could not be the Bishop; even though he was considered the most absent man in the whole kingdom, and people told the drollest anecdotes about him. Reflecting on the matter, and without looking right or left, the Councilor went through East Street and across the Habro-Platz. The bridge leading to Palace Square was not to be found; scarcely trusting his senses, the nocturnal wanderer discovered a shallow piece of water, and here fell in with two men who very comfortably were rocking to and fro in a boat.

"Does your honor want to cross the ferry to the Holme?" asked they.

"Across to the Holme!" said the Councilor, who knew nothing of the age in which he at that moment was. "No, I am going to Christianshafen, to Little Market Street."

Both men stared at him in astonishment.

"Only just tell me where the bridge is," said he. "It is really unpardonable that there are no lamps here; and it is as dirty as if one had to wade through a morass."

The longer he spoke with the boatmen, the more unintelligible did their language become to him.

"I don't understand your Bornholmish dialect," said he at last, angrily, and turning his back upon them. He was unable to find the bridge: there was no railway either. "It is really disgraceful what a state this place is in," muttered he to himself. Never had his age, with which, however, he was always grumbling, seemed so miserable as on this evening. "I'll take a hackney-coach!" thought he. But where were the hackney-coaches? Not one was to be seen.

"I must go back to the New Market; there, it is to be hoped, I shall find some coaches; for if I don't, I shall never get safe to Christianshafen."

So off he went in the direction of East Street and had nearly got to the end of it when the moon shone forth.

"God bless me! What wooden scaffolding is that which they have set up there?" cried he involuntarily, as he looked at East Gate, which, in those days, was at the end of East Street.

He found, however, a little side-door open, and through this he went, and stepped into our New Market of the present time. It was a huge desolate plain; some wild bushes stood up here and there, while across the field flowed a broad canal or river. Some wretched hovels for the Dutch sailors, resembling great boxes, and after which the place was named, lay about in confused disorder on the opposite bank.

"I either behold a fata morgana, or I am regularly tipsy," whimpered out the Councilor. "But what's this?"

He turned round anew, firmly convinced that he was seriously ill. He gazed at the street formerly so well known to him, and now so strange in appearance, and looked at the houses more attentively: most of them were of wood, slightly put together; and many had a thatched roof.

"No, I am far from well," sighed he, "and yet I drank only one glass of punch; but I cannot suppose it—it was, too, really very wrong to give us punch and hot salmon for supper. I shall speak about it at the first opportunity. I have half a mind to go back again and say what I suffer. But no, that would be too silly; and heaven only knows if they are up still."

He looked for the house, but it had vanished.

"It is really dreadful," groaned he with increasing anxiety; "I cannot recognize East Street again; there is not a single decent shop from one end to the other! Nothing but wretched huts can I see anywhere; just as if I were at Ringstead. Oh! I am ill! I can scarcely bear myself any longer. Where the deuce can the house be? It must be here on this very spot; yet there is not the slightest idea of resemblance, to such a degree has everything changed this night! At all events here are some people up and stirring. Oh! Oh! I am certainly very ill."

He now hit upon a half-open door, through a chink of which a faint light shone. It was a sort of hostelry of those times, a kind of public house. The room had some resemblance to the clay-floored halls in Holstein; a pretty numerous company, consisting of seamen, Copenhagen burghers, and a few scholars, sat here in deep converse over their pewter cans, and gave little heed to the person who entered.

"By your leave!" said the Councilor to the hostess, who came bustling towards him. "I've felt so odd all of a sudden; would you have the goodness to send for a hackney-coach to take me to Christianshafen?"

The woman examined him with eyes of astonishment and shook her head; she then addressed him in German. The Councilor thought she did not understand Danish and therefore repeated his wish in German. This, in connection with his costume, strengthened the good woman in the belief that he was a foreigner. That he was ill, she comprehended directly; so, she brought him a pitcher of water, which tasted certainly pretty strong of the sea, although it had been fetched from the well.

The Councilor supported his head on his hand, drew a long breath, and thought over all the wondrous things he saw around him.

"Is this the Daily News of this evening?" he asked mechanically, as he saw the hostess push aside a large sheet of paper.

The meaning of this councillorship query remained, of course, a riddle to her, yet she handed him the paper without replying. It was a coarse woodcut, representing a splendid meteor "as seen in the town of Cologne," which was to be read below in bright letters.

"That is very old!" said the Councilor, whom this piece of antiquity began to make considerably more cheerful. "Pray how did you come into possession of this rare print? It is extremely interesting, although the whole is a mere fable. Such meteorous appearances are to be explained in this way—that they are the reflections of the Aurora Borealis, and it is highly probable they are caused principally by electricity."

Those persons who were sitting nearest him and heard his speech, stared at him in wonderment; and one of them rose, took off his hat respectfully, and said with a serious countenance, "You are no doubt a very learned man, Monsieur."

"Oh no," answered the Councilor, "I can only join in conversation on this topic and on that, as indeed one must do according to the demands of the world at present."

"Modesty is a fine virtue," continued the gentleman, "however, as to your speech, I must say *mihi secus videtur*: yet I am willing to suspend my judicium."

"May I ask with whom I have the pleasure of speaking?" asked the Councilor.

"I am a Bachelor in Theologia," answered the gentleman with a stiff reverence.

This reply fully satisfied the Councilor; the title suited the dress. "He is certainly," thought he, "some village schoolmaster—some odd old fellow, such as one still often meets with in Jutland."

"This is no *locus docendi*, it is true," began the clerical gentleman, "yet I beg you earnestly to let us profit by your learning. Your reading in the ancients is, *sine dubio*, of vast extent?"

"Oh yes, I've read something, to be sure," replied the Councilor. "I like reading all useful works, but I do not on that account despise the modern ones; 'tis only the unfortunate 'Tales of Everyday Life' that I cannot bear. We have enough and more than enough such in reality."

"'Tales of Everyday Life?'" said our Bachelor inquiringly.

"I mean those newfangled novels, twisting and writhing themselves in the dust of commonplace, which also expect to find a reading public."

"Oh," exclaimed the clerical gentleman smiling, "there is much wit in them; besides they are read at court. The King likes the history of Sir Iffven and Sir Gaudian particularly, which treats of King Arthur, and his

Knights of the Round Table; he has more than once joked about it with his high vassals."

"I have not read that novel," said the Councilor. "It must be quite a new one, that Heiberg has published lately."

"No," answered the theologian of the time of King Hans. "That book is not written by a Heiberg, but was imprinted by Godfrey von Gehmen."

"Oh, is that the author's name?" said the Councilor. "It is a very old name, and, as well as I recollect, he was the first printer that appeared in Denmark."

"Yes, he is our first printer," replied the clerical gentleman hastily.

So far all went on well. Some one of the worthy burghers now spoke of the dreadful pestilence that had raged in the country a few years back, meaning that of 1484. The Councilor imagined it was the cholera that was meant, which people made so much fuss about; and the discourse passed off satisfactorily enough. The war of the buccaneers of 1490 was so recent that it could not fail being alluded to; the English pirates had, they said, most shamefully taken their ships while in the roadstead; and the Councilor, before whose eyes the Herostratic event of 1801 still floated vividly, agreed entirely with the others in abusing the rascally English. With other topics he was not so fortunate; every moment brought about some new confusion and threatened to become a perfect Babel; for the worthy Bachelor was really too ignorant, and the simplest observations of the Councilor sounded to him too daring and fantastical. They looked at one another from the crown of the head to the soles of the feet; and when matters grew to too high a pitch, then the Bachelor talked Latin, in the hope of being better understood—but it was of no use after all.

"What's the matter?" asked the hostess, plucking the Councilor by the sleeve; and now his recollection returned, for in the course of the conversation he had entirely forgotten all that had preceded it.

"Merciful God, where am I!" exclaimed he in agony; and while he so thought, all his ideas and feelings of overpowering dizziness, against which he struggled with the utmost power of desperation, encompassed him with renewed force. "Let us drink claret and mead, and Bremen beer," shouted one of the guests, "and you shall drink with us!"

Two maidens approached. One wore a cap of two staring colors, denoting the class of persons to which she belonged. They poured out the liquor, and made the friendliest gesticulations; while a cold perspiration trickled down the back of the poor Councilor.

"What's to be the end of this! What's to become of me!" groaned he. But he was forced, in spite of his opposition, to drink with the rest. They took hold of the worthy man; who, hearing on every side that he was intoxicated, did not in the least doubt the truth of this certainly not very polite assertion. But on the contrary, implored the ladies and gentlemen present to procure him a hackney-coach: they, however, imagined he was talking Russian.

Never before, he thought, had he been in such a coarse and ignorant company; one might almost fancy the people had turned heathens again. "It is the most dreadful moment of my life: the whole world is leagued against me!" But suddenly it occurred to him that he might stoop down under the table and then creep unobserved out of the door. He did so, but just as he was going, the others remarked what he was about; they laid hold of him by the legs, and now, happily for him, off fell his fatal shoes—and with them the charm was at an end.

The Councilor saw quite distinctly before him a lantern burning, and behind this a large handsome house. All seemed to him in proper order as usual; it was East Street, splendid and elegant as we now see it. He lay with his feet towards a doorway, and exactly opposite sat the watchman asleep.

"Gracious heaven!" said he. "Have I lain here in the street and dreamed? Yes; 'tis East Street! How splendid and light it is! But really it is terrible what an effect that one glass of punch must have had on me!"

Two minutes later, he was sitting in a hackney-coach and driving to Frederickshafen. He thought of the distress and agony he had endured and praised from the very bottom of his heart the happy reality—our own time—which, with all its deficiencies, is yet much better than that in which, so much against his inclination, he had lately been.

The Watchman's Adventure

Why, there is a pair of galoshes, as sure as I'm alive!" said the watchman, awaking from a gentle slumber. "They belong no doubt to the lieutenant who lives over the way. They lie close to the door."

The worthy man was inclined to ring and deliver them at the house, for there was still a light in the window; but he did not like disturbing the other people in their beds, and so very considerately he left the matter alone.

"Such a pair of shoes must be very warm and comfortable," said he. "The leather is so soft and supple." They fitted his feet as though they had been made for him. "It is a curious world we live in," continued he, soliloquizing. "There is the lieutenant, now, who might go quietly to bed if he chose, where no doubt he could stretch himself at his ease; but does he do it? No, he saunters up and down his room, because, probably, he has enjoyed too many of the good things of this world at his dinner. That's a happy fellow! He has neither an infirm mother, nor a whole troop of everlastingly hungry children to torment him. Every evening, he goes to a party, where his nice supper costs him nothing: would to heaven I could but change with him! How happy should I be!"

While expressing his wish, the charm of the shoes, which he had put on, began to work; the watchman entered into the being and nature of the lieutenant. He stood in the handsomely furnished apartment, and held between his fingers a small sheet of rose-colored paper, on which some verses were written—written indeed by the officer himself; for who has not, at least once in his life, had a lyrical moment? And if one then marks down one's thoughts, poetry is produced. But here was written:

Oh, Were I Rich!

Oh, were I rich! Such was my wish, yes such
When hardly three feet high, I longed for much.
Oh, were I rich! An officer were I,
With sword, and uniform, and plume so high.
And the time came, and officer was I!
But yet I grew not rich. Alas, poor me!
Have pity, You, who all man's wants does see.

I sat one evening sunk in dreams of bliss,
A maid gave me a kiss,
I at that time was rich in poesy
And tales of old, though poor as poor could be;
But all she asked for was this poesy.
Then was I rich, but not in gold, poor me!

As You don't know, who all men's hearts cannot see.
    Oh, were I rich! Oft asked I for this boon.
The child grew up to womanhood full soon.
She is so pretty, clever, and so kind
Oh, did she know what's hidden in my mind—
A tale of old. Would she to me were kind!
But I'm condemned to silence! Oh, poor me!
As you don't know, who all men's hearts cannot see.
    Oh, were I rich in calm and peace of mind,
My grief you then would not here written find!
O thou, to whom I do my heart devote,
Oh, read this page of glad days now remote,
A dark, dark tale, which I tonight devote!
Dark is the future now. Alas, poor me!
Have pity you, who all men's pains does see."

Such verses as these people write when they are in love! But no man in his senses ever thinks of printing them. Here one of the sorrows of life, in which there is real poetry, gave itself vent; not that barren grief which the poet may only hint at, but never depict in its detail—misery and want: that animal necessity, in short, to snatch at least at a fallen leaf of the bread-fruit tree, if not at the fruit itself. The higher the position in which one finds oneself transplanted, the greater is the suffering. Everyday necessity is the stagnant pool of life—no lovely picture reflects itself therein. Lieutenant, love, and lack of money—that is a symbolic triangle, or much the same as the half of the shattered die of Fortune. This the lieutenant felt most poignantly, and this was the reason he leant his head against the window and sighed so deeply.

"The poor watchman out there in the street is far happier than I. He knows not what I term privation. He has a home, a wife, and children, who weep with him over his sorrows, who rejoice with him when he is glad. Oh, far happier were I, could I exchange with him my being—with his desires and with his hopes perform the weary pilgrimage of life! Oh, he is a hundred times happier than I!"

In the same moment the watchman was again watchman. It was the shoes that caused the metamorphosis by means of which, unknown to himself, he took upon him the thoughts and feelings of the officer.

But, as we have just seen, he felt himself in his new situation much less contented, and now preferred the very thing which but some minutes before he had rejected. So then the watchman was again watchman.

"That was an unpleasant dream," said he, "but 'twas droll enough altogether. I fancied that I was the lieutenant over there: and yet the thing was not very much to my taste after all. I missed my good old mother and the dear little ones, who almost tear me to pieces for sheer love."

He seated himself once more and nodded: the dream continued to haunt him, for he still had the shoes on his feet. A falling star shone in the dark firmament.

"There falls another star," said he, "but what does it matter; there are always enough left. I should not much mind examining the little glimmering things somewhat nearer, especially the moon; for that would not slip so easily through a man's fingers. When we die—so at least says the student, for whom my wife does the washing—we shall fly about as light as a feather from one such a star to the other. That's, of course, not true: but 'twould be pretty enough if it were so. If I could but once take a leap up there, my body might stay here on the steps for what I care."

Behold—there are certain things in the world to which one ought never to give utterance except with the greatest caution; but doubly careful must one be when we have the Shoes of Fortune on our feet. Now just listen to what happened to the watchman.

As to ourselves, we all know the speed produced by the employment of steam; we have experienced it either on railroads, or in boats when crossing the sea; but such a flight is like the travelling of a sloth in comparison with the velocity with which light moves. It flies nineteen million times faster than the best racehorse; and yet electricity is quicker still. Death is an electric shock which our heart receives; the freed soul soars upwards on the wings of electricity. The sun's light wants eight minutes and some seconds to perform a journey of more than twenty million of our Danish miles; borne by electricity, the soul wants even some minutes less to accomplish the same flight. To it the space between the heavenly bodies is not greater than the distance between the homes of our friends in town is for us, even if they live a short way from each other; such an electric shock in the heart, however, costs us the use of the body here below; unless, like the watchman of East Street, we happen to have on the Shoes of Fortune.

In a few seconds the watchman had done the fifty-two thousands of our miles up to the moon, which, as everyone knows, was formed out of matter much lighter than our earth; and is, so we should say, as soft as newly fallen snow. He found himself on one of the many circumjacent mountain ridges with which we are acquainted by means of Dr. Madler's "Map of the Moon." Within, down it sunk perpendicularly into a caldron, about a Danish mile in depth; while below lay a town, whose appearance we can, in some measure, realize to ourselves by beating the white of an egg in a glass of water. The matter of which it was built was just as soft, and formed similar towers, and domes, and pillars, transparent and rocking in the thin air, while above his head our earth was rolling like a large fiery ball.

He perceived immediately a quantity of beings who were certainly what we call "men;" yet they looked different to us. A far more correct imagination than that of the pseudo-Herschel had created them; and if they had been placed in rank and file, and copied by some skillful painter's hand, one would, without doubt, have exclaimed involuntarily, "What a beautiful arabesque!"

They had a language too, but surely nobody can expect that the soul of the watchman should understand it. Be that as it may, it did comprehend it; for in our souls there germinate far greater powers than we poor mortals, despite all our cleverness, have any notion of. Does she not show us—she the queen in the land of enchantment—her astounding dramatic talent in all our dreams? There every acquaintance appears and speaks upon the stage, so entirely in character, and with the same tone of voice, that none of us, when awake, were able to imitate it. How well can she recall persons to our mind, of whom we have not thought for years; when suddenly they step forth "every inch a man," resembling the real personages, even to the finest features, and become the heroes or heroines of our world of dreams. In reality, such remembrances are rather unpleasant: every sin, every evil thought, may, like a clock with alarm or chimes, be repeated at pleasure; then the question is if we can trust ourselves to give an account of every unbecoming word in our heart and on our lips.

The watchman's spirit understood the language of the inhabitants of the moon pretty well. The Selenites disputed variously about our earth, and expressed their doubts if it could be inhabited: the air, they said, must certainly be too dense to allow any rational dweller in the moon the necessary free respiration. They considered the moon alone to be inhabited:

they imagined it was the real heart of the universe or planetary system, on which the genuine Cosmopolites, or citizens of the world, dwelt. What strange things men—no, what strange things Selenites sometimes take into their heads!

About politics they had a good deal to say. But little Denmark must take care what it is about and not run counter to the moon; that great realm, that might in an ill-humor bestir itself, and dash down a hailstorm in our faces, or force the Baltic to overflow the sides of its gigantic basin.

We will, therefore, not listen to what was spoken, and on no condition run in the possibility of telling tales out of school; but we will rather proceed, like good quiet citizens, to East Street, and observe what happened meanwhile to the body of the watchman.

He sat lifeless on the steps: the morning star, that is to say, the heavy wooden staff, headed with iron spikes, and which had nothing else in common with its sparkling brother in the sky, had glided from his hand; while his eyes were fixed with glassy stare on the moon, looking for the good old fellow of a spirit which still haunted it.

"What's the hour, watchman?" asked a passerby. But when the watchman gave no reply, the merry person took it into his head to try what a tweak of the nose would do, on which the supposed sleeper lost his balance, the body lay motionless, stretched out on the pavement. When the patrol came up, all his comrades, who comprehended nothing of the whole affair, were seized with a dreadful fright. The proper authorities were informed of the circumstance, people talked a good deal about it, and in the morning he was carried to the hospital.

The seemingly dead body of the watchman wandered, as we have said, to the hospital, where it was brought into the general viewing-room: and the first thing that was done here was naturally to pull off the galoshes—when the spirit, that was merely gone out on adventures, must have returned with the quickness of lightning to its earthly tenement. It took its direction towards the body in a straight line; and a few seconds after, life began to show itself in the man. He asserted that the preceding night had been the worst that ever the malice of fate had allotted him; he would not for two silver marks again go through what he had endured while moon-stricken; but now, however, it was over.

The same day he was discharged from the hospital as perfectly cured; but the Shoes meanwhile remained behind.

A Moment of Head Importance: An Evening's "Dramatic Readings" —A Most Strange Journey

Every inhabitant of Copenhagen knows, from personal inspection, how the entrance to Frederick's Hospital looks; but as it is possible that others, who are not Copenhagen people, may also read this little work, we will beforehand give a short description of it.

The extensive building is separated from the street by a pretty high railing, the thick iron bars of which are so far apart, that in all seriousness, it is said, some very thin fellow had of a night occasionally squeezed himself through to go and pay his little visits in the town. The part of the body most difficult to manage on such occasions was, no doubt, the head; here, as is so often the case in the world, long-headed people get through best. So much, then, for the introduction.

One of the young men, whose head, in a physical sense only, might be said to be of the thickest, had the watch that evening. The rain poured down in torrents; yet despite these two obstacles, the young man was obliged to go out, if it were but for a quarter of an hour; and as to telling the doorkeeper about it, that, he thought, was quite unnecessary, if, with a whole skin, he were able to slip through the railings. There, on the floor lay the galoshes, which the watchman had forgotten; he never dreamed for a moment that they were those of Fortune; and they promised to do him good service in the wet; so, he put them on. The question now was, if he could squeeze himself through the grating, for he had never tried before. Well, there he stood.

"Would to heaven I had got my head through!" said he, involuntarily; and instantly through it slipped, easily and without pain, notwithstanding it was pretty large and thick. But now the rest of the body was to be got through!

"Ah! I am much too stout," groaned he aloud, while fixed as in a vise. "I had thought the head was the most difficult part of the matter! I really cannot squeeze myself through!"

He now wanted to pull his over-hasty head back again, but he could not. For his neck there was room enough, but for nothing more. His first feeling was of anger; his next that his temper fell to zero. The Shoes of

Fortune had placed him in the most dreadful situation; and, unfortunately, it never occurred to him to wish himself free. The pitch-black clouds poured down their contents in still heavier torrents; not a creature was to be seen in the streets. To reach up to the bell was what he did not like; to cry aloud for help would have availed him little; besides, how ashamed would he have been to be found caught in a trap, like an outwitted fox! How was he to twist himself through! He saw clearly that it was his irrevocable destiny to remain a prisoner till dawn, or, perhaps, even late in the morning; then the smith must be fetched to file away the bars; but all that would not be done so quickly as he could think about it. The whole Charity School, just opposite, would be in motion; all the new booths, with their not very courtier-like swarm of seamen, would join them out of curiosity, and would greet him with a wild "hurrah!" while he was standing in his pillory: there would be a mob, a hissing, and rejoicing, and jeering. "Oh, my blood is mounting to my brain; 'tis enough to drive one mad! I shall go wild! I know not what to do. Oh, were I but loose; my dizziness would then cease. Oh, were my head but loose!"

You see he ought to have said that sooner, for the moment he expressed the wish his head was free, and cured of all his paroxysms of love, he hastened off to his room, where the pains consequent on the fright the Shoes had prepared for him, did not so soon take their leave.

But you must not think that the affair is over now; it grows much worse.

The night passed, the next day also, but nobody came to fetch the Shoes.

In the evening "Dramatic Readings" were to be given at the little theatre in King Street. The house was filled to suffocation; and among other pieces to be recited was a new poem by H. C. Andersen, called, My Aunt's Spectacles; the contents of which were pretty nearly as follows:

"A certain person had an aunt, who boasted of particular skill in fortune-telling with cards, and who was constantly being stormed by persons that wanted to have a peep into futurity. But she was full of mystery about her art, in which a certain pair of magic spectacles did her essential service. Her nephew, a merry boy, who was his aunt's darling, begged so long for these spectacles, that, at last, she lent him the treasure, after having informed him, with many exhortations, that in order to execute the interesting trick, he need only repair to some place where a great many persons were assembled; and then, from a higher position, whence he could overlook the crowd, pass the company in review before him through his spectacles. Immediately "the inner man" of each individual would be displayed before him, like a game of cards, in which he unerringly might read what the future of every person presented was to be. Well pleased the little magician hastened away to prove the powers of the spectacles in the theatre; no place seeming to him more fitted for such a trial. He begged permission of the worthy audience and set his spectacles on his nose. A motley phantasmagoria presents itself before him, which he describes in a few satirical touches, yet without expressing his opinion openly: he tells the people enough to set them all thinking and guessing; but in order to hurt nobody, he wraps his witty oracular judgments in a transparent veil, or rather in a lurid thundercloud, shooting forth bright sparks of wit, that they may fall in the powder-magazine of the expectant audience."

The humorous poem was admirably recited, and the speaker much applauded. Among the audience was the young man of the hospital, who seemed to have forgotten his adventure of the preceding night. He had on the Shoes; for as yet no lawful owner had appeared to claim them; and besides it was so very dirty out-of-doors, they were just the thing for him, he thought.

The beginning of the poem he praised with great generosity: he even found the idea original and effective. But that the end of it, like the Rhine, was very insignificant, proved, in his opinion, the author's want of invention; he was without genius, and so forth. This was an excellent opportunity to have said something clever.

Meanwhile he was haunted by the idea—he should like to possess such a pair of spectacles himself; then, perhaps, by using them circumspectly, one would be able to look into people's hearts, which, he thought, would be far more interesting than merely to see what was to happen next year; for that we should all know in proper time, but the other never.

"I can now," said he to himself, "fancy the whole row of ladies and gentlemen sitting there in the front row; if one could but see into their hearts—yes, that would be a revelation—a sort of bazaar. In that lady yonder, so strangely dressed, I should find for certain a large milliner's shop; in that one the shop is empty, but it wants cleaning plain enough. But there would also be some good stately shops among them. Alas!" sighed he, "I know one in which all is stately; but there sits already a spruce young shopman, which is the only thing that's amiss in the whole shop. All would be splendidly decked out, and we should hear, 'Walk in, gentlemen, pray walk in; here you will find all you please to want.' Ah! I wish to heaven I could walk in and take a trip right through the hearts of those present!"

And behold to the Shoes of Fortune this was the cue; the whole man shrunk together and a most uncommon journey through the hearts of the front row of spectators, now began. The first heart through which he came, was that of a middle-aged lady, but he instantly fancied himself in the room of the "Institution for the cure of the crooked and deformed," where casts of misshapen limbs are displayed in naked reality on the wall. Yet there was this difference, in the institution the casts were taken at the entry of the patient, but here they were retained and guarded in the heart while the sound persons went away. They were, namely, casts of female friends, whose bodily or mental deformities were here most faithfully preserved.

With the snake-like writhings of an idea he glided into another female heart; but this seemed to him like a large holy temple. The white dove of innocence fluttered over the altar. How gladly would he have sunk upon his knees; but he must away to the next heart; yet he still heard the pealing tones of the organ, and he himself seemed to have become a newer and a better man; he felt unworthy to tread the neighboring sanctuary which a poor garret, with a sick bed-rid mother, revealed. But God's warm sun streamed through the open window; lovely roses nodded from the wooden flowerboxes on the roof, and two sky-blue birds sang rejoicingly, while the sick mother implored God's richest blessings on her pious daughter.

He now crept on hands and feet through a butcher's shop; at least on every side, and above and below, there was nought but flesh. It was the heart of a most respectable rich man, whose name is certain to be found in the directory.

He was now in the heart of the wife of this worthy gentleman. It was an old, dilapidated, moldering dovecot. The husband's portrait was used as a weathercock, which was connected in some way or other with the doors, and so they opened and shut of their own accord, whenever the stern old husband turned round.

Hereupon he wandered into a boudoir formed entirely of mirrors, like the one in Castle Rosenburg; but here the glasses magnified to an astonishing degree. On the floor, in the middle of the room, sat, like a Dalai Lama, the insignificant "self" of the person, quite confounded at his own greatness. He then imagined he had got into a needle case full of pointed needles of every size.

"This is certainly the heart of an old maid," thought he. But he was mistaken. It was the heart of a young military man; a man, as people said, of talent and feeling.

In the greatest perplexity, he now came out of the last heart in the row; he was unable to put his thoughts in order and fancied that his too lively imagination had run away with him.

"Good Heavens!" sighed he. "I have surely a disposition to madness—'tis dreadfully hot here; my blood boils in my veins and my head is burning like a coal." And he now remembered the important event of the evening before, how his head had got jammed in between the iron railings of the hospital. "That's what it is, no doubt," said he. "I must do something in time: under such circumstances a Russian bath might do me good. I only wish I were already on the upper bank."

And so there he lay on the uppermost bank in the vapor-bath; but with all his clothes on, in his boots and galoshes, while the hot drops fell scalding from the ceiling on his face.

"Holloa!" cried he, leaping down. The bathing attendant, on his side, uttered a loud cry of astonishment when he beheld in the bath, a man completely dressed.

The other, however, retained sufficient presence of mind to whisper to him, "'Tis a bet, and I have won it!" But the first thing he did as soon as he got home, was to have a large blister put on his chest and back to draw out his madness.

The next morning, he had a sore chest and a bleeding back; and, excepting the fright, that was all that he had gained by the Shoes of Fortune.

Metamorphosis of the Copying-Clerk

The watchman, whom we have certainly not forgotten, thought meanwhile of the galoshes he had found and taken with him to the hospital; he now went to fetch them; and as neither the lieutenant, nor anybody else in the street, claimed them as his property, they were delivered over to the police office.

"Why, I declare the Shoes look just like my own," said one of the clerks, eying the newly found treasure, whose hidden powers, even he, sharp as he was, was not able to discover. "One must have more than the eye of a shoemaker to know one pair from the other," said he, soliloquizing; and putting, at the same time, the galoshes in search of an owner, beside his own in the corner.

"Here, sir!" said one of the men, who panting brought him a tremendous pile of papers.

The copying-clerk turned round and spoke awhile with the man about the reports and legal documents in question; but when he had finished, and his eye fell again on the Shoes, he was unable to say whether those to the left or those to the right belonged to him. "At all events it must be those which are wet," thought he; but this time, in spite of his cleverness, he guessed quite wrong, for it was just those of Fortune which played as it were into his hands, or rather on his feet. And why, I should like to know, are the police never to be wrong? So, he put them on quickly, stuck his papers in his pocket, and took besides a few under his arm, intending to look them through at home to make the necessary notes. It was noon and the weather, that had threatened rain, began to clear up, while gaily dressed holiday folks filled the streets. "A little trip to Fredericksburg would do me no great harm," thought he; "for I, poor beast of burden that I am, have so much to annoy me, that I don't know what a good appetite is. 'Tis a bitter crust, alas, at which I am condemned to gnaw!"

Nobody could be more steady or quiet than this young man; we therefore wish him joy of the excursion with all our heart; and it will certainly be beneficial for a person who leads so sedentary a life. In the park he met a friend, one of our young poets, who told him that the following day he should set out on his long-intended tour.

"So, you are going away again!" said the clerk. "You are a very free and happy being; we others are chained by the leg and held fast to our desk."

"Yes, but it is a chain, friend, which ensures you the blessed bread of existence," answered the poet. "You need feel no care for the coming morrow: when you are old, you receive a pension."

"True," said the clerk, shrugging his shoulders, "and yet you are the better off. To sit at one's ease and poetise—that is a pleasure; everybody has something agreeable to say to you, and you are always your own master. No, friend, you should but try what it is to sit from one year's end to the other occupied with and judging the most trivial matters."

The poet shook his head, the copying-clerk did the same. Each one kept to his own opinion, and so they separated.

"It's a strange race, those poets!" said the clerk, who was very fond of soliloquizing. "I should like some day, just for a trial, to take such nature upon me, and be a poet myself; I am very sure I should make no such miserable verses as the others. Today, methinks, is a most delicious day for a poet. Nature seems anew to celebrate her awakening into life. The air is so unusually clear, the clouds sail on so buoyantly, and from the green herbage a fragrance is exhaled that fills me with delight. For many a year have I not felt as at this moment."

We see already, by the foregoing effusion, that he is become a poet; to give further proof of it, however, would in most cases be insipid, for it is a most foolish notion to fancy a poet different from other men. Among the latter there may be far more poetical natures than many an acknowledged poet, when examined more closely, could boast of; the difference only is, that the poet possesses a better mental memory, on which account he is able to retain the feeling and the thought till they can be embodied by means of words; a faculty which the others do not possess. But the transition from a commonplace nature to one that is richly endowed, demands always a more or less breakneck leap over a certain abyss which yawns threateningly below; and thus, must the sudden change with the clerk strike the reader.

"The sweet air!" continued he of the police office, in his dreamy imaginings. "How it reminds me of the violets in the garden of my aunt Magdalena! Yes, then I was a little wild boy, who did not go to school very regularly. O heavens, 'tis a long time since I have thought on those times. The good old soul! She lived behind the Exchange. She always had a few twigs or green shoots in water—let the winter rage without as it might. The violets exhaled their sweet breath, whilst I pressed against the windowpanes covered with fantastic frostwork the copper coin I had heated on the stove, and so made peep holes. What splendid vistas were then opened to my view! What change—what magnificence! Yonder in the canal lay the ships frozen up, and deserted by their whole crews, with a screaming crow for the sole occupant. But when the spring, with a gentle stirring motion, announced her arrival, a new and busy life arose; with songs and hurrahs the ice was sawn asunder, the ships were fresh tarred and rigged, that they might sail away to distant lands. But I have remained here—must always remain here, sitting at my desk in the office, and patiently see other people fetch their passports to go abroad. Such is my fate! Alas!" sighed he and was again silent. "Great heaven! What is come to me! Never have I thought or felt like this before! It must be the summer air that affects me with feelings almost as disquieting as they are refreshing."

He felt in his pocket for the papers. "These police reports will soon stem the torrent of my ideas and effectually hinder any rebellious overflowing of the time-worn banks of official duties." He said to himself consolingly, while his eye ran over the first page. "DAME TIGBRITH, tragedy in five acts." "What is that? And yet it is undeniably my own handwriting. Have I written the tragedy? Wonderful, very wonderful! And this—what have I here? 'INTRIGUE ON THE RAMPARTS; or THE DAY OF REPENTANCE: vaudeville with new songs to the most favorite airs.' The deuce! Where did I get all this rubbish? Someone must have slipped it slyly into my pocket for a joke. There is too a letter to me; a crumpled letter and the seal broken."

Yes, it was not a very polite epistle from the manager of a theatre, in which both pieces were flatly refused.

"Hem! Hem!" said the clerk breathlessly, and quite exhausted he seated himself on a bank. His thoughts were so elastic, his heart so tender; and involuntarily he picked one of the nearest flowers. It is a simple daisy, just bursting out of the bud. What the botanist tells us after a number of imperfect lectures, the flower proclaimed in a minute. It related the myths of its birth, told of the power of the sunlight that spread out its delicate leaves, and forced them to impregnate the air with their incense—and then he thought of the manifold struggles of life, which in like manner awaken the budding flowers of feeling in our bosom. Light and air contend with chivalric emulation for the love of the fair flower that bestowed her chief favors on the latter; full of longing she turned towards the light, and as soon as it vanished, rolled her tender leaves together and slept in the embraces of the air. "It is the light which adorns me," said the flower.

"But 'tis the air which enables thee to breathe," said the poet's voice.

Close by stood a boy who dashed his stick into a wet ditch. The drops of water splashed up to the green leafy roof, and the clerk thought of the million of ephemera which in a single drop were thrown up to a height, that was as great doubtless for their size, as for us if we were to be hurled above the clouds. While he thought of this and of the whole metamorphosis he had undergone, he smiled and said, "I sleep and dream; but it is wonderful how one can dream so naturally and know besides so exactly that it is but a dream. If only tomorrow on awaking, I could again call all to mind so vividly! I seem in unusually good spirits; my perception of things is clear, I feel as light and cheerful as though I were in heaven; but I know for a certainty, that if tomorrow a dim remembrance of it should swim before my mind, it will then seem nothing but stupid nonsense, as I have often experienced already—especially before I enlisted under the banner of the police, for that dispels like a whirlwind all the visions of an unfettered imagination. All we hear or say in a dream that is fair and beautiful is like the gold of the subterranean spirits; it is rich and splendid when it is given us but viewed by daylight we find only withered leaves. Alas!" he sighed quite sorrowful and gazed at the chirping birds that hopped contentedly from branch to branch, "they are much better off than I! To fly must be a heavenly art; and happy do I prize that creature in which it is innate. Yes! Could I exchange my nature with any other creature, I fain would be such a happy little lark!"

He had hardly uttered these hasty words when the skirts and sleeves of his coat folded themselves together into wings; the clothes became feathers, and the galoshes claws. He observed it perfectly and laughed in his heart. "Now then, there is no doubt that I am dreaming; but I never before was aware of such mad freaks as these." And up he flew into the green roof and sang; but in the song there was no poetry, for the spirit of the poet was gone. The Shoes, as is the case with anybody who does what he has to do properly, could only attend to one thing at a time. He wanted to be a poet, and he was one; he now wished to be a merry chirping bird: but when he was metamorphosed into one, the former peculiarities ceased immediately. "It is really pleasant enough," said he, "the whole day long I sit in the office amid the driest law papers, and at night I fly in my dream as a lark in the gardens of Fredericksburg; one might really write a very pretty comedy upon it." He now fluttered down into the grass, turned his head gracefully on every side, and with his bill pecked the pliant blades of grass, which, in comparison to his present size, seemed as majestic as the palm branches of northern Africa.

Unfortunately, the pleasure lasted but a moment. Presently black night overshadowed our enthusiast, who had so entirely missed his part of copying-clerk at a police office; some vast object seemed to be thrown over him. It was a large oil-skin cap, which a sailor boy of the quay had thrown over the struggling bird; a coarse hand sought its way carefully in under the broad rim and seized the clerk over the back and wings. In the first moment of fear, he called, indeed, as loud as he could, "You impudent little blackguard! I am a copying-clerk at the police office, and you know you cannot insult any belonging to the constabulary force without a chastisement. Besides, you good-for-nothing rascal, it is strictly forbidden to catch birds in the royal gardens of Fredericksburg; but your blue uniform betrays where you come from." This fine tirade sounded, however, to the ungodly sailor boy like a mere "Pippi-pi." He gave the noisy bird a knock on his beak and walked on.

He was soon met by two schoolboys of the upper class—that is to say as individuals, for with regard to learning they were in the lowest class in the school; and they bought the stupid bird. So, the copying-clerk came to Copenhagen as guest, or rather as prisoner in a family living in Gother Street.

"'Tis well that I'm dreaming," said the clerk, "or I really should get angry. First I was a poet; now sold for a few pence as a lark; no doubt it was that accursed poetical nature which has metamorphosed me into such a poor harmless little creature. It is really pitiable, particularly when one gets into the hands of a little blackguard, perfect in all sorts of cruelty to animals: all I should like to know is, how the story will end."

The two schoolboys, the proprietors now of the transformed clerk, carried him into an elegant room. A stout stately dame received them with a smile; but she expressed much dissatisfaction that a common field-bird, as she called the lark, should appear in such high society. For today, however, she would allow it; and they must shut him in the empty cage that was standing in the window. "Perhaps he will amuse my good Polly," added the lady, looking with a benignant smile at a large green parrot that swung himself backwards and forwards most comfortably in his ring, inside a magnificent brass-wired cage. "Today is Polly's birthday," said she with stupid simplicity: "and the little brown field bird must wish him joy."

Mr. Polly uttered not a syllable in reply but swung to and fro with dignified condescension; while a pretty canary, as yellow as gold, that had lately been brought from his sunny fragrant home, began to sing aloud.

"Noisy creature! Will you be quiet!" screamed the lady of the house, covering the cage with an embroidered white pocket handkerchief.

"Chirp, chirp!" sighed he. "That was a dreadful snowstorm;" and he sighed again and was silent.

The copying-clerk, or, as the lady said, the brown field bird, was put into a small cage, close to the canary, and not far from "my good Polly." The only human sounds that the parrot could bawl out were, "Come, let us be men!" Everything else that he said was as unintelligible to everybody as the chirping of the canary, except to the clerk, who was now a bird too: he understood his companion perfectly.

"I flew about beneath the green palms, and the blossoming almond trees," sang the Canary; "I flew around, with my brothers and sisters, over the beautiful flowers, and over the glassy lakes, where the bright water-plants nodded to me from below. There, too, I saw many splendidly dressed paroquets, that told the drollest stories, and the wildest fairy tales without end."

"Oh, those were uncouth birds," answered the Parrot. "They had no education and talked of whatever came into their head.

"If my mistress and all her friends can laugh at what I say, so may you too, I should think. It is a great fault to have no taste for what is witty or amusing—come, let us be men."

"Ah, you have no remembrance of love for the charming maidens that danced beneath the outspread tents beside the bright fragrant flowers. Do you no longer remember the sweet fruits, and the cooling juice in the wild plants of our never-to-be-forgotten home?" said the former inhabitant of the Canary Isles, continuing his dithyrambic.

"Oh, yes," said the Parrot; "but I am far better off here. I am well fed and get friendly treatment. I know I am a clever fellow; and that is all I care about. Come, let us be men. You are of a poetical nature, as it is called—I, on the contrary, possess profound knowledge and inexhaustible wit. You have genius; but clear-sighted, calm discretion does not take such lofty flights and utter such high natural tones. For this they have covered you over—they never do the like to me; for I cost more. Besides, they are afraid of my beak; and I have always a witty answer at hand. Come, let us be men!"

"O warm spicy land of my birth," sang the Canary bird. "I will sing of thy dark-green bowers, of the calm bays where the pendent boughs kiss the surface of the water; I will sing of the rejoicing of all my brothers and sisters where the cactus grows in wanton luxuriance."

"Spare us your elegiac tones," said the Parrot giggling. "Rather speak of something at which one may laugh heartily. Laughing is an infallible sign of the highest degree of mental development. Can a dog, or a horse laugh? No, but they can cry. The gift of laughing was given to man alone. Ha! Ha! Ha!" screamed Polly and added his stereotype witticism. "Come, let us be men!"

"Poor little Danish grey bird," said the Canary, "you have been caught too. It is, no doubt, cold enough in your woods, but there at least is the breath of liberty; therefore, fly away. In the hurry they have forgotten to shut your cage, and the upper window is open. Fly, my friend; fly away. Farewell!"

Instinctively the Clerk obeyed; with a few strokes of his wings, he was out of the cage; but at the same moment the door, which was only ajar, and which led to the next room, began to creak, and supple and creeping came the large tomcat into the room, and began to pursue him. The frightened canary fluttered about in his cage; the parrot flapped his wings, and cried, "Come, let us be men!" The Clerk felt a mortal fright, and flew through the window, far away over the houses and streets. At last, he was forced to rest a little.

The neighboring house had a something familiar about it; a window stood open; he flew in; it was his own room. He perched upon the table.

"Come, let us be men!" said he, involuntarily imitating the chatter of the parrot, and at the same moment he was again a copying-clerk; but he was sitting in the middle of the table.

"Heaven help me!" cried he. "How did I get up here—and so buried in sleep, too? After all, that was a very unpleasant, disagreeable dream that haunted me! The whole story is nothing but silly, stupid nonsense!"

The Wild Swans

Far away in the land to which the swallows fly when it is winter, dwelt a king who had eleven sons, and one daughter, named Eliza. The eleven brothers were princes, and each went to school with a star on his breast, and a sword by his side. They wrote with diamond pencils on gold slates, and learnt their lessons so quickly and read so easily that everyone might know they were princes. Their sister Eliza sat on a little stool of plate-glass, and had a book full of pictures, which had cost as much as half a kingdom. Oh, these children were indeed happy, but it was not to remain so always. Their father, who was king of the country, married a very wicked queen, who did not love the poor children at all. They knew this from the very first day after the wedding.

In the palace there were great festivities, and the children played at receiving company; but instead of having, as usual, all the cakes and apples that were left, she gave them some sand in a teacup, and told them to pretend it was cake. The week after, she sent little Eliza into the country to a peasant and his wife, and then she told the king so many untrue things about the young princes, that he gave himself no more trouble respecting them.

"Go out into the world and get your own living," said the queen. "Fly like great birds, who have no voice." But she could not make them ugly as she wished, for they were turned into eleven beautiful wild swans. Then, with a strange cry, they flew through the windows of the palace, over the park, to the forest beyond. It was early morning when they passed the peasant's cottage, where their sister Eliza lay asleep in her room. They hovered over the roof, twisted their long necks and flapped their wings, but no one heard them or saw them, so they were at last obliged to fly away, high up in the clouds; and over the wide world they flew till they came to a thick, dark wood, which stretched far away to the seashore. Poor little Eliza was alone in her room playing with a green leaf, for she had no other playthings, and she pierced a hole through the leaf, and looked through it at the sun, and it was as if she saw her brothers' clear eyes, and when the warm sun shone on her cheeks, she thought of all the kisses they had given her.

One day passed just like another; sometimes the winds rustled through the leaves of the rosebush, and would whisper to the roses, "Who can be more beautiful than you!" But the roses would shake their heads, and say, "Eliza is." And when the old woman sat at the cottage door on Sunday, and read her hymnbook, the wind would flutter the leaves, and say to the book, "Who can be more pious than you?" and then the hymnbook would answer "Eliza." And the roses and the hymnbook told the real truth.

At fifteen she returned home, but when the queen saw how beautiful she was, she became full of spite and hatred towards her. Willingly would she have turned her into a swan, like her brothers, but she did not dare to do so yet, because the king wished to see his daughter. Early one morning the queen went into the bathroom; it was built of marble, and had soft cushions, trimmed with the most beautiful tapestry. She took three toads with her, and kissed them, and said to one, "When Eliza comes to the bath, seat yourself upon her head, that she may become as stupid as you are." Then she said to another, "Place yourself on her forehead, that she may become as ugly as you are, and that her father may not know her." "Rest on her heart," she whispered to the third, "then she will have evil inclinations, and suffer in consequence."

So she put the toads into the clear water, and they turned green immediately. She next called Eliza, and helped her to undress and get into the bath. As Eliza dipped her head under the water, one of the toads sat on her hair, a second on her forehead, and a third on her breast, but she did not seem to notice them, and when she rose out of the water, there were three red poppies floating upon it. Had not the creatures been venomous or been kissed by the witch, they would have been changed into red roses. At all events they became flowers, because they had rested on Eliza's head, and on her heart. She was too good and too innocent for witchcraft to have any power over her. When the wicked queen saw this, she rubbed mud on her face, so that she was quite brown; then she tangled her beautiful hair and smeared it with disgusting ointment, till it was quite impossible to recognize the beautiful Eliza.

When her father saw her, he was much shocked, and declared she was not his daughter. No one but the watchdog and the swallows knew her; and they were only poor animals, and could say nothing. Then poor Eliza wept, and thought of her eleven brothers, who were all away. Sorrowfully, she stole away from the palace, and walked, the whole day, over fields and moors, till she came to the great forest. She knew not in what direction to go; but she was so unhappy, and longed so for her brothers, who had been, like herself, driven out into the world, that she was determined to seek them. She had been but a short time in the wood when night came on, and she quite lost the path; so she laid herself down on the soft moss, offered up her evening prayer, and leaned her head against the stump of a tree. All nature was still, and the soft, mild air fanned her forehead. The light of hundreds of glowworms shone amidst the grass and the moss, like green fire; and if she touched a twig with her hand, ever so lightly, the brilliant insects fell down around her, like shooting stars.

All night long she dreamt of her brothers. She and they were children again, playing together. She saw them writing with their diamond pencils on golden slates, while she looked at the beautiful picture book which had cost half a kingdom. They were not writing lines and letters, as they used to do; but descriptions of the noble deeds they had performed, and of all they had discovered and seen. In the picture book, too, everything was living. The birds sang, and the people came out of the book, and spoke to Eliza and her brothers; but, as the leaves turned over, they darted back again to their places, that all might be in order.

When she awoke, the sun was high in the heavens; yet she could not see him, for the lofty trees spread their branches thickly over her head; but his beams were glancing through the leaves here and there, like a golden mist. There was a sweet fragrance from the fresh green verdure, and the birds almost perched upon her shoulders. She heard water rippling from a number of springs, all flowing in a lake with golden sands. Bushes grew thickly round the lake, and at one spot an opening had been made by a deer, through which Eliza went down to the water.

The lake was so clear that, had not the wind rustled the branches of the trees and the bushes, so that they moved, they would have appeared as if painted in the depths of the lake; for every leaf was reflected in the water, whether it stood in the shade or the sunshine.

As soon as Eliza saw her own face, she was quite terrified at finding it caked with mud; but when she wetted her little hand, and rubbed her eyes and forehead, her skin gleamed forth once more; and, after she had undressed, and dipped herself in the fresh water, a more beautiful king's daughter could not be found in the wide world.

As soon as she had dressed herself again, and braided her long hair, she went to the bubbling spring, and drank some water out of the hollow of her hand. Then she wandered far into the forest, not knowing whither she went. She thought of her brothers, and felt sure that God would not forsake her. It is God who makes the wild apples grow in the wood, to satisfy the hungry, and He now led her to one of these trees, which was so loaded with fruit, that the boughs bent beneath the weight. Here she held her noonday repast, placed props under the boughs, and then went into the gloomiest depths of the forest. It was so still that she could hear the sound of her own footsteps, as well as the rustling of every withered leaf which she crushed under her feet. Not a bird was to be seen, not a sunbeam could penetrate through the large, dark boughs of the trees. Their lofty trunks stood so close together, that, when she looked before her, it seemed as if she were enclosed within trelliswork. Such solitude she had never known before. The night was very dark. Not a single glow worm glittered in the moss.

Sorrowfully she laid herself down to sleep; and, after a while, it seemed to her as if the branches of the trees parted over her head, and that the mild eyes of angels looked down upon her from heaven. When she awoke in the morning, she knew not whether she had dreamt this, or if it had really been so. Then she continued her wandering; but she had not gone many steps forward, when she met an old woman with berries in her basket, and she gave her a few to eat. Then Eliza asked her if she had not seen eleven princes riding through the forest.

"No," replied the old woman, "But I saw yesterday eleven swans, with gold crowns on their heads, swimming on the river close by." Then she led Eliza a little distance farther to a sloping bank, and at the foot of it wound a little river. The trees on its banks stretched their long leafy branches across the water towards each other, and where the growth prevented them from meeting naturally, the roots had torn themselves away from the ground, so that the branches might mingle their foliage as they hung over the water. Eliza bade the old woman farewell, and walked by the flowing river, till she reached the shore of the open sea. And there, before the young maiden's eyes, lay the glorious ocean, but not a sail appeared on its surface, not even a boat could be seen. How was she to go farther? She noticed how the countless pebbles on the seashore had been smoothed and rounded by the action of the water. Glass, iron, stones, everything that lay there mingled together, had taken its shape from the same power, and felt as smooth, or even smoother than her own delicate hand. "The water rolls on without weariness," she said, "till all that is hard becomes smooth; so will I be unwearied in my task. Thanks for your lessons, bright rolling waves; my heart tells me you will lead me to my dear brothers."

On the foam-covered seaweeds, lay eleven white swan feathers, which she gathered up and placed together. Drops of water lay upon them; whether they were dewdrops or tears no one could say. Lonely as it was on the seashore, she did not observe it, for the ever-moving sea showed more changes in a few hours than the most varying lake could produce during a whole year. If a black heavy cloud arose, it was as if the sea said, "I can look dark and angry too;" and then the wind blew, and the waves turned to white foam as they rolled. When the wind slept, and the clouds glowed with the red sunlight, then the sea looked like a rose leaf. But however quietly its white glassy surface rested, there was still a motion on the shore, as its waves rose and fell like the breast of a sleeping child.

When the sun was about to set, Eliza saw eleven white swans with golden crowns on their heads, flying towards the land, one behind the other, like a long white ribbon. Then Eliza went down the slope from the shore, and hid herself behind the bushes. The swans alighted quite close to her and flapped their great white wings. As soon as the sun had disappeared under the water, the feathers of the swans fell off, and eleven beautiful princes, Eliza's brothers, stood near her. She uttered a loud cry, for, although they were very much changed, she knew them immediately. She sprang into their arms, and called them each by name. Then, how happy the princes were at meeting their little sister again, for they recognized her, although she had grown so tall and beautiful. They laughed, and they wept, and very soon understood how wickedly their mother had acted to them all. "We brothers," said the eldest, "fly about as wild swans, so long as the sun is in the sky; but as soon as it sinks behind the hills, we recover our human shape. Therefore must we always be near a resting place for our feet before sunset; for if we should be flying towards the clouds at the time we recovered our natural shape as men, we should sink deep into the sea. We do not dwell here, but in a land just as fair, that lies beyond the ocean, which we have to cross for a long distance; there is no island in our passage upon which we could pass the night; nothing but a little rock rising out of the sea, upon which we can scarcely stand with safety, even closely crowded together. If the sea is rough, the foam dashes over us, yet we thank God even for this rock; we have passed whole nights upon it, or we should never have reached our beloved fatherland, for our flight across the sea occupies two of the longest days in the year. We have permission to visit out home once in every year, and to remain eleven days, during which we fly across the forest to look once more at the palace where our father dwells, and where we were born, and at the church, where our mother lies buried. Here it seems as if the very trees and bushes were related to us. The wild horses leap over the plains as we have seen them in our childhood. The charcoal burners sing the old songs, to which we have danced as children. This is our fatherland, to which we are drawn by loving ties; and here we have found you, our dear little sister. Two days longer we can remain here, and then must we fly away to a beautiful land which is not our home; and how can we take you with us? We have neither ship nor boat."

"How can I break this spell?" said their sister. And then she talked about it nearly the whole night, only slumbering for a few hours.

Eliza was awakened by the rustling of the swans' wings as they soared above. Her brothers were again changed to swans, and they flew in circles wider and wider, till they were far away; but one of them, the youngest swan, remained behind, and laid his head in his sister's lap, while she stroked his wings; and they remained together the whole day.

Towards evening, the rest came back, and as the sun went down they resumed their natural forms. "Tomorrow," said one, "we shall fly away, not to return again till a whole year has passed. But we cannot leave you here. Have you courage to go with us? My arm is strong enough to carry you through the wood; and will not all our wings be strong enough to fly with you over the sea?"

"Yes, take me with you," said Eliza. Then they spent the whole night in weaving a net with the pliant willow and rushes. It was very large and strong. Eliza laid herself down on the net, and when the sun rose, and her brothers again became wild swans, they took up the net with their beaks, and flew up to the clouds with their dear sister, who still slept. The sunbeams fell on her face, therefore one of the swans soared over her head, so that his broad wings might shade her. They were far from the land when Eliza woke. She thought she must still be dreaming, it seemed so strange to her to feel herself being carried so high in the air over the sea. By her side lay a branch full of beautiful ripe berries, and a bundle of sweet roots; the youngest of her brothers had gathered them for her, and placed them by her side. She smiled her thanks to him; she knew it was the same who had hovered over her to shade her with his wings.

They were now so high, that a large ship beneath them looked like a white seagull skimming the waves. A great cloud floating behind them appeared like a vast mountain, and upon it Eliza saw her own shadow and those of the eleven swans, looking gigantic in size. Altogether it formed a more beautiful picture than she had ever seen; but as the sun rose higher, and the clouds were left behind, the shadowy picture vanished away. Onward the whole day they flew through the air like a winged arrow, yet more slowly than usual, for they had their sister to carry. The weather seemed inclined to be stormy, and Eliza watched the sinking sun with great anxiety, for the little rock in the ocean was not yet in sight. It appeared to her as if the swans were making great efforts with their wings. Alas! she was the cause of their not advancing more quickly. When the sun set, they would change to men, fall into the sea and be drowned. Then she offered a prayer from her inmost heart, but still no appearance of the rock. Dark clouds came nearer, the gusts of wind told of a coming storm, while from a thick, heavy mass of clouds the lightning burst forth flash after flash. The sun had reached the edge of the sea, when the swans darted down so swiftly, that Eliza's head trembled; she believed they were falling, but they again soared onward. Presently she caught sight of the rock just below them, and by this time the sun was half hidden by the waves. The rock did not appear larger than a seal's head thrust out of the water. They sunk so rapidly, that at the moment their feet touched the rock, it shone only like a star, and at last disappeared like the last spark in a piece of burnt paper. Then she saw her brothers standing closely round her with their arms linked together. There was but just room enough for them, and not the smallest space to spare.

The sea dashed against the rock, and covered them with spray. The heavens were lighted up with continual flashes, and peal after peal of thunder rolled. But the sister and brothers sat holding each other's hands, and singing hymns, from which they gained hope and courage. In the early dawn the air became calm and still, and at sunrise the swans flew away from the rock with Eliza. The sea was still rough, and from their high position in the air, the white foam on the dark green waves looked like millions of swans swimming on the water. As the sun rose higher, Eliza saw before her, floating on the air, a range of mountains, with shining masses of ice on their summits. In the centre rose a castle apparently a mile long, with rows of columns, rising one above another, while, around it, palm trees waved and flowers bloomed as large as mill wheels. She asked if this was the land to which they were hastening. The swans shook their heads, for what she beheld were the beautiful ever-changing cloud palaces of the "Fata Morgana," into which no mortal can enter. Eliza was still gazing at the scene, when mountains, forests, and castles melted away, and twenty stately churches rose in their stead, with high towers and pointed gothic windows. Eliza even fancied she could hear the tones of the organ, but it was the music of the murmuring sea which she heard. As they drew nearer to the churches, they also changed into a fleet of ships, which seemed to be sailing beneath her; but as she looked again, she found it was only a sea mist gliding over the ocean. So there continued to pass before her eyes a constant change of scene, till at last she saw the real land to which they were bound, with its blue mountains, its cedar forests, and its cities and palaces. Long before the sun went down, she sat on a rock, in front of a large cave, on the floor of which the overgrown yet delicate green creeping plants looked like an embroidered carpet. "Now we shall expect to hear what you dream of tonight," said the youngest brother, as he showed his sister her bedroom.

"Heaven grant that I may dream how to save you," she replied. And this thought took such hold upon her mind that she prayed earnestly to God for help, and even in her sleep she continued to pray. Then it appeared to her as if she were flying high in the air, towards the cloudy palace of the "Fata Morgana," and a fairy came out to meet her, radiant and beautiful in appearance, and yet very much like the old woman who had given her berries in the wood, and who had told her of the swans with golden crowns on their heads. "Your brothers can be released," said she, "if you have only courage and perseverance. True, water is softer than your own delicate hands, and yet it polishes stones into shapes; it feels no pain as your fingers would feel, it has no soul, and cannot suffer such agony and torment as you will have to endure. Do you see the stinging nettle which I hold in my hand? Quantities of the same sort grow round the cave in which you sleep, but none will be of any use to you unless they grow upon the graves in a churchyard. These you must gather even while they burn blisters on your hands. Break them to pieces with your hands and feet, and they will become flax, from which you must spin and weave eleven coats with long sleeves; if these are then thrown over the eleven swans, the spell will be broken. But remember, that from the moment you commence your task until it is finished, even should it occupy years of your life, you must not speak. The first word you utter will pierce through the hearts of your brothers like a deadly dagger. Their lives hang upon your tongue. Remember all I have told you." And as she finished speaking, she touched her hand lightly with the nettle, and a pain, as of burning fire, awoke Eliza.

It was broad daylight, and close by where she had been sleeping lay a nettle like the one she had seen in her dream. She fell on her knees and offered her thanks to God. Then she went forth from the cave to begin her work with her delicate hands. She groped in amongst the ugly nettles, which burnt great blisters on her hands and arms, but she determined to bear it gladly if she could only release her dear brothers. So she bruised the nettles with her bare feet and spun the flax. At sunset her brothers returned and were very much frightened when they found her dumb. They believed it to be some new sorcery of their wicked stepmother. But when they saw her hands they understood what she was doing on their behalf, and the youngest brother wept, and where his tears fell the pain ceased, and the burning blisters vanished. She kept to her work all night, for she could not rest till she had released her dear brothers. During the whole of the following day, while her brothers were absent, she sat in solitude, but never before had the time flown so quickly. One coat was already finished and she had begun the second, when she heard the huntsman's horn, and was struck with fear. The sound came nearer and nearer, she heard the dogs barking, and fled with terror into the cave. She hastily bound together the nettles she had gathered into a bundle and sat upon them. Immediately a great dog came bounding towards her out of the ravine, and then another and another; they barked loudly, ran back, and then came again. In a very few minutes all the huntsmen stood before the cave, and the handsomest of them was the king of the country. He advanced towards her, for he had never seen a more beautiful maiden.

"How did you come here, my sweet child?" he asked.

Eliza shook her head. She dared not speak, at the cost of her brothers' lives. And she hid her hands under her apron, so that the king might not see how she must be suffering.

"Come with me," he said; "here you cannot remain. If you are as good as you are beautiful, I will dress you in silk and velvet, I will place a golden crown upon your head, and you shall dwell, and rule, and make your home in my richest castle." And then he lifted her on his horse. She wept and wrung her hands, but the king said, "I wish only for your

happiness. A time will come when you will thank me for this." And then he galloped away over the mountains, holding her before him on this horse, and the hunters followed behind them.

As the sun went down, they approached a fair royal city, with churches, and cupolas. On arriving at the castle the king led her into marble halls, where large fountains played, and where the walls and the ceilings were covered with rich paintings. But she had no eyes for all these glorious sights, she could only mourn and weep. Patiently she allowed the women to array her in royal robes, to weave pearls in her hair, and draw soft gloves over her blistered fingers. As she stood before them in all her rich dress, she looked so dazzlingly beautiful that the court bowed low in her presence. Then the king declared his intention of making her his bride, but the archbishop shook his head, and whispered that the fair young maiden was only a witch who had blinded the king's eyes and bewitched his heart. But the king would not listen to this; he ordered the music to sound, the daintiest dishes to be served, and the loveliest maidens to dance. Afterwards he led her through fragrant gardens and lofty halls, but not a smile appeared on her lips or sparkled in her eyes. She looked the very picture of grief. Then the king opened the door of a little chamber in which she was to sleep; it was adorned with rich green tapestry, and resembled the cave in which he had found her. On the floor lay the bundle of flax which she had spun from the nettles, and under the ceiling hung the coat she had made. These things had been brought away from the cave as curiosities by one of the huntsmen.

"Here you can dream yourself back again in the old home in the cave," said the king; "here is the work with which you employed yourself. It will amuse you now in the midst of all this splendor to think of that time."

When Eliza saw all these things which lay so near her heart, a smile played around her mouth, and the crimson blood rushed to her cheeks. She thought of her brothers, and their release made her so joyful that she kissed the king's hand. Then he pressed her to his heart. Very soon the joyous church bells announced the marriage feast, and that the beautiful dumb girl out of the wood was to be made the queen of the country. Then the archbishop whispered wicked words in the king's ear, but they did not sink into his heart. The marriage was still to take place, and the archbishop himself had to place the crown on the bride's head; in his wicked spite, he pressed the narrow circlet so tightly on her forehead that it caused her pain. But a heavier weight encircled her heart—sorrow for her brothers. She felt not bodily pain. Her mouth was closed; a single word would cost the lives of her brothers. But she loved the kind, handsome king, who did everything to make her happy more and more each day; she loved him with all her heart, and her eyes beamed with the love she dared not speak. Oh! if she had only been able to confide in him and tell him of her grief. But dumb she must remain till her task was finished. Therefore at night she crept away into her little chamber, which had been decked out to look like the cave, and quickly wove one coat after another.

But when she began the seventh she found she had no more flax She knew that the nettles she wanted to use grew in the churchyard, and that she must pluck them herself. How should she get out there? "Oh, what is the pain in my fingers to the torment which my heart endures?" said she. "I must venture, I shall not be denied help from heaven." Then with a trembling heart, as if she were about to perform a wicked deed, she crept into the garden in the broad moonlight, and passed through the narrow walks and the deserted streets, till she reached the churchyard. Then she saw on one of the broad tombstones a group of ghouls. These hideous creatures took off their rags, as if they intended to bathe, and then clawing open the fresh graves with their long, skinny fingers, pulled out the dead bodies and ate the flesh! Eliza had to pass close by them, and they fixed their wicked glances upon her, but she prayed silently, gathered the burning nettles, and carried them home with her to the castle. One person only had seen her, and that was the archbishop—he was awake while everybody was asleep. Now he thought his opinion was evidently correct. All was not right with the queen. She was a witch, and had bewitched the king and all the people. Secretly he told the king what he had seen and what he feared, and as the hard words came from his tongue, the carved images of the saints shook their heads as if they would say. "It is not so. Eliza is innocent."

But the archbishop interpreted it in another way; he believed that they witnessed against her, and were shaking their heads at her wickedness. Two large tears rolled down the king's cheeks, and he went home with doubt in his heart, and at night he pretended to sleep, but there came no real sleep to his eyes, for he saw Eliza get up every night and disappear in her own chamber. From day to day his brow became darker, and Eliza saw it and did not understand the reason, but it alarmed her and made her heart tremble for her brothers. Her hot tears glittered like pearls on the regal velvet and diamonds, while all who saw her were wishing they could be queens. In the meantime she had almost finished her task; only one coat of mail was wanting, but she had no flax left, and not a single nettle. Once more only, and for the last time, must she venture to the churchyard and pluck a few handfuls. She thought with terror of the solitary walk, and of the horrible ghouls, but her will was firm, as well as her trust in Providence. Eliza went, and the king and the archbishop followed her. They saw her vanish through the wicket gate into the churchyard, and when they came nearer they saw the ghouls sitting on the tombstone, as Eliza had seen them, and the king turned away his head, for he thought she was with them—she whose head had rested on his breast that very evening.

"The people must condemn her," said he, and she was very quickly condemned by everyone to suffer death by fire. Away from the gorgeous regal halls was she led to a dark, dreary cell, where the wind whistled through the iron bars. Instead of the velvet and silk dresses, they gave her the coats of mail which she had woven to cover her, and the bundle of nettles for a pillow; but nothing they could give her would have pleased her more. She continued her task with joy, and prayed for help, while the street-boys sang jeering songs about her, and not a soul comforted her with a kind word. Towards evening, she heard at the grating the flutter of a swan's wing, it was her youngest brother—he had found his sister, and she sobbed for joy, although she knew that very likely this would be the last night she would have to live. But still she could hope, for her task was almost finished, and her brothers were come. Then the archbishop arrived, to be with her during her last hours, as he had promised the king. But she shook her head, and begged him, by looks and gestures, not to stay; for in this night she knew she must finish her task, otherwise all her pain and tears and sleepless nights would have been suffered in vain. The archbishop withdrew, uttering bitter words against her; but poor Eliza knew that she was innocent, and diligently continued her work.

The little mice ran about the floor, they dragged the nettles to her feet, to help as well as they could; and the thrush sat outside the grating of the window, and sang to her the whole night long, as sweetly as possible, to keep up her spirits.

It was still twilight, and at least an hour before sunrise, when the eleven brothers stood at the castle gate, and demanded to be brought before the king. They were told it could not be, it was yet almost night, and as the king slept they dared not disturb him. They threatened, they entreated. Then the guard appeared, and even the king himself, inquiring what all the noise meant. At this moment the sun rose. The eleven brothers were seen no more, but eleven wild swans flew away over the castle.

And now all the people came streaming forth from the gates of the city, to see the witch burnt. An old horse drew the cart on which she sat. They had dressed her in a garment of coarse sackcloth. Her lovely hair hung loose on her shoulders, her cheeks were deadly pale, her lips moved silently, while her fingers still worked at the green flax. Even on the way to death, she would not give up her task. The ten coats of mail lay at her feet, she was working hard at the eleventh, while the mob jeered her and said, "See the witch, how she mutters! She has no hymnbook in her hand. She sits there with her ugly sorcery. Let us tear it in a thousand pieces."

And then they pressed towards her, and would have destroyed the coats of mail, but at the same moment eleven wild swans flew over her, and alighted on the cart. Then they flapped their large wings, and the crowd drew on one side in alarm.

"It is a sign from heaven that she is innocent," whispered many of them; but they ventured not to say it aloud.

As the executioner seized her by the hand, to lift her out of the cart, she hastily threw the eleven coats of mail over the swans, and they immediately became eleven handsome princes; but the youngest had a swan's wing, instead of an arm; for she had not been able to finish the last sleeve of the coat.

"Now I may speak," she exclaimed. "I am innocent."

Then the people, who saw what happened, bowed to her, as before a saint; but she sank lifeless in her brothers' arms, overcome with suspense, anguish, and pain.

"Yes, she is innocent," said the eldest brother; and then he related all that had taken place; and while he spoke there rose in the air a fragrance as from millions of roses. Every piece of faggot in the pile had taken root, and threw out branches, and appeared a thick hedge, large and high, covered with roses; while above all bloomed a white and shining flower, that glittered like a star. This flower the king plucked, and placed in Eliza's bosom, when she awoke from her swoon, with peace and happiness in her heart. And all the church bells rang of themselves, and the birds came in great troops. And a marriage procession returned to the castle, such as no king had ever before seen.

The Fir Tree

Far down in the forest, where the warm sun and the fresh air made a sweet resting-place, grew a pretty little fir tree; and yet it was not happy, it wished so much to be tall like its companions—the pines and firs which grew around it. The sun shone, and the soft air fluttered its leaves, and the little peasant children passed by, prattling merrily, but the fir tree heeded them not. Sometimes the children would bring a large basket of raspberries or strawberries, wreathed on a straw, and seat themselves near the fir tree, and say, "Is it not a pretty little tree?" which made it feel more unhappy than before. And yet all this while the tree grew a notch or joint taller every year; for by the number of joints in the stem of a fir tree we can discover its age. Still, as it grew, it complained, "Oh! how I wish I were as tall as the other trees, then I would spread out my branches on every side, and my top would overlook the wide world. I should have the birds building their nests on my boughs, and when the wind blew, I should bow with stately dignity like my tall companions."

The tree was so discontented, that it took no pleasure in the warm sunshine, the birds, or the rosy clouds that floated over it morning and evening. Sometimes, in winter, when the snow lay white and glittering on the ground, a hare would come springing along, and jump right over the little tree; and then how mortified it would feel! Two winters passed, and when the third arrived, the tree had grown so tall that the hare was obliged to run round it. Yet it remained unsatisfied, and would exclaim, "Oh, if I could but keep on growing tall and old! There is nothing else worth caring for in the world!" In the autumn, as usual, the woodcutters came and cut down several of the tallest trees, and the young fir tree, which was now grown to its full height, shuddered as the noble trees fell to the earth with a crash. After the branches were lopped off, the trunks looked so slender and bare, that they could scarcely be recognized. Then they were placed upon wagons, and drawn by horses out of the forest. "Where were they going? What would become of them?" The young fir tree wished very much to know; so in the spring, when the swallows and the storks came, it asked, "Do you know where those trees were taken? Did you meet them?"

The swallows knew nothing, but the stork, after a little reflection, nodded his head, and said, "Yes, I think I do. I met several new ships when I flew from Egypt, and they had fine masts that smelt like fir. I think these must have been the trees; I assure you they were stately, very stately."

"Oh, how I wish I were tall enough to go on the sea," said the fir tree. "What is the sea, and what does it look like?"

"It would take too much time to explain," said the stork, flying quickly away.

"Rejoice in thy youth," said the sunbeam; "rejoice in thy fresh growth, and the young life that is in thee."

And the wind kissed the tree, and the dew watered it with tears; but the fir tree regarded them not.

Christmastime drew near, and many young trees were cut down, some even smaller and younger than the fir tree who enjoyed neither rest nor peace with longing to leave its forest home. These young trees, which were chosen for their beauty, kept their branches, and were also laid on wagons and drawn by horses out of the forest.

"Where are they going?" asked the fir tree. "They are not taller than I am: indeed, one is much less; and why are the branches not cut off? Where are they going?"

"We know, we know," sang the sparrows; "we have looked in at the windows of the houses in the town, and we know what is done with them. They are dressed up in the most splendid manner. We have seen them standing in the middle of a warm room, and adorned with all sorts of beautiful things—honey cakes, gilded apples, playthings, and many hundreds of wax tapers."

"And then," asked the fir tree, trembling through all its branches, "and then what happens?"

"We did not see any more," said the sparrows; "but this was enough for us."

"I wonder whether anything so brilliant will ever happen to me," thought the fir tree. "It would be much better than crossing the sea. I long for it almost with pain. Oh! when will Christmas be here? I am now as tall and well grown as those which were taken away last year. Oh! that I were now laid on the wagon, or standing in the warm room, with all that brightness and splendor around me! Something better and more beautiful is to come after, or the trees would not be so decked out. Yes, what follows will be grander and more splendid. What can it be? I am weary with longing. I scarcely know how I feel."

"Rejoice with us," said the air and the sunlight. "Enjoy thine own bright life in the fresh air."

But the tree would not rejoice, though it grew taller every day; and, winter and summer, its dark-green foliage might be seen in the forest, while passersby would say, "What a beautiful tree!"

A short time before Christmas, the discontented fir tree was the first to fall. As the axe cut through the stem, and divided the pith, the tree fell with a groan to the earth, conscious of pain and faintness, and forgetting all its anticipations of happiness, in sorrow at leaving its home in the forest. It knew that it should never again see its dear old companions, the trees, nor the little bushes and many-colored flowers that had grown by its side; perhaps not even the birds. Neither was the journey at all pleasant. The tree first recovered itself while being unpacked in the courtyard of a house, with several other trees; and it heard a man say, "We only want one, and this is the prettiest."

Then came two servants in grand livery, and carried the fir tree into a large and beautiful apartment. On the walls hung pictures, and near the great stove stood great china vases, with lions on the lids. There were rocking chairs, silken sofas, large tables, covered with pictures, books, and playthings, worth a great deal of money—at least, the children said so. Then the fir tree was placed in a large tub, full of sand; but green baize hung all around it, so that no one could see it was a tub, and it stood on a very handsome carpet. How the fir tree trembled! "What was going to happen to him now?" Some young ladies came, and the servants helped them to adorn the tree. On one branch they hung little bags cut out of colored paper, and each bag was filled with sweetmeats; from other branches hung gilded apples and walnuts, as if they had grown there; and above, and all round, were hundreds of red, blue, and white tapers, which were fastened on the branches. Dolls, exactly like real babies, were placed under the green leaves,—the tree had never seen such things before. And at the very top was fastened a glittering star, made of tinsel. Oh, it was very beautiful!

"This evening," they all exclaimed, "how bright it will be!" "Oh, that the evening were come," thought the tree, "and the tapers lighted! then I shall know what else is going to happen. Will the trees of the forest come to see me? I wonder if the sparrows will peep in at the windows as they fly? shall I grow faster here, and keep on all these ornaments summer and winter?" But guessing was of very little use; it made his bark ache, and this pain is as bad for a slender fir tree, as headache is for us. At last the tapers were lighted, and then what a glistening blaze of light the tree presented! It trembled so with joy in all its branches, that one of the candles fell among the green leaves and burnt some of them. "Help! help!" exclaimed the young ladies, but there was no danger, for they quickly extinguished the fire. After this, the tree tried not to tremble at all, though the fire frightened him; he was so anxious not to hurt any of the beautiful ornaments, even while their brilliancy dazzled him. And now the folding doors were thrown open, and a troop of children rushed in as if they intended to upset the tree; they were followed more silently by their elders. For a moment the little ones stood silent with astonishment, and then they shouted for joy, till the room rang, and they danced merrily round the tree, while one present after another was taken from it.

"What are they doing? What will happen next?" thought the fir. At last the candles burnt down to the branches and were put out. Then the children received permission to plunder the tree.

Oh, how they rushed upon it, till the branches cracked, and had it not been fastened with the glistening star to the ceiling, it must have been thrown down. The children then danced about with their pretty toys, and no one noticed the tree, except the children's maid who came and peeped among the branches to see if an apple or a fig had been forgotten.

"A story, a story," cried the children, pulling a little fat man towards the tree.

"Now we shall be in the green shade," said the man, as he seated himself under it, "and the tree will have the pleasure of hearing also, but I shall only relate one story; what shall it be? Ivede-Avede, or Humpty Dumpty, who fell downstairs, but soon got up again, and at last married a princess."

"Ivede-Avede," cried some. "Humpty Dumpty," cried others, and there was a fine shouting and crying out. But the fir tree remained quite still, and thought to himself, "Shall I have anything to do with all this?" but he had already amused them as much as they wished. Then the old man told them the story of Humpty Dumpty, how he fell downstairs, and was raised up again, and married a princess. And the children clapped their hands and cried, "Tell another, tell another," for they wanted to hear the story of "Ivede-Avede;" but they only had "Humpty Dumpty." After this the fir tree became quite silent and thoughtful; never had the birds in the forest told such tales as "Humpty Dumpty," who fell downstairs, and yet married a princess.

"Ah! yes, so it happens in the world," thought the fir tree; he believed it all, because it was related by such a nice man. "Ah! well," he thought, "who knows? perhaps I may fall down too, and marry a princess;" and he looked forward joyfully to the next evening, expecting to be again decked out with lights and playthings, gold and fruit. "Tomorrow I will not tremble," thought he; "I will enjoy all my splendor, and I shall hear the story of Humpty Dumpty again, and perhaps Ivede-Avede." And the tree remained quiet and thoughtful all night.

In the morning the servants and the housemaid came in. "Now," thought the fir, "all my splendor is going to begin again." But they dragged him out of the room and upstairs to the garret, and threw him on the floor, in a dark corner, where no daylight shone, and there they left him. "What does this mean?" thought the tree, "what am I to do here? I can hear nothing in a place like this," and he had time enough to think, for days and nights passed and no one came near him, and when at last somebody did come, it was only to put away large boxes in a corner. So the tree was completely hidden from sight as if it had never existed. "It is winter now," thought the tree, "the ground is hard and covered with snow, so that people cannot plant me. I shall be sheltered here, I dare say, until spring comes. How thoughtful and kind everybody is to me! Still I wish this place were not so dark, as well as lonely, with not even a little hare to look at. How pleasant it was out in the forest while the snow lay on the ground, when the hare would run by, yes, and jump over me too, although I did not like it then. Oh! it is terrible lonely here."

"Squeak, squeak," said a little mouse, creeping cautiously towards the tree; then came another; and they both sniffed at the fir tree and crept between the branches.

"Oh, it is very cold," said the little mouse, "or else we should be so comfortable here, shouldn't we, you old fir tree?"

"I am not old," said the fir tree, "there are many who are older than I am."

"Where do you come from? and what do you know?" asked the mice, who were full of curiosity. "Have you seen the most beautiful places in the world, and can you tell us all about them? and have you been in the storeroom, where cheeses lie on the shelf, and hams hang from the ceiling? One can run about on tallow candles there, and go in thin and come out fat."

"I know nothing of that place," said the fir tree, "but I know the wood where the sun shines and the birds sing." And then the tree told the little mice all about its youth. They had never heard such an account in their lives; and after they had listened to it attentively, they said, "What a number of things you have seen? you must have been very happy."

"Happy!" exclaimed the fir tree, and then as he reflected upon what he had been telling them, he said, "Ah, yes! after all those were happy days." But when he went on and related all about Christmas Eve, and how he had been dressed up with cakes and lights, the mice said, "How happy you must have been, you old fir tree."

"I am not old at all," replied the tree, "I only came from the forest this winter, I am now checked in my growth."

"What splendid stories you can relate," said the little mice. And the next night four other mice came with them to hear what the tree had to tell. The more he talked the more he remembered, and then he thought to himself, "Those were happy days, but they may come again. Humpty Dumpty fell downstairs, and yet he married the princess; perhaps I may marry a princess too." And the fir tree thought of the pretty little birch tree that grew in the forest, which was to him a real beautiful princess.

"Who is Humpty Dumpty?" asked the little mice. And then the tree related the whole story; he could remember every single word, and the little mice were so delighted with it, that they were ready to jump to the top of the tree. The next night a great many more mice made their appearance, and on Sunday two rats came with them; but they said, it was not a pretty story at all, and the little mice were very sorry, for it made them also think less of it.

"Do you know only one story?" asked the rats.

"Only one," replied the fir tree; "I heard it on the happiest evening of my life; but I did not know I was so happy at the time."

"We think it is a very miserable story," said the rats. "Don't you know any story about bacon, or tallow in the storeroom?"

"No," replied the tree.

"Many thanks to you then," replied the rats, and they marched off.

The little mice also kept away after this, and the tree sighed, and said, "It was very pleasant when the merry little mice sat round me and listened while I talked. Now that is all passed too. However, I shall consider myself happy when someone comes to take me out of this place." But would this ever happen? Yes; one morning people came to clear out the garret, the boxes were packed away, and the tree was pulled out of the corner, and thrown roughly on the garret floor; then the servant dragged it out upon the staircase where the daylight shone. "Now life is beginning again," said the tree, rejoicing in the sunshine and fresh air. Then it was carried downstairs and taken into the courtyard so quickly, that it forgot to think of itself, and could only look about, there was so much to be seen. The court was close to a garden, where everything looked blooming. Fresh and fragrant roses hung over the little palings. The linden trees were in blossom; while the swallows flew here and there, crying, "Twit, twit, twit, my mate is coming"—but it was not the fir tree they meant. "Now I shall live," cried the tree, joyfully spreading out its branches; but alas! they were all withered and yellow, and it lay in a corner amongst weeds and nettles. The star of gold paper still stuck in the top of the tree and glittered in the sunshine. In the same courtyard two of the merry children were playing who had danced round the tree at Christmas, and had been so happy.

The youngest saw the gilded star, and ran and pulled it off the tree. "Look what is sticking to the ugly old fir tree," said the child, treading on the branches till they crackled under his boots. And the tree saw all the fresh bright flowers in the garden, and then looked at itself, and wished it had remained in the dark corner of the garret. It thought of its fresh youth in the forest, of the merry Christmas evening, and of the little mice who had listened to the story of "Humpty Dumpty."

"Past! past!" said the old tree; "Oh, had I but enjoyed myself while I could have done so! but now it is too late." Then a lad came and chopped the tree into small pieces, till a large bundle lay in a heap on the ground.

The pieces were placed in a fire under the copper, and they quickly blazed up brightly, while the tree sighed so deeply that each sigh was like a pistol-shot.

Then the children, who were at play, came and seated themselves in front of the fire, and looked at it and cried, "Pop, pop." But at each "pop," which was a deep sigh, the tree was thinking of a summer day in the forest; and of Christmas evening, and of "Humpty Dumpty," the only story it had ever heard or knew how to relate, till at last it was consumed. The boys still played in the garden, and the youngest wore the golden star on his breast, with which the tree had been adorned during the happiest evening of its existence. Now all was past; the tree's life was past, and the story also—for all stories must come to an end at last.

The Snow Queen

First Story: Which Describes a Looking Glass and Its Broken Fragments

You must attend to the beginning of this story, for when we get to the end we shall know more than we now do about a very wicked hobgoblin; he was one of the most mischievous of all sprites, for he was a real demon.

One day when he was in a merry mood he made a looking glass which had the power of making everything good or beautiful that was reflected in it shrink almost to nothing, while everything that was worthless and bad was magnified so as to look ten times worse than it really was.

The most lovely landscapes appeared like boiled spinach, and all the people became hideous and looked as if they stood on their heads and had no bodies. Their countenances were so distorted that no one could recognize them, and even one freckle on the face appeared to spread over the whole of the nose and mouth. The demon said this was very amusing. When a good or holy thought passed through the mind of any one a wrinkle was seen in the mirror, and then how the demon laughed at his cunning invention.

All who went to the demon's school—for he kept a school—talked everywhere of the wonders they had seen, and declared that people could now, for the first time, see what the world and its inhabitants were really like. They carried the glass about everywhere, till at last there was not a land nor a people who had not been looked at through this distorted mirror.

They wanted even to fly with it up to heaven to see the angels, but the higher they flew the more slippery the glass became, and they could scarcely hold it. At last it slipped from their hands, fell to the earth, and was broken into millions of pieces.

But now the looking glass caused more unhappiness than ever, for some of the fragments were not so large as a grain of sand, and they flew about the world into every country. And when one of these tiny atoms flew into a person's eye it stuck there, unknown to himself, and from that moment he viewed everything the wrong way, and could see only the worst side of what he looked at, for even the smallest fragment retained the same power which had belonged to the whole mirror.

Some few persons even got a splinter of the looking glass in their hearts, and this was terrible, for their hearts became cold and hard like a lump of ice. A few of the pieces were so large that they could be used as windowpanes; it would have been a sad thing indeed to look at our friends through them. Other pieces were made into spectacles, and this was dreadful, for those who wore them could see nothing either rightly or justly. At all this the wicked demon laughed till his sides shook, to see the mischief he had done. There are still a number of these little fragments of glass floating about in the air, and now you shall hear what happened with one of them.

Second Story: A Little Boy and a Little Girl

In a large town full of houses and people there is not room for everybody to have even a little garden. Most people are obliged to content themselves with a few flowers in flowerpots.

In one of these large towns lived two poor children who had a garden somewhat larger and better than a few flowerpots. They were not brother and sister, but they loved each other almost as much as if they had been. Their parents lived opposite each other in two garrets where the roofs of neighboring houses nearly joined each other, and the water pipe ran between them. In each roof was a little window, so that anyone could step across the gutter from one window to the other.

The parents of each of these children had a large wooden box in which they cultivated kitchen vegetables for their own use, and in each box was a little rosebush which grew luxuriantly.

After a while the parents decided to place these two boxes across the water pipe, so that they reached from one window to the other and looked like two banks of flowers. Sweet peas drooped over the boxes, and the rosebushes shot forth long branches, which were trained about the windows and clustered together almost like a triumphal arch of leaves and flowers.

The boxes were very high, and the children knew they must not climb upon them without permission; but they often had leave to step out and sit upon their little stools under the rosebushes or play quietly together.

In winter all this pleasure came to an end, for the windows were sometimes quite frozen over. But they would warm copper pennies on the stove and hold the warm pennies against the frozen pane; then there would soon be a little round hole through which they could peep, and the soft, bright eyes of the little boy and girl would sparkle through the hole at each window as they looked at each other. Their names were Kay and Gerda. In summer they could be together with one jump from the window, but in winter they had to go up and down the long staircase and out through the snow before they could meet.

"See! there are the white bees swarming," said Kay's old grandmother one day when it was snowing.

"Have they a queen bee?" asked the little boy, for he knew that the real bees always had a queen.

"To be sure they have," said the grandmother. "She is flying there where the swarm is thickest. She is the largest of them all and never remains on the earth, but flies up to the dark clouds. Often at midnight she flies through the streets of the town and breathes with her frosty breath upon the windows; then the ice freezes on the panes into wonderful forms that look like flowers and castles."

"Yes, I have seen them," said both the children; and they knew it must be true.

"Can the Snow Queen come in here?" asked the little girl.

"Only let her come," said the boy. "I'll put her on the warm stove, and then she'll melt."

The grandmother smoothed his hair and told him more stories.

That same evening when little Kay was at home, half undressed, he climbed upon a chair by the window and peeped out through the little round hole. A few flakes of snow were falling, and one of them, rather larger than the rest, alighted on the edge of one of the flower boxes. Strange to say, this snowflake grew larger and larger till at last it took the form of a woman dressed in garments of white gauze, which looked like millions of starry snowflakes linked together. She was fair and beautiful, but made of ice—glittering, dazzling ice. Still, she was alive, and her eyes sparkled like bright stars, though there was neither peace nor rest in them. She nodded toward the window and waved her hand. The little boy was frightened and sprang from the chair, and at the same moment it seemed as if a large bird flew by the window.

On the following day there was a clear frost, and very soon came the spring. The sun shone; the young green leaves burst forth; the swallows built their nests; windows were opened, and the children sat once more in the garden on the roof, high above all the other rooms.

How beautifully the roses blossomed this summer! The little girl had learned a hymn in which roses were spoken of. She thought of their own roses, and she sang the hymn to the little boy, and he sang, too:

"Roses bloom and fade away;
The Christ-child shall abide alway.
Blessed are we his face to see
And ever little children be."

Then the little ones held each other by the hand, and kissed the roses, and looked at the bright sunshine, and spoke to it as if the Christ-child were really there. Those were glorious summer days. How beautiful and fresh it was out among the rosebushes, which seemed as if they would never leave off blooming.

One day Kay and Gerda sat looking at a book of pictures of animals and birds. Just then, as the clock in the church tower struck twelve, Kay said, "Oh, something has struck my heart!" and soon after, "There is certainly something in my eye."

The little girl put her arm round his neck and looked into his eye, but she could see nothing.

"I believe it is gone," he said. But it was not gone; it was one of those bits of the looking glass—that magic mirror of which we have spoken—the ugly glass which made everything great and good appear small and ugly, while all that was wicked and bad became more visible, and every little fault could be plainly seen. Poor little Kay had also received a small splinter in his heart, which very quickly turned to a lump of ice. He felt no more pain, but the glass was there still. "Why do you cry?" said he at last. "It makes you look ugly. There is nothing the matter with me now. Oh, fie!" he cried suddenly; "that rose is worm-eaten, and this one is quite crooked. After all, they are ugly roses, just like the box in which they stand." And then he kicked the boxes with his foot and pulled off the two roses.

"Why, Kay, what are you doing?" cried the little girl; and then when he saw how grieved she was he tore off another rose and jumped through his own window, away from sweet little Gerda.

When afterward she brought out the picture book he said, "It is only fit for babies in long clothes," and when grandmother told stories he would interrupt her with "but;" or sometimes when he could manage it he would get behind her chair, put on a pair of spectacles, and imitate her very cleverly to make the people laugh. By and by he began to mimic the speech and gait of persons in the street. All that was peculiar or disagreeable in a person he would imitate directly, and people said, "That boy will be very clever; he has a remarkable genius." But it was the piece of glass in his eye and the coldness in his heart that made him act like this. He would even tease little Gerda, who loved him with all her heart.

His games too were quite different; they were not so childlike. One winter's day, when it snowed, he brought out a burning glass, then, holding out the skirt of his blue coat, let the snowflakes fall upon it.

"Look in this glass, Gerda," said he, and she saw how every flake of snow was magnified and looked like a beautiful flower or a glittering star.

"Is it not clever," said Kay, "and much more interesting than looking at real flowers? There is not a single fault in it. The snowflakes are quite perfect till they begin to melt."

Soon after, Kay made his appearance in large, thick gloves and with his sledge at his back. He called upstairs to Gerda, "I've got leave to go into the great square, where the other boys play and ride." And away he went.

In the great square the boldest among the boys would often tie their sledges to the wagons of the country people and so get a ride. This was capital. But while they were all amusing themselves, and Kay with them, a great sledge came by; it was painted white, and in it sat someone wrapped in a rough white fur and wearing a white cap. The sledge drove twice round the square, and Kay fastened his own little sledge to it, so that when it went away he went with it. It went faster and faster right through the next street, and the person who drove turned round and nodded pleasantly to Kay as if they were well acquainted with each other; but whenever Kay wished to loosen his little sledge the driver turned and nodded as if to signify that he was to stay, so Kay sat still, and they drove out through the town gate.

Then the snow began to fall so heavily that the little boy could not see a hand's breadth before him, but still they drove on. He suddenly loosened the cord so that the large sledge might go on without him, but it was of no use; his little carriage held fast, and away they went like the wind. Then he called out loudly, but nobody heard him, while the snow beat upon him, and the sledge flew onward. Every now and then it gave a jump, as if they were going over hedges and ditches. The boy was frightened and tried to say a prayer, but he could remember nothing but the multiplication table.

The snowflakes became larger and larger, till they appeared like great white birds. All at once they sprang on one side, the great sledge stopped, and the person who had driven it rose up. The fur and the cap, which were made entirely of snow, fell off, and he saw a lady, tall and white; it was the Snow Queen.

"We have driven well," said she; "but why do you tremble so? Here, creep into my warm fur." Then she seated him beside her in the sledge, and as she wrapped the fur about him, he felt as if he were sinking into a snowdrift.

"Are you still cold?" she asked, as she kissed him on the forehead. The kiss was colder than ice; it went quite through to his heart, which was almost a lump of ice already. He felt as if he were going to die, but only for a moment—he soon seemed quite well and did not notice the cold all around him.

"My sledge! Don't forget my sledge," was his first thought, and then he looked and saw that it was bound fast to one of the white birds which flew behind him. The Snow Queen kissed little Kay again, and by this time he had forgotten little Gerda, his grandmother, and all at home.

"Now you must have no more kisses," she said, "or I should kiss you to death."

Kay looked at her. She was so beautiful, he could not imagine a more lovely face; she did not now seem to be made of ice as when he had seen her through his window and she had nodded to him.

In his eyes she was perfect, and he did not feel at all afraid. He told her he could do mental arithmetic as far as fractions, and that he knew the number of square miles and the number of inhabitants in the country. She smiled, and it occurred to him that she thought he did not yet know so very much.

He looked around the vast expanse as she flew higher and higher with him upon a black cloud, while the storm blew and howled as if it were singing songs of olden time. They flew over woods and lakes, over sea and land; below them roared the wild wind; wolves howled, and the snow crackled; over them flew the black, screaming crows, and above all shone the moon, clear and bright—and so Kay passed through the long, long winter's night, and by day he slept at the feet of the Snow Queen.

Third Story: The Enchanted Flower Garden

But how fared little Gerda in Kay's absence?

What had become of him no one knew, nor could anyone give the slightest information, excepting the boys, who said that he had tied his sledge to another very large one, which had driven through the street and out at the town gate. No one knew where it went. Many tears were shed for him, and little Gerda wept bitterly for a long time. She said she knew he must be dead, that he was drowned in the river which flowed close by the school. The long winter days were very dreary. But at last spring came with warm sunshine.

"Kay is dead and gone," said little Gerda.

"I don't believe it," said the sunshine.

"He is dead and gone," she said to the sparrows.

"We don't believe it," they replied, and at last little Gerda began to doubt it herself.

"I will put on my new red shoes," she said one morning, "those that Kay has never seen, and then I will go down to the river and ask for him."

It was quite early when she kissed her old grandmother, who was still asleep; then she put on her red shoes and went, quite alone, out of the town gate, toward the river.

"Is it true that you have taken my little playmate away from me?" she said to the river. "I will give you my red shoes if you will give him back to me."

And it seemed as if the waves nodded to her in a strange manner. Then she took off her red shoes, which she liked better than anything else, and threw them both into the river, but they fell near the bank, and the little waves carried them back to land just as if the river would not take from her what she loved best, because it could not give her back little Kay.

But she thought the shoes had not been thrown out far enough. Then she crept into a boat that lay among the reeds, and threw the shoes again from the farther end of the boat into the water; but it was not fastened, and her movement sent it gliding away from the land. When she saw this she hastened to reach the end of the boat, but before she could do so it was more than a yard from the bank and drifting away faster than ever.

Little Gerda was very much frightened. She began to cry, but no one heard her except the sparrows, and they could not carry her to land, but they flew along by the shore and sang as if to comfort her: "Here we are! Here we are!"

The boat floated with the stream, and little Gerda sat quite still with only her stockings on her feet; the red shoes floated after her, but she could not reach them because the boat kept so much in advance.

The banks on either side of the river were very pretty. There were beautiful flowers, old trees, sloping fields in which cows and sheep were grazing, but not a human being to be seen.

"Perhaps the river will carry me to little Kay," thought Gerda, and then she became more cheerful, and raised her head and looked at the beautiful green banks; and so the boat sailed on for hours. At length she came to a large cherry orchard, in which stood a small house with strange red and blue windows. It had also a thatched roof, and outside were two wooden soldiers that presented arms to her as she sailed past. Gerda called out to them, for she thought they were alive; but of course they did not answer, and as the boat drifted nearer to the shore she saw what they really were.

Then Gerda called still louder, and there came a very old woman out of the house, leaning on a crutch. She wore a large hat to shade her from the sun, and on it were painted all sorts of pretty flowers.

"You poor little child," said the old woman, "how did you manage to come this long, long distance into the wide world on such a rapid, rolling stream?" And then the old woman walked into the water, seized the boat with her crutch, drew it to land, and lifted little Gerda out. And Gerda was glad to feel herself again on dry ground, although she was rather afraid of the strange old woman.

"Come and tell me who you are," said she, "and how you came here."

Then Gerda told her everything, while the old woman shook her head and said, "Hem-hem;" and when Gerda had finished she asked the old woman if she had not seen little Kay. She told her he had not passed that way, but he very likely would come. She told Gerda not to be sorrowful, but to taste the cherries and look at the flowers; they were better than any picture book, for each of them could tell a story. Then she took Gerda by the hand, and led her into the little house, and closed the door. The windows were very high, and as the panes were red, blue, and yellow, the daylight shone through them in all sorts of singular colors. On the table stood some beautiful cherries, and Gerda had permission to eat as many as she would. While she was eating them the old woman combed out her long flaxen ringlets with a golden comb, and the glossy curls hung down on each side of the little round, pleasant face, which looked fresh and blooming as a rose.

"I have long been wishing for a dear little maiden like you," said the old woman, "and now you must stay with me and see how happily we shall live together." And while she went on combing little Gerda's hair the child thought less and less about her adopted brother Kay, for the old woman was an enchantress, although she was not a wicked witch; she conjured only a little for her own amusement, and, now, because she wanted to keep Gerda. Therefore she went into the garden and stretched out her crutch toward all the rose trees, beautiful though they were, and they immediately sank into the dark earth, so that no one could tell where they had once stood. The old woman was afraid that if little Gerda saw roses, she would think of those at home and then remember little Kay and run away.

Then she took Gerda into the flower garden. How fragrant and beautiful it was! Every flower that could be thought of, for every season of the year, was here in full bloom; no picture book could have more beautiful colors. Gerda jumped for joy, and played till the sun went down behind the tall cherry trees; then she slept in an elegant bed, with red silk pillows embroidered with colored violets, and she dreamed as pleasantly as a queen on her wedding day.

The next day, and for many days after, Gerda played with the flowers in the warm sunshine. She knew every flower, and yet, although there were so many of them, it seemed as if one were missing, but what it was she could not tell. One day, however, as she sat looking at the old woman's hat with the painted flowers on it, she saw that the prettiest of them all was a rose. The old woman had forgotten to take it from her hat when she made all the roses sink into the earth. But it is difficult to keep the thoughts together in everything, and one little mistake upsets all our arrangements.

"What! are there no roses here?" cried Gerda, and she ran out into the garden and examined all the beds, and searched and searched. There was not one to be found. Then she sat down and wept, and her tears fell just on the place where one of the rose trees had sunk down. The warm tears moistened the earth, and the rose tree sprouted up at once, as blooming as when it had sunk; and Gerda embraced it, and kissed the roses, and thought of the beautiful roses at home, and, with them, of little Kay.

"Oh, how I have been detained!" said the little maiden. "I wanted to seek for little Kay. Do you know where he is?" she asked the roses; "do you think he is dead?"

And the roses answered: "No, he is not dead. We have been in the ground, where all the dead lie, but Kay is not there."

"Thank you," said little Gerda, and then she went to the other flowers and looked into their little cups and asked, "Do you know where little Kay is?" But each flower as it stood in the sunshine dreamed only of its own little fairy tale or history. Not one knew anything of Kay. Gerda heard many stories from the flowers, as she asked them one after another about him.

And then she ran to the other end of the garden. The door was fastened, but she pressed against the rusty latch, and it gave way. The door sprang open, and little Gerda ran out with bare feet into the wide world.

She looked back three times, but no one seemed to be following her. At last she could run no longer, so she sat down to rest on a great stone, and when she looked around she saw that the summer was over and autumn very far advanced. She had known nothing of this in the beautiful garden where the sun shone and the flowers grew all the year round.

"Oh, how I have wasted my time!" said little Gerda. "It is autumn; I must not rest any longer," and she rose to go on. But her little feet were wounded and sore, and everything around her looked cold and bleak. The long willow leaves were quite yellow, the dewdrops fell like water, leaf after leaf dropped from the trees; the sloe thorn alone still bore fruit, but the sloes were sour and set the teeth on edge. Oh, how dark and weary the whole world appeared!

Fourth Story: The Prince and Princess

Gerda was obliged to rest again, and just opposite the place where she sat she saw a great crow come hopping toward her across the snow. He stood looking at her for some time, and then he wagged his head and said, "Caw, caw, good day, good day." He pronounced the words as plainly as he could, because he meant to be kind to the little girl, and then he asked her where she was going all alone in the wide world.

The word "alone" Gerda understood very well and felt how much it expressed. So she told the crow the whole story of her life and adventures and asked him if he had seen little Kay.

The crow nodded his head very gravely and said, "Perhaps I have—it may be."

"No! Do you really think you have?" cried little Gerda, and she kissed the crow and hugged him almost to death, with joy.

"Gently, gently," said the crow. "I believe I know. I think it may be little Kay; but he has certainly forgotten you by this time, for the princess."

"Does he live with a princess?" asked Gerda.

"Yes, listen," replied the crow; "but it is so difficult to speak your language. If you understand the crows' language, then I can explain it better. Do you?"

"No, I have never learned it," said Gerda, "but my grandmother understands it, and used to speak it to me. I wish I had learned it."

"It does not matter," answered the crow. "I will explain as well as I can, although it will be very badly done;" and he told her what he had heard.

"In this kingdom where we now are," said he, "there lives a princess who is so wonderfully clever that she has read all the newspapers in the world—and forgotten them too, although she is so clever.

"A short time ago, as she was sitting on her throne, which people say is not such an agreeable seat as is often supposed, she began to sing a song which commences with these words:

"Why should I not be married?

"Why not, indeed?" said she, and so she determined to marry if she could find a husband who knew what to say when he was spoken to, and not one who could only look grand, for that was so tiresome. She assembled all her court ladies at the beat of the drum, and when they heard of her intentions they were very much pleased.

"We are so glad to hear of it," said they. "We were talking about it ourselves the other day."

"You may believe that every word I tell you is true," said the crow, "for I have a tame sweetheart who hops freely about the palace, and she told me all this."

Of course his sweetheart was a crow, for "birds of a feather flock together," and one crow always chooses another crow.

"Newspapers were published immediately with a border of hearts and the initials of the princess among them. They gave notice that every young man who was handsome was free to visit the castle and speak with the princess, and those who could reply loud enough to be heard when spoken to were to make themselves quite at home at the palace, and the one who spoke best would be chosen as a husband for the princess.

"Yes, yes, you may believe me. It is all as true as I sit here," said the crow.

"The people came in crowds. There was a great deal of crushing and running about, but no one succeeded either on the first or the second day. They could all speak very well while they were outside in the streets, but when they entered the palace gates and saw the guards in silver uniforms and the footmen in their golden livery on the staircase and the great halls lighted up, they became quite confused. And when they stood before the throne on which the princess sat they could do nothing but repeat the last words she had said, and she had no particular wish to hear her own words over again. It was just as if they had all taken something to make them sleepy while they were in the palace, for they did not recover themselves nor speak till they got back again into the street. There was a long procession of them, reaching from the town gate to the palace.

"I went myself to see them," said the crow. "They were hungry and thirsty, for at the palace they did not even get a glass of water. Some of the wisest had taken a few slices of bread and butter with them, but they did not share it with their neighbors; they thought if the others went in to the princess looking hungry, there would be a better chance for themselves."

"But Kay! tell me about little Kay!" said Gerda. "Was he among the crowd?"

"Stop a bit; we are just coming to him. It was on the third day that there came marching cheerfully along to the palace a little personage without horses or carriage, his eyes sparkling like yours. He had beautiful long hair, but his clothes were very poor."

"That was Kay," said Gerda, joyfully. "Oh, then I have found him!" and she clapped her hands.

"He had a little knapsack on his back," added the crow.

"No, it must have been his sledge," said Gerda, "for he went away with it."

"It may have been so," said the crow; "I did not look at it very closely. But I know from my tame sweetheart that he passed through the palace gates, saw the guards in their silver uniform and the servants in their liveries of gold on the stairs, but was not in the least embarrassed.

"It must be very tiresome to stand on the stairs," he said. "I prefer to go in."

"The rooms were blazing with light; councilors and ambassadors walked about with bare feet, carrying golden vessels; it was enough to make anyone feel serious. His boots creaked loudly as he walked, and yet he was not at all uneasy."

"It must be Kay," said Gerda; "I know he had new boots on. I heard them creak in grandmother's room."

"They really did creak," said the crow, "yet he went boldly up to the princess herself, who was sitting on a pearl as large as a spinning wheel. And all the ladies of the court were present with their maids and all the cavaliers with their servants, and each of the maids had another maid to wait upon her, and the cavaliers' servants had their own servants as well as each a page. They all stood in circles round the princess, and the nearer they stood to the door the prouder they looked. The servants' pages, who always wore slippers, could hardly be looked at, they held themselves up so proudly by the door."

"It must be quite awful," said little Gerda; "but did Kay win the princess?"

"If I had not been a crow," said he, "I would have married her myself, although I am engaged. He spoke as well as I do when I speak the crows' language. I heard this from my tame sweetheart. He was quite free and agreeable and said he had not come to woo the princess, but to hear her wisdom. And he was as pleased with her as she was with him."

"Oh, certainly that was Kay," said Gerda; "he was so clever; he could work mental arithmetic and fractions. Oh, will you take me to the palace?"

"It is very easy to ask that," replied the crow, "but how are we to manage it? However, I will speak about it to my tame sweetheart and ask her advice, for, I must tell you, it will be very difficult to gain permission for a little girl like you to enter the palace."

"Oh, yes, but I shall gain permission easily," said Gerda, "for when Kay hears that I am here he will come out and fetch me in immediately."

"Wait for me here by the palings," said the crow, wagging his head as he flew away.

It was late in the evening before the crow returned. "Caw, caw!" he said; "she sends you greeting, and here is a little roll which she took from the kitchen for you. There is plenty of bread there, and she thinks you must be hungry. It is not possible for you to enter the palace by the front entrance. The guards in silver uniform and the servants in gold livery would not allow it. But do not cry; we will manage to get you in. My sweetheart knows a little back staircase that leads to the sleeping apartments, and she knows where to find the key."

Then they went into the garden, through the great avenue, where the leaves were falling one after another, and they could see the lights in the palace being put out in the same manner. And the crow led little Gerda to a back door which stood ajar. Oh, how her heart beat with anxiety and longing; it was as if she were going to do something wrong, and yet she only wanted to know where little Kay was.

"It must be he," she thought, "with those clear eyes and that long hair."

She could fancy she saw him smiling at her as he used to at home when they sat among the roses. He would certainly be glad to see her, and to hear what a long distance she had come for his sake, and to know how sorry they had all been at home because he did not come back. Oh, what joy and yet what fear she felt!

They were now on the stairs, and in a small closet at the top a lamp was burning. In the middle of the floor stood the tame crow, turning her head from side to side and gazing at Gerda, who curtsied as her grandmother had taught her to do.

"My betrothed has spoken so very highly of you, my little lady," said the tame crow. "Your story is very touching. If you will take the lamp, I will walk before you. We will go straight along this way; then we shall meet no one."

"I feel as if somebody were behind us," said Gerda, as something rushed by her like a shadow on the wall; and then it seemed to her that horses with flying manes and thin legs, hunters, ladies and gentlemen on horseback, glided by her like shadows.

"They are only dreams," said the crow; "they are coming to carry the thoughts of the great people out hunting. All the better, for if their thoughts are out hunting, we shall be able to look at them in their beds more safely. I hope that when you rise to honor and favor you will show a grateful heart."

"You may be quite sure of that," said the crow from the forest.

They now came into the first hall, the walls of which were hung with rose-colored satin embroidered with artificial flowers. Here the dreams again flitted by them, but so quickly that Gerda could not distinguish the royal persons. Each hall appeared more splendid than the last. It was enough to bewilder one. At length they reached a bedroom. The ceiling was like a great palm tree, with glass leaves of the most costly crystal, and over the center of the floor two beds, each resembling a lily, hung from a stem of gold. One, in which the princess lay, was white; the other was red. And in this Gerda had to seek for little Kay.

She pushed one of the red leaves aside and saw a little brown neck. Oh, that must be Kay! She called his name loudly and held the lamp over him. The dreams rushed back into the room on horseback. He woke and turned his head round—it was not little Kay! The prince was only like him; still he was young and pretty. Out of her white-lily bed peeped the princess, and asked what was the matter. Little Gerda wept and told her story, and all that the crows had done to help her.

"You poor child," said the prince and princess; then they praised the crows, and said they were not angry with them for what they had done, but that it must not happen again, and that this time they should be rewarded.

"Would you like to have your freedom?" asked the princess, "or would you prefer to be raised to the position of court crows, with all that is left in the kitchen for yourselves?"

Then both the crows bowed and begged to have a fixed appointment; for they thought of their old age, and it would be so comfortable, they said, to feel that they had made provision for it.

And then the prince got out of his bed and gave it up to Gerda—he could not do more—and she lay down. She folded her little hands and thought, "How good everybody is to me, both men and animals;" then she closed her eyes and fell into a sweet sleep. All the dreams came flying back again to her, looking like angels now, and one of them drew a little sledge, on which sat Kay, who nodded to her. But all this was only a dream. It vanished as soon as she awoke.

The following day she was dressed from head to foot in silk and velvet and invited to stay at the palace for a few days and enjoy herself; but she only begged for a pair of boots and a little carriage and a horse to draw it, so that she might go out into the wide world to seek for Kay.

And she obtained not only boots but a muff, and was neatly dressed; and when she was ready to go, there at the door she found a coach made of pure gold with the coat of arms of the prince and princess shining upon it like a star, and the coachman, footman, and outriders all wearing golden crowns upon their heads. The prince and princess themselves helped her into the coach and wished her success.

The forest crow, who was now married, accompanied her for the first three miles; he sat by Gerda's side, as he could not bear riding backwards. The tame crow stood in the doorway flapping her wings. She could not go with them, because she had been suffering from headache ever since the new appointment, no doubt from overeating. The coach was well stored with sweet cakes, and under the seat were fruit and gingerbread nuts.

"Farewell, farewell," cried the prince and princess, and little Gerda wept, and the crow wept; and then, after a few miles, the crow also said farewell, and this parting was even more sad. However he flew to a tree and stood flapping his black wings as long as he could see the coach, which glittered like a sunbeam.

Fifth Story: The Little Robber Girl

The coach drove on through a thick forest, where it lighted up the way like a torch and dazzled the eyes of some robbers, who could not bear to let it pass them unmolested.

"It is gold! it is gold!" cried they, rushing forward and seizing the horses. Then they struck dead the little jockeys, the coachman, and the footman, and pulled little Gerda out of the carriage.

"She is plump and pretty. She has been fed with the kernels of nuts," said the old robber woman, who had a long beard, and eyebrows that hung over her eyes. "She is as good as a fatted lamb; how nice she will taste!" and as she said this she drew forth a shining knife, that glittered horribly. "Oh!" screamed the old woman at the same moment, for her own daughter, who held her back, had bitten her in the ear. "You naughty girl," said the mother, and now she had not time to kill Gerda.

"She shall play with me," said the little robber girl. "She shall give me her muff and her pretty dress, and sleep with me in my bed." And then she bit her mother again, and all the robbers laughed.

"I will have a ride in the coach," said the little robber girl, and she would have her own way, for she was self-willed and obstinate.

She and Gerda seated themselves in the coach and drove away over stumps and stones, into the depths of the forest. The little robber girl was about the same size as Gerda, but stronger; she had broader shoulders and a darker skin; her eyes were quite black, and she had a mournful look. She clasped little Gerda round the waist and said:

"They shall not kill you as long as you don't make me vexed with you. I suppose you are a princess."

"No," said Gerda; and then she told her all her history and how fond she was of little Kay.

The robber girl looked earnestly at her, nodded her head slightly, and said, "They shan't kill you even if I do get angry with you, for I will do it myself." And then she wiped Gerda's eyes and put her own hands into the beautiful muff, which was so soft and warm.

The coach stopped in the courtyard of a robber's castle, the walls of which were full of cracks from top to bottom. Ravens and crows flew in and out of the holes and crevices, while great bulldogs, each of which looked as if it could swallow a man, were jumping about; but they were not allowed to bark.

In the large old smoky hall a bright fire was burning on the stone floor. There was no chimney, so the smoke went up to the ceiling and found a way out for itself. Soup was boiling in a large cauldron, and hares and rabbits were roasting on the spit.

"You shall sleep with me and all my little animals tonight," said the robber girl after they had had something to eat and drink. So she took Gerda to a corner of the hall where some straw and carpets were laid down. Above them, on laths and perches, were more than a hundred pigeons that all seemed to be asleep, although they moved slightly when the two little girls came near them. "These all belong to me," said the robber girl, and she seized the nearest to her, held it by the feet, and shook it till it flapped its wings. "Kiss it," cried she, flapping it in Gerda's face.

"There sit the wood pigeons," continued she, pointing to a number of laths and a cage which had been fixed into the walls, near one of the openings. "Both rascals would fly away directly, if they were not closely locked up. And here is my old sweetheart 'Ba,'" and she dragged out a reindeer by the horn; he wore a bright copper ring round his neck and was tethered to the spot. "We are obliged to hold him tight too, else he would run away from us also. I tickle his neck every evening with my sharp knife, which frightens him very much." And the robber girl drew a long knife from a chink in the wall and let it slide gently over the reindeer's neck. The poor animal began to kick, and the little robber girl laughed and pulled down Gerda into bed with her.

"Will you have that knife with you while you are asleep?" asked Gerda, looking at it in great fright.

"I always sleep with the knife by me," said the robber girl. "No one knows what may happen. But now tell me again all about little Kay, and why you went out into the world."

Then Gerda repeated her story over again, while the wood pigeons in the cage over her cooed, and the other pigeons slept. The little robber girl put one arm across Gerda's neck, and held the knife in the other, and was soon fast asleep and snoring. But Gerda could not close her eyes at all; she knew not whether she was to live or to die. The robbers sat round the fire, singing and drinking. It was a terrible sight for a little girl to witness.

Then the wood pigeons said: "Coo, coo, we have seen little Kay. A white fowl carried his sledge, and he sat in the carriage of the Snow Queen, which drove through the wood while we were lying in our nest. She blew upon us, and all the young ones died, excepting us two. Coo, coo."

"What are you saying up there?" cried Gerda. "Where was the Snow Queen going? Do you know anything about it?"

"She was most likely traveling to Lapland, where there is always snow and ice. Ask the reindeer that is fastened up there with a rope."

"Yes, there is always snow and ice," said the reindeer, "and it is a glorious place; you can leap and run about freely on the sparkling icy plains. The Snow Queen has her summer tent there, but her strong castle is at the North Pole, on an island called Spitzbergen."

"O Kay, little Kay!" sighed Gerda.

"Lie still," said the robber girl, "or you shall feel my knife."

In the morning Gerda told her all that the wood pigeons had said, and the little robber girl looked quite serious, and nodded her head and said: "That is all talk, that is all talk. Do you know where Lapland is?" she asked the reindeer.

"Who should know better than I do?" said the animal, while his eyes sparkled. "I was born and brought up there and used to run about the snow-covered plains."

"Now listen," said the robber girl; "all our men are gone away; only mother is here, and here she will stay; but at noon she always drinks out of a great bottle, and afterwards sleeps for a little while; and then I'll do something for you." She jumped out of bed, clasped her mother round the neck, and pulled her by the beard, crying, "My own little nanny goat, good morning!" And her mother pinched her nose till it was quite red; yet she did it all for love.

When the mother had gone to sleep the little robber maiden went to the reindeer and said: "I should like very much to tickle your neck a few times more with my knife, for it makes you look so funny, but never mind—I will untie your cord and set you free, so that you may run away to Lapland; but you must make good use of your legs and carry this little maiden to the castle of the Snow Queen, where her playfellow is. You have heard what she told me, for she spoke loud enough, and you were listening."

The reindeer jumped for joy, and the little robber girl lifted Gerda on his back and had the forethought to tie her on and even to give her own little cushion to sit upon.

"Here are your fur boots for you," said she, "for it will be very cold; but I must keep the muff, it is so pretty. However, you shall not be frozen for the want of it; here are my mother's large warm mittens; they will reach up to your elbows. Let me put them on. There, now your hands look just like my mother's."

But Gerda wept for joy.

"I don't like to see you fret," said the little robber girl. "You ought to look quite happy now. And here are two loaves and a ham, so that you need not starve."

These were fastened upon the reindeer, and then the little robber maiden opened the door, coaxed in all the great dogs, cut the string with which the reindeer was fastened, with her sharp knife, and said, "Now run, but mind you take good care of the little girl." And Gerda stretched out her hand, with the great mitten on it, toward the little robber girl and said "Farewell," and away flew the reindeer over stumps and stones, through the great forest, over marshes and plains, as quickly as he could. The wolves howled and the ravens screamed, while up in the sky quivered red lights like flames of fire. "There are my old northern lights," said the reindeer; "see how they flash!" And he ran on day and night still faster and faster, but the loaves and the ham were all eaten by the time they reached Lapland.

Sixth Story: The Lapland Woman and the Finland Woman

They stopped at a little hut; it was very mean looking. The roof sloped nearly down to the ground, and the door was so low that the family had to creep in on their hands and knees when they went in and out.

There was no one at home but an old Lapland woman who was dressing fish by the light of a train-oil lamp.

The reindeer told her all about Gerda's story after having first told his own, which seemed to him the most important. But Gerda was so pinched with the cold that she could not speak.

"Oh, you poor things," said the Lapland woman, "you have a long way to go yet. You must travel more than a hundred miles farther, to Finland. The Snow Queen lives there now, and she burns Bengal lights every evening. I will write a few words on a dried stockfish, for I have no paper, and you can take it from me to the Finland woman who lives there. She can give you better information than I can."

So when Gerda was warmed and had taken something to eat and drink, the woman wrote a few words on the dried fish and told Gerda to take great care of it. Then she tied her again on the back of the reindeer, and he sprang high into the air and set off at full speed. Flash, flash, went the beautiful blue northern lights the whole night long.

And at length they reached Finland and knocked at the chimney of the Finland woman's hut, for it had no door above the ground. They crept in, but it was so terribly hot inside that the woman wore scarcely any clothes. She was small and very dirty looking. She loosened little Gerda's dress and took off the fur boots and the mittens, or Gerda would have been unable to bear the heat; and then she placed a piece of ice on the reindeer's head and read what was written on the dried fish. After she had read it three times she knew it by heart, so she popped the fish into the soup saucepan, as she knew it was good to eat, and she never wasted anything.

The reindeer told his own story first and then little Gerda's, and the Finlander twinkled with her clever eyes, but said nothing.

"You are so clever," said the reindeer; "I know you can tie all the winds of the world with a piece of twine. If a sailor unties one knot, he has a fair wind; when he unties the second, it blows hard; but if the third and fourth are loosened, then comes a storm which will root up whole forests. Cannot you give this little maiden something which will make her as strong as twelve men, to overcome the Snow Queen?"

"The power of twelve men!" said the Finland woman. "That would be of very little use." But she went to a shelf and took down and unrolled a large skin on which were inscribed wonderful characters, and she read till the perspiration ran down from her forehead.

But the reindeer begged so hard for little Gerda, and Gerda looked at the Finland woman with such tender, tearful eyes, that her own eyes began to twinkle again. She drew the reindeer into a corner and whispered to him while she laid a fresh piece of ice on his head: "Little Kay is really with the Snow Queen, but he finds everything there so much to his taste and his liking that he believes it is the finest place in the world; and this is because he has a piece of broken glass in his heart and a little splinter of glass in his eye. These must be taken out, or he will never be a human being again, and the Snow Queen will retain her power over him."

"But can you not give little Gerda something to help her to conquer this power?"

"I can give her no greater power than she has already," said the woman; "don't you see how strong that is? how men and animals are obliged to serve her, and how well she has gotten through the world, barefooted as she is? She cannot receive any power from me greater than she now has, which consists in her own purity and innocence of heart. If she cannot herself obtain access to the Snow Queen and remove the glass fragments from little Kay, we can do nothing to help her. Two miles from here the Snow Queen's garden begins. You can carry the little girl so far, and set her down by the large bush which stands in the snow, covered with red berries. Do not stay gossiping, but come back here as quickly as you can." Then the Finland woman lifted little Gerda upon the reindeer, and he ran away with her as quickly as he could.

"Oh, I have forgotten my boots and my mittens," cried little Gerda, as soon as she felt the cutting cold; but the reindeer dared not stop, so he ran on till he reached the bush with the red berries. Here he set Gerda down, and he kissed her, and the great bright tears trickled over the animal's cheeks; then he left her and ran back as fast as he could

There stood poor Gerda, without shoes, without gloves, in the midst of cold, dreary, ice-bound Finland. She ran forward as quickly as she could, when a whole regiment of snowflakes came round her. They did not, however, fall from the sky, which was quite clear and glittered with the northern lights. The snowflakes ran along the ground, and the nearer they came to her the larger they appeared. Gerda remembered how large and beautiful they looked through the burning glass. But these were really larger and much more terrible, for they were alive and were the guards of the Snow Queen and had the strangest shapes. Some were like great porcupines, others like twisted serpents with their heads stretching out, and some few were like little fat bears with their hair bristled; but all were dazzlingly white, and all were living snowflakes.

Little Gerda repeated the Lord's Prayer, and the cold was so great that she could see her own breath come out of her mouth like steam, as she uttered the words. The steam appeared to increase as she continued her prayer, till it took the shape of little angels, who grew larger the moment they touched the earth. They all wore helmets on their heads and carried spears and shields. Their number continued to increase more and more, and by the time Gerda had finished her prayers a whole legion stood round her. They thrust their spears into the terrible snowflakes so that they shivered into a hundred pieces, and little Gerda could go forward with courage and safety. The angels stroked her hands and feet, so that she felt the cold less as she hastened on to the Snow Queen's castle.

But now we must see what Kay is doing. In truth he thought not of little Gerda, and least of all that she could be standing at the front of the palace.

Seventh Story: The Palace of the Snow Queen and What Happened There at Last

The walls of the palace were formed of drifted snow, and the windows and doors of cutting winds. There were more than a hundred rooms in it, all as if they had been formed of snow blown together. The largest of them extended for several miles. They were all lighted up by the vivid light of the aurora, and were so large and empty, so icy cold and glittering!

There were no amusements here; not even a little bear's ball, when the storm might have been the music, and the bears could have danced on their hind legs and shown their good manners. There were no pleasant games of snapdragon, or touch, nor even a gossip over the tea table for the young-lady foxes. Empty, vast, and cold were the halls of the Snow Queen.

The flickering flames of the northern lights could be plainly seen, whether they rose high or low in the heavens, from every part of the castle. In the midst of this empty, endless hall of snow was a frozen lake, broken on its surface into a thousand forms; each piece resembled another, because each was in itself perfect as a work of art, and in the center of this lake sat the Snow Queen when she was at home. She called the lake "The Mirror of Reason," and said that it was the best, and indeed the only one, in the world.

Little Kay was quite blue with cold, indeed, almost black, but he did not feel it; for the Snow Queen had kissed away the icy shiverings, and his heart was already a lump of ice. He dragged some sharp, flat pieces of ice to and fro and placed them together in all kinds of positions, as if he wished to make something out of them—just as we try to form various figures with little tablets of wood, which we call a "Chinese puzzle." Kay's figures were very artistic; it was the icy game of reason at which he played, and in his eyes the figures were very remarkable and of the highest importance; this opinion was owing to the splinter of glass still sticking in his eye. He composed many complete figures, forming different words, but there was one word he never could manage to form, although he wished it very much. It was the word "Eternity."

The Snow Queen had said to him, "When you can find out this, you shall be your own master, and I will give you the whole world and a new pair of skates." But he could not accomplish it.

"Now I must hasten away to warmer countries," said the Snow Queen. "I will go and look into the black craters of the tops of the burning mountains, Etna and Vesuvius, as they are called. I shall make them look white, which will be good for them and for the lemons and the grapes." And away flew the Snow Queen, leaving little Kay quite alone in the great hall which was so many miles in length. He sat and looked at his pieces of ice and was thinking so deeply and sat so still that anyone might have supposed he was frozen.

Just at this moment it happened that little Gerda came through the great door of the castle. Cutting winds were raging around her, but she offered up a prayer, and the winds sank down as if they were going to sleep. On she went till she came to the large, empty hall and caught sight of Kay. She knew him directly; she flew to him and threw her arms around his neck and held him fast while she exclaimed, "Kay, dear little Kay, I have found you at last!"

But he sat quite still, stiff and cold.

Then little Gerda wept hot tears, which fell on his breast, and penetrated into his heart, and thawed the lump of ice, and washed away the little piece of glass which had stuck there. Then he looked at her, and she sang:

"Roses bloom and fade away,
But we the Christ-child see alway."

Then Kay burst into tears. He wept so that the splinter of glass swam out of his eye. Then he recognized Gerda and said joyfully, "Gerda, dear little Gerda, where have you been all this time, and where have I been?" And he looked all around him and said, "How cold it is, and how large and empty it all looks," and he clung to Gerda, and she laughed and wept for joy.

It was so pleasing to see them that even the pieces of ice danced, and when they were tired and went to lie down they formed themselves into the letters of the word which the Snow Queen had said he must find out before he could be his own master and have the whole world and a pair of new skates.

Gerda kissed his cheeks, and they became blooming; and she kissed his eyes till they shone like her own; she kissed his hands and feet, and he became quite healthy and cheerful. The Snow Queen might come home now when she pleased, for there stood his certainty of freedom, in the word she wanted, written in shining letters of ice.

Then they took each other by the hand and went forth from the great palace of ice. They spoke of the grandmother and of the roses on the roof, and as they went on the winds were at rest, and the sun burst forth. When they arrived at the bush with red berries, there stood the reindeer waiting for them, and he had brought another young reindeer with him, whose udders were full, and the children drank her warm milk and kissed her on the mouth.

They carried Kay and Gerda first to the Finland woman, where they warmed themselves thoroughly in the hot room and had directions about their journey home. Next they went to the Lapland woman, who had made some new clothes for them and put their sleighs in order. Both the reindeer ran by their side and followed them as far as the boundaries of the country, where the first green leaves were budding.

And here they took leave of the two reindeer and the Lapland woman, and all said farewell.

Then birds began to twitter, and the forest too was full of green young leaves, and out of it came a beautiful horse, which Gerda remembered, for it was one which had drawn the golden coach. A young girl was riding upon it, with a shining red cap on her head and pistols in her belt. It was the little robber maiden, who had got tired of staying at home; she was going first to the north, and if that did not suit her, she meant to try some other part of the world. She knew Gerda directly, and Gerda remembered her; it was a joyful meeting.

"You are a fine fellow to go gadding about in this way," said she to little Kay. "I should like to know whether you deserve that anyone should go to the end of the world to find you."

But Gerda patted her cheeks and asked after the prince and princess.

"They are gone to foreign countries," said the robber girl.

"And the crow?" asked Gerda.

"Oh, the crow is dead," she replied. "His tame sweetheart is now a widow and wears a bit of black worsted round her leg. She mourns very pitifully, but it is all stuff. But now tell me how you managed to get him back."

Then Gerda and Kay told her all about it.

"Snip, snap, snurre! it's all right at last," said the robber girl.

She took both their hands and promised that if ever she should pass through the town, she would call and pay them a visit. And then she rode away into the wide world.

But Gerda and Kay went hand in hand toward home, and as they advanced, spring appeared more lovely with its green verdure and its beautiful flowers. Very soon they recognized the large town where they lived, and the tall steeples of the churches in which the sweet bells were ringing a merry peal, as they entered it and found their way to their grandmother's door.

They went upstairs into the little room, where all looked just as it used to do. The old clock was going "Tick, tick," and the hands pointed to the time of day, but as they passed through the door into the room they perceived that they were both grown up and become a man and woman. The roses out on the roof were in full bloom and peeped in at the window, and there stood the little chairs on which they had sat when children, and

Kay and Gerda seated themselves each on their own chair and held each other by the hand, while the cold, empty grandeur of the Snow Queen's palace vanished from their memories like a painful dream.

The grandmother sat in God's bright sunshine, and she read aloud from the Bible, "Except ye become as little children, ye shall in no wise enter into the kingdom of God." And Kay and Gerda looked into each other's eyes and all at once understood the words of the old song:

Roses bloom and fade away,
But we the Christ-child see alway.

And they both sat there, grown up, yet children at heart, and it was summer—warm, beautiful summer.

The Leaping Match

A Flea, the Grasshopper, and the Frog once wanted to see which of them could jump the highest. They made a festival, and invited the whole world and everyone else besides who liked to come and see the grand sight. Three famous jumpers they were, as all should say, when they met together in the room.

"I will give my daughter to him who shall jump highest," said the King; "it would be too bad for you to have the jumping, and for us to offer no prize."

The Flea was the first to come forward. He had most exquisite manners, and bowed to the company on every side; for he was of noble blood, and, besides, was accustomed to the society of man, and that, of course, had been an advantage to him.

Next came the Grasshopper. He was not quite so elegantly formed as the Flea, but he knew perfectly well how to conduct himself, and he wore the green uniform which belonged to him by right of birth. He said, moreover, that he came of a very ancient Egyptian family, and that in the house where he then lived he was much thought of.

The fact was that he had been just brought out of the fields and put in a card-house three stories high, and built on purpose for him, with the colored sides inwards, and doors and windows cut out of the Queen of Hearts. "And I sing so well," said he, "that sixteen parlor-bred crickets, who have chirped from infancy and yet got no one to build them card-houses to live in, have fretted themselves thinner even than before, from sheer vexation on hearing me."

It was thus that the Flea and the Grasshopper made the most of themselves, each thinking himself quite an equal match for the princess.

The Leapfrog said not a word; but people said that perhaps he thought the more; and the housedog who snuffed at him with his nose allowed that he was of good family. The old councilor, who had had three orders given him in vain for keeping quiet, asserted that the Leapfrog was a prophet, for that one could see on his back whether the coming winter was to be severe or mild, which is more than one can see on the back of the man who writes the almanac.

"I say nothing for the present," exclaimed the King; "yet I have my own opinion, for I observe everything."

And now the match began. The Flea jumped so high that no one could see what had become of him; and so they insisted that he had not jumped at all—which was disgraceful after all the fuss he had made.

The Grasshopper jumped only half as high; but he leaped into the King's face, who was disgusted by his rudeness.

The Leapfrog stood for a long time, as if lost in thought; people began to think he would not jump at all.

"I'm afraid he is ill!" said the dog and he went to snuff at him again; when lo! he suddenly made a sideways jump into the lap of the princess, who sat close by on a little golden stool.

"There is nothing higher than my daughter," said the King; "therefore to bound into her lap is the highest jump that can be made. Only one of good understanding would ever have thought of that. Thus the Frog has shown that he has sense. He has brains in his head, that he has."

And so he won the princess.

"I jumped the highest, for all that," said the Flea; "but it's all the same to me. The princess may have the stiff-legged, slimy creature, if she likes. In this world merit seldom meets its reward. Dullness and heaviness win the day. I am too light and airy for a stupid world."

And so the Flea went into foreign service.

The Grasshopper sat without on a green bank and reflected on the world and its ways; and he too said, "Yes, dullness and heaviness win the day; a fine exterior is what people care for nowadays." And then he began to sing in his own peculiar way—and it is from his song that we have taken this little piece of history, which may very possibly be all untrue, although it does stand printed here in black and white.

The Little Match Girl

It was dreadfully cold; it was snowing fast, and was almost dark, as evening came on—the last evening of the year. In the cold and the darkness, there went along the street a poor little girl, bareheaded and with naked feet. When she left home she had slippers on, it is true; but they were much too large for her feet—slippers that her mother had used till then, and the poor little girl lost them in running across the street when two carriages were passing terribly fast. When she looked for them, one was not to be found, and a boy seized the other and ran away with it, saying he would use it for a cradle someday, when he had children of his own.

So on the little girl went with her bare feet, that were red and blue with cold. In an old apron that she wore were bundles of matches, and she carried a bundle also in her hand. No one had bought so much as a bunch all the long day, and no one had given her even a penny.

Poor little girl! Shivering with cold and hunger she crept along, a perfect picture of misery.

The snowflakes fell on her long flaxen hair, which hung in pretty curls about her throat; but she thought not of her beauty nor of the cold. Lights gleamed in every window, and there came to her the savory smell of roast goose, for it was New Year's Eve. And it was this of which she thought.

In a corner formed by two houses, one of which projected beyond the other, she sat cowering down. She had drawn under her little feet, but still she grew colder and colder; yet she dared not go home, for she had sold no matches and could not bring a penny of money. Her father would certainly beat her; and, besides, it was cold enough at home, for they had only the house-roof above them, and though the largest holes had been stopped with straw and rags, there were left many through which the cold wind could whistle.

And now her little hands were nearly frozen with cold. Alas! a single match might do her good if she might only draw it from the bundle, rub it against the wall, and warm her fingers by it. So at last she drew one out. Whisht! How it blazed and burned! It gave out a warm, bright flame like a little candle, as she held her hands over it. A wonderful little light it was. It really seemed to the little girl as if she sat before a great iron stove with polished brass feet and brass shovel and tongs. So blessedly it burned that the little maiden stretched out her feet to warm them also.

How comfortable she was! But lo, the flame went out, the stove vanished, and nothing remained but the little burned match in her hand.

She rubbed another match against the wall. It burned brightly, and where the light fell upon the wall it became transparent like a veil, so that she could see through it into the room. A snow-white cloth was spread upon the table, on which was a beautiful china dinner-service, while a roast goose, stuffed with apples and prunes, steamed famously and sent forth a most savory smell. And what was more delightful still, and wonderful, the goose jumped from the dish, with knife and fork still in its breast, and waddled along the floor straight to the little girl.

But the match went out then, and nothing was left to her but the thick, damp wall.

She lighted another match. And now she was under a most beautiful Christmas tree, larger and far more prettily trimmed than the one she had seen through the glass doors at the rich merchant's. Hundreds of wax tapers were burning on the green branches, and gay figures, such as she had seen in shop windows, looked down upon her. The child stretched out her hands to them; then the match went out.

Still the lights of the Christmas tree rose higher and higher. She saw them now as stars in heaven, and one of them fell, forming a long trail of fire.

"Now someone is dying," murmured the child softly; for her grandmother, the only person who had loved her, and who was now dead, had told her that whenever a star falls a soul mounts up to God.

She struck yet another match against the wall, and again it was light; and in the brightness there appeared before her the dear old grandmother, bright and radiant, yet sweet and mild, and happy as she had never looked on earth.

"Oh, grandmother," cried the child, "take me with you. I know you will go away when the match burns out. You, too, will vanish, like the warm stove, the splendid New Year's feast, the beautiful Christmas tree." And lest her grandmother should disappear, she rubbed the whole bundle of matches against the wall.

And the matches burned with such a brilliant light that it became brighter than noonday. Her grandmother had never looked so grand and beautiful. She took the little girl in her arms, and both flew together, joyously and gloriously, mounting higher and higher, far above the earth;

and for them there was neither hunger, nor cold, nor care—they were with God.

But in the corner, at the dawn of day, sat the poor girl, leaning against the wall, with red cheeks and smiling mouth—frozen to death on the last evening of the old year. Stiff and cold she sat, with the matches, one bundle of which was burned.

"She wanted to warm herself, poor little thing," people said. No one imagined what sweet visions she had had, or how gloriously she had gone with her grandmother to enter upon the joys of a new year.

The Dream of Little Tuk

Little Tuk! An odd name, to be sure! However, it was not the little boy's real name. His real name was Carl; but when he was so young that he could not speak plainly, he used to call himself Tuk. It would be hard to say why, for it is not at all like "Carl;" but the name does as well as any, if one only knows it.

Little Tuk was left at home to take care of his sister Gustava, who was much younger than himself; and he had also to learn his lesson. Here were two things to be done at the same time, and they did not at all suit each other. The poor boy sat with his sister in his lap, singing to her all the songs he knew, yet giving, now and then, a glance into his geography, which lay open beside him. By tomorrow morning he must know the names of all the towns in Seeland by heart, and be able to tell about them all that could be told.

His mother came at last, and took little Gustava in her arms. Tuk ran quickly to the window and read and read till he had almost read his eyes out—for it was growing dark, and his mother could not afford to buy candles.

"There goes the old washerwoman down the lane," said the mother, as she looked out of the window. "She can hardly drag herself along, poor thing; and now she has to carry that heavy pail from the pump. Be a good boy, little Tuk, and run across to help the poor creature, will you not?" And little Tuk ran quickly and helped to bear the weight of the pail. But when he came back into the room, it was quite dark. Nothing was said about a candle, and it was of no use to wish for one; he must go to his little trundle-bed, which was made of an old settle.

There he lay, still thinking of the geography lesson, of Seeland, and of all that the master had said. He could not read the book again, as he should by rights have done, for want of a light. So he put the geography book under his pillow. Somebody had once told him that would help him wonderfully to remember his lesson, but he had never yet found that one could depend upon it.

There he lay and thought and thought, till all at once he felt as though some one were gently sealing his mouth and eyes with a kiss. He slept and yet did not sleep, for he seemed to see the old washerwoman's mild, kind eyes fixed upon him, and to hear her say: "It would be a shame, indeed, for you not to know your lesson tomorrow, little Tuk. You helped me; now I will help you, and our Lord will help us both."

All at once the leaves of the book began to rustle under little Tuk's head, and he heard something crawling about under his pillow.

"Cluck, cluck, cluck!" cried a hen, as she crept towards him. (She came from the town of Kjöge.) "I'm a Kjöge hen," she said. And then she told him how many inhabitants the little town contained, and about the battle that had once been fought there, and how it was now hardly worth mentioning, there were so many greater things.

Scratch, scratch! kribbley crabbley! and now a great wooden bird jumped down upon the bed. It was the popinjay from the shooting ground at Præstö. He had reckoned the number of inhabitants in Præstö, and found that there were as many as he had nails in his body. He was a proud bird. "Thorwaldsen lived in one corner of Præstö, close by me. Am I not a pretty bird, a merry popinjay?"

And now little Tuk no longer lay in bed. All in a moment he was on horseback, and on he went, gallop, gallop! A splendid knight, with a bright helmet and waving plume—a knight of the olden time—held him on his own horse; and on they rode together, through the wood of the ancient city of Vordingborg, and it was once again a great and busy town. The high towers of the king's castle rose against the sky, and bright lights were seen gleaming through the windows. Within were music and merrymaking. King Waldemar was leading out the noble ladies of his court to dance with him.

Suddenly the morning dawned, the lamps grew pale, the sun rose, the outlines of the buildings faded away, and at last one high tower alone remained to mark the spot where the royal castle had stood. The vast city had shrunk into a poor, mean-looking little town. The schoolboys, coming out of school with their geography books under their arms, said,

"Two thousand inhabitants;" but that was a mere boast, for the town had not nearly so many.

And little Tuk lay in his bed. He knew not whether he had been dreaming or not, but again there was someone close by his side.

"Little Tuk! little Tuk!" cried a voice; it was the voice of a young sailor boy. "I am come to bring you greeting from Korsör. Korsör is a new town, a living town, with steamers and mail coaches. Once people used to call it a low, ugly place, but they do so no longer.

"'I dwell by the seaside,' says Korsör; 'I have broad highroads and pleasure gardens; and I have given birth to a poet, a witty one, too, which is more than all poets are. I once thought of sending a ship all round the world; but I did not do it, though I might as well have done so. I dwell so pleasantly, close by the port; and I am fragrant with perfume, for the loveliest roses bloom round about me, close to my gates.'"

And little Tuk could smell the roses and see them and their fresh green leaves. But in a moment they had vanished; the green leaves spread and thickened—a perfect grove had grown up above the bright waters of the bay, and above the grove rose the two high-pointed towers of a glorious old church. From the side of the grass-grown hill gushed a fountain in rainbow-hued streams, with a merry, musical voice, and close beside it sat a king, wearing a gold crown upon his long dark hair. This was King Hroar of the springs; and hard by was the town of Roskilde (Hroar's Fountain). And up the hill, on a broad highway, went all the kings and queens of Denmark, wearing golden crowns; hand in hand they passed on into the church, and the deep music of the organ mingled with the clear rippling of the fountain. For nearly all the kings and queens of Denmark lie buried in this beautiful church. And little Tuk saw and heard it all.

"Don't forget the towns," said King Hroar.

Then all vanished; though where it went he knew not. It seemed like turning the leaves of a book.

And now there stood before him an old peasant woman from Sorö, the quiet little town where grass grows in the very marketplace. Her green linen apron was thrown over her head and back, and the apron was very wet, as if it had been raining heavily.

"And so it has," she said. And she told a great many pretty things from Holberg's comedies, and recited ballads about Waldemar and Absalon; for Holberg had founded an academy in her native town.

All at once she cowered down and rocked her head as if she were a frog about to spring. "Koax!" cried she; "it is wet, it is always wet, and it is as still as the grave in Sorö." She had changed into a frog. "Koax!" and again she was an old woman. "One must dress according to the weather," she said.

"It is wet! it is wet! My native town is like a bottle; one goes in at the cork, and by the cork one must come out. In old times we had the finest of fish; now we have fresh, rosy-cheeked boys at the bottom of the bottle. There they learn wisdom—Greek, Greek, and Hebrew! Koax!"

It sounded exactly as if frogs were croaking, or as if someone were walking over the great swamp with heavy boots. So tiresome was her tone, all on the same note, that little Tuk fell fast asleep; and a very good thing it was for him.

But even in sleep there came a dream, or whatever else it may be called. His little sister Gustava, with her blue eyes and flaxen ringlets, was grown into a tall, beautiful girl, who, though she had no wings, could fly; and away they now flew over Seeland—over its green woods and blue waters.

"Hark! Do you hear the cock crow, little Tuk? 'Cock-a-doodle-do!' The fowls are flying hither from Kjöge, and you shall have a farmyard, a great, great poultry yard of your own! You shall never suffer hunger or want. The golden goose, the bird of good omen, shall be yours; you shall become a rich and happy man. Your house shall rise up like King Waldemar's towers and be richly decked with statues like those of Thorwaldsen at Præstö.

"Understand me well; your good name shall be borne round the world, like the ship that was to sail from Korsör, and at Roskilde you shall speak and give counsel wisely and well, little Tuk, like King Hroar; and when at last you shall lie in your peaceful grave you shall sleep as quietly."

"As if I lay sleeping in Sorö," said Tuk, and he woke. It was a bright morning, and he could not remember his dream, but it was not necessary that he should. One has no need to know what one will live to see.

And now he sprang quickly out of bed and sought his book, that had lain under his pillow. He read his lesson and found that he knew the towns perfectly well.

And the old washerwoman put her head in at the door and said, with a friendly nod: "Thank you, my good child, for yesterday's help. May the Lord fulfill your brightest and most beautiful dreams! I know he will."

Little Tuk had forgotten what he had dreamed, but it did not matter. There was One above who knew it all.

The Naughty Boy

A long time ago, there lived an old poet, a thoroughly kind old poet. As he was sitting one evening in his room, a dreadful storm arose without, and the rain streamed down from heaven; but the old poet sat warm and comfortable in his chimney-corner, where the fire blazed and the roasting apple hissed.

"Those who have not a roof over their heads will be wetted to the skin," said the good old poet.

"Oh let me in! Let me in! I am cold, and I'm so wet!" exclaimed suddenly a child that stood crying at the door and knocking for admittance, while the rain poured down, and the wind made all the windows rattle.

"Poor thing!" said the old poet, as he went to open the door. There stood a little boy, quite naked, and the water ran down from his long golden hair; he trembled with cold, and had he not come into a warm room he would most certainly have perished in the frightful tempest.

"Poor child!" said the old poet, as he took the boy by the hand. "Come in, come in, and I will soon restore thee! Thou shalt have wine and roasted apples, for thou art verily a charming child!" And the boy was so really. His eyes were like two bright stars; and although the water trickled down his hair, it waved in beautiful curls. He looked exactly like a little angel, but he was so pale, and his whole body trembled with cold. He had a nice little bow in his hand, but it was quite spoiled by the rain, and the tints of his many-colored arrows ran one into the other.

The old poet seated himself beside his hearth and took the little fellow on his lap; he squeezed the water out of his dripping hair, warmed his hands between his own, and boiled for him some tea. Then the boy recovered, his cheeks again grew rosy, he jumped down from the lap where he was sitting and danced round the kind old poet.

"You are a merry fellow," said the old man. "What's your name?"

"My name is Cupid," answered the boy. "Don't you know me? There lies my bow; it shoots well, I can assure you! Look, the weather is now clearing up, and the moon is shining clear again through the window."

"Why, your bow is quite spoiled," said the old poet.

"That were sad indeed," said the boy, and he took the bow in his hand and examined it on every side. "Oh, it is dry again and is not hurt at all; the string is quite tight. I will try it directly." And he bent his bow, took aim, and shot an arrow at the old poet. "You see now that my bow was not spoiled," said he laughing and away he ran.

The naughty boy, to shoot the old poet in that way; he who had taken him into his warm room, who had treated him so kindly, and who had given him warm tea and the very best apples!

The poor poet lay on the earth and wept, for the arrow had flown into his heart.

"Fie!" said he. "How naughty a boy Cupid is! I will tell all children about him, that they may take care and not play with him, for he will only cause them sorrow and many a heartache."

And all good children to whom he related this story, took great heed of this naughty Cupid; but he made fools of them still, for he is astonishingly cunning. When the university students come from the lectures, he runs beside them in a black coat, and with a book under his arm. It is quite impossible for them to know him, and they walk along with him arm in arm, as if he, too, were a student like themselves; and then, unperceived, he thrusts an arrow to their bosom. When the young maidens come from being examined by the clergyman, or go to church to be confirmed, there he is again close behind them. Yes, he is forever following people. At the play, he sits in the great chandelier and burns in bright flames, so that people think it is really a flame, but they soon discover it is something else. He roves about in the garden of the palace and upon the ramparts: yes, once he even shot your father and mother right in the heart. Ask them only and you will hear what they'll tell you. Oh, he is a naughty boy, that Cupid; you must never have anything to do with him. He is forever running after everybody. Only think, he shot an arrow once at your old grandmother! But that is a long time ago, and it is all past now; however, a thing of that sort she never forgets. Fie, naughty Cupid! But now you know him, and you know, too, how ill-behaved he is!

The Butterfly

There was once a butterfly who wished for a bride, and, as may be supposed, he wanted to choose a very pretty one from among the flowers. He glanced, with a very critical eye, at all the flowerbeds, and found that the flowers were seated quietly and demurely on their stalks, just as maidens should sit before they are engaged; but there was a great number of them, and it appeared as if his search would become very wearisome. The butterfly did not like to take too much trouble, so he flew off on a visit to the daisies. The French call this flower "Marguerite," and they say that the little daisy can prophesy. Lovers pluck off the leaves, and as they pluck each leaf, they ask a question about their lovers; thus: "Does he or she love me? Ardently? Distractedly? Very much? A little? Not at all?" and so on. Everyone speaks these words in his own language. The butterfly came also to Marguerite to inquire, but he did not pluck off her leaves; he pressed a kiss on each of them, for he thought there was always more to be done by kindness.

"Darling Marguerite daisy," he said to her, "you are the wisest woman of all the flowers. Pray tell me which of the flowers I shall choose for my wife. Which will be my bride? When I know, I will fly directly to her, and propose."

But Marguerite did not answer him; she was offended that he should call her a woman when she was only a girl; and there is a great difference. He asked her a second time, and then a third; but she remained dumb, and answered not a word. Then he would wait no longer, but flew away, to commence his wooing at once. It was in the early spring, when the crocus and the snowdrop were in full bloom.

"They are very pretty," thought the butterfly; "charming little lasses; but they are rather formal."

Then, as the young lads often do, he looked out for the elder girls. He next flew to the anemones; these were rather sour to his taste. The violet, a little too sentimental. The lime blossoms, too small, and besides, there was such a large family of them. The apple blossoms, though they looked like roses, bloomed today, but might fall off tomorrow, with the first wind that blew; and he thought that a marriage with one of them might last too short a time. The pea blossom pleased him most of all; she was white and red, graceful and slender, and belonged to those domestic maidens who have a pretty appearance, and can yet be useful in the kitchen. He was just about to make her an offer, when, close by the maiden, he saw a pod, with a withered flower hanging at the end.

"Who is that?" he asked.

"That is my sister," replied the pea blossom.

"Oh, indeed; and you will be like her someday," said he; and he flew away directly, for he felt quite shocked.

A honeysuckle hung forth from the hedge, in full bloom; but there were so many girls like her, with long faces and sallow complexions. No; he did not like her. But which one did he like?

Spring went by, and summer drew towards its close; autumn came; but he had not decided. The flowers now appeared in their most gorgeous robes, but all in vain; they had not the fresh, fragrant air of youth. For the heart asks for fragrance, even when it is no longer young; and there is very little of that to be found in the dahlias or the dry chrysanthemums; therefore the butterfly turned to the mint on the ground. You know, this plant has no blossom; but it is sweetness all over, full of fragrance from head to foot, with the scent of a flower in every leaf.

"I will take her," said the butterfly; and he made her an offer. But the mint stood silent and stiff, as she listened to him. At last she said,

"Friendship, if you please; nothing more. I am old, and you are old, but we may live for each other just the same; as to marrying—no; don't let us appear ridiculous at our age."

And so it happened that the butterfly got no wife at all. He had been too long choosing, which is always a bad plan. And the butterfly became what is called an old bachelor.

It was late in the autumn, with rainy and cloudy weather. The cold wind blew over the bowed backs of the willows, so that they creaked again. It was not the weather for flying about in summer clothes; but fortunately the butterfly was not out in it. He had got a shelter by chance. It was in a room heated by a stove, and as warm as summer. He could exist here, he said, well enough.

"But it is not enough merely to exist," said he, "I need freedom, sunshine, and a little flower for a companion."

Then he flew against the windowpane, and was seen and admired by those in the room, who caught him, and stuck him on a pin, in a box of curiosities. They could not do more for him.

"Now I am perched on a stalk, like the flowers," said the butterfly. "It is not very pleasant, certainly; I should imagine it is something like being married; for here I am stuck fast." And with this thought he consoled himself a little.

"That seems very poor consolation," said one of the plants in the room, that grew in a pot.

"Ah," thought the butterfly, "one can't very well trust these plants in pots; they have too much to do with mankind."

Little Ida's Flowers

My poor flowers are quite dead," said little Ida, "they were so pretty yesterday evening, and now all the leaves are hanging down quite withered. What do they do that for?" she asked, of the student who sat on the sofa; she liked him very much, he could tell the most amusing stories, and cut out the prettiest pictures; hearts, and ladies dancing, castles with doors that opened, as well as flowers; he was a delightful student. "Why do the flowers look so faded today?" she asked again, and pointed to her nosegay, which was quite withered.

"Don't you know what is the matter with them?" said the student. "The flowers were at a ball last night, and therefore, it is no wonder they hang their heads."

"But flowers cannot dance?" cried little Ida.

"Yes indeed, they can," replied the student. "When it grows dark, and everybody is asleep, they jump about quite merrily. They have a ball almost every night."

"Can children go to these balls?"

"Yes," said the student, "little daisies and lilies of the valley."

"Where do the beautiful flowers dance?" asked little Ida.

"Have you not often seen the large castle outside the gates of the town, where the king lives in summer, and where the beautiful garden is full of flowers? And have you not fed the swans with bread when they swam towards you? Well, the flowers have capital balls there, believe me."

"I was in the garden out there yesterday with my mother," said Ida, "but all the leaves were off the trees, and there was not a single flower left. Where are they? I used to see so many in the summer."

"They are in the castle," replied the student. "You must know that as soon as the king and all the court are gone into the town, the flowers run out of the garden into the castle, and you should see how merry they are. The two most beautiful roses seat themselves on the throne, and are called the king and queen, then all the red cockscombs range themselves on each side, and bow, these are the lords-in-waiting. After that the pretty flowers come in, and there is a grand ball. The blue violets represent little naval cadets, and dance with hyacinths and crocuses which they call young ladies. The tulips and tiger-lilies are the old ladies who sit and watch the dancing, so that everything may be conducted with order and propriety."

"But," said little Ida, "is there no one there to hurt the flowers for dancing in the king's castle?"

"No one knows anything about it," said the student. "The old steward of the castle, who has to watch there at night, sometimes comes in; but he carries a great bunch of keys, and as soon as the flowers hear the keys rattle, they run and hide themselves behind the long curtains, and stand quite still, just peeping their heads out. Then the old steward says, 'I smell flowers here,' but he cannot see them."

"Oh how capital," said little Ida, clapping her hands. "Should I be able to see these flowers?"

"Yes," said the student, "mind you think of it the next time you go out, no doubt you will see them, if you peep through the window. I did so today, and I saw a long yellow lily lying stretched out on the sofa. She was a court lady."

"Can the flowers from the Botanical Gardens go to these balls?" asked Ida. "It is such a distance!"

"Oh yes," said the student, "whenever they like, for they can fly. Have you not seen those beautiful red, white, and yellow butterflies, that look like flowers? They were flowers once. They have flown off their stalks into the air, and flap their leaves as if they were little wings to make them fly. Then, if they behave well, they obtain permission to fly about during the day, instead of being obliged to sit still on their stems at home, and so in time their leaves become real wings. It may be, however, that the flowers in the Botanical Gardens have never been to the king's palace, and, therefore, they know nothing of the merry doings at night, which take place there. I will tell you what to do, and the botanical professor, who lives close by here, will be so surprised. You know him very well, do you not? Well, next time you go into his garden, you must tell one of the flowers that there is going to be a grand ball at the castle, then that flower will tell all the others, and they will fly away to the castle as soon as possible. And when the professor walks into his garden, there will not be a single flower left. How he will wonder what has become of them!"

"But how can one flower tell another? Flowers cannot speak?"

"No, certainly not," replied the student; "but they can make signs. Have you not often seen that when the wind blows they nod at one another, and rustle all their green leaves?"

"Can the professor understand the signs?" asked Ida.

"Yes, to be sure he can. He went one morning into his garden, and saw a stinging nettle making signs with its leaves to a beautiful red carnation. It was saying, 'You are so pretty, I like you very much.' But the professor did not approve of such nonsense, so he clapped his hands on the nettle to stop it. Then the leaves, which are its fingers, stung him so sharply that he has never ventured to touch a nettle since."

"Oh how funny!" said Ida, and she laughed.

"How can anyone put such notions into a child's head?" said a tiresome lawyer, who had come to pay a visit, and sat on the sofa. He did not like the student, and would grumble when he saw him cutting out droll or amusing pictures. Sometimes it would be a man hanging on a gibbet and holding a heart in his hand as if he had been stealing hearts. Sometimes it was an old witch riding through the air on a broom and carrying her husband on her nose. But the lawyer did not like such jokes, and he would say as he had just said, "How can anyone put such nonsense into a child's head! what absurd fancies there are!"

But to little Ida, all these stories which the student told her about the flowers, seemed very droll, and she thought over them a great deal. The flowers did hang their heads, because they had been dancing all night, and were very tired, and most likely they were ill. Then she took them into the room where a number of toys lay on a pretty little table, and the whole of the table drawer besides was full of beautiful things. Her doll Sophy lay in the doll's bed asleep, and little Ida said to her, "You must really get up Sophy, and be content to lie in the drawer tonight; the poor flowers are ill, and they must lie in your bed, then perhaps they will get well again." So she took the doll out, who looked quite cross, and said not a single word, for she was angry at being turned out of her bed. Ida placed the flowers in the doll's bed, and drew the quilt over them. Then she told them to lie quite still and be good, while she made some tea for them, so that they might be quite well and able to get up the next morning. And she drew the curtains close round the little bed, so that the sun might not shine in their eyes. During the whole evening she could not help thinking of what the student had told her. And before she went to bed herself, she was obliged to peep behind the curtains into the garden where all her mother's beautiful flowers grew, hyacinths and tulips, and many others. Then she whispered to them quite softly, "I know you are going to a ball

tonight." But the flowers appeared as if they did not understand, and not a leaf moved; still Ida felt quite sure she knew all about it. She lay awake a long time after she was in bed, thinking how pretty it must be to see all the beautiful flowers dancing in the king's garden. "I wonder if my flowers have really been there," she said to herself, and then she fell asleep. In the night she awoke; she had been dreaming of the flowers and of the student, as well as of the tiresome lawyer who found fault with him. It was quite still in Ida's bedroom; the night-lamp burnt on the table, and her father and mother were asleep. "I wonder if my flowers are still lying in Sophy's bed," she thought to herself; "how much I should like to know."

She raised herself a little, and glanced at the door of the room where all her flowers and playthings lay; it was partly open, and as she listened, it seemed as if someone in the room was playing the piano, but softly and more prettily than she had ever before heard it. "Now all the flowers are certainly dancing in there," she thought, "oh how much I should like to see them," but she did not dare move for fear of disturbing her father and mother. "If they would only come in here," she thought; but they did not come, and the music continued to play so beautifully, and was so pretty, that she could resist no longer. She crept out of her little bed, went softly to the door, and looked into the room. Oh what a splendid sight there was to be sure! There was no night-lamp burning, but the room appeared quite light, for the moon shone through the window upon the floor, and made it almost like day. All the hyacinths and tulips stood in two long rows down the room, not a single flower remained in the window, and the flowerpots were all empty. The flowers were dancing gracefully on the floor, making turns and holding each other by their long green leaves as they swung round. At the piano sat a large yellow lily which little Ida was sure she had seen in the summer, for she remembered the student saying she was very much like Miss Lina, one of Ida's friends. They all laughed at him then, but now it seemed to little Ida as if the tall, yellow flower was really like the young lady. She had just the same manners while playing, bending her long yellow face from side to side, and nodding in time to the beautiful music. Then she saw a large purple crocus jump into the middle of the table where the playthings stood, go up to the doll's bedstead, and draw back the curtains; there lay the sick flowers, but they got up directly, and nodded to the others as a sign that they wished to dance with them. The old rough doll, with the broken mouth, stood up and bowed to the pretty flowers. They did not look ill at all now, but jumped about and were very merry, yet none of them noticed little Ida. Presently it seemed as if something fell from the table. Ida looked that way, and saw a slight carnival rod jumping down among the flowers as if it belonged to them; it was, however, very smooth and neat, and a little wax doll with a broad brimmed hat on her head, like the one worn by the lawyer, sat upon it. The carnival rod hopped about among the flowers on its three red stilted feet, and stamped quite loud when it danced the Mazurka; the flowers could not perform this dance, they were too light to stamp in that manner. All at once the wax doll which rode on the carnival rod seemed to grow larger and taller, and it turned round and said to the paper flowers, "How can you put such things in a child's head? they are all foolish fancies;" and then the doll was exactly like the lawyer with the broad brimmed hat, and looked as yellow and as cross as he did; but the paper dolls struck him on his thin legs, and he shrunk up again and became quite a little wax doll. This was very amusing, and Ida could not help laughing. The carnival rod went on dancing, and the lawyer was obliged to dance also. It was no use, he might make himself great and tall, or remain a little wax doll with a large black hat; still he must dance. Then at last the other flowers interceded for him, especially those who had lain in the doll's bed, and the carnival rod gave up his dancing. At the same moment a loud knocking was heard in the drawer, where Ida's doll Sophy lay with many other toys. Then the rough doll ran to the end of the table, laid himself flat down upon it, and began to pull the drawer out a little way.

Then Sophy raised himself, and looked round quite astonished, "There must be a ball here tonight," said Sophy. "Why did not somebody tell me?"

"Will you dance with me?" said the rough doll.

"You are the right sort to dance with, certainly," said she, turning her back upon him.

Then she seated herself on the edge of the drawer, and thought that perhaps one of the flowers would ask her to dance; but none of them came. Then she coughed, "Hem, hem, a-hem"; but for all that not one came. The shabby doll now danced quite alone, and not very badly, after all. As none of the flowers seemed to notice Sophy, she let herself down from the drawer to the floor, so as to make a very great noise. All the flowers came round her directly, and asked if she had hurt herself, especially those who had lain in her bed. But she was not hurt at all, and Ida's flowers thanked her for the use of the nice bed, and were very kind to her. They led her into the middle of the room, where the moon shone, and danced with her, while all the other flowers formed a circle round them. Then Sophy was very happy, and said they might keep her bed; she did not mind lying in the drawer at all. But the flowers thanked her very much, and said,

"We cannot live long. Tomorrow morning we shall be quite dead; and you must tell little Ida to bury us in the garden, near to the grave of the canary; then, in the summer we shall wake up and be more beautiful than ever."

"No, you must not die," said Sophy, as she kissed the flowers.

Then the door of the room opened, and a number of beautiful flowers danced in. Ida could not imagine where they could come from, unless they were the flowers from the king's garden. First came two lovely roses, with little golden crowns on their heads; these were the king and queen. Beautiful stocks and carnations followed, bowing to every one present. They had also music with them. Large poppies and peonies had pea-shells for instruments, and blew into them till they were quite red in the face. The bunches of blue hyacinths and the little white snowdrops jingled their bell-like flowers, as if they were real bells. Then came many more flowers: blue violets, purple heart's-ease, daisies, and lilies of the valley, and they all danced together, and kissed each other. It was very beautiful to behold.

At last the flowers wished each other good night. Then little Ida crept back into her bed again, and dreamt of all she had seen. When she arose the next morning, she went quickly to the little table, to see if the flowers were still there. She drew aside the curtains of the little bed. There they all lay, but quite faded; much more so than the day before. Sophy was lying in the drawer where Ida had placed her; but she looked very sleepy.

"Do you remember what the flowers told you to say to me?" said little Ida. But Sophy looked quite stupid, and said not a single word.

"You are not kind at all," said Ida; "and yet they all danced with you."

Then she took a little paper box, on which were painted beautiful birds, and laid the dead flowers in it.

"This shall be your pretty coffin," she said; "and by and by, when my cousins come to visit me, they shall help me to bury you out in the garden; so that next summer you may grow up again more beautiful than ever."

Her cousins were two good-tempered boys, whose names were James and Adolphus. Their father had given them each a bow and arrow, and they had brought them to show Ida. She told them about the poor flowers which were dead; and as soon as they obtained permission, they went with her to bury them. The two boys walked first, with their crossbows on their shoulders, and little Ida followed, carrying the pretty box containing the dead flowers. They dug a little grave in the garden. Ida kissed her flowers and then laid them, with the box, in the earth. James and Adolphus then fired their crossbows over the grave, as they had neither guns nor cannons.

The Girl Who Trod on the Loaf

There was once a girl who trod on a loaf to avoid soiling her shoes, and the misfortunes that happened to her in consequence are well known. Her name was Inge; she was a poor child, but proud and presuming, and with a bad and cruel disposition. When she was little, she was often cruel to animals and grew worse instead of better with years. Unfortunately, she was pretty, which caused her to be excused, when she should have been sharply reproved.

"Your headstrong will requires severity to conquer it," her mother often said to her. "As a little child you used to trample on my apron, but one day I fear you will trample on my heart." And, alas! this fear was realized.

Inge was taken to the house of some rich people, who lived at a distance, and who treated her as their own child, and dressed her so fine that her pride and arrogance increased.

When she had been there about a year, her patroness said to her, "You ought to go, for once, and see your parents, Inge."

So, Inge started to go and visit her parents, but she only wanted to show herself in her native place, that the people might see how fine she was. She reached the entrance of the village and saw the young laboring men and maidens standing together chatting, and her own mother amongst them. Inge's mother was sitting on a stone to rest, with a faggot of sticks lying before her, which she had picked up in the wood. Then Inge turned back; she who was so finely dressed she felt ashamed of her mother, a poorly clad woman, who picked up wood in the forest. She did not turn back out of pity for her mother's poverty, but from pride.

Another half-year went by, and her mistress said, "You ought to go home again, and visit your parents, Inge, and I will give you a large wheaten loaf to take to them, they will be glad to see you, I am sure."

So, Inge put on her best clothes, and her new shoes, drew her dress up around her, and set out, stepping very carefully, that she might be clean and neat about the feet, and there was nothing wrong in doing so. But when she came to the place where the footpath led across the moor, she found small pools of water, and a great deal of mud, so she threw the loaf into the mud, and trod upon it, that she might pass without wetting her feet. But as she stood with one foot on the loaf and the other lifted up to step forward, the loaf began to sink under her, lower and lower, till

she disappeared altogether, and only a few bubbles on the surface of the muddy pool remained to show where she had sunk. And this is the story.

But where did Inge go? She sank into the ground, and went down to the Marsh Woman, who is always brewing there.

The Marsh Woman is related to the elf maidens, who are well-known, for songs are sung and pictures painted about them. But of the Marsh Woman nothing is known, excepting that when a mist arises from the meadows, in summertime, it is because she is brewing beneath them. To the Marsh Woman's brewery Inge sunk down to a place which no one can endure for long. A heap of mud is a palace compared with the Marsh Woman's brewery; and as Inge fell, she shuddered in every limb and soon became cold and stiff as marble. Her foot was still fastened to the loaf, which bowed her down as a golden ear of corn bends the stem.

An evil spirit soon took possession of Inge, and carried her to a still worse place, in which she saw crowds of unhappy people, waiting in a state of agony for the gates of mercy to be opened to them, and in every heart was a miserable and eternal feeling of unrest. It would take too much time to describe the various tortures these people suffered, but Inge's punishment consisted in standing there as a statue, with her foot fastened to the loaf. She could move her eyes about, and see all the misery around her, but she could not turn her head; and when she saw the people looking at her, she thought they were admiring her pretty face and fine clothes, for she was still vain and proud. But she had forgotten how soiled her clothes had become while in the Marsh Woman's brewery, and that they were covered with mud; a snake had also fastened itself in her hair, and hung down her back, while from each fold in her dress a great toad peeped out and croaked like an asthmatic poodle. Worse than all was the terrible hunger that tormented her, and she could not stoop to break off a piece of the loaf on which she stood. No, her back was too stiff, and her whole body like a pillar of stone.

"If this lasts much longer," she said, "I shall not be able to bear it." But it did last, and she had to bear it, without being able to help herself.

A tear, followed by many scalding tears, fell upon her head, and rolled over her face and neck, down to the loaf on which she stood. Who could be weeping for Inge? She had a mother in the world still, and the tears of sorrow which a mother sheds for her child will always find their way to the child's heart, but they often increase the torment instead of being a relief.

And Inge could hear all that was said about her in the world she had left, and everyone seemed cruel to her. The sin she had committed in treading on the loaf was known on earth, for she had been seen by the cowherd from the hill, when she was crossing the marsh and had disappeared.

When her mother wept and exclaimed, "Ah, Inge! What grief you have caused your mother," she would say, "Oh that I had never been born! My mother's tears are useless now."

And then the words of the kind people who had adopted her came to her ears, when they said, "Inge was a sinful girl, who did not value the gifts of God, but trampled them under her feet."

"Ah," thought Inge, "they should have punished me, and driven all my naughty tempers out of me."

A song was made about "the girl who trod on a loaf to keep her shoes from being soiled," and this song was sung everywhere. The story of her sin was also told to the little children, and they called her "wicked Inge," and said she was so naughty that she ought to be punished. Inge heard all this, and her heart became hardened and full of bitterness.

But one day, while hunger and grief were gnawing in her hollow frame, she heard a little, innocent child, while listening to the tale of the vain, haughty Inge, burst into tears and exclaim, "But will she never come up again?"

And she heard the reply, "No, she will never come up again."

"But if she were to say she was sorry, and ask pardon, and promise never to do so again?" asked the little one.

"Yes, then she might come; but she will not beg pardon," was the answer.

"Oh, I wish she would!" said the child, who was quite unhappy about it. "I should be so glad. I would give up my doll and all my playthings, if she could only come here again. Poor Inge! It is so dreadful for her."

These pitying words penetrated to Inge's inmost heart and seemed to do her good. It was the first time anyone had said, "Poor Inge!" without saying something about her faults. A little innocent child was weeping and praying for mercy for her. It made her feel quite strange, and she would gladly have wept herself, and it added to her torment to find she could not do so. And while she thus suffered in a place where nothing changed, years passed away on earth, and she heard her name less frequently mentioned. But one day a sigh reached her ear, and the words, "Inge! Inge! What a grief you have been to me! I said it would be so." It was the last sigh of her dying mother.

After this, Inge heard her kind mistress say, "Ah, poor Inge! Shall I ever see you again? Perhaps I may, for we know not what may happen in the future." But Inge knew right well that her mistress would never come to that dreadful place.

Time passed—a long bitter time—then Inge heard her name pronounced once more and saw what seemed two bright stars shining above her. They were two gentle eyes closing on earth. Many years had passed since the little girl had lamented and wept about "poor Inge." That child was now an old woman, whom God was taking to Himself. In the last hour of existence, the events of a whole life often appear before us; and this hour the old woman remembered how, when a child, she had shed tears over the story of Inge, and she prayed for her now. As the eyes of the old woman closed to earth, the eyes of the soul opened upon the hidden things of eternity, and then she, in whose last thoughts Inge had been so vividly present, saw how deeply the poor girl had sunk. She burst into tears at the sight, and in heaven, as she had done when a little child on earth, she wept and prayed for poor Inge. Her tears and her prayers echoed through the dark void that surrounded the tormented captive soul, and the unexpected mercy was obtained for it through an angel's tears. As in thought Inge seemed to act over again every sin she had committed on earth, she trembled and tears she had never yet been able to weep rushed to her eyes. It seemed impossible that the gates of mercy could ever be opened to her; but while she acknowledged this in deep penitence, a beam of radiant light shot suddenly into the depths upon her. More powerful than the sunbeam that dissolves the man of snow which the children have raised, more quickly than the snowflake melts and becomes a drop of water on the warm lips of a child, was the stony form of Inge changed, and as a little bird she soared, with the speed of lightning, upward to the world of mortals. A bird that felt timid and shy to all things around it, that seemed to shrink with shame from meeting any living creature, and hurriedly sought to conceal itself in a dark corner of an old, ruined wall; there it sat cowering and unable to utter a sound, for it was voiceless. Yet how quickly the little bird discovered the beauty of everything around it. The sweet, fresh air; the soft radiance of the moon, as its light spread over the earth; the fragrance which exhaled from bush and tree, made it feel happy as it sat there clothed in its fresh, bright plumage. All creation seemed to speak of beneficence and love. The bird wanted to give utterance to thoughts that stirred in his breast, as the cuckoo and the nightingale in the spring, but it could not. Yet in heaven can be heard the song of praise, even from a worm; and the notes trembling in the breast of the bird were as audible to heaven even as the psalms of David before they had fashioned themselves into words and song.

Christmastime drew near, and a peasant who dwelt close by the old wall stuck up a pole with some ears of corn fastened to the top, that the birds of heaven might have feast, and rejoice in the happy, blessed time. And on Christmas morning the sun arose and shone upon the ears of corn, which were quickly surrounded by a number of twittering birds. Then, from a hole in the wall, gushed forth in song the swelling thoughts of the bird as he issued from his hiding place to perform his first good deed on earth, and in heaven it was well known who that bird was.

The winter was very hard; the ponds were covered with ice, and there was very little food for either the beasts of the field or the birds of the air. Our little bird flew away into the public roads, and found here and there, in the ruts of the sledges, a grain of corn, and at the halting places some crumbs. Of these he ate only a few, but he called around him the other birds and the hungry sparrows, that they too might have food. He flew into the towns, and looked about, and wherever a kind hand had strewed bread on the windowsill for the birds, he only ate a single crumb himself, and gave all the rest to the rest of the other birds. In the course of the winter the bird had in this way collected many crumbs and given them to other birds, till they equaled the weight of the loaf on which Inge had trod to keep her shoes clean; and when the last breadcrumb had been found and given, the gray wings of the bird became white, and spread themselves out for flight.

"See, yonder is a seagull!" cried the children, when they saw the white bird, as it dived into the sea, and rose again into the clear sunlight, white and glittering. But no one could tell whither it went then although some declared it flew straight to the sun.

The Darning-Needle

There was once a darning-needle who thought herself so fine that she fancied she must be fit for embroidery. "Hold me tight," she would say to the fingers, when they took her up, "don't let me fall; if you do I shall never be found again, I am so very fine."

"That is your opinion, is it?" said the fingers, as they seized her round the body.

"See, I am coming with a train," said the darning-needle, drawing a long thread after her; but there was no knot in the thread.

The fingers then placed the point of the needle against the cook's slipper. There was a crack in the upper leather, which had to be sewn together.

"What coarse work!" said the darning-needle, "I shall never get through. I shall break! — I am breaking!" and sure enough she broke. "Did I not say so?" said the darning-needle, "I know I am too fine for such work as that."

"This needle is quite useless for sewing now," said the fingers; but they still held it fast, and the cook dropped some sealing-wax on the needle, and fastened her handkerchief with it in front.

"So now I am a breastpin," said the darning-needle; "I knew very well I should come to honor some day: merit is sure to rise;" and she laughed, quietly to herself, for of course no one ever saw a darning-needle laugh. And there she sat as proudly as if she were in a state coach, and looked all around her. "May I be allowed to ask if you are made of gold?" she inquired of her neighbor, a pin; "you have a very pretty appearance, and a curious head, although you are rather small. You must take pains to grow, for it is not everyone who has sealing-wax dropped upon him;" and as she spoke, the darning-needle drew herself up so proudly that she fell out of the handkerchief right into the sink, which the cook was cleaning. "Now I am going on a journey," said the needle, as she floated away with the dirty water, "I do hope I shall not be lost." But she really was lost in a gutter. "I am too fine for this world," said the darning-needle, as she lay in the gutter; "but I know who I am, and that is always some comfort."

So the darning-needle kept up her proud behavior, and did not lose her good humor. Then there floated over her all sorts of things—chips and straws, and pieces of old newspaper. "See how they sail," said the darning-needle; "they do not know what is under them. I am here, and here I shall stick. See, there goes a chip, thinking of nothing in the world but himself—only a chip. There's a straw going by now; how he turns and twists about! Don't be thinking too much of yourself, or you may chance to run against a stone. There swims a piece of newspaper; what is written upon it has been forgotten long ago, and yet it gives itself airs. I sit here patiently and quietly. I know who I am, so I shall not move."

One day something lying close to the darning-needle glittered so splendidly that she thought it was a diamond; yet it was only a piece of broken bottle. The darning-needle spoke to it, because it sparkled, and represented herself as a breastpin. "I suppose you are really a diamond?" she said.

"Why yes, something of the kind," he replied; and so each believed the other to be very valuable, and then they began to talk about the world, and the conceited people in it.

"I have been in a lady's workbox," said the darning-needle, "and this lady was the cook. She had on each hand five fingers, and anything so conceited as these five fingers I have never seen; and yet they were only employed to take me out of the box and to put me back again."

"Were they not high-born?"

"High-born!" said the darning-needle, "no indeed, but so haughty. They were five brothers, all born fingers; they kept very proudly together, though they were of different lengths. The one who stood first in the rank was named the thumb, he was short and thick, and had only one joint in his back, and could therefore make but one bow; but he said that if he were cut off from a man's hand, that man would be unfit for a soldier. Sweet tooth, his neighbor, dipped himself into sweet or sour, pointed to the sun and moon, and formed the letters when the fingers wrote. Longman, the middle finger, looked over the heads of all the others. Gold-band, the next finger, wore a golden circle round his waist. And little Playman did nothing at all, and seemed proud of it. They were boasters, and boasters they will remain; and therefore I left them."

"And now we sit here and glitter," said the piece of broken bottle.

At the same moment more water streamed into the gutter, so that it overflowed, and the piece of bottle was carried away.

"So he is promoted," said the darning-needle, "while I remain here; I am too fine, but that is my pride, and what do I care?" And so she sat there in her pride, and had many such thoughts as these, "I could almost fancy that I came from a sunbeam, I am so fine. It seems as if the sunbeams were always looking for me under the water. Ah! I am so fine that even my mother cannot find me. Had I still my old eye, which was broken off, I believe I should weep; but no, I would not do that, it is not genteel to cry."

One day a couple of street boys were paddling in the gutter, for they sometimes found old nails, farthings, and other treasures. It was dirty work, but they took great pleasure in it. "Hallo!" cried one, as he pricked himself with the darning-needle, "here's a fellow for you."

"I am not a fellow, I am a young lady," said the darning-needle; but no one heard her.

The sealing-wax had come off, and she was quite black; but black makes a person look slender, so she thought herself even finer than before.

"Here comes an eggshell sailing along," said one of the boys; so they stuck the darning-needle into the eggshell.

"White walls, and I am black myself," said the darning-needle, "that looks well; now I can be seen, but I hope I shall not be seasick, or I shall break again." She was not seasick, and she did not break. "It is a good thing against seasickness to have a steel stomach, and not to forget one's own importance. Now my seasickness has past: delicate people can bear a great deal."

Crack went the eggshell, as a wagon passed over it. "Good heavens, how it crushes!" said the darning-needle. "I shall be sick now. I am breaking!" but she did not break, though the wagon went over her as she lay at full length; and there let her lie.

The Brave Tin Soldier

There were once five-and-twenty tin soldiers, who were all brothers, for they had been made out of the same old tin spoon. They shouldered arms and looked straight before them, and wore a splendid uniform, red and blue. The first thing in the world they ever heard were the words, "Tin soldiers!" uttered by a little boy, who clapped his hands with delight when the lid of the box, in which they lay, was taken off. They were given him for a birthday present, and he stood at the table to set them up. The soldiers were all exactly alike, excepting one, who had only one leg; he had been left to the last, and then there was not enough of the melted tin to finish him, so they made him to stand firmly on one leg, and this caused him to be very remarkable.

The table on which the tin soldiers stood, was covered with other playthings, but the most attractive to the eye was a pretty little paper castle. Through the small windows the rooms could be seen. In front of the castle a number of little trees surrounded a piece of looking glass, which was intended to represent a transparent lake. Swans, made of wax, swam on the lake, and were reflected in it. All this was very pretty, but the prettiest of all was a tiny little lady, who stood at the open door of the castle; she, also, was made of paper, and she wore a dress of clear muslin, with a narrow blue ribbon over her shoulders just like a scarf. In front of these was fixed a glittering tinsel rose, as large as her whole face. The little lady was a dancer, and she stretched out both her arms, and raised one of her legs so high, that the tin soldier could not see it at all, and he thought that she, like himself, had only one leg. "That is the wife for me," he thought; "but she is too grand, and lives in a castle, while I have only a box to live in, five-and-twenty of us altogether, that is no place for her. Still I must try and make her acquaintance." Then he laid himself at full length on the table behind a snuffbox that stood upon it, so that he could peep at the little delicate lady, who continued to stand on one leg without losing her balance. When evening came, the other tin soldiers were all placed in the box, and the people of the house went to bed. Then the playthings began to have their own games together, to pay visits, to have sham fights, and to give balls. The tin soldiers rattled in their box; they wanted to get out and join the amusements, but they could not open the lid. The nutcrackers played at leapfrog, and the pencil jumped about the table. There was such a noise that the canary woke up and began to talk, and in poetry too. Only the tin soldier and the dancer remained in their places. She stood on tiptoe, with her legs stretched out, as firmly as he did on his one leg. He never took his eyes from her for even a moment. The clock struck twelve, and, with a bounce, up sprang the lid of the snuffbox; but, instead of snuff, there jumped up a little black goblin; for the snuffbox was a toy puzzle.

"Tin soldier," said the goblin, "don't wish for what does not belong to you."

But the tin soldier pretended not to hear.

"Very well; wait till tomorrow, then," said the goblin.

When the children came in the next morning, they placed the tin soldier in the window. Now, whether it was the goblin who did it, or the draught, is not known, but the window flew open, and out fell the tin soldier, heels over head, from the third story, into the street beneath. It was a terrible fall; for he came head downwards, his helmet and his bayonet stuck in between the flagstones, and his one leg up in the air. The servant maid and the little boy went downstairs directly to look for him; but he was nowhere to be seen, although once they nearly trod upon him. If he had called out, "Here I am," it would have been all right, but he was too proud to cry out for help while he wore a uniform.

Presently it began to rain, and the drops fell faster and faster, till there was a heavy shower. When it was over, two boys happened to pass by, and one of them said, "Look, there is a tin soldier. He ought to have a boat to sail in."

So they made a boat out of a newspaper, and placed the tin soldier in it, and sent him sailing down the gutter, while the two boys ran by the side of it, and clapped their hands. Good gracious, what large waves arose in that gutter! and how fast the stream rolled on! for the rain had been very heavy. The paper boat rocked up and down, and turned itself round sometimes so quickly that the tin soldier trembled; yet he remained firm; his countenance did not change; he looked straight before him, and shouldered his musket. Suddenly the boat shot under a bridge which formed a part of a drain, and then it was as dark as the tin soldier's box.

"Where am I going now?" thought he. "This is the black goblin's fault, I am sure. Ah, well, if the little lady were only here with me in the boat, I should not care for any darkness."

Suddenly there appeared a great water-rat, who lived in the drain.

"Have you a passport?" asked the rat, "give it to me at once." But the tin soldier remained silent and held his musket tighter than ever. The boat sailed on and the rat followed it. How he did gnash his teeth and cry out to the bits of wood and straw, "Stop him, stop him; he has not paid toll, and has not shown his pass." But the stream rushed on stronger and stronger. The tin soldier could already see daylight shining where the arch ended. Then he heard a roaring sound quite terrible enough to frighten the bravest man. At the end of the tunnel the drain fell into a large canal over a steep place, which made it as dangerous for him as a waterfall would be to us. He was too close to it to stop, so the boat rushed on, and the poor tin soldier could only hold himself as stiffly as possible, without moving an eyelid, to show that he was not afraid. The boat whirled round three or four times, and then filled with water to the very edge; nothing could save it from sinking. He now stood up to his neck in water, while deeper and deeper sank the boat, and the paper became soft and loose with the wet, till at last the water closed over the soldier's head. He thought of the elegant little dancer whom he should never see again, and the words of the song sounded in his ears —

"Farewell, warrior! ever brave,
Drifting onward to thy grave."

Then the paper boat fell to pieces, and the soldier sank into the water and immediately afterwards was swallowed up by a great fish. Oh how dark it was inside the fish! A great deal darker than in the tunnel, and narrower too, but the tin soldier continued firm, and lay at full length shouldering his musket. The fish swam to and fro, making the most wonderful movements, but at last he became quite still. After a while, a flash of lightning seemed to pass through him, and then the daylight approached, and a voice cried out, "I declare here is the tin soldier." The fish had been caught, taken to the market, and sold to the cook, who took him into the kitchen and cut him open with a large knife. She picked up the soldier and held him by the waist between her finger and thumb, and carried him into the room. They were all anxious to see this wonderful soldier who had travelled about inside a fish; but he was not at all proud. They placed him on the table, and—how many curious things do happen in the world!—there he was in the very same room from the window of which he had fallen, there were the same children, the same playthings,

standing on the table, and the pretty castle with the elegant little dancer at the door; she still balanced herself on one leg, and held up the other, so she was as firm as himself. It touched the tin soldier so much to see her that he almost wept tin tears, but he kept them back. He only looked at her and they both remained silent.

Presently one of the little boys took up the tin soldier, and threw him into the stove. He had no reason for doing so, therefore it must have been the fault of the black goblin who lived in the snuffbox. The flames lighted up the tin soldier, as he stood, the heat was very terrible, but whether it proceeded from the real fire or from the fire of love he could not tell. Then he could see that the bright colors were faded from his uniform, but whether they had been washed off during his journey or from the effects of his sorrow, no one could say. He looked at the little lady, and she looked at him. He felt himself melting away, but he still remained firm with his gun on his shoulder. Suddenly the door of the room flew open and the draught of air caught up the little dancer, she fluttered like a sylph right into the stove by the side of the tin soldier, and was instantly in flames and was gone. The tin soldier melted down into a lump, and the next morning, when the maidservant took the ashes out of the stove, she found him in the shape of a little tin heart. But of the little dancer nothing remained but the tinsel rose, which was burnt black as a cinder.

The Flax

The flax was in full bloom; it had pretty little blue flowers as delicate as the wings of a moth, or even more so. The sun shone, and the showers watered it; and this was just as good for the flax as it is for little children to be washed and then kissed by their mother. They look much prettier for it, and so did the flax.

"People say that I look exceedingly well," said the flax, "and that I am so fine and long that I shall make a beautiful piece of linen. How fortunate I am; it makes me so happy, it is such a pleasant thing to know that something can be made of me. How the sunshine cheers me, and how sweet and refreshing is the rain; my happiness overpowers me, no one in the world can feel happier than I am."

"Ah, yes, no doubt," said the fern, "but you do not know the world yet as well as I do, for my sticks are knotty;" and then it sung quite mournfully,

"Snip, snap, snurre,
Basse lurre:
The song is ended."

"No, it is not ended," said the flax. "Tomorrow the sun will shine, or the rain descend. I feel that I am growing. I feel that I am in full blossom. I am the happiest of all creatures."

Well, one day some people came, who took hold of the flax, and pulled it up by the roots; this was painful; then it was laid in water as if they intended to drown it; and, after that, placed near a fire as if it were to be roasted; all this was very shocking. "We cannot expect to be happy always," said the flax; "by experiencing evil as well as good, we become wise." And certainly there was plenty of evil in store for the flax. It was steeped, and roasted, and broken, and combed; indeed, it scarcely knew what was done to it. At last it was put on the spinning wheel. "Whirr, whirr," went the wheel so quickly that the flax could not collect its thoughts. "Well, I have been very happy," he thought in the midst of his pain, "and must be contented with the past;" and contented he remained till he was put on the loom, and became a beautiful piece of white linen. All the flax, even to the last stalk, was used in making this one piece. "Well, this is quite wonderful; I could not have believed that I should be so favored by fortune. The fern was not wrong with its song of:

'Snip, snap, snurre,
Basse lurre.'

"But the song is not ended yet, I am sure; it is only just beginning. How wonderful it is, that after all I have suffered, I am made something of at last; I am the luckiest person in the world—so strong and fine; and how white, and what a length! This is something different to being a mere plant and bearing flowers. Then I had no attention, nor any water unless it rained; now, I am watched and taken care of. Every morning the maid turns me over, and I have a shower-bath from the watering-pot every evening. Yes, and the clergyman's wife noticed me, and said I was the best piece of linen in the whole parish. I cannot be happier than I am now."

After some time, the linen was taken into the house, placed under the scissors, and cut and torn into pieces, and then pricked with needles. This certainly was not pleasant; but at last it was made into twelve garments of that kind which people do not like to name, and yet everybody should wear one. "See, now, then," said the flax; "I have become something of importance. This was my destiny; it is quite a blessing. Now I shall be of some use in the world, as everyone ought to be; it is the only way to be happy. I am now divided into twelve pieces, and yet we are all one and the same in the whole dozen. It is most extraordinary good fortune."

Years passed away, and at last the linen was so worn it could scarcely hold together. "It must end very soon," said the pieces to each other; "we would gladly have held together a little longer, but it is useless to expect impossibilities." And at length they fell into rags and tatters, and thought it was all over with them, for they were torn to shreds, and steeped in water, and made into a pulp, and dried, and they knew not what besides, till all at once they found themselves beautiful white paper. "Well, now, this is a surprise; a glorious surprise too," said the paper. "I am now finer than ever, and I shall be written upon, and who can tell what fine things I may have written upon me. This is wonderful luck!" And sure enough the most beautiful stories and poetry were written upon it, and only once was there a blot, which was very fortunate. Then people heard the stories and poetry read, and it made them wiser and better; for all that was written had a good and sensible meaning, and a great blessing was contained in the words on this paper.

"I never imagined anything like this," said the paper, "when I was only a little blue flower, growing in the fields. How could I fancy that I should ever be the means of bringing knowledge and joy to man? I cannot understand it myself, and yet it is really so. Heaven knows that I have done nothing myself, but what I was obliged to do with my weak powers for my own preservation; and yet I have been promoted from one joy and honor to another. Each time I think that the song is ended; and then something higher and better begins for me. I suppose now I shall be sent on my travels about the world, so that people may read me. It cannot be otherwise; indeed, it is more than probable; for I have more splendid thoughts written upon me, than I had pretty flowers in olden times. I am happier than ever."

But the paper did not go on its travels; it was sent to the printer, and all the words written upon it were set up in type, to make a book, or rather, many hundreds of books; for so many more persons could derive pleasure and profit from a printed book, than from the written paper; and if the paper had been sent around the world, it would have been worn out before it had got half through its journey.

"This is certainly the wisest plan," said the written paper; "I really did not think of that. I shall remain at home, and be held in honor, like some old grandfather, as I really am to all these new books. They will do some good. I could not have wandered about as they do. Yet he who wrote all this has looked at me, as every word flowed from his pen upon my surface. I am the most honored of all."

Then the paper was tied in a bundle with other papers, and thrown into a tub that stood in the washhouse.

"After work, it is well to rest," said the paper, "and a very good opportunity to collect one's thoughts. Now I am able, for the first time, to think of my real condition; and to know one's self is true progress. What will be done with me now, I wonder? No doubt I shall still go forward. I have always progressed hitherto, as I know quite well."

Now it happened one day that all the paper in the tub was taken out, and laid on the hearth to be burnt. People said it could not be sold at the shop, to wrap up butter and sugar, because it had been written upon. The children in the house stood round the stove; for they wanted to see the paper burn, because it flamed up so prettily, and afterwards, among the ashes, so many red sparks could be seen running one after the other, here and there, as quick as the wind. They called it seeing the children come out of school, and the last spark was the schoolmaster. They often thought the last spark had come; and one would cry, "There goes the schoolmaster;" but the next moment another spark would appear, shining so beautifully. How they would like to know where the sparks all went to! Perhaps we shall find out some day, but we don't know now.

The whole bundle of paper had been placed on the fire, and was soon alight. "Ugh," cried the paper, as it burst into a bright flame; "ugh." It was certainly not very pleasant to be burning; but when the whole was wrapped in flames, the flames mounted up into the air, higher than the flax had ever been able to raise its little blue flower, and they glistened as the white linen never could have glistened. All the written letters became quite red in a moment, and all the words and thoughts turned to fire.

"Now I am mounting straight up to the sun," said a voice in the flames; and it was as if a thousand voices echoed the words; and the flames darted up through the chimney, and went out at the top. Then a number of tiny beings, as many in number as the flowers on the flax had been, and invisible to mortal eyes, floated above them. They were even lighter and more delicate than the flowers from which they were born; and as the flames were extinguished, and nothing remained of the paper but black ashes, these little beings danced upon it; and whenever they touched it, bright red sparks appeared.

"The children are all out of school, and the schoolmaster was the last of all," said the children. It was good fun, and they sang over the dead ashes,

"Snip, snap, snurre,
Basse lure:
The song is ended."

But the little invisible beings said, "The song is never ended; the most beautiful is yet to come."

But the children could neither hear nor understand this, nor should they; for children must not know everything.

The Daisy

Now listen! In the country, close by the high road, stood a farm-house; perhaps you have passed by and seen it yourself. There was a little flower garden with painted wooden palings in front of it; close by was a ditch, on its fresh green bank grew a little daisy; the sun shone as warmly and brightly upon it as on the magnificent garden flowers, and therefore it thrived well. One morning it had quite opened, and its little snow-white petals stood round the yellow centre, like the rays of the sun. It did not mind that nobody saw it in the grass, and that it was a poor despised flower; on the contrary, it was quite happy, and turned towards the sun, looking upward and listening to the song of the lark high up in the air.

The little daisy was as happy as if the day had been a great holiday, but it was only Monday. All the children were at school, and while they were sitting on the forms and learning their lessons, it sat on its thin green stalk and learnt from the sun and from its surroundings how kind God is, and it rejoiced that the song of the little lark expressed so sweetly and distinctly its own feelings. With a sort of reverence the daisy looked up to the bird that could fly and sing, but it did not feel envious. "I can see and hear," it thought; "the sun shines upon me, and the forest kisses me. How rich I am!"

In the garden close by grew many large and magnificent flowers, and, strange to say, the less fragrance they had the haughtier and prouder they were. The peonies puffed themselves up in order to be larger than the roses, but size is not everything! The tulips had the finest colours, and they knew it well, too, for they were standing bolt upright like candles, that one might see them the better. In their pride they did not see the little daisy, which looked over to them and thought, "How rich and beautiful they are! I am sure the pretty bird will fly down and call upon them. Thank God, that I stand so near and can at least see all the splendour." And while the daisy was still thinking, the lark came flying down, crying "Tweet," but not to the peonies and tulips—no, into the grass to the poor daisy. Its joy was so great that it did not know what to think. The little bird hopped round it and sang, "How beautifully soft the grass is, and what a lovely little flower with its golden heart and silver dress is growing here." The yellow centre in the daisy did indeed look like gold, while the little petals shone as brightly as silver.

How happy the daisy was! No one has the least idea. The bird kissed it with its beak, sang to it, and then rose again up to the blue sky. It was certainly more than a quarter of an hour before the daisy recovered its senses. Half ashamed, yet glad at heart, it looked over to the other flowers in the garden; surely they had witnessed its pleasure and the honour that had been done to it; they understood its joy. But the tulips stood more stiffly than ever, their faces were pointed and red, because they were vexed. The peonies were sulky; it was well that they could not speak, otherwise they would have given the daisy a good lecture. The little flower could very well see that they were ill at ease, and pitied them sincerely.

Shortly after this a girl came into the garden, with a large sharp knife. She went to the tulips and began cutting them off, one after another. "Ugh!" sighed the daisy, "that is terrible; now they are done for."

The girl carried the tulips away. The daisy was glad that it was outside, and only a small flower—it felt very grateful. At sunset it folded its petals, and fell asleep, and dreamt all night of the sun and the little bird.

On the following morning, when the flower once more stretched forth its tender petals, like little arms, towards the air and light, the daisy recognised the bird's voice, but what it sang sounded so sad. Indeed the poor bird had good reason to be sad, for it had been caught and put into a cage close by the open window. It sang of the happy days when it could merrily fly about, of fresh green corn in the fields, and of the time when it could soar almost up to the clouds. The poor lark was most unhappy as a prisoner in a cage. The little daisy would have liked so much to help it, but what could be done? Indeed, that was very difficult for such a small flower to find out. It entirely forgot how beautiful everything around it was, how warmly the sun was shining, and how splendidly white its own petals were. It could only think of the poor captive bird, for which it could do nothing. Then two little boys came out of the garden; one of them had a large sharp knife, like that with which the girl had cut the tulips. They came straight towards the little daisy, which could not understand what they wanted.

"Here is a fine piece of turf for the lark," said one of the boys, and began to cut out a square round the daisy, so that it remained in the centre of the grass.

"Pluck the flower off," said the other boy, and the daisy trembled for fear, for to be pulled off meant death to it; and it wished so much to live, as it was to go with the square of turf into the poor captive lark's cage.

"No let it stay," said the other boy, "it looks so pretty."

And so it stayed, and was brought into the lark's cage. The poor bird was lamenting its lost liberty, and beating its wings against the wires; and the little daisy could not speak or utter a consoling word, much as it would have liked to do so. So the forenoon passed.

"I have no water," said the captive lark, "they have all gone out, and forgotten to give me anything to drink. My throat is dry and burning. I feel as if I had fire and ice within me, and the air is so oppressive. Alas! I must die, and part with the warm sunshine, the fresh green meadows, and all the beauty that God has created." And it thrust its beak into the piece of grass, to refresh itself a little. Then it noticed the little daisy, and nodded to it, and kissed it with its beak and said: "You must also fade in here, poor little flower. You and the piece of grass are all they have given me in exchange for the whole world, which I enjoyed outside. Each little blade of grass shall be a green tree for me, each of your white petals a fragrant flower. Alas! you only remind me of what I have lost."

"I wish I could console the poor lark," thought the daisy. It could not move one of its leaves, but the fragrance of its delicate petals streamed forth, and was much stronger than such flowers usually have: the bird noticed it, although it was dying with thirst, and in its pain tore up the green blades of grass, but did not touch the flower.

The evening came, and nobody appeared to bring the poor bird a drop of water; it opened its beautiful wings, and fluttered about in its anguish; a faint and mournful "Tweet, tweet" was all it could utter, then it bent its little head towards the flower, and its heart broke for want and longing. The flower could not, as on the previous evening, fold up its petals and sleep; it dropped sorrowfully. The boys only came the next morning; when they saw the dead bird, they began to cry bitterly, dug a nice grave for it, and adorned it with flowers. The bird's body was placed in a pretty red box; they wished to bury it with royal honours. While it was alive and sang they forgot it, and let it suffer want in the cage; now, they cried over it and covered it with flowers. The piece of turf, with the little daisy in it, was thrown out on the dusty highway. Nobody thought of the flower which had felt so much for the bird and had so greatly desired to comfort it.

Under the Willow Tree

The region round the little town of Kjoge is very bleak and cold. The town lies on the seashore, which is always beautiful; but here it might be more beautiful than it is, for on every side the fields are flat, and it is a long way to the forest. But when persons reside in a place and get used to it, they can always find something beautiful in it—something for which they long, even in the most charming spot in the world which is not home. It must be owned that there are in the outskirts of the town some humble gardens on the banks of a little stream that runs on towards the sea, and in summer these gardens look very pretty. Such indeed was the opinion of two little children, whose parents were neighbors, and who played in these gardens, and forced their way from one garden to the other through the gooseberry bushes that divided them. In one of the gardens grew an elder tree, and in the other an old willow, under which the children were very fond of playing. They had permission to do so, although the tree stood close by the stream, and they might easily have fallen into the water; but the eye of God watches over the little ones, otherwise they would never be safe. At the same time, these children were very careful not to go too near the water; indeed, the boy was so afraid of it, that in the summer, while the other children were splashing about in the sea, nothing could entice him to join them. They jeered and laughed at him, and he was obliged to bear it all as patiently as he could. Once the neighbor's little girl, Joanna, dreamed that she was sailing in a boat, and the boy—Knud was his name—waded out in the water to join her, and the water came up to his neck, and at last closed over his head, and in a moment he had disappeared. When little Knud heard this dream, it seemed as if he could not bear the mocking and jeering again; how could he dare to go into the water now, after Joanna's dream! He never would do it, for this dream always satisfied him. The parents of these children, who were poor, often sat together while Knud and Joanna played in the gardens or in the road. Along this road—a row of willow trees had been planted to separate it from a ditch on one side of it. They were not very handsome trees, for the tops had been cut off; however, they were intended for use, and not for show. The old willow tree in the garden was much handsomer, and therefore the children were very fond of sitting under it. The town had a large marketplace; and at the fair-time there would be whole rows, like streets, of tents and booths containing silks and ribbons, and toys and cakes, and everything that could be wished for. There were crowds of people, and sometimes the weather would be rainy, and splash with moisture the woollen jackets of the peasants; but it did not destroy the beautiful fragrance of the honey-cakes and gingerbread with which one booth was filled; and the best of it was, that the man who sold these cakes always lodged during the fair-time with little Knud's parents. So every now and then he had a present of gingerbread, and of course Joanna always had a share. And, more delightful still, the gingerbread seller knew all sorts of things to tell and could even relate stories about his own gingerbread. So one evening he told them a story that made such a deep impression on the children that they never forgot it; and therefore I think we may as well hear it too, for it is not very long.

"Once upon a time," said he, "there lay on my counter two gingerbread cakes, one in the shape of a man wearing a hat, the other of a maiden without a bonnet. Their faces were on the side that was uppermost, for on the other side they looked very different. Most people have a best side to their characters, which they take care to show to the world. On the left, just where the heart is, the gingerbread man had an almond stuck in to represent it, but the maiden was honey cake all over. They were placed on the counter as samples, and after lying there a long time they at last fell in love with each other; but neither of them spoke of it to the other, as they should have done if they expected anything to follow. 'He is a man, he ought to speak the first word,' thought the gingerbread maiden; but she felt quite happy—she was sure that her love was returned. But his thoughts were far more ambitious, as the thoughts of a man often are. He dreamed that he was a real street boy, that he possessed four real pennies, and that he had bought the gingerbread lady, and ate her up.

And so they lay on the counter for days and weeks, till they grew hard and dry; but the thoughts of the maiden became ever more tender and womanly. 'Ah well, it is enough for me that I have been able to live on the same counter with him,' said she one day; when suddenly, 'crack,' and she broke in two. 'Ah,' said the gingerbread man to himself, 'if she had only known of my love, she would have kept together a little longer.' And here they both are, and that is their history," said the cake man. "You think the history of their lives and their silent love, which never came to anything, very remarkable; and there they are for you." So saying, he gave Joanna the gingerbread man, who was still quite whole—and to Knud the broken maiden; but the children had been so much impressed by the story, that they had not the heart to eat the lovers up.

The next day they went into the churchyard, and took the two cake figures with them, and sat down under the church wall, which was covered with luxuriant ivy in summer and winter, and looked as if hung with rich tapestry. They stuck up the two gingerbread figures in the sunshine among the green leaves, and then told the story, and all about the silent love which came to nothing, to a group of children. They called it, "love," because the story was so lovely, and the other children had the same opinion. But when they turned to look at the gingerbread pair, the broken maiden was gone! A great boy, out of wickedness, had eaten her up. At first the children cried about it; but afterwards, thinking very probably that the poor lover ought not to be left alone in the world, they ate him up too: but they never forgot the story.

The two children still continued to play together by the elder tree, and under the willow; and the little maiden sang beautiful songs, with a voice that was as clear as a bell. Knud, on the contrary, had not a note of music in him, but knew the words of the songs, and that of course is something. The people of Kjoge, and even the rich wife of the man who kept the fancy shop, would stand and listen while Joanna was singing, and say, "She has really a very sweet voice."

Those were happy days; but they could not last forever. The neighbors were separated, the mother of the little girl was dead, and her father had thoughts of marrying again and of residing in the capital, where he had been promised a very lucrative appointment as messenger. The neighbors parted with tears, the children wept sadly; but their parents promised that they should write to each other at least once a year.

After this, Knud was bound apprentice to a shoemaker; he was growing a great boy, and could not be allowed to run wild any longer. Besides, he was going to be confirmed. Ah, how happy he would have been on that festal day in Copenhagen with little Joanna; but he still remained at Kjoge, and had never seen the great city, though the town is not five miles from it. But far across the bay, when the sky was clear, the towers of Copenhagen could be seen; and on the day of his confirmation he saw distinctly the golden cross on the principal church glittering in the sun. How often his thoughts were with Joanna! but did she think of him? Yes. About Christmas came a letter from her father to Knud's parents, which stated that they were going on very well in Copenhagen, and mentioning particularly that Joanna's beautiful voice was likely to bring her a brilliant fortune in the future. She was engaged to sing at a concert, and she had already earned money by singing, out of which she sent her dear neighbors at Kjoge a whole dollar, for them to make merry on Christmas Eve, and they were to drink her health. She had herself added this in a postscript, and in the same postscript she wrote, "Kind regards to Knud."

The good neighbors wept, although the news was so pleasant; but they wept tears of joy. Knud's thoughts had been daily with Joanna, and now he knew that she also had thought of him; and the nearer the time came for his apprenticeship to end, the clearer did it appear to him that he loved Joanna, and that she must be his wife; and a smile came on his lips at the thought, and at one time he drew the thread so fast as he worked, and pressed his foot so hard against the knee strap, that he ran the awl into his finger; but what did he care for that? He was determined not to play the dumb lover as both the gingerbread cakes had done; the story was a good lesson to him.

At length he become a journeyman, and then, for the first time, he prepared for a journey to Copenhagen, with his knapsack packed and ready. A master was expecting him there, and he thought of Joanna, and how glad she would be to see him. She was now seventeen, and he nineteen years old. He wanted to buy a gold ring for her in Kjoge, but then he recollected how far more beautiful such things would be in Copenhagen. So he took leave of his parents, and on a rainy day, late in the autumn, wandered forth on foot from the town of his birth. The leaves were falling from the trees; and, by the time he arrived at his new master's in the great metropolis, he was wet through. On the following Sunday he intended to pay his first visit to Joanna's father. When the day came, the new journeyman's clothes were brought out, and a new hat, which he had brought in Kjoge. The hat became him very well, for hitherto he had only worn a cap. He found the house that he sought easily, but had to mount so many stairs that he became quite giddy; it surprised him to find how people lived over one another in this dreadful town.

On entering a room in which everything denoted prosperity, Joanna's father received him very kindly. The new wife was a stranger to him, but she shook hands with him, and offered him coffee.

"Joanna will be very glad to see you," said her father. "You have grown quite a nice young man, you shall see her presently; she is a good child, and is the joy of my heart, and, please God, she will continue to be so; she has her own room now, and pays us rent for it." And the father knocked quite politely at a door, as if he were a stranger, and then they both went in. How pretty everything was in that room! A more beautiful apartment could not be found in the whole town of Kjoge; the queen herself could scarcely be better accommodated. There were carpets, and rugs, and window curtains hanging to the ground. Pictures and flowers were scattered about. There was a velvet chair, and a looking glass against the wall, into which a person might be in danger of stepping, for it was as large as a door. All this Knud saw at a glance, and yet, in truth, he saw nothing but Joanna. She was quite grown up, and very different from what Knud had fancied her, and a great deal more beautiful. In all Kjoge there was not a girl like her; and how graceful she looked, although her glance at first was odd, and not familiar; but for a moment only, then she rushed towards him as if she would have kissed him; she did not, however, although she was very near it. Yes, she really was joyful at seeing the friend of her childhood once more, and the tears even stood in her eyes. Then she asked so many questions about Knud's parents, and everything, even to the elder tree and the willow, which she called "elder-mother and willow-father," as if they had been human beings; and so, indeed, they might be, quite as much as the gingerbread cakes. Then she talked about them, and the story of their silent love, and how they lay on the counter together and split in two; and then she laughed heartily; but the blood rushed into Knud's cheeks, and his heartbeat quickly. Joanna was not proud at all; he noticed that through her he was invited by her parents to remain the whole evening with them, and she poured out the tea and gave him a cup herself; and afterwards she took a book and read aloud to them, and it seemed to Knud as if the story was all about himself and his love, for it agreed so well with his own thoughts. And then she sang a simple song, which, through her singing, became a true story, and as if she poured forth the feelings of her own heart.

"Oh," he thought, "she knows I am fond of her." The tears he could not restrain rolled down his cheeks, and he was unable to utter a single word; it seemed as if he had been struck dumb.

When he left, she pressed his hand, and said, "You have a kind heart, Knud: remain always as you are now." What an evening of happiness this had been; to sleep after it was impossible, and Knud did not sleep.

At parting, Joanna's father had said, "Now, you won't quite forget us; you must not let the whole winter go by without paying us another visit;" so that Knud felt himself free to go again the following Sunday evening, and so he did. But every evening after working hours—and they worked by candlelight then—he walked out into the town, and through the street in which Joanna lived, to look up at her window. It was almost always lighted up; and one evening he saw the shadow of her face quite plainly on the window blind; that was a glorious evening for him. His master's wife did not like his always going out in the evening, idling, wasting time, as she called it, and she shook her head.

But his master only smiled, and said, "He is a young man, my dear, you know."

"On Sunday I shall see her," said Knud to himself, "and I will tell her that I love her with my whole heart and soul, and that she must be my little wife. I know I am now only a poor journeyman shoemaker, but I will work and strive, and become a master in time. Yes, I will speak to her; nothing comes from silent love. I learnt that from the gingerbread-cake story."

Sunday came, but when Knud arrived, they were all unfortunately invited out to spend the evening, and were obliged to tell him so.

Joanna pressed his hand, and said, "Have you ever been to the theatre? you must go once; I sing there on Wednesday, and if you have time on that day, I will send you a ticket; my father knows where your master lives." How kind this was of her! And on Wednesday, about noon, Knud received a sealed packet with no address, but the ticket was inside; and in the evening Knud went, for the first time in his life, to a theatre. And what did he see? He saw Joanna, and how beautiful and charming she looked! He certainly saw her being married to a stranger, but that was all in the play, and only a pretence; Knud well knew that. She could never have the heart, he thought, to send him a ticket to go and see it, if it had been real. So he looked on, and when all the people applauded and clapped their hands, he shouted "hurrah." He could see that even the king smiled at Joanna, and seemed delighted with her singing. How small Knud felt; but then he loved her so dearly, and thought she loved him, and the man must speak the first word, as the gingerbread maiden had thought. Ah, how much there was for him in that childish story. As soon as Sunday arrived, he went again, and felt as if he were about to enter on holy ground. Joanna was alone to welcome him, nothing could be more fortunate.

"I am so glad you are come," she said. "I was thinking of sending my father for you, but I had a presentiment that you would be here this evening. The fact is, I wanted to tell you that I am going to France. I shall start on Friday. It is necessary for me to go there, if I wish to become a first-rate performer."

Poor Knud! It seemed to him as if the whole room was whirling round with him. His courage failed, and he felt as if his heart would burst. He kept down the tears, but it was easy to see how sorrowful he was.

"You honest, faithful soul," she exclaimed; and the words loosened Knud's tongue, and he told her how truly he had loved her, and that she must be his wife; and as he said this, he saw Joanna change color, and turn pale. She let his hand fall, and said, earnestly and mournfully, "Knud, do not make yourself and me unhappy. I will always be a good sister to you, one in whom you can trust; but I can never be anything more." And she drew her white hand over his burning forehead, and said, "God gives strength to bear a great deal, if we only strive ourselves to endure."

At this moment her stepmother came into the room, and Joanna said quickly, "Knud is so unhappy, because I am going away;" and it appeared as if they had only been talking of her journey. "Come, be a man," she added, placing her hand on his shoulder; "you are still a child, and you must be good and reasonable, as you were when we were both children, and played together under the willow tree."

Knud listened, but he felt as if the world had slid out of its course. His thoughts were like a loose thread fluttering to and fro in the wind. He stayed, although he could not tell whether she had asked him to do so. But she was kind and gentle to him; she poured out his tea, and sang to him; but the song had not the old tone in it, although it was wonderfully beautiful, and made his heart feel ready to burst. And then he rose to go. He did not offer his hand, but she seized it, and said, "Will you not shake hands with your sister at parting, my old playfellow?" and she smiled through the tears that were rolling down her cheeks. Again she repeated the word "brother," which was a great consolation certainly; and thus they parted.

She sailed to France, and Knud wandered about the muddy streets of Copenhagen. The other journeymen in the shop asked him why he looked so gloomy, and wanted him to go and amuse himself with them, as he was still a young man. So he went with them to a dancing room. He saw many handsome girls there, but none like Joanna; and here, where he thought to forget her, she was more lifelike before his mind than ever. "God gives us strength to bear much, if we try to do our best," she had said; and as he thought of this, a devout feeling came into his mind, and he folded his hands. Then, as the violins played and the girls danced round the room, he started; for it seemed to him as if he were in a place where he ought not to have brought Joanna, for she was here with him in his heart; and so he went out at once. As he went through the streets at a quick pace, he passed the house where she used to live; it was all dark, empty, and lonely. But the world went on its course, and Knud was obliged to go on too.

Winter came; the water was frozen, and everything seemed buried in a cold grave. But when spring returned, and the first steamer prepared to sail, Knud was seized with a longing to wander forth into the world, but not to France. So he packed his knapsack, and travelled through Germany, going from town to town, but finding neither rest or peace. It was not till he arrived at the glorious old town of Nuremberg that he gained the mastery over himself, and rested his weary feet; and here he remained.

Nuremberg is a wonderful old city, and looks as if it had been cut out of an old picture book. The streets seem to have arranged themselves according to their own fancy, and as if the houses objected to stand in rows or rank and file. Gables, with little towers, ornamented columns, and statues, can be seen even to the city gate; and from the singular-shaped roofs, waterspouts, formed like dragons, or long lean dogs, extend far across to the middle of the street. Here, in the marketplace, stood Knud, with his knapsack on his back, close to one of the old fountains which are so beautifully adorned with figures, scriptural and historical, and which spring up between the sparkling jets of water. A pretty servant-maid was just filling her pails, and she gave Knud a refreshing draught; she had a handful of roses, and she gave him one, which appeared to him like a good omen for the future. From a neighboring church came the sounds of music, and the familiar tones reminded him of the organ at home at Kjoge; so he passed into the great cathedral. The sunshine streamed through the painted glass windows, and between two lofty slender pillars. His thoughts became prayerful, and calm peace rested on his soul. He next sought and found a good master in Nuremberg, with whom he stayed and learnt the German language.

The old moat round the town had been converted into a number of little kitchen gardens; but the high walls, with their heavy-looking towers, are still standing. Inside these walls the ropemaker twisted his ropes along a walk built like a gallery, and in the cracks and crevices of the walls elderbushes grow and stretch their green boughs over the small houses which stand below. In one of these houses lived the master for whom Knud worked; and over the little garret window where he sat, the elder tree waved its branches. Here he dwelt through one summer and winter, but when spring came again, he could endure it no longer. The elder was in blossom, and its fragrance was so homelike, that he fancied himself back again in the gardens of Kjoge. So Knud left his master, and went to work for another who lived farther in the town, where no elder grew. His workshop was quite close to one of the old stone bridges, near to a watermill, round which the roaring stream rushed and foamed always, yet restrained by the neighboring houses, whose old, decayed balconies hung over, and seemed ready to fall into the water. Here grew no elder; here was not even a flowerpot, with its little green plant; but just opposite the workshop stood a great willow tree, which seemed to hold fast to the house for fear of being carried away by the water. It stretched its branches over the stream just as those of the willow tree in the garden at Kjoge had spread over the river. Yes, he had indeed gone from elder-mother to willow-father. There was a something about the tree here, especially in the moonlight nights, that went direct to his heart; yet it was not in reality the moonlight, but the old tree itself. However, he could not endure it: and why? Ask the willow, ask the blossoming elder! At all events, he bade farewell to Nuremberg and journeyed onwards. He never spoke of Joanna to anyone; his sorrow was hidden in his heart. The old childish story of the two cakes had a deep meaning for him. He understood now why the gingerbread man had a bitter almond in his left side; his was the feeling of bitterness, and Joanna, so mild and friendly, was represented by the honeycake maiden. As he thought upon all this, the strap of his knapsack pressed across his chest so that he could hardly breathe; he loosened it, but gained no relief. He saw but half the world around him; the other half he carried with him in his inward thoughts; and this is the condition in which he left Nuremberg. Not till he caught sight of the lofty mountains did the world appear more free to him; his thoughts were attracted to outer objects, and tears came into his eyes. The Alps appeared to him like the wings of earth folded together; unfolded, they would display the variegated pictures of dark woods, foaming waters, spreading clouds, and masses of snow. "At the last day," thought he, "the earth will unfold its great wings, and soar upwards to the skies, there to burst like a soap bubble in the radiant glance of the Deity. Oh," sighed he, "that the last day were come!"

Silently he wandered on through the country of the Alps, which seemed to him like a fruit garden, covered with soft turf. From the wooden balconies of the houses the young lacemakers nodded as he passed. The summits of the mountains glowed in the red evening sunset, and the green lakes beneath the dark trees reflected the glow. Then he thought of the seacoast by the bay Kjoge, with a longing in his heart that was, however, without pain. There, where the Rhine rolls onward like a great billow, and dissolves itself into snowflakes, where glistening clouds are ever changing as if here was the place of their creation, while the rainbow flutters about them like a many-colored ribbon, there did Knud think of the watermill at Kjoge, with its rushing, foaming waters. Gladly would he have remained in the quiet Rhenish town, but there were too many elders and willow trees.

So he travelled onwards, over a grand, lofty chain of mountains, over rugged—rocky precipices, and along roads that hung on the mountain's side like a swallow's nest. The waters foamed in the depths below him. The clouds lay beneath him. He wandered on, treading upon Alpine roses, thistles, and snow, with the summer sun shining upon him, till at length he bid farewell to the lands of the north. Then he passed on under the shade of blooming chestnut trees, through vineyards, and fields of Indian corn, till conscious that the mountains were as a wall between him and his early recollections; and he wished it to be so.

Before him lay a large and splendid city, called Milan, and here he found a German master who engaged him as a workman. The master and his wife, in whose workshop he was employed, were an old, pious couple; and the two old people became quite fond of the quiet journeyman, who spoke but little, but worked more, and led a pious, Christian life; and even to himself it seemed as if God had removed the heavy burden from his heart. His greatest pleasure was to climb, now and then, to the roof of the noble church, which was built of white marble. The pointed towers, the decorated and open cloisters, the stately columns, the white statues which smiled upon him from every corner and porch and arch—all, even the church itself, seemed to him to have been formed from the snow of his native land. Above him was the blue sky; below him, the city and the wide-spreading plains of Lombardy; and towards the north, the lofty mountains, covered with perpetual snow. And then he thought of the church of Kjoge, with its red, ivy-clad walls, but he had no longing to go there; here, beyond the mountains, he would die and be buried.

Three years had passed away since he left his home; one year of that time he had dwelt at Milan.

One day his master took him into the town; not to the circus in which riders performed, but to the opera, a large building, itself a sight well worth seeing. The seven tiers of boxes, which reached from the ground to a dizzy height, near the ceiling, were hung with rich, silken curtains; and in them were seated elegantly dressed ladies, with bouquets of flowers in their hands. The gentlemen were also in full dress, and many of them wore decorations of gold and silver. The place was so brilliantly lighted that it seemed like sunshine, and glorious music rolled through the building. Everything looked more beautiful than in the theatre at Copenhagen, but then Joanna had been there, and—could it be? Yes, it was like magic. She was here also, for when the curtain rose, there stood Joanna, dressed in silk and gold, and with a golden crown upon her head.

She sang, he thought, as only an angel could sing; and then she stepped forward to the front and smiled, as only Joanna could smile, and looked directly at Knud. Poor Knud! he seized his master's hand, and cried out loud, "Joanna," but no one heard him, excepting his master, for the music sounded above everything.

"Yes, yes, it is Joanna," said his master; and he drew forth a printed bill, and pointed to her name, which was there in full. Then it was not a dream. All the audience applauded her, and threw wreaths of flowers at her; and every time she went away they called for her again, so that she was always coming and going. In the street the people crowded round her carriage, and drew it away themselves without the horses. Knud was in the foremost row, and shouted as joyously as the rest; and when the carriage stopped before a brilliantly lighted house, Knud placed himself close to the door of her carriage. It flew open, and she stepped out; the light fell upon her dear face, and he could see that she smiled as she thanked them, and appeared quite overcome. Knud looked straight in her face, and she looked at him, but she did not recognize him. A man, with a glittering star on his breast, gave her his arm, and people said the two were engaged to be married. Then Knud went home and packed up his knapsack; he felt he must return to the home of his childhood, to the elder tree and the willow. "Ah, under that willow tree!" A man may live a whole life in one single hour.

The old couple begged him to remain, but words were useless. In vain they reminded him that winter was coming, and that the snow had already fallen on the mountains. He said he could easily follow the track of the closely moving carriages, for which a path must be kept clear, and with nothing but his knapsack on his back, and leaning on his stick, he could step along briskly. So he turned his steps to the mountains, ascended one side and descended the other, still going northward till his strength began to fail, and not a house or village could be seen. The stars shone in the sky above him, and down in the valley lights glittered like stars, as if another sky were beneath him; but his head was dizzy and his feet stumbled, and he felt ill. The lights in the valley grew brighter and brighter, and more numerous, and he could see them moving to and fro, and then he understood that there must be a village in the distance; so he exerted his failing strength to reach it, and at length obtained shelter in a humble lodging. He remained there that night and the whole of the following day, for his body required rest and refreshment, and in the valley there was rain and a thaw. But early in the morning of the third day, a man came with an organ and played one of the melodies of home; and after that Knud could remain there no longer, so he started again on his journey toward the north. He travelled for many days with hasty steps, as if he were trying to reach home before all whom he remembered should die; but he spoke to no one of this longing. No one would have believed or understood this sorrow of his heart, the deepest that can be felt by human nature. Such grief is not for the world; it is not entertaining even to friends, and poor Knud had no friends; he was a stranger, wandering through strange lands to his home in the north.

He was walking one evening through the public roads, the country around him was flatter, with fields and meadows, the air had a frosty feeling. A willow tree grew by the roadside, everything reminded him of home. He felt very tired; so he sat down under the tree, and very soon began to nod, then his eyes closed in sleep. Yet still he seemed conscious that the willow tree was stretching its branches over him; in his dreaming state the tree appeared like a strong, old man—the "willow-father" himself, who had taken his tired son up in his arms to carry him back to the land of home, to the garden of his childhood, on the bleak open shores of Kjoge. And then he dreamed that it was really the willow tree itself from Kjoge, which had travelled out in the world to seek him, and now had found him and carried him back into the little garden on the banks of the streamlet; and there stood Joanna, in all her splendor, with the golden crown on her head, as he had last seen her, to welcome him back. And then there appeared before him two remarkable shapes, which looked much more like human beings than when he had seen them in his childhood; they were changed, but he remembered that they were the two gingerbread cakes, the man and the woman, who had shown their best sides to the world and looked so good.

"We thank you," they said to Knud, "for you have loosened our tongues; we have learnt from you that thoughts should be spoken freely, or nothing will come of them; and now something has come of our thoughts, for we are engaged to be married." Then they walked away, hand-in-hand, through the streets of Kjoge, looking very respectable on the best side, which they were quite right to show. They turned their steps to the church, and Knud and Joanna followed them, also walking hand-in-hand; there stood the church, as of old, with its red walls, on which the green ivy grew.

The great church door flew open wide, and as they walked up the broad aisle, soft tones of music sounded from the organ. "Our master first," said the gingerbread pair, making room for Knud and Joanna. As they knelt at the altar, Joanna bent her head over him, and cold, icy tears fell on his face from her eyes. They were indeed tears of ice, for her heart was melting towards him through his strong love, and as her tears fell on his burning cheeks he awoke. He was still sitting under the willow tree in a strange land, on a cold winter evening, with snow and hail falling from the clouds, and beating upon his face.

"That was the most delightful hour of my life," said he, "although it was only a dream. Oh, let me dream again." Then he closed his eyes once more, and slept and dreamed.

Towards morning there was a great fall of snow; the wind drifted it over him, but he still slept on. The villagers came forth to go to church; by the roadside they found a workman seated, but he was dead! frozen to death under a willow tree.

The Marsh King's Daughter

The storks relate to their little ones a great many stories, and they are all about moors and reed banks, and suited to their age and capacity. The youngest of them are quite satisfied with "kribble, krabble," or such nonsense, and think it very grand; but the elder ones want something with a deeper meaning, or at least something about their own family.

We are only acquainted with one of the two longest and oldest stories which the storks relate—it is about Moses, who was exposed by his mother on the banks of the Nile, and was found by the king's daughter, who gave him a good education, and he afterwards became a great man; but where he was buried is still unknown.

Everyone knows this story, but not the second; very likely because it is quite an inland story. It has been repeated from mouth to mouth, from one stork-mamma to another, for thousands of years; and each has told it better than the last; and now we mean to tell it better than all.

The first stork pair who related it lived at the time it happened, and had their summer residence on the rafters of the Viking's house, which stood near the wild moorlands of Wendsyssell; that is, to speak more correctly, the great moorheath, high up in the north of Jutland, by the Skjagen peak. This wilderness is still an immense wild heath of marshy ground, about which we can read in the "Official Directory." It is said that in olden times the place was a lake, the ground of which had heaved up from beneath, and now the moorland extends for miles in every direction, and is surrounded by damp meadows, trembling, undulating swamps, and marshy ground covered with turf, on which grow bilberry bushes and stunted trees. Mists are almost always hovering over this region, which, seventy years ago, was overrun with wolves. It may well be called the Wild Moor; and one can easily imagine, with such a wild expanse of marsh and lake, how lonely and dreary it must have been a thousand years ago. Many things may be noticed now that existed then. The reeds grow to the same height, and bear the same kind of long, purple-brown leaves, with their feathery tips. There still stands the birch, with its white bark and its delicate, loosely hanging leaves; and with regard to the living beings who frequented this spot, the fly still wears a gauzy dress of the same cut, and the favorite colors of the stork are white, with black and red for stockings. The people, certainly, in those days, wore very different dresses to those they now wear, but if any of them, be he huntsman or squire, master or servant, ventured on the wavering, undulating, marshy ground of the moor, they met with the same fate a thousand years ago as they would now. The wanderer sank, and went down to the Marsh King, as he is named, who rules in the great moorland empire beneath. They also called him "Gunkel King," but we like the name of "Marsh King" better, and we will give him that name as the storks do. Very little is known of the Marsh King's rule, but that, perhaps, is a good thing.

In the neighborhood of the moorlands, and not far from the great arm of the North Sea and the Cattegat which is called the Lumfjorden, lay the castle of the Viking, with its watertight stone cellars, its tower, and its three projecting stories. On the ridge of the roof the stork had built his nest, and there the stork-mamma sat on her eggs and felt sure her hatching would come to something.

One evening, stork-papa stayed out rather late, and when he came home he seemed quite busy, bustling, and important. "I have something very dreadful to tell you," said he to the stork-mamma.

"Keep it to yourself then," she replied. "Remember that I am hatching eggs; it may agitate me, and will affect them."

"You must know it at once," said he. "The daughter of our host in Egypt has arrived here. She has ventured to take this journey, and now she is lost."

"She who sprung from the race of the fairies, is it?" cried the mother stork. "Oh, tell me all about it; you know I cannot bear to be kept waiting at a time when I am hatching eggs."

"Well, you see, mother," he replied, "she believed what the doctors said, and what I have heard you state also, that the moor-flowers which grow about here would heal her sick father; and she has flown to the north in swan's plumage, in company with some other swan-princesses, who come to these parts every year to renew their youth. She came, and where is she now!"

"You enter into particulars too much," said the mamma stork, "and the eggs may take cold; I cannot bear such suspense as this."

"Well," said he, "I have kept watch; and this evening I went among the rushes where I thought the marshy ground would bear me, and while I was there three swans came. Something in their manner of flying seemed to say to me, 'Look carefully now; there is one not all swan, only swan's feathers.' You know, mother, you have the same intuitive feeling that I have; you know whether a thing is right or not immediately."

"Yes, of course," said she; "but tell me about the princess; I am tired of hearing about the swan's feathers."

"Well, you know that in the middle of the moor there is something like a lake," said the stork-papa. "You can see the edge of it if you raise yourself a little. Just there, by the reeds and the green banks, lay the trunk of an elder tree; upon this the three swans stood flapping their wings, and looking about them; one of them threw off her plumage, and I immediately recognized her as one of the princesses of our home in Egypt. There she sat, without any covering but her long, black hair. I heard her tell the two others to take great care of the swan's plumage, while she dipped down into the water to pluck the flowers which she fancied she saw there. The others nodded, and picked up the feather dress, and took possession of it. I wonder what will become of it? thought I, and she most likely asked herself the same question. If so, she received an answer, a very practical one; for the two swans rose up and flew away with her swan's plumage. 'Dive down now!' they cried; 'thou shalt never more fly in the swan's plumage, thou shalt never again see Egypt; here, on the moor, thou wilt remain.' So saying, they tore the swan's plumage into a thousand pieces, the feathers drifted about like a snow-shower, and then the two deceitful princesses flew away."

"Why, that is terrible," said the stork-mamma; "I feel as if I could hardly bear to hear any more, but you must tell me what happened next."

"The princess wept and lamented aloud; her tears moistened the elder stump, which was really not an elder stump but the Marsh King himself, he who in marshy ground lives and rules. I saw myself how the stump of the tree turned round, and was a tree no more, while long, clammy branches like arms, were extended from it. Then the poor child was terribly frightened, and started up to run away. She hastened to cross the green, slimy ground; but it will not bear any weight, much less hers. She quickly sank, and the elder stump dived immediately after her; in fact, it was he who drew her down. Great black bubbles rose up out of the moor-slime, and with these every trace of the two vanished. And now the princess is buried in the wild marsh, she will never now carry flowers to Egypt to cure her father. It would have broken your heart, mother, had you seen it."

"You ought not to have told me," said she, "at such a time as this; the eggs might suffer. But I think the princess will soon find help; someone will rise up to help her. Ah! if it had been you or I, or one of our people, it would have been all over with us."

"I mean to go every day," said he, "to see if anything comes to pass;" and so he did.

A long time went by, but at last he saw a green stalk shooting up out of the deep, marshy ground. As it reached the surface of the marsh, a leaf spread out, and unfolded itself broader and broader, and close to it came forth a bud.

One morning, when the stork-papa was flying over the stem, he saw that the power of the sun's rays had caused the bud to open, and in the cup of the flower lay a charming child—a little maiden, looking as if she had just come out of a bath. The little one was so like the Egyptian princess, that the stork, at the first moment, thought it must be the princess herself, but after a little reflection he decided that it was much more likely to be the daughter of the princess and the Marsh King; and this explained also her being placed in the cup of a waterlily. "But she cannot be left to lie here," thought the stork, "and in my nest there are already so many. But stay, I have thought of something: the wife of the Viking has no children, and how often she has wished for a little one. People always say the stork brings the little ones; I will do so in earnest this time. I shall fly with the child to the Viking's wife; what rejoicing there will be!"

And then the stork lifted the little girl out of the flower-cup, flew to the castle, picked a hole with his beak in the bladder-covered window, and laid the beautiful child in the bosom of the Viking's wife. Then he flew back quickly to the stork-mamma and told her what he had seen and done; and the little storks listened to it all, for they were then quite old enough to do so. "So you see," he continued, "that the princess is not dead, for she must have sent her little one up here; and now I have found a home for her."

"Ah, I said it would be so from the first," replied the stork-mamma; "but now think a little of your own family. Our travelling time draws near, and I sometimes feel a little irritation already under the wings. The cuckoos and the nightingale are already gone, and I heard the quails say they should go too as soon as the wind was favorable. Our youngsters will go through all the manoeuvres at the review very well, or I am much mistaken in them."

The Viking's wife was above measure delighted when she awoke the next morning and found the beautiful little child lying in her bosom. She kissed it and caressed it; but it cried terribly, and struck out with its arms and legs, and did not seem to be pleased at all. At last it cried itself to sleep; and as it lay there so still and quiet, it was a most beautiful sight to see. The Viking's wife was so delighted, that body and soul were full of joy. Her heart felt so light within her, that it seemed as if her husband and his soldiers, who were absent, must come home as suddenly and unexpectedly as the little child had done. She and her whole household therefore busied themselves in preparing everything for the reception of her lord. The long, colored tapestry, on which she and her maidens had worked pictures of their idols, Odin, Thor, and Friga, was hung up. The slaves polished the old shields that served as ornaments; cushions were placed on the seats, and dry wood laid on the fireplaces in the centre of the hall, so that the flames might be fanned up at a moment's notice. The Viking's wife herself assisted in the work, so that at night she felt very tired, and quickly fell into a sound sleep. When she awoke, just before morning, she was terribly alarmed to find that the infant had vanished.

She sprang from her couch, lighted a pine chip, and searched all round the room, when, at last, in that part of the bed where her feet had been, lay, not the child, but a great, ugly frog. She was quite disgusted at this sight, and seized a heavy stick to kill the frog; but the creature looked at her with such strange, mournful eyes, that she was unable to strike the blow. Once more she searched round the room; then she started at hearing the frog utter a low, painful croak. She sprang from the couch and opened the window hastily; at the same moment the sun rose, and threw its beams through the window, till it rested on the couch where the great frog lay. Suddenly it appeared as if the frog's broad mouth contracted, and became small and red. The limbs moved and stretched out and extended themselves till they took a beautiful shape; and behold there was the pretty child lying before her, and the ugly frog was gone. "How is this?" she cried, "have I had a wicked dream? Is it not my own lovely cherub that lies there?" Then she kissed it and fondled it; but the child struggled and fought, and bit as if she had been a little wild cat.

The Viking did not return on that day, nor the next; he was, however, on the way home; but the wind, so favorable to the storks, was against him; for it blew towards the south. A wind in favor of one is often against another.

After two or three days had passed, it became clear to the Viking's wife how matters stood with the child; it was under the influence of a powerful sorcerer. By day it was charming in appearance as an angel of light, but with a temper wicked and wild; while at night, in the form of an ugly frog, it was quiet and mournful, with eyes full of sorrow. Here were two natures, changing inwardly and outwardly with the absence and return of sunlight. And so it happened that by day the child, with the actual form of its mother, possessed the fierce disposition of its father; at night, on the contrary, its outward appearance plainly showed its descent on the father's side, while inwardly it had the heart and mind of its mother. Who would be able to loosen this wicked charm which the sorcerer had worked upon it? The wife of the Viking lived in constant pain and sorrow about it. Her heart clung to the little creature, but she could not explain to her husband the circumstances in which it was placed. He was expected to return shortly; and were she to tell him, he would very likely, as was the custom at that time, expose the poor child in the public highway, and let anyone take it away who would. The good wife of the Viking could not let that happen, and she therefore resolved that the Viking should never see the child excepting by daylight.

One morning there sounded a rushing of storks' wings over the roof. More than a hundred pair of storks had rested there during the night, to recover themselves after their excursion; and now they soared aloft, and prepared for the journey southward.

"All the husbands are here, and ready!" they cried; "wives and children also!"

"How light we are!" screamed the young storks in chorus. "Something pleasant seems creeping over us, even down to our toes, as if we were full of live frogs. Ah, how delightful it is to travel into foreign lands!"

"Hold yourselves properly in the line with us," cried papa and mamma. "Do not use your beaks so much; it tries the lungs." And then the storks flew away.

About the same time sounded the clang of the warriors' trumpets across the heath. The Viking had landed with his men. They were returning home, richly laden with spoil from the Gallic coast, where the people, as did also the inhabitants of Britain, often cried in alarm, "Deliver us from the wild northmen."

Life and noisy pleasure came with them into the castle of the Viking on the moorland. A great cask of mead was drawn into the hall, piles of wood blazed, cattle were slain and served up, that they might feast in reality, The priest who offered the sacrifice sprinkled the devoted parishioners with the warm blood; the fire crackled, and the smoke rolled along beneath the roof; the soot fell upon them from the beams; but they were used to all these things. Guests were invited, and received handsome presents. All wrongs and unfaithfulness were forgotten. They drank deeply, and threw in each other's faces the bones that were left, which was looked upon as a sign of good feeling amongst them. A bard, who was a kind of musician as well as warrior, and who had been with the Viking in his expedition, and knew what to sing about, gave them one of his best songs, in which they heard all their warlike deeds praised, and every wonderful action brought forward with honor. Every verse ended with this refrain,

Gold and possessions will flee away,
Friends and foes must die one day;
Every man on earth must die,
But a famous name will never die.

And with that they beat upon their shields, and hammered upon the table with knives and bones, in a most outrageous manner.

The Viking's wife sat upon a raised cross seat in the open hall. She wore a silk dress, golden bracelets, and large amber beads. She was in costly attire, and the bard named her in his song, and spoke of the rich treasure of gold which she had brought to her husband. Her husband had already seen the wonderfully beautiful child in the daytime, and was delighted with her beauty; even her wild ways pleased him. He said the little maiden would grow up to be a heroine, with the strong will and determination of a man. She would never wink her eyes, even if, in joke, an expert hand should attempt to cut off her eyebrows with a sharp sword.

The full cask of mead soon became empty, and a fresh one was brought in; for these were people who liked plenty to eat and drink. The old proverb, which everyone knows, says that "the cattle know when to leave their pasture, but a foolish man knows not the measure of his own appetite." Yes, they all knew this; but men may know what is right, and yet often do wrong. They also knew "that even the welcome guest becomes wearisome when he sits too long in the house." But there they remained; for pork and mead are good things. And so at the Viking's house they stayed, and enjoyed themselves; and at night the bondmen slept in the ashes, and dipped their fingers in the fat, and licked them. Oh, it was a delightful time!

Once more in the same year the Viking went forth, though the storms of autumn had already commenced to roar. He went with his warriors to the coast of Britain; he said that it was but an excursion of pleasure across the water, so his wife remained at home with the little girl. After a while, it is quite certain the foster-mother began to love the poor frog, with its gentle eyes and its deep sighs, even better than the little beauty who bit and fought with all around her.

The heavy, damp mists of autumn, which destroy the leaves of the wood, had already fallen upon forest and heath. Feathers of plucked birds, as they call the snow, flew about in thick showers, and winter was coming. The sparrows took possession of the stork's nest, and conversed about the absent owners in their own fashion; and they, the stork pair and all their young ones, where were they staying now? The storks might have been found in the land of Egypt, where the sun's rays shone forth bright and warm, as it does here at midsummer. Tamarinds and acacias were in full bloom all over the country, the crescent of Mahomet glittered brightly from the cupolas of the mosques, and on the slender pinnacles sat many of the storks, resting after their long journey. Swarms of them took divided possession of the nests—nests which lay close to each other between the venerable columns, and crowded the arches of temples in forgotten cities. The date and the palm lifted themselves as a screen or as a sunshade over them. The gray pyramids looked like broken shadows in the clear air and the far-off desert, where the ostrich wheels his rapid flight, and the lion, with his subtle eyes, gazes at the marble sphinx which lies half buried in sand. The waters of the Nile had retreated, and the whole bed of the river was covered with frogs, which was a most acceptable prospect for the stork families. The young storks thought their eyes deceived them, everything around appeared so beautiful.

"It is always like this here, and this is how we live in our warm country," said the stork-mamma; and the thought made the young ones almost beside themselves with pleasure.

"Is there anything more to see?" they asked; "are we going farther into the country?"

"There is nothing further for us to see," answered the stork-mamma. "Beyond this delightful region there are immense forests, where the branches of the trees entwine round each other, while prickly, creeping plants cover the paths, and only an elephant could force a passage for himself with his great feet. The snakes are too large, and the lizards too lively for us to catch. Then there is the desert; if you went there, your eyes would soon be full of sand with the lightest breeze, and if it should blow great guns, you would most likely find yourself in a sand drift. Here is the best place for you, where there are frogs and locusts; here I shall remain, and so must you." And so they stayed.

The parents sat in the nest on the slender minaret, and rested, yet still were busily employed in cleaning and smoothing their feathers, and in sharpening their beaks against their red stockings; then they would stretch out their necks, salute each other, and gravely raise their heads with the high-polished forehead, and soft, smooth feathers, while their brown eyes shone with intelligence. The female young ones strutted about amid the moist rushes, glancing at the other young storks and making acquaintances, and swallowing a frog at every third step, or tossing a little snake about with their beaks, in a way they considered very becoming, and besides it tasted very good. The young male storks soon began to quarrel; they struck at each other with their wings, and pecked with their beaks till the blood came. And in this manner many of the young ladies and gentlemen were betrothed to each other: it was, of course, what they wanted, and indeed what they lived for. Then they returned to a nest, and there the quarrelling began afresh; for in hot countries people are almost all violent and passionate. But for all that it was pleasant, especially for the old people, who watched them with great joy: all that their young ones did suited them. Every day here there was sunshine, plenty to eat, and nothing to think of but pleasure. But in the rich castle of their Egyptian host, as they called him, pleasure was not to be found. The rich and mighty lord of the castle lay on his couch, in the midst of the great hall, with its many colored walls looking like the centre of a great tulip; but he was stiff and powerless in all his limbs, and lay stretched out like a mummy. His family and servants stood round him; he was not dead, although he could scarcely be said to live. The healing moor-flower from the north, which was to have been found and brought to him by her who loved him so well, had not arrived. His young and beautiful daughter who, in swan's plumage, had flown over land and seas to the distant north, had never returned. She is dead, so the two swan-maidens had said when they came home; and they made up quite a story about her, and this is what they told,

"We three flew away together through the air," said they: "a hunter caught sight of us, and shot at us with an arrow. The arrow struck our young friend and sister, and slowly singing her farewell song she sank down, a dying swan, into the forest lake. On the shores of the lake, under a spreading birch tree, we laid her in the cold earth. We had our revenge; we bound fire under the wings of a swallow, who had a nest on the thatched roof of the huntsman. The house took fire, and burst into flames; the hunter was burnt with the house, and the light was reflected over the sea as far as the spreading birch, beneath which we laid her sleeping dust. She will never return to the land of Egypt." And then they both wept. And stork-papa, who heard the story, snapped with his beak so that it might be heard a long way off.

"Deceit and lies!" cried he; "I should like to run my beak deep into their chests."

"And perhaps break it off," said the mamma stork, "then what a sight you would be. Think first of yourself, and then of your family; all others are nothing to us."

"Yes, I know," said the stork-papa; "but tomorrow I can easily place myself on the edge of the open cupola, when the learned and wise men assemble to consult on the state of the sick man; perhaps they may come a little nearer to the truth." And the learned and wise men assembled together, and talked a great deal on every point; but the stork could make no sense out of anything they said; neither were there any good results from their consultations, either for the sick man, or for his daughter in the marshy heath. When we listen to what people say in this world, we shall hear a great deal; but it is an advantage to know what has been said and done before, when we listen to a conversation. The stork did, and we know at least as much as he, the stork.

"Love is a life-giver. The highest love produces the highest life. Only through love can the sick man be cured." This had been said by many, and even the learned men acknowledged that it was a wise saying.

"What a beautiful thought!" exclaimed the papa stork immediately.

"I don't quite understand it," said the mamma stork, when her husband repeated it; "however, it is not my fault, but the fault of the thought; whatever it may be, I have something else to think of."

Now the learned men had spoken also of love between this one and that one; of the difference of the love which we have for our neighbor, to the love that exists between parents and children; of the love of the plant for the light, and how the germ springs forth when the sunbeam kisses the ground. All these things were so elaborately and learnedly explained, that it was impossible for stork-papa to follow it, much less to talk about it. His thoughts on the subject quite weighed him down; he stood the whole of the following day on one leg, with half-shut eyes, thinking deeply. So much learning was quite a heavy weight for him to carry. One thing, however, the papa stork could understand. Everyone, high and low, had from their inmost hearts expressed their opinion that it was a great misfortune for so many thousands of people—the whole country indeed—to have this man so sick, with no hopes of his recovery. And what joy and blessing it would spread around if he could by any means be cured! But where bloomed the flower that could bring him health? They had searched for it everywhere; in learned writings, in the shining stars, in the weather and wind. Inquiries had been made in every by-way that could be thought of, until at last the wise and learned men has asserted, as we have been already told, that "love, the life-giver, could alone give new life to a father;" and in saying this, they had overdone it, and said more than they understood themselves. They repeated it, and wrote it down as a recipe, "Love is a life-giver." But how could such a recipe be prepared—that was a difficulty they could not overcome. At last it was decided that help could only come from the princess herself, whose whole soul was wrapped up in her father, especially as a plan had been adopted by her to enable her to obtain a remedy.

More than a year had passed since the princess had set out at night, when the light of the young moon was soon lost beneath the horizon. She had gone to the marble sphinx in the desert, shaking the sand from her sandals, and then passed through the long passage, which leads to the centre of one of the great pyramids, where the mighty kings of antiquity, surrounded with pomp and splendor, lie veiled in the form of mummies. She had been told by the wise men, that if she laid her head on the breast of one of them, from the head she would learn where to find life and recovery for her father. She had performed all this, and in a dream had learnt that she must bring home to her father the lotus flower, which grows in the deep sea, near the moors and heath in the Danish land. The very place and situation had been pointed out to her, and she was told that the flower would restore her father to health and strength. And, therefore, she had gone forth from the land of Egypt, flying over to the open marsh and the wild moor in the plumage of a swan.

The papa and mamma storks knew all this, and we also know it now. We know, too, that the Marsh King has drawn her down to himself, and that to the loved ones at home she is forever dead. One of the wisest of them said, as the stork-mamma also said, "That in some way she would, after all, manage to succeed;" and so at last they comforted themselves with this hope, and would wait patiently; in fact, they could do nothing better.

"I should like to get away the swan's feathers from those two treacherous princesses," said the papa stork; "then, at least, they would not be able to fly over again to the wild moor, and do more wickedness. I can hide the two suits of feathers over yonder, till we find some use for them."

"But where will you put them?" asked the mamma stork.

"In our nest on the moor. I and the young ones will carry them by turns during our flight across; and as we return, should they prove too heavy for us, we shall be sure to find plenty of places on the way in which we can conceal them till our next journey. Certainly one suit of swan's feathers would be enough for the princess, but two are always better. In those northern countries no one can have too many travelling wrappers."

"No one will thank you for it," said stork-mamma; "but you are master; and, excepting at breeding time, I have nothing to say."

In the Viking's castle on the wild moor, to which the storks directed their flight in the following spring, the little maiden still remained. They had named her Helga, which was rather too soft a name for a child with a temper like hers, although her form was still beautiful. Every month this temper showed itself in sharper outlines; and in the course of years, while the storks still made the same journeys in autumn to the hill, and in spring to the moors, the child grew to be almost a woman, and before anyone seemed aware of it, she was a wonderfully beautiful maiden of sixteen. The casket was splendid, but the contents were worthless. She

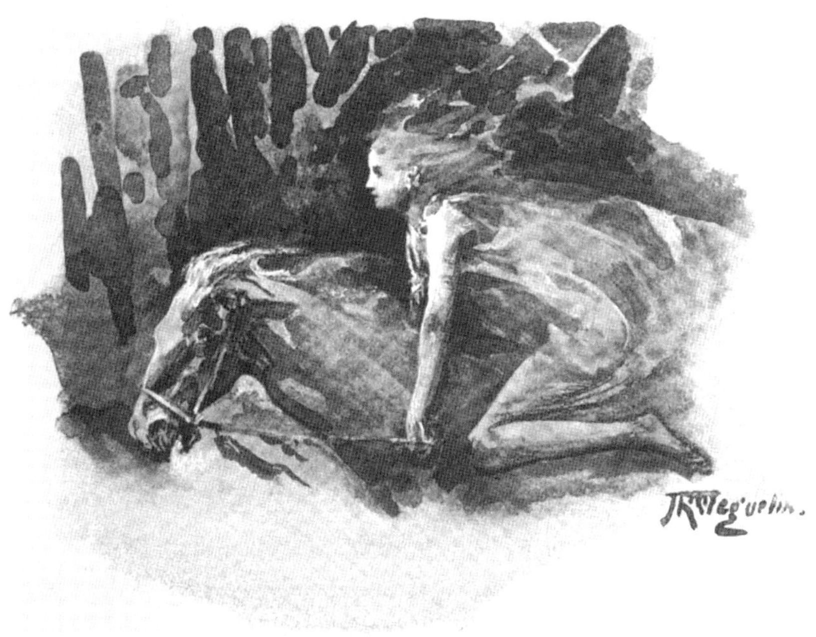

was, indeed, wild and savage even in those hard, uncultivated times. It was a pleasure to her to splash about with her white hands in the warm blood of the horse which had been slain for sacrifice. In one of her wild moods she bit off the head of the black cock, which the priest was about to slay for the sacrifice. To her foster-father she said one day, "If thine enemy were to pull down thine house about thy ears, and thou shouldest be sleeping in unconscious security, I would not wake thee; even if I had the power I would never do it, for my ears still tingle with the blow that thou gavest me years ago. I have never forgotten it." But the Viking treated her words as a joke; he was, like everyone else, bewitched with her beauty, and knew nothing of the change in the form and temper of Helga at night. Without a saddle, she would sit on a horse as if she were a part of it, while it rushed along at full speed; nor would she spring from its back, even when it quarrelled with other horses and bit them. She would often leap from the high shore into the sea with all her clothes on, and swim to meet the Viking, when his boat was steering home towards the shore. She once cut off a long lock of her beautiful hair, and twisted it into a string for her bow. "If a thing is to be done well," said she, "I must do it myself."

The Viking's wife was, for the time in which she lived, a woman of strong character and will; but, compared to her daughter, she was a gentle, timid woman, and she knew that a wicked sorcerer had the terrible child in his power. It was sometimes as if Helga acted from sheer wickedness; for often when her mother stood on the threshold of the door, or stepped into the yard, she would seat herself on the brink of the well, wave her arms and legs in the air, and suddenly fall right in. Here she was able, from her frog nature, to dip and dive about in the water of the deep well, until at last she would climb forth like a cat, and come back into the hall dripping with water, so that the green leaves that were strewed on the floor were whirled round, and carried away by the streams that flowed from her.

But there was one time of the day which placed a check upon Helga. It was the evening twilight; when this hour arrived she became quiet and thoughtful, and allowed herself to be advised and led; then also a secret feeling seemed to draw her towards her mother. And as usual, when the sun set, and the transformation took place, both in body and mind, inwards and outwards, she would remain quiet and mournful, with her form shrunk together in the shape of a frog. Her body was much larger than those animals ever are, and on this account it was much more hideous in appearance; for she looked like a wretched dwarf, with a frog's head, and webbed fingers. Her eyes had a most piteous expression; she was without a voice, excepting a hollow, croaking sound, like the smothered sobs of a dreaming child.

Then the Viking's wife took her on her lap, and forgot the ugly form, as she looked into the mournful eyes, and often said, "I could wish that thou wouldst always remain my dumb frog child, for thou art too terrible when thou art clothed in a form of beauty." And the Viking woman wrote Runic characters against sorcery and spells of sickness, and threw them over the wretched child; but they did no good.

"One can scarcely believe that she was ever small enough to lie in the cup of the waterlily," said the papa stork; "and now she is grown up, and the image of her Egyptian mother, especially about the eyes. Ah, we shall never see her again; perhaps she has not discovered how to help herself, as you and the wise men said she would. Year after year have I flown across and across the moor, but there was no sign of her being still alive. Yes, and I may as well tell you that each year, when I arrived a few days before you to repair the nest, and put everything in its place, I have spent a whole night flying here and there over the marshy lake, as if I had been an owl or a bat, but all to no purpose. The two suit of swan's plumage, which I and the young ones dragged over here from the land of the Nile, are of no use; trouble enough it was to us to bring them here in three journeys, and now they are lying at the bottom of the nest; and if a fire should happen to break out, and the wooden house be burnt down, they would be destroyed."

"And our good nest would be destroyed, too," said the mamma stork; "but you think less of that than of your plumage stuff and your moor-princess. Go and stay with her in the marsh if you like. You are a bad father to your own children, as I have told you already, when I hatched my first brood. I only hope neither we nor our children may have an arrow sent through our wings, owing to that wild girl. Helga does not know in the least what she is about. We have lived in this house longer than she has, she should think of that, and we have never forgotten our duty. We have paid every year our toll of a feather, an egg, and a young one, as it is only right we should do. You don't suppose I can wander about the courtyard, or go everywhere as I used to do in old times. I can do it in Egypt, where I can be a companion of the people, without forgetting myself. But here I cannot go and peep into the pots and kettles as I do there. No, I can only sit up here and feel angry with that girl, the little wretch; and I am angry with you, too; you should have left her lying in the water lily, then no one would have known anything about her."

"You are far better than your conversation," said the papa stork; "I know you better than you know yourself." And with that he gave a hop, and flapped his wings twice, proudly; then he stretched his neck and flew, or rather soared away, without moving his outspread wings. He went on for some distance, and then he gave a great flap with his wings and flew on his course at a rapid rate, his head and neck bending proudly before him, while the sun's rays fell on his glossy plumage.

"He is the handsomest of them all," said the mamma stork, as she watched him; "but I won't tell him so."

Early in the autumn, the Viking again returned home laden with spoil, and bringing prisoners with him. Among them was a young Christian priest, one of those who condemned the gods of the north. Often lately there had been, both in hall and chamber, a talk of the new faith which was spreading far and wide in the south, and which, through the means of the holy Ansgarius, had already reached as far as Hedeby on the Schlei. Even Helga had heard of this belief in the teachings of One who was named Christ, and who for the love of mankind, and for their redemption, had given up His life. But to her all this had, as it were, gone in one ear and out the other. It seemed that she only understood the meaning of the word "love," when in the form of a miserable frog she crouched together in the corner of the sleeping chamber; but the Viking's wife had listened to the wonderful story, and had felt herself strangely moved by it.

On their return, after this voyage, the men spoke of the beautiful temples built of polished stone, which had been raised for the public worship of this holy love. Some vessels, curiously formed of massive gold, had been brought home among the booty. There was a peculiar fragrance about them all, for they were incense vessels, which had been swung before the altars in the temples by the Christian priests. In the deep stony cellars of the castle, the young Christian priest was immured, and his hands and feet tied together with strips of bark. The Viking's wife considered him as beautiful as Baldur, and his distress raised her pity; but Helga said he ought to have ropes fastened to his heels, and be tied to the tails of wild animals.

"I would let the dogs loose after him" she said, "over the moor and across the heath. Hurrah! that would be a spectacle for the gods, and better still to follow in its course."

But the Viking would not allow him to die such a death as that, especially as he was the disowned and despiser of the high gods. In a few days, he had decided to have him offered as a sacrifice on the bloodstone in the grove. For the first time, a man was to be sacrificed here. Helga begged to be allowed to sprinkle the assembled people with the blood of the priest. She sharpened her glittering knife; and when one of the great, savage dogs, who were running about the Viking's castle in great numbers, sprang towards her, she thrust the knife into his side, merely, as she said, to prove its sharpness.

The Viking's wife looked at the wild, badly disposed girl, with great sorrow; and when night came on, and her daughter's beautiful form and disposition were changed, she spoke in eloquent words to Helga of the sorrow and deep grief that was in her heart. The ugly frog, in its monstrous shape, stood before her, and raised its brown mournful eyes to her face, listening to her words, and seeming to understand them with the intelligence of a human being.

"Never once to my lord and husband has a word passed my lips of what I have to suffer through you; my heart is full of grief about you," said the Viking's wife. "The love of a mother is greater and more powerful than I ever imagined. But love never entered thy heart; it is cold and clammy, like the plants on the moor."

Then the miserable form trembled; it was as if these words had touched an invisible bond between body and soul, for great tears stood in the eyes.

"A bitter time will come for thee at last," continued the Viking's wife; "and it will be terrible for me too. It had been better for thee if thou hadst been left on the high road, with the cold night wind to lull thee to sleep." And the Viking's wife shed bitter tears, and went away in anger and sorrow, passing under the partition of furs, which hung loose over the beam and divided the hall.

The shrivelled frog still sat in the corner alone. Deep silence reigned around. At intervals, a half-stifled sigh was heard from its inmost soul; it was the soul of Helga. It seemed in pain, as if a new life were arising in her heart. Then she took a step forward and listened; then stepped again forward, and seized with her clumsy hands the heavy bar which was laid across the door. Gently, and with much trouble, she pushed back the bar, as silently lifted the latch, and then took up the glimmering lamp which stood in the antechamber of the hall. It seemed as if a stronger will than her own gave her strength. She removed the iron bolt from the closed cellar door, and slipped in to the prisoner. He was slumbering. She touched him with her cold, moist hand, and as he awoke and caught sight of the hideous form, he shuddered as if he beheld a wicked apparition. She drew her knife, cut through the bonds which confined his hands and feet, and beckoned to him to follow her. He uttered some holy names and made the sign of the cross, while the form remained motionless by his side.

"Who art thou?" he asked, "whose outward appearance is that of an animal, while thou willingly performest acts of mercy?"

The frog-figure beckoned to him to follow her, and led him through a long gallery concealed by hanging drapery to the stables, and then pointed to a horse. He mounted upon it, and she sprang up also before him, and held tightly by the animal's mane. The prisoner understood her, and they rode on at a rapid trot, by a road which he would never have found by himself, across the open heath. He forgot her ugly form, and only thought how the mercy and loving-kindness of the Almighty was acting through this hideous apparition. As he offered pious prayers and sang holy songs of praise, she trembled. Was it the effect of prayer and praise that caused this? or, was she shuddering in the cold morning air at the thought of approaching twilight? What were her feelings? She raised herself up, and wanted to stop the horse and spring off, but the Christian priest held her back with all his might, and then sang a pious song, as if this could loosen the wicked charm that had changed her into the semblance of a frog.

And the horse galloped on more wildly than before. The sky painted itself red, the first sunbeam pierced through the clouds, and in the clear flood of sunlight the frog became changed. It was Helga again, young and beautiful, but with a wicked demoniac spirit. He held now a beautiful young woman in his arms, and he was horrified at the sight. He stopped the horse, and sprang from its back. He imagined that some new sorcery was at work. But Helga also leaped from the horse and stood on the ground. The child's short garment reached only to her knee. She snatched the sharp knife from her girdle, and rushed like lightning at the astonished priest. "Let me get at thee!" she cried; "let me get at thee, that I may plunge this knife into thy body. Thou art pale as ashes, thou beardless slave." She pressed in upon him. They struggled with each other in heavy combat, but it was as if an invisible power had been given to the Christian in the struggle. He held her fast, and the old oak under which they stood seemed to help him, for the loosened roots on the ground became entangled in the maiden's feet, and held them fast. Close by rose a bubbling spring, and he sprinkled Helga's face and neck with the water, commanded the unclean spirit to come forth, and pronounced upon her a Christian blessing. But the water of faith has no power unless the well-spring of faith flows within. And yet even here its power was shown; something more than the mere strength of a man opposed itself, through his means, against the evil which struggled within her. His holy action seemed to overpower her. She dropped her arms, glanced at him with pale cheeks and looks of amazement. He appeared to her a mighty magician skilled in secret arts; his language was the darkest magic to her, and the movements of his hands in the air were as the secret signs of a magician's wand. She would not have blinked had he waved over her head a sharp knife or a glittering axe; but she shrunk from him as he signed her with the sign of the cross on her forehead and breast, and sat before him like a tame bird, with her head bowed down. Then he spoke to her, in gentle words, of the deed of love she had performed for him during the night, when she had come to him in the form of an ugly frog, to loosen his bonds, and to lead him forth to life and light; and he told her that she was bound in closer fetters than he had been, and that she could recover also life and light by his means. He would take her to Hedeby to St. Ansgarius, and there, in that Christian town, the spell of the sorcerer would be removed. But he would not let her sit before him on the horse, though of her own free will she wished to do so. "Thou must sit behind me, not before me," said he. "Thy magic beauty has a magic power which comes from an evil origin, and I fear it; still I am sure to overcome through my faith in Christ." Then he knelt down, and prayed with pious fervor. It was as if the quiet woodland were a holy church

consecrated by his worship. The birds sang as if they were also of this new congregation; and the fragrance of the wildflowers was as the ambrosial perfume of incense; while, above all, sounded the words of Scripture, "A light to them that sit in darkness and in the shadow of death, to guide their feet into the way of peace." And he spoke these words with the deep longing of his whole nature.

Meanwhile, the horse that had carried them in wild career stood quietly by, plucking at the tall bramble bushes, till the ripe young berries fell down upon Helga's hands, as if inviting her to eat. Patiently she allowed herself to be lifted on the horse, and sat there like a somnambulist—as one who walked in his sleep. The Christian bound two branches together with bark, in the form of a cross, and held it on high as they rode through the forest. The way gradually grew thicker of brushwood, as they rode along, till at last it became a trackless wilderness. Bushes of the wild sloe here and there blocked up the path, so that they had to ride over them. The bubbling spring formed not a stream, but a marsh, round which also they were obliged to guide the horse; still there were strength and refreshment in the cool forest breeze, and no trifling power in the gentle words spoken in faith and Christian love by the young priest, whose inmost heart yearned to lead this poor lost one into the way of light and life. It is said that raindrops can make a hollow in the hardest stone, and the waves of the sea can smooth and round the rough edges of the rocks; so did the dew of mercy fall upon Helga, softening what was hard, and smoothing what was rough in her character. These effects did not yet appear; she was not herself aware of them; neither does the seed in the lap of earth know, when the refreshing dew and the warm sunbeams fall upon it, that it contains within itself power by which it will flourish and bloom. The song of the mother sinks into the heart of the child, and the little one prattles the words after her, without understanding their meaning; but after a time the thoughts expand, and what has been heard in childhood seems to the mind clear and bright. So now the "Word," which is all-powerful to create, was working in the heart of Helga.

They rode forth from the thick forest, crossed the heath, and again entered a pathless wood. Here, towards evening, they met with robbers.

"Where hast thou stolen that beauteous maiden?" cried the robbers, seizing the horse by the bridle, and dragging the two riders from its back.

The priest had nothing to defend himself with, but the knife he had taken from Helga, and with this he struck out right and left. One of the robbers raised his axe against him; but the young priest sprang on one side, and avoided the blow, which fell with great force on the horse's neck, so that the blood gushed forth, and the animal sunk to the ground. Then Helga seemed suddenly to awake from her long, deep reverie; she threw herself hastily upon the dying animal. The priest placed himself before her, to defend and shelter her; but one of the robbers swung his iron axe against the Christian's head with such force that it was dashed to pieces, the blood and brains were scattered about, and he fell dead upon the ground. Then the robbers seized beautiful Helga by her white arms and slender waist; but at that moment the sun went down, and as its last ray disappeared, she was changed into the form of a frog. A greenish white mouth spread half over her face; her arms became thin and slimy; while broad hands, with webbed fingers, spread themselves out like fans. Then the robbers, in terror, let her go, and she stood among them, a hideous monster; and as is the nature of frogs to do, she hopped up as high as her own size, and disappeared in the thicket. Then the robbers knew that this must be the work of an evil spirit or some secret sorcery, and, in a terrible fright, they ran hastily from the spot.

The full moon had already risen, and was shining in all her radiant splendor over the earth, when from the thicket, in the form of a frog, crept poor Helga. She stood still by the corpse of the Christian priest, and the carcase of the dead horse. She looked at them with eyes that seemed to weep, and from the frog's head came forth a croaking sound, as when a child bursts into tears. She threw herself first upon one, and then upon the other; brought water in her hand, which, from being webbed, was large and hollow, and poured it over them; but they were dead, and dead they would remain. She understood that at last. Soon wild animals would come and tear their dead bodies; but no, that must not happen. Then she dug up the earth, as deep as she was able, that she might prepare a grave for them. She had nothing but a branch of a tree and her two hands, between the fingers of which the webbed skin stretched, and they were torn by the work, while the blood ran down her hands. She saw at last that her work would be useless, more than she could accomplish; so she fetched more water, and washed the face of the dead, and then covered it with fresh green leaves; she also brought large boughs and spread over him, and scattered dried leaves between the branches. Then she brought the heaviest stones that she could carry, and laid them over the dead body, filling up the crevices with moss, till she thought she had fenced in his resting-place strongly enough. The difficult task had employed her the whole night; and as the sun broke forth, there stood the beautiful Helga in all her loveliness, with her bleeding hands, and, for the first time, with tears on her maiden cheeks. It was, in this transformation, as if two natures were striving together within her; her whole frame trembled, and she looked around her as if she had just awoke from a painful dream. She leaned for support against the trunk of a slender tree, and at last climbed to the topmost branches, like a cat, and seated herself firmly upon them. She remained there the whole day, sitting alone, like a frightened squirrel, in the silent solitude of the wood, where the rest and stillness is as the calm of death.

Butterflies fluttered around her, and close by were several anthills, each with its hundreds of busy little creatures moving quickly to and fro. In the air, danced myriads of gnats, swarm upon swarm, troops of buzzing flies, ladybirds, dragonflies with golden wings, and other little winged creatures. The worm crawled forth from the moist ground, and the moles crept out; but, excepting these, all around had the stillness of death: but when people say this, they do not quite understand themselves what they mean. None noticed Helga but a flock of magpies, which flew chattering round the top of the tree on which she sat. These birds hopped close to her on the branches with bold curiosity. A glance from her eyes was a signal to frighten them away, and they were not clever enough to find out who she was; indeed she hardly knew herself.

When the sun was near setting, and the evening's twilight about to commence, the approaching transformation aroused her to fresh exertion. She let herself down gently from the tree, and, as the last sunbeam vanished, she stood again in the wrinkled form of a frog, with the torn, webbed skin on her hands, but her eyes now gleamed with more radiant beauty than they had ever possessed in her most beautiful form of loveliness; they were now pure, mild maidenly eyes that shone forth in the face of a frog. They showed the existence of deep feeling and a human heart, and the beauteous eyes overflowed with tears, weeping precious drops that lightened the heart.

On the raised mound which she had made as a grave for the dead priest, she found the cross made of the branches of a tree, the last work of him who now lay dead and cold beneath it. A sudden thought came to Helga, and she lifted up the cross and planted it upon the grave, between the stones that covered him and the dead horse. The sad recollection brought the tears to her eyes, and in this gentle spirit she traced the same sign in the sand round the grave; and as she formed, with both her hands, the sign of the cross, the web skin fell from them like a torn glove. She washed her hands in the water of the spring, and gazed with astonishment at their delicate whiteness. Again she made the holy sign in the air, between herself and the dead man; her lips trembled, her tongue moved, and the name which she in her ride through the forest had so often heard spoken, rose to her lips, and she uttered the words, "Jesus Christ." Then the frog skin fell from her; she was once more a lovely maiden. Her head bent wearily, her tired limbs required rest, and then she slept.

Her sleep, however, was short. Towards midnight, she awoke; before her stood the dead horse, prancing and full of life, which shone forth from his eyes and from his wounded neck. Close by his side appeared the murdered Christian priest, more beautiful than Baldur, as the Viking's wife had said; but now he came as if in a flame of fire. Such gravity, such stern justice, such a piercing glance shone from his large, gentle eyes, that it seemed to penetrate into every corner of her heart. Beautiful Helga trembled at the look, and her memory returned with a power as if it had been the day of judgment. Every good deed that had been done for her, every loving word that had been said, were vividly before her mind. She understood now that love had kept her here during the day of her trial; while the creature formed of dust and clay, soul and spirit, had wrestled and struggled with evil. She acknowledged that she had only followed the impulses of an evil disposition, that she had done nothing to cure herself; everything had been given her, and all had happened as it were by the ordination of Providence. She bowed herself humbly, confessed her great imperfections in the sight of Him who can read every fault of the heart, and then the priest spoke. "Daughter of the moorland, thou hast come from the swamp and the marshy earth, but from this thou shalt arise. The sunlight shining into thy inmost soul proves the origin from which thou hast really sprung, and has restored the body to its natural form. I am come to thee from the land of the dead, and thou also must pass through the valley to reach the holy mountains where mercy and perfection dwell. I cannot lead thee to Hedeby that thou mayst receive

Christian baptism, for first thou must remove the thick veil with which the waters of the moorland are shrouded, and bring forth from its depths the living author of thy being and thy life. Till this is done, thou canst not receive consecration."

Then he lifted her on the horse and gave her a golden censer, similar to those she had already seen at the Viking's house. A sweet perfume arose from it, while the open wound in the forehead of the slain priest, shone with the rays of a diamond. He took the cross from the grave, and held it aloft, and now they rode through the air over the rustling trees, over the hills where warriors lay buried each by his dead war-horse; and the brazen monumental figures rose up and galloped forth, and stationed themselves on the summits of the hills. The golden crescent on their foreheads, fastened with golden knots, glittered in the moonlight, and their mantles floated in the wind. The dragon, that guards buried treasure, lifted his head and gazed after them. The goblins and the satyrs peeped out from beneath the hills, and flitted to and fro in the fields, waving blue, red, and green torches, like the glowing sparks in burning paper. Over woodland and heath, flood and fen, they flew on, till they reached the wild moor, over which they hovered in broad circles. The Christian priest held the cross aloft, and it glittered like gold, while from his lips sounded pious prayers. Beautiful Helga's voice joined with his in the hymns he sung, as a child joins in her mother's song. She swung the censer, and a wonderful fragrance of incense arose from it; so powerful, that the reeds and rushes of the moor burst forth into blossom. Each germ came forth from the deep ground: all that had life raised itself. Blooming waterlilies spread themselves forth like a carpet of wrought flowers, and upon them lay a slumbering woman, young and beautiful. Helga fancied that it was her own image she saw reflected in the still water. But it was her mother she beheld, the wife of the Marsh King, the princess from the land of the Nile.

The dead Christian priest desired that the sleeping woman should be lifted on the horse, but the horse sank beneath the load, as if he had been a funeral pall fluttering in the wind. But the sign of the cross made the airy phantom strong, and then the three rode away from the marsh to firm ground.

At the same moment the cock crew in the Viking's castle, and the dream figures dissolved and floated away in the air, but mother and daughter stood opposite to each other.

"Am I looking at my own image in the deep water?" said the mother.

"Is it myself that I see represented on a white shield?" cried the daughter.

Then they came nearer to each other in a fond embrace. The mother's heart beat quickly, and she understood the quickened pulses. "My child!" she exclaimed, "the flower of my heart—my lotus flower of the deep water!" and she embraced her child again and wept, and the tears were as a baptism of new life and love for Helga. "In swan's plumage I came here," said the mother, "and here I threw off my feather dress. Then I sank down through the wavering ground, deep into the marsh beneath, which closed like a wall around me; I found myself after a while in fresher water; still a power drew me down deeper and deeper. I felt the weight of sleep upon my eyelids. Then I slept, and dreams hovered round me. It seemed to me as if I were again in the pyramids of Egypt, and yet the waving elder trunk that had frightened me on the moor stood ever before me. I observed the clefts and wrinkles in the stem; they shone forth in strange colors, and took the form of hieroglyphics. It was the mummy case on which I gazed. At last it burst, and forth stepped the thousand years' old king, the mummy form, black as pitch, black as the shining wood-snail, or the slimy mud of the swamp. Whether it was really the mummy or the Marsh King I know not. He seized me in his arms, and I felt as if I must die. When I recovered myself, I found in my bosom a little bird, flapping its wings, twittering and fluttering. The bird flew away from my bosom, upwards towards the dark, heavy canopy above me, but a long, green band kept it fastened to me. I heard and understood the tenor of its longings. Freedom! sunlight! to my father! Then I thought of my father, and the sunny land of my birth, my life, and my love. Then I loosened the band, and let the bird fly away to its home—to a father. Since that hour I have ceased to dream; my sleep has been long and heavy, till in this very hour, harmony and fragrance awoke me, and set me free."

The green band which fastened the wings of the bird to the mother's heart, where did it flutter now? whither had it been wafted? The stork only had seen it. The band was the green stalk, the cup of the flower the cradle in which lay the child, that now in blooming beauty had been folded to the mother's heart.

And while the two were resting in each other's arms, the old stork flew round and round them in narrowing circles, till at length he flew away swiftly to his nest, and fetched away the two suits of swan's feathers, which he had preserved there for many years. Then he returned to the mother and daughter, and threw the swan's plumage over them; the feathers immediately closed around them, and they rose up from the earth in the form of two white swans.

"And now we can converse with pleasure," said the stork-papa; "we can understand one another, although the beaks of birds are so different in shape. It is very fortunate that you came tonight. Tomorrow we should have been gone. The mother, myself and the little ones, we're about to fly to the south. Look at me now: I am an old friend from the Nile, and a mother's heart contains more than her beak. She always said that the princess would know how to help herself. I and the young ones carried the swan's feathers over here, and I am glad of it now, and how lucky it is that I am here still. When the day dawns we shall start with a great company of other storks. We'll fly first, and you can follow in our track, so that you cannot miss your way. I and the young ones will have an eye upon you."

"And the lotus flower which I was to take with me," said the Egyptian princess, "is flying here by my side, clothed in swan's feathers. The flower of my heart will travel with me; and so the riddle is solved. Now for home! now for home!"

But Helga said she could not leave the Danish land without once more seeing her foster-mother, the loving wife of the Viking. Each pleasing recollection, each kind word, every tear from the heart which her foster-mother had wept for her, rose in her mind, and at that moment she felt as if she loved this mother the best.

"Yes, we must go to the Viking's castle," said the stork; "mother and the young ones are waiting for me there. How they will open their eyes and flap their wings! My wife, you see, does not say much; she is short and abrupt in her manner; but she means well, for all that. I will flap my wings at once, that they may hear us coming." Then stork-papa flapped his wings in first-rate style, and he and the swans flew away to the Viking's castle.

In the castle, everyone was in a deep sleep. It had been late in the evening before the Viking's wife retired to rest. She was anxious about Helga, who, three days before, had vanished with the Christian priest. Helga must have helped him in his flight, for it was her horse that was missed from the stable; but by what power had all this been accomplished? The Viking's wife thought of it with wonder, thought on the miracles which they said could be performed by those who believed in the Christian faith, and followed its teachings. These passing thoughts formed themselves into a vivid dream, and it seemed to her that she was still lying awake on her couch, while without darkness reigned. A storm arose; she heard the lake dashing and rolling from east and west, like the waves of the North Sea or the Cattegat. The monstrous snake which, it is said, surrounds the earth in the depths of the ocean, was trembling in spasmodic convulsions. The night of the fall of the gods was come, "Ragnorock," as the heathens call the judgment day, when everything shall pass away, even the high gods themselves. The war trumpet sounded; riding upon the rainbow, came the gods, clad in steel, to fight their last battle on the last battlefield. Before them flew the winged vampires, and the dead warriors closed up the train. The whole firmament was ablaze with the northern lights, and yet the darkness triumphed. It was a terrible hour. And, close to the terrified woman, Helga seemed to be seated on the floor, in the hideous form of a frog, yet trembling, and clinging to her foster-mother, who took her on her lap, and lovingly caressed her, hideous and frog-like as she was. The air was filled with the clashing of arms and the hissing of arrows, as if a storm of hail was descending upon the earth. It seemed to her the hour when earth and sky would burst asunder, and all things be swallowed up in Saturn's fiery lake; but she knew that a new heaven and a new earth would arise, and that cornfields would wave where now the lake rolled over desolate sands, and the ineffable God reign. Then she saw rising from the region of the dead, Baldur the gentle, the loving, and as the Viking's wife gazed upon him, she recognized his countenance. It was the captive Christian priest. "White Christian!" she exclaimed aloud, and with the words, she pressed a kiss on the forehead of the hideous frog-child. Then the frog-skin fell off, and Helga stood before her in all her beauty, more lovely and gentle-looking, and with eyes beaming with love. She kissed the hands of her foster-mother, blessed her for all her fostering love and care during the days of her trial and misery, for the thoughts she had suggested and awoke in her heart, and for naming the Name which she now repeated. Then beautiful Helga rose as a mighty swan, and spread her wings with the rushing sound of troops of birds of passage flying through the air.

Then the Viking's wife awoke, but she still heard the rushing sound without. She knew it was the time for the storks to depart, and that it must be their wings which she heard. She felt she should like to see them once more, and bid them farewell. She rose from her couch, stepped out on the threshold, and beheld, on the ridge of the roof, a party of storks ranged side by side. Troops of the birds were flying in circles over the castle and the highest trees; but just before her, as she stood on the threshold and close to the well where Helga had so often sat and alarmed her with her wildness, now stood two swans, gazing at her with intelligent eyes. Then she remembered her dream, which still appeared to her as a reality. She thought of Helga in the form of a swan. She thought of a Christian priest, and suddenly a wonderful joy arose in her heart. The swans flapped their wings and arched their necks as if to offer her a greeting, and the Viking's wife spread out her arms towards them, as if she accepted it, and smiled through her tears. She was roused from deep thought by a rustling of wings and snapping of beaks; all the storks arose, and started on their journey towards the south.

"We will not wait for the swans," said the mamma stork; "if they want to go with us, let them come now; we can't sit here till the plovers start. It is a fine thing after all to travel in families, not like the finches and the partridges. There the male and the female birds fly in separate flocks, which, to speak candidly, I consider very unbecoming."

"What are those swans flapping their wings for?"

"Well, everyone flies in his own fashion," said the papa stork. "The swans fly in an oblique line; the cranes, in the form of a triangle; and the plovers, in a curved line like a snake."

"Don't talk about snakes while we are flying up here," said stork-mamma. "It puts ideas into the children's heads that cannot be realized."

"Are those the high mountains I have heard spoken of?" asked Helga, in the swan's plumage.

"They are storm clouds driving along beneath us," replied her mother.

"What are yonder white clouds that rise so high?" again inquired Helga.

"Those are mountains covered with perpetual snows, that you see yonder," said her mother. And then they flew across the Alps towards the blue Mediterranean.

"Africa's land! Egyptia's strand!" sang the daughter of the Nile, in her swan's plumage, as from the upper air she caught sight of her native land, a narrow, golden, wavy strip on the shores of the Nile; the other birds espied it also and hastened their flight.

"I can smell the Nile mud and the wet frogs," said the stork-mamma, "and I begin to feel quite hungry. Yes, now you shall taste something nice, and you will see the marabout bird, and the ibis, and the crane. They all belong to our family, but they are not nearly so handsome as we are. They give themselves great airs, especially the ibis. The Egyptians have spoilt him. They make a mummy of him, and stuff him with spices. I would rather be stuffed with live frogs, and so would you, and so you shall. Better have something in your inside while you are alive, than to be made a parade of after you are dead. That is my opinion, and I am always right."

"The storks are come," was said in the great house on the banks of the Nile, where the lord lay in the hall on his downy cushions, covered with a leopard skin, scarcely alive, yet not dead, waiting and hoping for the lotus flower from the deep moorland in the far north. Relatives and servants were standing by his couch, when the two beautiful swans who had come with the storks flew into the hall. They threw off their soft white plumage, and two lovely female forms approached the pale, sick old man, and threw back their long hair, and when Helga bent over her grandfather, redness came back to his cheeks, his eyes brightened, and life returned to his benumbed limbs. The old man rose up with health and energy renewed; daughter and grandchild welcomed him as joyfully as if with a morning greeting after a long and troubled dream.

Joy reigned through the whole house, as well as in the stork's nest; although there the chief cause was really the good food, especially the quantities of frogs, which seemed to spring out of the ground in swarms.

Then the learned men hastened to note down, in flying characters, the story of the two princesses, and spoke of the arrival of the health-giving flower as a mighty event, which had been a blessing to the house and the land. Meanwhile, the stork-papa told the story to his family in his own way; but not till they had eaten and were satisfied; otherwise they would have had something else to do than to listen to stories.

"Well," said the stork-mamma, when she had heard it, "you will be made something of at last; I suppose they can do nothing less."

"What could I be made?" said stork-papa; "what have I done? Just nothing."

"You have done more than all the rest," she replied. "But for you and the youngsters the two young princesses would never have seen Egypt again, and the recovery of the old man would not have been affected. You will become something. They must certainly give you a doctor's hood, and our young ones will inherit it, and their children after them, and so on. You already look like an Egyptian doctor, at least in my eyes."

"I cannot quite remember the words I heard when I listened on the roof," said stork-papa, while relating the story to his family; "all I know is, that what the wise men said was so complicated and so learned, that they received not only rank, but presents; even the head cook at the great house was honored with a mark of distinction, most likely for the soup."

"And what did you receive?" said the stork-mamma. "They certainly ought not to forget the most important person in the affair, as you really are. The learned men have done nothing at all but use their tongues. Surely they will not overlook you."

Late in the night, while the gentle sleep of peace rested on the now happy house, there was still one watcher. It was not stork-papa, who, although he stood on guard on one leg, could sleep soundly. Helga alone was awake. She leaned over the balcony, gazing at the sparkling stars that shone clearer and brighter in the pure air than they had done in the north, and yet they were the same stars. She thought of the Viking's wife in the wild moorland, of the gentle eyes of her foster-mother, and of the tears she had shed over the poor frog-child that now lived in splendor and starry beauty by the waters of the Nile, with air balmy and sweet as spring. She thought of the love that dwelt in the breast of the heathen woman, love that had been shown to a wretched creature, hateful as a human being, and hideous when in the form of an animal. She looked at the glittering stars, and thought of the radiance that had shone forth on the forehead of the dead man, as she had fled with him over the woodland and moor. Tones were awakened in her memory; words which she had heard him speak as they rode onward, when she was carried, wondering and trembling, through the air; words from the great Fountain of love, the highest love that embraces all the human race. What had not been won and achieved by this love?

Day and night beautiful Helga was absorbed in the contemplation of the great amount of her happiness, and lost herself in the contemplation, like a child who turns hurriedly from the giver to examine the beautiful gifts. She was overpowered with her good fortune, which seemed always increasing, and therefore what might it become in the future? Had she not been brought by a wonderful miracle to all this joy and happiness? And in these thoughts she indulged, until at last she thought no more of the Giver. It was the over-abundance of youthful spirits unfolding its wings for a daring flight. Her eyes sparkled with energy, when suddenly arose a loud noise in the court below, and the daring thought vanished. She looked down, and saw two large ostriches running round quickly in narrow circles; she had never seen these creatures before—great, coarse, clumsy-looking birds with curious wings that looked as if they had been clipped, and the birds themselves had the appearance of having been roughly used. She inquired about them, and for the first time heard the legend which the Egyptians relate respecting the ostrich.

Once, say they, the ostriches were a beautiful and glorious race of birds, with large, strong wings. One evening the other large birds of the forest said to the ostrich, "Brother, shall we fly to the river tomorrow morning to drink, God willing?" and the ostrich answered, "I will."

With the break of day, therefore, they commenced their flight; first rising high in the air, towards the sun, which is the eye of God; still higher and higher the ostrich flew, far above the other birds, proudly approaching the light, trusting in its own strength, and thinking not of the Giver, or saying, "if God will." When suddenly the avenging angel drew back the veil from the flaming ocean of sunlight, and in a moment the wings of the proud bird were scorched and shrivelled, and they sunk miserably to the earth. Since that time the ostrich and his race have never been able to rise in the air; they can only fly terror-stricken along the ground, or run round and round in narrow circles. It is a warning to mankind, that in all our thoughts and schemes, and in every action we undertake, we should say, "if God will."

Then Helga bowed her head thoughtfully and seriously, and looked at the circling ostrich, as with timid fear and simple pleasure it glanced at its own great shadow on the sunlit walls. And the story of the ostrich sunk deeply into the heart and mind of Helga: a life of happiness, both in the present and in the future, seemed secure for her, and what was yet to come might be the best of all, God willing.

Early in the spring, when the storks were again about to journey northward, beautiful Helga took off her golden bracelets, scratched her name on them, and beckoned to the stork-father. He came to her, and she placed the golden circlet round his neck, and begged him to deliver it safely to the Viking's wife, so that she might know that her foster-daughter still lived, was happy, and had not forgotten her.

"It is rather heavy to carry," thought stork-papa, when he had it on his neck; "but gold and honor are not to be flung into the street. The stork brings good fortune—they'll be obliged to acknowledge that at last."

"You lay gold, and I lay eggs," said stork-mamma; "with you it is only once in a way, I lay eggs every year But no one appreciates what we do; I call it very mortifying."

"But then we have a consciousness of our own worth, mother," replied stork-papa.

"What good will that do you?" retorted stork-mamma; "it will neither bring you a fair wind, nor a good meal."

"The little nightingale, who is singing yonder in the tamarind grove, will soon be going north, too." Helga said she had often heard her singing on the wild moor, so she determined to send a message by her. While flying in the swan's plumage she had learnt the bird language; she had often conversed with the stork and the swallow, and she knew that the nightingale would understand. So she begged the nightingale to fly to the beechwood, on the peninsula of Jutland, where a mound of stone and twigs had been raised to form the grave, and she begged the nightingale to persuade all the other little birds to build their nests round the place, so that evermore should resound over that grave music and song. And the nightingale flew away, and time flew away also.

In the autumn, an eagle, standing upon a pyramid, saw a stately train of richly laden camels, and men attired in armor on foaming Arabian steeds, whose glossy skins shone like silver, their nostrils were pink, and their thick, flowing manes hung almost to their slender legs. A royal prince of Arabia, handsome as a prince should be, and accompanied by distinguished guests, was on his way to the stately house, on the roof of which the storks' empty nests might be seen. They were away now in the far north, but expected to return very soon. And, indeed, they returned on a day that was rich in joy and gladness.

A marriage was being celebrated, in which the beautiful Helga, glittering in silk and jewels, was the bride, and the bridegroom the young Arab prince. Bride and bridegroom sat at the upper end of the table, between the bride's mother and grandfather. But her gaze was not on the bridegroom, with his manly, sunburnt face, round which curled a black beard, and whose dark fiery eyes were fixed upon her; but away from him, at a twinkling star, that shone down upon her from the sky. Then was heard the sound of rushing wings beating the air. The storks were coming home; and the old stork pair, although tired with the journey and requiring rest, did not fail to fly down at once to the balustrades of the verandah, for they knew already what feast was being celebrated. They had heard of it on the borders of the land, and also that Helga had caused their figures to be represented on the walls, for they belonged to her history.

"I call that very sensible and pretty," said stork-papa.

"Yes, but it is very little," said mamma stork; "they could not possibly have done less."

But, when Helga saw them, she rose and went out into the verandah to stroke the backs of the storks. The old stork pair bowed their heads, and curved their necks, and even the youngest among the young ones felt honored by this reception.

Helga continued to gaze upon the glittering star, which seemed to glow brighter and purer in its light; then between herself and the star floated a form, purer than the air, and visible through it. It floated quite near to her, and she saw that it was the dead Christian priest, who also was coming to her wedding feast—coming from the heavenly kingdom.

"The glory and brightness, yonder, outshines all that is known on earth," said he.

Then Helga the fair prayed more gently, and more earnestly, than she had ever prayed in her life before, that she might be permitted to gaze, if only for a single moment, at the glory and brightness of the heavenly kingdom. Then she felt herself lifted up, as it were, above the earth, through a sea of sound and thought; not only around her, but within her, was there light and song, such as words cannot express.

"Now we must return;" he said, "you will be missed."

"Only one more look," she begged; "but one short moment more."

"We must return to earth; the guests will have all departed. Only one more look—the last!"

Then Helga stood again in the verandah. But the marriage lamps in the festive hall had been all extinguished, and the torches outside had vanished. The storks were gone; not a guest could be seen; no bridegroom—all in those few short moments seemed to have died. Then a great dread fell upon her. She stepped from the verandah through the empty hall into the next chamber, where slept strange warriors. She opened a side door, which once led into her own apartment, but now, as she passed through, she found herself suddenly in a garden which she had never before seen here, the sky blushed red, it was the dawn of morning. Three minutes only in heaven, and a whole night on earth had passed away! Then she saw the storks, and called to them in their own language.

Then stork-papa turned his head towards her, listened to her words, and drew near. "You speak our language," said he, "what do you wish? Why do you appear—you—a strange woman?"

"It is I—it is Helga! Dost thou not know me? Three minutes ago we were speaking together yonder in the verandah."

"That is a mistake," said the stork, "you must have dreamed all this."

"No, no," she exclaimed. Then she reminded him of the Viking's castle, of the great lake, and of the journey across the ocean.

Then stork-papa winked his eyes, and said, "Why that's an old story which happened in the time of my grandfather. There certainly was a princess of that kind here in Egypt once, who came from the Danish land, but she vanished on the evening of her wedding day, many hundred years ago, and never came back. You may read about it yourself yonder, on a monument in the garden. There you will find swans and storks sculptured, and on the top is a figure of the princess Helga, in marble."

And so it was; Helga understood it all now, and sank on her knees. The sun burst forth in all its glory, and, as in olden times, the form of the frog vanished in his beams, and the beautiful form stood forth in all its loveliness; so now, bathed in light, rose a beautiful form, purer, clearer than air—a ray of brightness—from the Source of light Himself. The body crumbled into dust, and a faded lotus flower lay on the spot on which Helga had stood.

"Now that is a new ending to the story," said stork-papa; "I really never expected it would end in this way, but it seems a very good ending."

"And what will the young ones say to it, I wonder?" said stork-mamma.

"Ah, that is a very important question," replied the stork.

The Pea Blossom

There were once five peas in one shell, they were green, the shell was green, and so they believed that the whole world must be green also, which was a very natural conclusion. The shell grew, and the peas grew, they accommodated themselves to their position, and sat all in a row. The sun shone without and warmed the shell, and the rain made it clear and transparent; it was mild and agreeable in broad daylight, and dark at night, as it generally is; and the peas as they sat there grew bigger and bigger, and more thoughtful as they mused, for they felt there must be something else for them to do.

"Are we to sit here forever?" asked one; "shall we not become hard by sitting so long? It seems to me there must be something outside, and I feel sure of it."

And as weeks passed by, the peas became yellow, and the shell became yellow.

"All the world is turning yellow, I suppose," said they, and perhaps they were right.

Suddenly they felt a pull at the shell; it was torn off, and held in human hands, then slipped into the pocket of a jacket in company with other full pods.

"Now we shall soon be opened," said one, just what they all wanted.

"I should like to know which of us will travel furthest," said the smallest of the five; "we shall soon see now."

"What is to happen will happen," said the largest pea.

"Crack" went the shell as it burst, and the five peas rolled out into the bright sunshine. There they lay in a child's hand. A little boy was holding them tightly, and said they were fine peas for his peashooter. And immediately he put one in and shot it out.

"Now I am flying out into the wide world," said he; "catch me if you can;" and he was gone in a moment.

"I," said the second, "intend to fly straight to the sun, that is a shell that lets itself be seen, and it will suit me exactly;" and away he went.

"We will go to sleep wherever we find ourselves," said the two next, "we shall still be rolling onwards;" and they did certainly fall on the floor, and roll about before they got into the peashooter; but they were put in for all that. "We shall go farther than the others," said they.

"What is to happen will happen," exclaimed the last, as he was shot out of the peashooter; and as he spoke he flew up against an old board under a garret-window, and fell into a little crevice, which was almost filled up with moss and soft earth. The moss closed itself round him, and there he lay, a captive indeed, but not unnoticed by God.

"What is to happen will happen," said he to himself.

Within the little garret lived a poor woman, who went out to clean stoves, chop wood into small pieces, and perform such-like hard work, for she was strong and industrious. Yet she remained always poor, and at home in the garret lay her only daughter, not quite grown up, and very delicate and weak. For a whole year she had kept her bed, and it seemed as if she could neither live nor die.

"She is going to her little sister," said the woman; "I had but the two children, and it was not an easy thing to support both of them; but the good God helped me in my work, and took one of them to Himself and provided for her. Now I would gladly keep the other that was left to me, but I suppose they are not to be separated, and my sick girl will very soon go to her sister above." But the sick girl still remained where she was, quietly and patiently she lay all the day long, while her mother was away from home at her work.

Spring came, and one morning early the sun shone brightly through the little window, and threw its rays over the floor of the room. Just as the mother was going to her work, the sick girl fixed her gaze on the lowest pane of the window. "Mother," she exclaimed, "what can that little green thing be that peeps in at the window? It is moving in the wind."

The mother stepped to the window and half opened it. "Oh!" she said, "there is actually a little pea which has taken root and is putting out its green leaves. How could it have got into this crack? Well now, here is a little garden for you to amuse yourself with." So the bed of the sick girl was drawn nearer to the window, that she might see the budding plant; and the mother went out to her work.

"Mother, I believe I shall get well," said the sick child in the evening, "the sun has shone in here so brightly and warmly today, and the little pea is thriving so well: I shall get on better, too, and go out into the warm sunshine again."

"God grant it!" said the mother, but she did not believe it would be so. But she propped up with the little stick the green plant which had given her child such pleasant hopes of life, so that it might not be broken by the winds; she tied the piece of string to the windowsill and to the upper part of the frame, so that the pea-tendrils might twine round it when it shot up. And it did shoot up, indeed it might almost be seen to grow from day to day.

"Now really here is a flower coming," said the old woman one morning, and now at last she began to encourage the hope that her sick daughter might really recover. She remembered that for some time the child had spoken more cheerfully, and during the last few days had raised herself in bed in the morning to look with sparkling eyes at her little garden which contained only a single pea plant. A week after, the invalid sat up for the first time a whole hour, feeling quite happy by the open window in the warm sunshine, while outside grew the little plant, and on it a pink pea blossom in full bloom. The little maiden bent down and gently kissed the delicate leaves. This day was to her like a festival.

"Our heavenly Father Himself has planted that pea, and made it grow and flourish, to bring joy to you and hope to me, my blessed child," said the happy mother, and she smiled at the flower, as if it had been an angel from God.

But what became of the other peas? Why the one who flew out into the wide world, and said, "Catch me if you can," fell into a gutter on the roof of a house, and ended his travels in the crop of a pigeon. The two lazy ones were carried quite as far, for they also were eaten by pigeons, so they were at least of some use; but the fourth, who wanted to reach the sun, fell into a sink and lay there in the dirty water for days and weeks, till he had swelled to a great size.

"I am getting beautifully fat," said the pea, "I expect I shall burst at last; no pea could do more that, I think; I am the most remarkable of all the five which were in the shell." And the sink confirmed the opinion.

But the young maiden stood at the open garret window, with sparkling eyes and the rosy hue of health on her cheeks, she folded her thin hands over the pea blossom, and thanked God for what He had done.

"I," said the sink, "shall stand up for my pea."

The Storks

On the last house in a little village the storks had built a nest, and the mother stork sat in it with her four young ones, who stretched out their necks and pointed their black beaks, which had not yet turned red like those of the parent birds. A little way off, on the edge of the roof, stood the father stork, quite upright and stiff; not liking to be quite idle, he drew up one leg, and stood on the other, so still that it seemed almost as if he were carved in wood. "It must look very grand," thought he, "for my wife to have a sentry guarding her nest. They do not know that I am her husband; they will think I have been commanded to stand here, which is quite aristocratic;" and so he continued standing on one leg.

In the street below were a number of children at play, and when they caught sight of the storks, one of the boldest amongst the boys began to sing a song about them, and very soon he was joined by the rest. These are the words of the song, but each only sang what he could remember of them in his own way.

Stork, stork, fly away,
Stand not on one leg, I pray,
See your wife is in her nest,
With her little ones at rest.
They will hang one,
And fry another;
They will shoot a third,
And roast his brother.

"Just hear what those boys are singing," said the young storks; "they say we shall be hanged and roasted."

"Never mind what they say; you need not listen," said the mother. "They can do no harm."

But the boys went on singing and pointing at the storks, and mocking at them, excepting one of the boys whose name was Peter; he said it was a shame to make fun of animals, and would not join with them at all. The mother stork comforted her young ones, and told them not to mind. "See," she said, "how quiet your father stands, although he is only on one leg."

"But we are very much frightened," said the young storks, and they drew back their heads into the nests.

The next day when the children were playing together, and saw the storks, they sang the song again—

They will hang one,
And roast another.

"Shall we be hanged and roasted?" asked the young storks.

"No, certainly not," said the mother. "I will teach you to fly, and when you have learnt, we will fly into the meadows, and pay a visit to the frogs, who will bow themselves to us in the water, and cry 'Croak, croak,' and then we shall eat them up; that will be fun."

"And what next?" asked the young storks.

"Then," replied the mother, "all the storks in the country will assemble together, and go through their autumn manoeuvres, so that it is very important for everyone to know how to fly properly. If they do not, the general will thrust them through with his beak, and kill them. Therefore you must take pains and learn, so as to be ready when the drilling begins."

"Then we may be killed after all, as the boys say; and hark! they are singing again."

"Listen to me, and not to them," said the mother stork. "After the great review is over, we shall fly away to warm countries far from hence, where there are mountains and forests. To Egypt, where we shall see three-cornered houses built of stone, with pointed tops that reach nearly to the clouds. They are called Pyramids, and are older than a stork could imagine; and in that country, there is a river that overflows its banks, and then goes back, leaving nothing but mire; there we can walk about, and eat frogs in abundance."

"Oh, oh!" cried the young storks.

"Yes, it is a delightful place; there is nothing to do all day long but eat, and while we are so well off out there, in this country there will not be a single green leaf on the trees, and the weather will be so cold that the clouds will freeze, and fall on the earth in little white rags." The stork meant snow, but she could not explain it in any other way.

"Will the naughty boys freeze and fall in pieces?" asked the young storks.

"No, they will not freeze and fall into pieces," said the mother, "but they will be very cold, and be obliged to sit all day in a dark, gloomy room, while we shall be flying about in foreign lands, where there are blooming flowers and warm sunshine."

Time passed on, and the young storks grew so large that they could stand upright in the nest and look about them. The father brought them, every day, beautiful frogs, little snakes, and all kinds of stork-dainties that he could find. And then, how funny it was to see the tricks he would perform to amuse them. He would lay his head quite round over his tail, and clatter with his beak, as if it had been a rattle; and then he would tell them stories all about the marshes and fens.

"Come," said the mother one day, "now you must learn to fly." And all the four young ones were obliged to come out on the top of the roof. Oh, how they tottered at first, and were obliged to balance themselves with their wings, or they would have fallen to the ground below.

"Look at me," said the mother, "you must hold your heads in this way, and place your feet so. Once, twice, once, twice—that is it. Now you will be able to take care of yourselves in the world."

Then she flew a little distance from them, and the young ones made a spring to follow her; but down they fell plump, for their bodies were still too heavy.

"I don't want to fly," said one of the young storks, creeping back into the nest. "I don't care about going to warm countries."

"Would you like to stay here and freeze when the winter comes?" said the mother, "or till the boys comes to hang you, or to roast you? Well then, I'll call them."

"Oh no, no," said the young stork, jumping out on the roof with the others; and now they were all attentive, and by the third day could fly a little. Then they began to fancy they could soar, so they tried to do so, resting on their wings, but they soon found themselves falling, and had to flap their wings as quickly as possible. The boys came again in the street singing their song:

Stork, stork, fly away.

"Shall we fly down, and pick their eyes out?" asked the young storks.

"No; leave them alone," said the mother. "Listen to me; that is much more important. Now then. One-two-three. Now to the right. One-two-three. Now to the left, round the chimney. There now, that was very good. That last flap of the wings was so easy and graceful, that I shall give you permission to fly with me tomorrow to the marshes. There will be a number of very superior storks there with their families, and I expect you to show them that my children are the best brought up of any who may be present. You must strut about proudly—it will look well and make you respected."

"But may we not punish those naughty boys?" asked the young storks.

"No; let them scream away as much as they like. You can fly from them now up high amid the clouds, and will be in the land of the pyramids when they are freezing, and have not a green leaf on the trees or an apple to eat."

"We will revenge ourselves," whispered the young storks to each other, as they again joined the exercising.

Of all the boys in the street who sang the mocking song about the storks, not one was so determined to go on with it as he who first began it. Yet he was a little fellow not more than six years old. To the young storks he appeared at least a hundred, for he was so much bigger than their father and mother. To be sure, storks cannot be expected to know how old children and grown-up people are. So they determined to have their revenge on this boy, because he began the song first and would keep on with it. The young storks were very angry, and grew worse as they grew older; so at last their mother was obliged to promise that they should be revenged, but not until the day of their departure.

"We must see first, how you acquit yourselves at the grand review," said she. "If you get on badly there, the general will thrust his beak through you, and you will be killed, as the boys said, though not exactly in the same manner. So we must wait and see."

"You shall see," said the young birds, and then they took such pains and practised so well every day, that at last it was quite a pleasure to see them fly so lightly and prettily. As soon as the autumn arrived, all the storks began to assemble together before taking their departure for warm countries during the winter. Then the review commenced. They flew over forests and villages to show what they could do, for they had a long journey before them. The young storks performed their part so well that they received a mark of honor, with frogs and snakes as a present. These presents were the best part of the affair, for they could eat the frogs and snakes, which they very quickly did.

"Now let us have our revenge," they cried.

"Yes, certainly," cried the mother stork. "I have thought upon the best way to be revenged. I know the pond in which all the little children lie, waiting till the storks come to take them to their parents. The prettiest little babies lie there dreaming more sweetly than they will ever dream in the time to come. All parents are glad to have a little child, and children are so pleased with a little brother or sister. Now we will fly to the pond and fetch a little baby for each of the children who did not sing that naughty song to make game of the storks."

"But the naughty boy, who began the song first, what shall we do to him?" cried the young storks.

"There lies in the pond a little dead baby who has dreamed itself to death," said the mother. "We will take it to the naughty boy, and he will cry because we have brought him a little dead brother. But you have not forgotten the good boy who said it was a shame to laugh at animals: we will take him a little brother and sister too, because he was good. He is called Peter, and you shall all be called Peter in future."

So they all did what their mother had arranged, and from that day, even till now, all the storks have been called Peter.

The Tinderbox

A soldier came marching along the high road: "Left, right—left, right." He had his knapsack on his back, and a sword at his side; he had been to the wars, and was now returning home.

As he walked on, he met a very frightful-looking old witch in the road. Her under-lip hung quite down on her breast, and she stopped and said, "Good evening, soldier; you have a very fine sword, and a large knapsack, and you are a real soldier; so you shall have as much money as ever you like."

"Thank you, old witch," said the soldier.

"Do you see that large tree," said the witch, pointing to a tree which stood beside them. "Well, it is quite hollow inside, and you must climb to the top, when you will see a hole, through which you can let yourself down into the tree to a great depth. I will tie a rope round your body, so that I can pull you up again when you call out to me."

"But what am I to do, down there in the tree?" asked the soldier.

"Get money," she replied, "for you must know that when you reach the ground under the tree, you will find yourself in a large hall, lighted up by three hundred lamps; you will then see three doors, which can be easily opened, for the keys are in all the locks. On entering the first of the chambers, to which these doors lead, you will see a large chest, standing in the middle of the floor, and upon it a dog seated, with a pair of eyes as large as teacups. But you need not be at all afraid of him; I will give you my blue checked apron, which you must spread upon the floor, and then boldly seize hold of the dog, and place him upon it. You can then open the chest, and take from it as many pence as you please, they are only copper pence; but if you would rather have silver money, you must go into the second chamber. Here you will find another dog, with eyes as big as millwheels; but do not let that trouble you. Place him upon my apron, and then take what money you please. If, however, you like gold best, enter the third chamber, where there is another chest full of it. The dog who sits on this chest is very dreadful; his eyes are as big as a tower, but do not mind him. If he also is placed upon my apron, he cannot hurt you, and you may take from the chest what gold you will."

"This is not a bad story," said the soldier; "but what am I to give you, you old witch? for, of course, you do not mean to tell me all this for nothing."

"No," said the witch; "but I do not ask for a single penny. Only promise to bring me an old tinderbox, which my grandmother left behind the last time she went down there."

"Very well; I promise. Now tie the rope round my body."

"Here it is," replied the witch; "and here is my blue checked apron."

As soon as the rope was tied, the soldier climbed up the tree, and let himself down through the hollow to the ground beneath; and here he found, as the witch had told him, a large hall, in which many hundred lamps were all burning. Then he opened the first door. "Ah!" there sat the dog, with the eyes as large as teacups, staring at him.

"You're a pretty fellow," said the soldier, seizing him, and placing him on the witch's apron, while he filled his pockets from the chest with as many pieces as they would hold. Then he closed the lid, seated the dog upon it again, and walked into another chamber, And, sure enough, there sat the dog with eyes as big as millwheels.

"You had better not look at me in that way," said the soldier; "you will make your eyes water;" and then he seated him also upon the apron, and opened the chest. But when he saw what a quantity of silver money it contained, he very quickly threw away all the coppers he had taken, and filled his pockets and his knapsack with nothing but silver.

Then he went into the third room, and there the dog was really hideous; his eyes were, truly, as big as towers, and they turned round and round in his head like wheels.

"Good morning," said the soldier, touching his cap, for he had never seen such a dog in his life. But after looking at him more closely, he thought he had been civil enough, so he placed him on the floor, and opened the chest. Good gracious, what a quantity of gold there was! enough to buy all the sugar-sticks of the sweet-stuff women; all the tin soldiers, whips, and rocking horses in the world, or even the whole town itself. There was, indeed, an immense quantity. So the soldier now threw away all the silver money he had taken, and filled his pockets and his knapsack with gold instead; and not only his pockets and his knapsack, but even his cap and boots, so that he could scarcely walk.

He was really rich now; so he replaced the dog on the chest, closed the door, and called up through the tree, "Now pull me out, you old witch."

"Have you got the tinderbox?" asked the witch.

"No; I declare I quite forgot it." So he went back and fetched the tinderbox, and then the witch drew him up out of the tree, and he stood again in the high road, with his pockets, his knapsack, his cap, and his boots full of gold.

"What are you going to do with the tinderbox?" asked the soldier.

"That is nothing to you," replied the witch; "you have the money, now give me the tinderbox."

"I tell you what," said the soldier, "if you don't tell me what you are going to do with it, I will draw my sword and cut off your head."

"No," said the witch.

The soldier immediately cut off her head, and there she lay on the ground. Then he tied up all his money in her apron, and slung it on his back like a bundle, put the tinderbox in his pocket, and walked off to the nearest town. It was a very nice town, and he put up at the best inn, and ordered a dinner of all his favorite dishes, for now he was rich and had plenty of money.

The servant, who cleaned his boots, thought they certainly were a shabby pair to be worn by such a rich gentleman, for he had not yet bought any new ones. The next day, however, he procured some good clothes and proper boots, so that our soldier soon became known as a fine gentleman, and the people visited him, and told him all the wonders that were to be seen in the town, and of the king's beautiful daughter, the princess.

"Where can I see her?" asked the soldier.

"She is not to be seen at all," they said; "she lives in a large copper castle, surrounded by walls and towers. No one but the king himself can pass in or out, for there has been a prophecy that she will marry a common soldier, and the king cannot bear to think of such a marriage."

"I should like very much to see her," thought the soldier; but he could not obtain permission to do so. However, he passed a very pleasant time; went to the theatre, drove in the king's garden, and gave a great deal of money to the poor, which was very good of him; he remembered what it had been in olden times to be without a shilling. Now he was rich, had fine clothes, and many friends, who all declared he was a fine fellow and a real gentleman, and all this gratified him exceedingly. But his money would not last forever; and as he spent and gave away a great deal daily, and received none, he found himself at last with only two shillings left. So he was obliged to leave his elegant rooms, and live in a little garret under the roof, where he had to clean his own boots, and even mend them with a large needle. None of his friends came to see him, there were too many stairs to mount up. One dark evening, he had not even a penny to buy a candle; then all at once he remembered that there was a piece of candle stuck in the tinderbox, which he had brought from the old tree, into which the witch had helped him.

He found the tinderbox, but no sooner had he struck a few sparks from the flint and steel, than the door flew open and the dog with eyes as big as teacups, whom he had seen while down in the tree, stood before him, and said, "What orders, master?"

"Hallo," said the soldier; "well this is a pleasant tinderbox, if it brings me all I wish for."

"Bring me some money," said he to the dog.

He was gone in a moment, and presently returned, carrying a large bag of coppers in his month. The soldier very soon discovered after this the value of the tinderbox. If he struck the flint once, the dog who sat on the chest of copper money made his appearance; if twice, the dog came from the chest of silver; and if three times, the dog with eyes like towers, who watched over the gold. The soldier had now plenty of money; he returned to his elegant rooms, and reappeared in his fine clothes, so that his friends knew him again directly, and made as much of him as before.

After a while he began to think it was very strange that no one could get a look at the princess. "Everyone says she is very beautiful," thought he to himself; "but what is the use of that if she is to be shut up in a copper castle surrounded by so many towers. Can I by any means get to see her? Stop! where is my tinderbox?" Then he struck a light, and in a moment the dog, with eyes as big as teacups, stood before him.

"It is midnight," said the soldier, "yet I should very much like to see the princess, if only for a moment."

The dog disappeared instantly, and before the soldier could even look round, he returned with the princess. She was lying on the dog's back asleep, and looked so lovely, that everyone who saw her would know she was a real princess. The soldier could not help kissing her, true soldier as he was. Then the dog ran back with the princess; but in the morning, while at breakfast with the king and queen, she told them what a singular dream she had had during the night, of a dog and a soldier, that she had ridden on the dog's back, and been kissed by the soldier.

"That is a very pretty story, indeed," said the queen. So the next night one of the old ladies of the court was set to watch by the princess's bed, to discover whether it really was a dream, or what else it might be.

The soldier longed very much to see the princess once more, so he sent for the dog again in the night to fetch her, and to run with her as fast as ever he could. But the old lady put on water boots, and ran after him as quickly as he did, and found that he carried the princess into a large house. She thought it would help her to remember the place if she made a large cross on the door with a piece of chalk. Then she went home to bed, and the dog presently returned with the princess. But when he saw that a cross had been made on the door of the house, where the soldier lived, he took another piece of chalk and made crosses on all the doors in the town, so that the lady-in-waiting might not be able to find out the right door.

Early the next morning the king and queen accompanied the lady and all the officers of the household, to see where the princess had been.

"Here it is," said the king, when they came to the first door with a cross on it.

"No, my dear husband, it must be that one," said the queen, pointing to a second door having a cross also.

"And here is one, and there is another!" they all exclaimed; for there were crosses on all the doors in every direction.

So they felt it would be useless to search any farther. But the queen was a very clever woman; she could do a great deal more than merely ride in a carriage. She took her large gold scissors, cut a piece of silk into squares, and made a neat little bag. This bag she filled with buckwheat flour, and tied it round the princess's neck; and then she cut a small hole in the bag, so that the flour might be scattered on the ground as the princess went along. During the night, the dog came again and carried the princess on his back, and ran with her to the soldier, who loved her very much, and wished that he had been a prince, so that he might have her for a wife. The dog did not observe how the flour ran out of the bag all the way from the castle wall to the soldier's house, and even up to the window, where he had climbed with the princess. Therefore in the morning the king and queen found out where their daughter had been, and the soldier was taken up and put in prison.

Oh, how dark and disagreeable it was as he sat there, and the people said to him, "Tomorrow you will be hanged." It was not very pleasant news, and besides, he had left the tinderbox at the inn. In the morning he could see through the iron grating of the little window how the people were hastening out of the town to see him hanged; he heard the drums beating, and saw the soldiers marching. Everyone ran out to look at them, and a shoemaker's boy, with a leather apron and slippers on, galloped by so fast, that one of his slippers flew off and struck against the wall where the soldier sat looking through the iron grating. "Hallo, you shoemaker's boy, you need not be in such a hurry," cried the soldier to him. "There will be nothing to see till I come; but if you will run to the house where I have been living, and bring me my tinderbox, you shall have four shillings, but you must put your best foot foremost."

The shoemaker's boy liked the idea of getting the four shillings, so he ran very fast and fetched the tinderbox, and gave it to the soldier. And now we shall see what happened. Outside the town a large gibbet had been erected, round which stood the soldiers and several thousands of people. The king and the queen sat on splendid thrones opposite to the judges and the whole council. The soldier already stood on the ladder; but as they were about to place the rope around his neck, he said that an innocent request was often granted to a poor criminal before he suffered death. He wished very much to smoke a pipe, as it would be the last pipe he should ever smoke in the world. The king could not refuse this request, so the soldier took his tinderbox, and struck fire, once, twice, thrice,—and there in a moment stood all the dogs; the one with eyes as big as teacups, the one with eyes as large as millwheels, and the third, whose eyes were like towers. "Help me now, that I may not be hanged," cried the soldier.

And the dogs fell upon the judges and all the councillors; seized one by the legs, and another by the nose, and tossed them many feet high in the air, so that they fell down and were dashed to pieces.

"I will not be touched," said the king. But the largest dog seized him, as well as the queen, and threw them after the others. Then the soldiers and all the people were afraid, and cried, "Good soldier, you shall be our king, and you shall marry the beautiful princess."

So they placed the soldier in the king's carriage, and the three dogs ran on in front and cried "Hurrah!" and the little boys whistled through their fingers, and the soldiers presented arms. The princess came out of the copper castle, and became queen, which was very pleasing to her. The wedding festivities lasted a whole week, and the dogs sat at the table, and stared with all their eyes.

The Pen and the Inkstand

In a poet's room, where his inkstand stood on the table, the remark was once made, "It is wonderful what can be brought out of an inkstand. What will come next? It is indeed wonderful."

"Yes, certainly," said the inkstand to the pen, and to the other articles that stood on the table; "that's what I always say. It is wonderful and extraordinary what a number of things come out of me. It's quite incredible, and I really don't know what is coming next when that man dips his pen into me. One drop out of me is enough for half a page of paper, and what cannot half a page contain? From me, all the works of a poet are produced; all those imaginary characters whom people fancy they have known or met. All the deep feeling, the humor, and the vivid pictures of nature. I myself don't understand how it is, for I am not acquainted with nature, but it is certainly in me. From me have gone forth to the world those wonderful descriptions of troops of charming maidens, and of brave knights on prancing steeds; of the halt and the blind, and I know not what more, for I assure you I never think of these things."

"There you are right," said the pen, "for you don't think at all; if you did, you would see that you can only provide the means. You give the fluid that I may place upon the paper what dwells in me, and what I wish to bring to light. It is the pen that writes: no man doubts that; and, indeed, most people understand as much about poetry as an old inkstand."

"You have had very little experience," replied the inkstand. "You have hardly been in service a week, and are already half worn out. Do you imagine you are a poet? You are only a servant, and before you came I had many like you, some of the goose family, and others of English manufacture. I know a quill pen as well as I know a steel one. I have had both sorts in my service, and I shall have many more when he comes—the man who performs the mechanical part—and writes down what he obtains from me. I should like to know what will be the next thing he gets out of me."

"Inkpot!" exclaimed the pen contemptuously.

Late in the evening the poet came home. He had been to a concert, and had been quite enchanted with the admirable performance of a famous violin player whom he had heard there. The performer had produced from his instrument a richness of tone that sometimes sounded like tinkling waterdrops or rolling pearls; sometimes like the birds twittering in chorus, and then rising and swelling in sound like the wind through the fir trees. The poet felt as if his own heart were weeping, but in tones of melody like the sound of a woman's voice. It seemed not only the strings, but every part of the instrument from which these sounds were produced. It was a wonderful performance and a difficult piece, and yet the bow seemed to glide across the strings so easily that it was as if anyone could do it who tried. Even the violin and the bow appeared to perform independently of their master who guided them; it was as if soul and spirit had been breathed into the instrument, so the audience forgot the performer in the beautiful sounds he produced. Not so the poet; he remembered him, and named him, and wrote down his thoughts on the subject. "How foolish it would be for the violin and the bow to boast of their performance, and yet we men often commit that folly. The poet, the artist, the man of science in his laboratory, the general,—we all do it; and yet we are only the instruments which the Almighty uses; to Him alone the honor is due. We have nothing of ourselves of which we should be proud." Yes, this is what the poet wrote down. He wrote it in the form of a parable, and called it "The Master and the Instruments."

"That is what you have got, madam," said the pen to the inkstand, when the two were alone again. "Did you hear him read aloud what I had written down?"

"Yes, what I gave you to write," retorted the inkstand. "That was a cut at you because of your conceit. To think that you could not understand that you were being quizzed. I gave you a cut from within me. Surely I must know my own satire."

"Ink-pitcher!" cried the pen.

"Writing-stick!" retorted the inkstand. And each of them felt satisfied that he had given a good answer. It is pleasing to be convinced that you have settled a matter by your reply; it is something to make you sleep well, and they both slept well upon it. But the poet did not sleep. Thoughts rose up within him like the tones of the violin, falling like pearls, or rushing like the strong wind through the forest. He understood his own heart in these thoughts; they were as a ray from the mind of the Great Master of all minds.

"To Him be all the honor."

The Teapot

There was once a proud teapot; it was proud of being porcelain, proud of its long spout, proud of its broad handle. It had something before and behind—the spout before and the handle behind—and that was what it talked about. But it did not talk of its lid, which was cracked and riveted; these were defects, and one does not talk of one's defects, for there are plenty of others to do that. The cups, the cream pot, and the sugar bowl, the whole tea service, would think much oftener of the lid's imperfections—and talk about them—than of the sound handle and the remarkable spout. The teapot knew it.

"I know you," it said within itself. "I know, too, my imperfection, and I am well aware that in that very thing is seen my humility, my modesty. Imperfections we all have, but we also have compensations. The cups have a handle, the sugar bowl a lid; I have both, and one thing besides, in front, which they can never have. I have a spout, and that makes me the queen of the tea table. I spread abroad a blessing on thirsting mankind, for in me the Chinese leaves are brewed in the boiling, tasteless water."

All this said the teapot in its fresh young life. It stood on the table that was spread for tea; it was lifted by a very delicate hand, but the delicate hand was awkward. The teapot fell, the spout snapped off, and the handle snapped off. The lid was no worse to speak of; the worst had been spoken of that.

The teapot lay in a swoon on the floor, while the boiling water ran out of it. It was a horrid shame, but the worst was that everybody jeered at it; they jeered at the teapot and not at the awkward hand.

"I never shall forget that experience," said the teapot, when it afterward talked of its life. "I was called an invalid, and placed in a corner, and the next day was given to a woman who begged for victuals. I fell into poverty, and stood dumb both outside and in. But then, just as I was, began my better life. One can be one thing and still become quite another.

"Earth was placed in me. For a teapot, this is the same as being buried, but in the earth was placed a flower bulb. Who placed it there, who gave it, I know not; but given it was, and it became a compensation for the Chinese leaves and the boiling water, a compensation for the broken handle and spout.

"And the bulb lay in the earth, the bulb lay in me; it became my heart, my living heart, such as I had never before possessed. There was life in me, power and might. The heart pulsed, and the bulb put forth sprouts; it was the springing up of thoughts and feelings which burst forth into flower.

"I saw it, I bore it, I forgot myself in its delight. Blessed is it to forget oneself in another. The flower gave me no thanks; it did not think of me. It was admired and praised, and I was glad at that. How happy it must have been! One day I heard someone say that the flower deserved a better pot. I was thumped hard on my back, which was a great affliction, and the flower was put into a better pot. I was thrown out into the yard, where I lie as an old potsherd. But I have the memory, and that I can never lose."

The Flying Trunk

There was once a merchant who was so rich that he could have paved the whole street with gold, and would even then have had enough for a small alley. But he did not do so; he knew the value of money better than to use it in this way. So clever was he, that every shilling he put out brought him a crown; and so he continued till he died. His son inherited his wealth, and he lived a merry life with it; he went to a masquerade every night, made kites out of five pound notes, and threw pieces of gold into the sea instead of stones, making ducks and drakes of them. In this manner he soon lost all his money. At last he had nothing left but a pair of slippers, an old dressing gown, and four shillings. And now all his friends deserted him, they could not walk with him in the streets; but one of them, who was very good-natured, sent him an old trunk with this message, "Pack up!" "Yes," he said, "it is all very well to say, 'pack up,'" but he had nothing left to pack up, therefore he seated himself in the trunk.

It was a very wonderful trunk; no sooner did anyone press on the lock than the trunk could fly. He shut the lid and pressed the lock, when away flew the trunk up the chimney with the merchant's son in it, right up into the clouds. Whenever the bottom of the trunk cracked, he was in a great fright, for if the trunk fell to pieces he would have made a tremendous somerset over the trees. However, he got safely in his trunk to the land of Turkey. He hid the trunk in the wood under some dry leaves, and then went into the town: he could so this very well, for the Turks always go about dressed in dressing gowns and slippers, as he was himself. He happened to meet a nurse with a little child. "I say, you Turkish nurse," cried he, "what castle is that near the town, with the windows placed so high?"

"The king's daughter lives there," she replied, "it has been prophesied that she will be very unhappy about a lover, and therefore no one is allowed to visit her, unless the king and queen are present."

"Thank you," said the merchant's son. So he went back to the wood, seated himself in his trunk, flew up to the roof of the castle, and crept through the window into the princess's room. She lay on the sofa asleep, and she was so beautiful that the merchant's son could not help kissing her. Then she awoke, and was very much frightened; but he told her he was a Turkish angel, who had come down through the air to see her, which pleased her very much. He sat down by her side and talked to her: he said her eyes were like beautiful dark lakes, in which the thoughts swam about like little mermaids, and he told her that her forehead was a snowy mountain, which contained splendid halls full of pictures. And then he related to her about the stork who brings the beautiful children from the rivers. These were delightful stories; and when he asked the princess if she would marry him, she consented immediately.

"But you must come on Saturday," she said; "for then the king and queen will take tea with me. They will be very proud when they find that I am going to marry a Turkish angel; but you must think of some very pretty stories to tell them, for my parents like to hear stories better than anything. My mother prefers one that is deep and moral; but my father likes something funny, to make him laugh."

"Very well," he replied, "I shall bring you no other marriage portion than a story," and so they parted. But the princess gave him a sword which was studded with gold coins, and these he could use.

Then he flew away to the town and bought a new dressing gown, and afterwards returned to the wood, where he composed a story, so as to be ready for Saturday, which was no easy matter. It was ready however by Saturday, when he went to see the princess. The king, and queen, and the whole court, were at tea with the princess; and he was received with great politeness.

"Will you tell us a story?" said the queen, "one that is instructive and full of deep learning."

"Yes, but with something in it to laugh at," said the king.

"Certainly," he replied, and commenced at once, asking them to listen attentively. "There was once a bundle of matches that were exceedingly proud of their high descent. Their genealogical tree, that is, a large pine tree from which they had been cut, was at one time a large, old tree in the wood. The matches now lay between a tinderbox and an old iron saucepan, and were talking about their youthful days. 'Ah! then we grew on the green boughs, and were as green as they; every morning and evening we were fed with diamond drops of dew. Whenever the sun shone, we felt his warm rays, and the little birds would relate stories to us as they sung. We knew that we were rich, for the other trees only wore their green dress in summer, but our family

were able to array themselves in green, summer and winter. But the woodcutter came, like a great revolution, and our family fell under the axe. The head of the house obtained a situation as mainmast in a very fine ship, and can sail round the world when he will. The other branches of the family were taken to different places, and our office now is to kindle a light for common people. This is how such high-born people as we came to be in a kitchen.'

"'Mine has been a very different fate,' said the iron pot, which stood by the matches; 'from my first entrance into the world I have been used to cooking and scouring. I am the first in this house, when anything solid or useful is required. My only pleasure is to be made clean and shining after dinner, and to sit in my place and have a little sensible conversation with my neighbors. All of us, excepting the water bucket, which is sometimes taken into the courtyard, live here together within these four walls. We get our news from the market-basket, but he sometimes tells us very unpleasant things about the people and the government. Yes, and one day an old pot was so alarmed, that he fell down and was broken to pieces. He was a liberal, I can tell you.'

"'You are talking too much,' said the tinderbox, and the steel struck against the flint till some sparks flew out, crying, 'We want a merry evening, don't we?'

"'Yes, of course,' said the matches, 'let us talk about those who are the highest born.'

"'No, I don't like to be always talking of what we are,' remarked the saucepan; 'let us think of some other amusement; I will begin. We will tell something that has happened to ourselves; that will be very easy, and interesting as well. On the Baltic Sea, near the Danish shore.'

"'What a pretty commencement!' said the plates; 'we shall all like that story, I am sure.'

"'Yes; well in my youth, I lived in a quiet family, where the furniture was polished, the floors scoured, and clean curtains put up every fortnight.'

"'What an interesting way you have of relating a story,' said the carpet broom; 'it is easy to perceive that you have been a great deal in women's society, there is something so pure runs through what you say.'

"'That is quite true,' said the water bucket; and he made a spring with joy, and splashed some water on the floor.

"Then the saucepan went on with his story, and the end was as good as the beginning.

"The plates rattled with pleasure, and the carpet broom brought some green parsley out of the dust-hole and crowned the saucepan, for he knew it would vex the others; and he thought, 'If I crown him today he will crown me tomorrow.'

"'Now, let us have a dance,' said the fire tongs; and then how they danced and stuck up one leg in the air. The chair cushion in the corner burst with laughter when she saw it.

"'Shall I be crowned now?' asked the fire tongs; so the broom found another wreath for the tongs.

"'They were only common people after all,' thought the matches. The tea urn was now asked to sing, but she said she had a cold, and could not sing without boiling heat. They all thought this was affectation, and because she did not wish to sing excepting in the parlor, when on the table with the grand people.

"In the window sat an old quill pen, with which the maid generally wrote. There was nothing remarkable about the pen, excepting that it had been dipped too deeply in the ink, but it was proud of that.

"'If the tea urn won't sing,' said the pen, 'she can leave it alone; there is a nightingale in a cage who can sing; she has not been taught much, certainly, but we need not say anything this evening about that.'

"'I think it highly improper,' said the teakettle, who was kitchen singer, and half-brother to the tea urn, 'that a rich foreign bird should be listened to here. Is it patriotic? Let the market-basket decide what is right.'

"'I certainly am vexed,' said the basket; 'inwardly vexed, more than any one can imagine. Are we spending the evening properly? Would it not be more sensible to put the house in order? If each were in his own place I would lead a game; this would be quite another thing.'

"'Let us act a play,' said they all. At the same moment the door opened, and the maid came in. Then not one stirred; they all remained quite still; yet, at the same time, there was not a single pot amongst them who had not a high opinion of himself, and of what he could do if he chose.

"'Yes, if we had chosen,' they each thought, 'we might have spent a very pleasant evening.'

"The maid took the matches and lighted them; dear me, how they sputtered and blazed up!

"'Now then,' they thought, 'everyone will see that we are the first. How we shine; what a light we give!' Even while they spoke their light went out."

"What a capital story," said the queen, "I feel as if I were really in the kitchen, and could see the matches; yes, you shall marry our daughter."

"Certainly," said the king, "thou shalt have our daughter." The king said thou to him because he was going to be one of the family. The wedding day was fixed, and, on the evening before, the whole city was illuminated. Cakes and sweetmeats were thrown among the people. The street boys stood on tiptoe and shouted "hurrah," and whistled between their fingers; altogether it was a very splendid affair.

"I will give them another treat," said the merchant's son. So he went and bought rockets and crackers, and all sorts of fireworks that could be thought of, packed them in his trunk, and flew up with it into the air. What a whizzing and popping they made as they went off! The Turks, when they saw such a sight in the air, jumped so high that their slippers flew about their ears. It was easy to believe after this that the princess was really going to marry a Turkish angel.

As soon as the merchant's son had come down in his flying trunk to the wood after the fireworks, he thought, "I will go back into the town now, and hear what they think of the entertainment." It was very natural that he should wish to know. And what strange things people did say, to be sure! Everyone whom he questioned had a different tale to tell, though they all thought it very beautiful.

"'I saw the Turkish angel myself," said one; "he had eyes like glittering stars, and a head like foaming water."

"He flew in a mantle of fire," cried another, "and lovely little cherubs peeped out from the folds."

He heard many more fine things about himself, and that the next day he was to be married. After this he went back to the forest to rest himself in his trunk. It had disappeared! A spark from the fireworks which remained had set it on fire; it was burnt to ashes! So the merchant's son could not fly any more, nor go to meet his bride. She stood all day on the roof waiting for him, and most likely she is waiting there still; while he wanders through the world telling fairy tales, but none of them so amusing as the one he related about the matches.

The Last Pearl

We are in a rich, happy house, where the master, the servants, the friends of the family are full of joy and felicity. For on this day a son and heir has been born, and mother and child are doing well. The lamp in the bedchamber had been partly shaded, and the windows were covered with heavy curtains of some costly silken material. The carpet was thick and soft, like a covering of moss. Everything invited to slumber, everything had a charming look of repose; and so the nurse had discovered, for she slept; and well she might sleep, while everything around her told of happiness and blessing. The guardian angel of the house leaned against the head of the bed; while over the child was spread, as it were, a net of shining stars, and each star was a pearl of happiness. All the good stars of life had brought their gifts to the newly born; here sparkled health, wealth, fortune, and love; in short, there seemed to be everything for which man could wish on earth.

"Everything has been bestowed here," said the guardian angel.

"No, not everything," said a voice near him—the voice of the good angel of the child; "one fairy has not yet brought her gift, but she will, even if years should elapse, she will bring her gift; it is the last pearl that is wanting."

"Wanting!" cried the guardian angel; "nothing must be wanting here; and if it is so, let us fetch it; let us seek the powerful fairy; let us go to her."

"She will come, she will come someday unsought!"

"Her pearl must not be missing; it must be there, that the crown, when worn, may be complete. Where is she to be found? Where does she dwell?" said the guardian angel. "Tell me, and I will procure the pearl."

"Will you do that?" replied the good angel of the child. "Then I will lead you to her directly, wherever she may be. She has no abiding place;

she rules in the palace of the emperor, sometimes she enters the peasant's humble cot; she passes no one without leaving a trace of her presence. She brings her gift with her, whether it is a world or a bauble. To this child she must come. You think that to wait for this time would be long and useless. Well, then, let us go for this pearl—the only one lacking amidst all this wealth."

Then hand-in-hand they floated away to the spot where the fairy was now lingering. It was in a large house with dark windows and empty rooms, in which a peculiar stillness reigned. A whole row of windows stood open, so that the rude wind could enter at its pleasure, and the long white curtains waved to and fro in the current of air. In the centre of one of the rooms stood an open coffin, in which lay the body of a woman, still in the bloom of youth and very beautiful. Fresh roses were scattered over her. The delicate folded hands and the noble face glorified in death by the solemn, earnest look, which spoke of an entrance into a better world, were alone visible. Around the coffin stood the husband and children, a whole troop, the youngest in the father's arms. They were come to take a last farewell look of their mother. The husband kissed her hand, which now lay like a withered leaf, but which a short time before had been diligently employed in deeds of love for them all. Tears of sorrow rolled down their cheeks, and fell in heavy drops on the floor, but not a word was spoken. The silence which reigned here expressed a world of grief. With silent steps, still sobbing, they left the room. A burning light remained in the room, and a long, red wick rose far above the flame, which fluttered in the draught of air. Strange men came in and placed the lid of the coffin over the dead, and drove the nails firmly in; while the blows of the hammer resounded through the house, and echoed in the hearts that were bleeding.

"Whither art thou leading me?" asked the guardian angel. "Here dwells no fairy whose pearl could be counted amongst the best gifts of life."

"Yes, she is here; here in this sacred hour," replied the angel, pointing to a corner of the room; and there—where in her lifetime, the mother had taken her seat amidst flowers and pictures: in that spot, where she, like the blessed fairy of the house, had welcomed husband, children, and friends, and, like a sunbeam, had spread joy and cheerfulness around her, the centre and heart of them all—there, in that very spot, sat a strange woman, clothed in long, flowing garments, and occupying the place of the dead wife and mother. It was the fairy, and her name was "Sorrow." A hot tear rolled into her lap, and formed itself into a pearl, glowing with all the colors of the rainbow. The angel seized it: the pearl glittered like a star with seven-fold radiance. The pearl of Sorrow, the last, which must not be wanting, increases the lustre, and explains the meaning of all the other pearls.

"Do you see the shimmer of the rainbow, which unites earth to heaven?" So has there been a bridge built between this world and the next. Through the night of the grave we gaze upwards beyond the stars to the end of all things. Then we glance at the pearl of Sorrow, in which are concealed the wings which shall carry us away to eternal happiness.

The Loving Pair

A whipping Top and a Ball lay close together in a drawer among other playthings. One day the Top said to the Ball, "Since we are living so much together, why should we not be lovers?"

But the Ball, being made of Morocco leather, thought herself a very high-bred lady, and would hear nothing of such a proposal. On the next day the little boy to whom the playthings belonged came to the drawer; he painted the Top red and yellow, and drove a bright brass nail right through the head of it; it looked very smart indeed as it spun around after that.

"Look at me," said he to the Ball. "What do you say to me now; why should we not make a match of it, and become man and wife? We suit each other so well! You can jump and I can dance. There would not be a happier pair in the whole world!"

"Do you think so?" said the Ball. "Perhaps you do not know that my father and mother were Morocco slippers, and that I have a Spanish cork in my body!"

"Yes, but then I am made of mahogany," said the Top; "the Mayor himself turned me. He has a turning lathe of his own, and he took great pleasure in making me."

"Can I trust you in this?" asked the Ball.

"May I never be whipped again, if what I tell you is not true," returned the Top.

"You plead your cause well," said the Ball; "but I am not free to listen to your proposal. I am as good as engaged to a swallow. As often as I fly up into the air, he puts his head out of his nest, and says, 'Will you?' In my heart I have said Yes to him, and that is almost the same as an engagement; but I'll promise never to forget you."

"A deal of good that will do me," said the Top, and they left off speaking to each other.

Next day the Ball was taken out. The Top saw it fly like a bird into the air—so high that it passed quite out of sight. It came back again; but each time that it touched the earth, it sprang higher than before. This must have been either from its longing to mount higher, like the swallow, or because it had the Spanish cork in its body. On the ninth time the little Ball did not return. The boy sought and sought, but all in vain, for it was gone.

"I know very well where she is," sighed the Top. "She is in the swallow's nest, celebrating her wedding."

The more the Top thought of this the more lovely the Ball became to him; that she could not be his bride seemed to make his love for her the greater. She had preferred another rather than himself, but he could not forget her. He twirled round and round, spinning and humming, but always thinking of the Ball, who grew more and more beautiful the more he thought of her. And thus several years passed—it came to be an old love—and now the Top was no longer young!

One day he was gilded all over; never in his life had he been half so handsome. He was now a golden top, and bravely he spun, humming all the time. But once he sprang too high—and was gone!

They looked everywhere for him—even in the cellar—but he was nowhere to be found. Where was he?

He had jumped into the dustbin, and lay among cabbage stalks, sweepings, dust, and all sorts of rubbish that had fallen from the gutter in the roof.

"Alas! my gay gilding will soon be spoiled here. What sort of trumpery can I have got among?" And then he peeped at a long cabbage stalk which lay much too near him, and at something strange and round, which appeared like an apple, but was not. It was an old Ball that must have lain for years in the gutter, and been soaked through and through with water.

"Thank goodness! at last I see an equal; one of my own sort, with whom I can talk," said the Ball, looking earnestly at the gilded Top. "I am myself made of real morocco, sewed together by a young lady's hands, and within my body is a Spanish cork; though no one would think it now. I was very near marrying the swallow, when by a sad chance I fell into the gutter on the roof. I have lain there five years, and I am now wet through and through. You may think what a wearisome situation it has been for a young lady like me."

The Top made no reply. The more he thought of his old love, and the more he heard, the more sure he became that this was indeed she.

Then came the housemaid to empty the dustbin. "Hullo!" she cried; "why, here's the gilt Top." And so the Top was brought again to the play-room, to be used and honored as before, while nothing was again heard of the Ball.

And the Top never spoke again of his old love—the feeling must have passed away. And it is not strange, when the object of it has lain five years in a gutter, and been drenched through and through, and when one meets her again in a dustbin.

Holger Danske

In Denmark there stands an old castle named Kronenburg, close by the Sound of Elsinore, where large ships, both English, Russian, and Prussian, pass by hundreds every day. And they salute the old castle with cannons, "Boom, boom," which is as if they said, "Good day." And the cannons of the old castle answer "Boom," which means "Many thanks." In winter no ships sail by, for the whole Sound is covered with ice as far as the Swedish coast, and has quite the appearance of a high road. The Danish and the Swedish flags wave, and Danes and Swedes say, "Good day," and "Thank you" to each other, not with cannons, but with a friendly shake of the hand; and they exchange white bread and biscuits with each other, because foreign articles taste the best.

But the most beautiful sight of all is the old castle of Kronenburg, where Holger Danske sits in the deep, dark cellar, into which no one goes. He is clad in iron and steel, and rests his head on his strong arm; his long beard hangs down upon the marble table, into which it has become firmly rooted; he sleeps and dreams, but in his dreams he sees everything that happens in Denmark. On each Christmas Eve an angel comes to him and tells him that all he has dreamed is true, and that he may go to sleep again in peace, as Denmark is not yet in any real danger; but should danger ever come, then Holger Danske will rouse himself, and the table will burst asunder as he draws out his beard. Then he will come forth in his strength, and strike a blow that shall sound in all the countries of the world.

An old grandfather sat and told his little grandson all this about Holger Danske, and the boy knew that what his grandfather told him must be true. As the old man related this story, he was carving an image in wood to represent Holger Danske, to be fastened to the prow

of a ship; for the old grandfather was a carver in wood, that is, one who carved figures for the heads of ships, according to the names given to them. And now he had carved Holger Danske, who stood there erect and proud, with his long beard, holding in one hand his broad battle-axe, while with the other he leaned on the Danish arms. The old grandfather told the little boy a great deal about Danish men and women who had distinguished themselves in olden times, so that he fancied he knew as much even as Holger Danske himself, who, after all, could only dream; and when the little fellow went to bed, he thought so much about it that he actually pressed his chin against the counterpane, and imagined that he had a long beard which had become rooted to it. But the old grandfather remained sitting at his work and carving away at the last part of it, which was the Danish arms. And when he had finished he looked at the whole figure, and thought of all he had heard and read, and what he had that evening related to his little grandson. Then he nodded his head, wiped his spectacles and put them on, and said, "Ah, yes; Holger Danske will not appear in my lifetime, but the boy who is in bed there may very likely live to see him when the event really comes to pass." And the old grandfather nodded again; and the more he looked at Holger Danske, the more satisfied he felt that he had carved a good image of him. It seemed to glow with the color of life; the armor glittered like iron and steel.

The hearts in the Danish arms grew more and more red; while the lions, with gold crowns on their heads, were leaping up. "That is the most beautiful coat of arms in the world," said the old man. "The lions represent strength; and the hearts, gentleness and love." And as he gazed on the uppermost lion, he thought of King Canute, who chained great England to Denmark's throne; and he looked at the second lion, and thought of Waldemar, who untied Denmark and conquered the Vandals. The third lion reminded him of Margaret, who united Denmark, Sweden, and Norway. But when he gazed at the red hearts, their colors glowed more deeply, even as flames, and his memory followed each in turn. The first led him to a dark, narrow prison, in which sat a prisoner, a beautiful woman, daughter of Christian the Fourth, Eleanor Ulfeld, and the flame became a rose on her bosom, and its blossoms were not more pure than the heart of this noblest and best of all Danish women.

"Ah, yes; that is indeed a noble heart in the Danish arms," said the grandfather, and his spirit followed the second flame, which carried him out to sea, where cannons roared and the ships lay shrouded in smoke, and the flaming heart attached itself to the breast of Hvitfeldt in the form of the ribbon of an order, as he blew himself and his ship into the air in order to save the fleet. And the third flame led him to Greenland's wretched

Frie

huts, where the preacher, Hans Egede, ruled with love in every word and action. The flame was as a star on his breast, and added another heart to the Danish arms. And as the old grandfather's spirit followed the next hovering flame, he knew whither it would lead him. In a peasant woman's humble room stood Frederick the Sixth, writing his name with chalk on the beam. The flame trembled on his breast and in his heart, and it was in the peasant's room that his heart became one for the Danish arms.

The old grandfather wiped his eyes, for he had known King Frederick, with his silvery locks and his honest blue eyes, and had lived for him, and he folded his hands and remained for some time silent. Then his daughter came to him and said it was getting late, that he ought to rest for a while, and that the supper was on the table.

"What you have been carving is very beautiful, grandfather," said she. "Holger Danske and the old coat of arms; it seems to me as if I have seen the face somewhere."

"No, that is impossible," replied the old grandfather; "but I have seen it, and I have tried to carve it in wood, as I have retained it in my memory. It was a long time ago, while the English fleet lay in the roads, on the second of April, when we showed that we were true, ancient Danes. I was on board the Denmark, in Steene Bille's squadron; I had a man by my side whom even the cannon balls seemed to fear. He sung old songs in a merry voice, and fired and fought as if he were something more than a man. I still remember his face, but from whence he came, or whither he went, I know not; no one knows. I have often thought it might have been Holger Danske himself, who had swam down to us from Kronenburg to help us in the hour of danger. That was my idea, and there stands his likeness."

The wooden figure threw a gigantic shadow on the wall, and even on part of the ceiling; it seemed as if the real Holger Danske stood behind it, for the shadow moved; but this was no doubt caused by the flame of the lamp not burning steadily. Then the daughter-in-law kissed the old grandfather, and led him to a large armchair by the table; and she, and her husband, who was the son of the old man and the father of the little boy who lay in bed, sat down to supper with him. And the old grandfather talked of the Danish lions and the Danish hearts, emblems of strength and gentleness, and explained quite clearly that there is another strength than that which lies in a sword, and he pointed to a shelf where lay a number of old books, and amongst them a collection of Holberg's plays, which are much read and are so clever and amusing that it is easy to fancy we have known the people of those days, who are described in them.

"He knew how to fight also," said the old man; "for he lashed the follies and prejudices of people during his whole life."

Then the grandfather nodded to a place above the looking glass, where hung an almanac, with a representation of the Round Tower upon it, and said "Tycho Brahe was another of those who used a sword, but not one to cut into the flesh and bone, but to make the way of the stars of heaven clear, and plain to be understood. And then he whose father belonged to my calling—yes, he, the son of the old image-carver, he whom we ourselves have seen, with his silvery locks and his broad shoulders, whose name is known in all lands; yes, he was a sculptor, while I am only a carver. Holger Danske can appear in marble, so that people in all countries of the world may hear of the strength of Denmark. Now let us drink the health of Bertel."

But the little boy in bed saw plainly the old castle of Kronenburg, and the Sound of Elsinore, and Holger Danske, far down in the cellar, with his beard rooted to the table, and dreaming of everything that was passing above him.

And Holger Danske did dream of the little humble room in which the image-carver sat; he heard all that had been said, and he nodded in his dream, saying, "Ah, yes, remember me, you Danish people, keep me in your memory, I will come to you in the hour of need."

The bright morning light shone over Kronenburg, and the wind brought the sound of the hunting-horn across from the neighboring shores. The ships sailed by and saluted the castle with the boom of the cannon, and Kronenburg returned the salute, "Boom, boom." But the roaring cannons did not awake Holger Danske, for they meant only "Good morning," and "Thank you." They must fire in another fashion before he awakes; but wake he will, for there is energy yet in Holger Danske.

Ib and Little Christina

In the forest that extends from the banks of the Gudenau, in North Jutland, a long way into the country, and not far from the clear stream, rises a great ridge of land, which stretches through the wood like a wall. Westward of this ridge, and not far from the river, stands a farmhouse, surrounded by such poor land that the sandy soil shows itself between the scanty ears of rye and wheat which grow in it. Some years have passed since the people who lived here cultivated these fields; they kept three sheep, a pig, and two oxen; in fact they maintained themselves very well, they had quite enough to live upon, as people generally have who are content with their lot. They even could have afforded to keep two horses, but it was a saying among the farmers in those parts, "The horse eats himself up;" that is to say, he eats as much as he earns. Jeppe Jans cultivated his fields in summer, and in the winter he made wooden shoes. He also had an assistant, a lad who understood as well as he himself did how to make wooden shoes strong, but light, and in the fashion. They carved shoes and spoons, which paid well; therefore no one could justly call Jeppe Jans and his family poor people. Little Ib, a boy of seven years old and the only child, would sit by, watching the workmen, or cutting a stick, and sometimes his finger instead of the stick. But one day Ib succeeded so well in his carving that he made two pieces of wood look really like two little wooden shoes, and he determined to give them as a present to Little Christina.

"And who was Little Christina?" She was the boatman's daughter, graceful and delicate as the child of a gentleman; had she been dressed differently, no one would have believed that she lived in a hut on the neighboring heath with her father. He was a widower, and earned his living by carrying firewood in his large boat from the forest to the eel pond and eel weir, on the estate of Silkborg, and sometimes even to the distant town of Randers. There was no one under whose care he could leave Little Christina; so she was almost always with him in his boat, or playing in the wood among the blossoming heath, or picking the ripe wild berries. Sometimes, when her father had to go as far as the town, he would take Little Christina, who was a year younger than Ib, across the heath to the cottage of Jeppe Jans, and leave her there. Ib and Christina agreed together in everything; they divided their bread and berries when they were hungry; they were partners in digging their little gardens; they ran, and crept, and played about everywhere. Once they wandered a long way into the forest, and even ventured together to climb the high ridge. Another time they found a few snipes' eggs in the wood, which was a great event. Ib had never been on the heath where Christina's father lived, nor on the river; but at last came an opportunity. Christina's father invited him to go for a sail in his boat; and the evening before, he accompanied the boatman across the heath to his house. The next morning early, the two children were placed on the top of a high pile of firewood in the boat, and sat eating bread and wild strawberries, while Christina's father and his man drove the boat forward with poles. They floated on swiftly, for the tide was in their favor, passing over lakes, formed by the stream in its course; sometimes they seemed quite enclosed by reeds and water plants, yet there was always room for them to pass out, although the old trees overhung the water and the old oaks stretched out their bare branches, as if they had turned up their sleeves and wished to show their knotty, naked arms. Old alder trees, whose roots were loosened from the banks, clung with their fibres to the bottom of the stream, and the tops of the branches above the water looked like little woody islands. The waterlilies waved themselves to and fro on the river, everything made the excursion beautiful, and at last they came to the great eel weir, where the water rushed through the floodgates; and the children thought this a beautiful sight. In those days there was no factory nor any town house, nothing but the great farm, with its scanty-bearing fields, in which could be seen a few herd of cattle, and one or two farm laborers. The rushing of the water through the sluices, and the scream of the wild ducks, were almost the only signs of active life at Silkborg. After the firewood had been unloaded, Christina's father bought a whole bundle of eels and a sucking-pig, which were all placed in a basket in the stern of the boat.

Then they returned again up the stream; and as the wind was favorable, two sails were hoisted, which carried the boat on as well as if two horses had been harnessed to it. As they sailed on, they came by chance to the place where the boatman's assistant lived, at a little distance from the bank of the river. The boat was moored; and the two men, after desiring the children to sit still, both went on shore. They obeyed this order for a very short time, and then forgot it altogether. First they peeped into the basket containing the eels and the sucking-pig; then they must needs pull out the pig and take it in their hands, and feel it, and touch it; and as they both wanted to hold it at the same time, the consequence was that they let it fall into the water, and the pig sailed away with the stream.

Here was a terrible disaster. Ib jumped ashore, and ran a little distance from the boat.

"Oh, take me with you," cried Christina; and she sprang after him. In a few minutes they found themselves deep in a thicket, and could no longer see the boat or the shore. They ran on a little farther, and then Christina fell down, and began to cry.

Ib helped her up, and said, "Never mind; follow me. Yonder is the house." But the house was not yonder; and they wandered still farther, over the dry rustling leaves of the last year, and treading on fallen branches that crackled under their little feet; then they heard a loud, piercing cry, and they stood still to listen. Presently the scream of an eagle sounded through the wood; it was an ugly cry, and it frightened the children; but before them, in the thickest part of the forest, grew the most beautiful blackberries, in wonderful quantities. They looked so inviting that the children could not help stopping; and they remained there so long eating, that their mouths and cheeks became quite black with the juice.

Presently they heard the frightful scream again, and Christina said, "We shall get into trouble about that pig."

"Oh, never mind," said Ib; "we will go home to my father's house. It is here in the wood." So they went on, but the road led them out of the way; no house could be seen, it grew dark, and the children were afraid. The solemn stillness that reigned around them was now and then broken by the shrill cries of the great horned owl and other birds that they knew nothing of. At last they both lost themselves in the thicket; Christina began to cry, and then Ib cried too; and, after weeping and lamenting for some time, they stretched themselves down on the dry leaves and fell asleep.

The sun was high in the heavens when the two children woke. They felt cold; but not far from their resting place, on a hill, the sun was shining through the trees. They thought if they went there they should be warm, and Ib fancied he should be able to see his father's house from such a high spot. But they were far away from home now, in quite another part of the forest. They clambered to the top of the rising ground, and found themselves on the edge of a declivity, which sloped down to a clear transparent lake. Great quantities of fish could be seen through the clear water, sparkling in the sun's rays; they were quite surprised when they came so suddenly upon such an unexpected sight.

Close to where they stood grew a hazel bush, covered with beautiful nuts. They soon gathered some, cracked them, and ate the fine young kernels, which were only just ripe. But there was another surprise and fright in store for them. Out of the thicket stepped a tall old woman, her face quite brown, and her hair of a deep shining black; the whites of her eyes glittered like a Moor's; on her back she carried a bundle, and in her hand a knotted stick. She was a gypsy. The children did not at first understand what she said. She drew out of her pocket three large nuts, in which she told them were hidden the most beautiful and lovely things in the world, for they were wishing nuts. Ib looked at her, and as she spoke so kindly, he took courage, and asked her if she would give him the nuts; and the woman gave them to him, and then gathered some more from the bushes for herself, quite a pocket full. Ib and Christina looked at the wishing nuts with wide open eyes.

"Is there in this nut a carriage, with a pair of horses?" asked Ib.

"Yes, there is a golden carriage, with two golden horses," replied the woman.

"Then give me that nut," said Christina; so Ib gave it to her, and the strange woman tied up the nut for her in her handkerchief.

Ib held up another nut. "Is there, in this nut, a pretty little neckerchief like the one Christina has on her neck?" asked Ib.

"There are ten neckerchiefs in it," she replied, "as well as beautiful dresses, stockings, and a hat and veil."

"Then I will have that one also," said Christina; "and it is a pretty one too." And then Ib gave her the second nut.

The third was a little black thing. "You may keep that one," said Christina; "it is quite as pretty."

"What is in it?" asked Ib.

"The best of all things for you," replied the gypsy. So Ib held the nut very tight.

Then the woman promised to lead the children to the right path, that they might find their way home: and they went forward certainly in quite another direction to the one they meant to take; therefore no one ought to speak against the woman, and say that she wanted to steal the children. In the wild wood path they met a forester who knew Ib, and, by his help, Ib and Christina reached home, where they found everyone had been very anxious about them. They were pardoned and forgiven, although they really had both done wrong, and deserved to get into trouble; first, because they had let the sucking-pig fall into the water; and, secondly, because they had run away. Christina was taken back to her father's house on the heath, and Ib remained in the farmhouse on the borders of the wood, near the great land ridge.

The first thing Ib did that evening was to take out of his pocket the little black nut, in which the best thing of all was said to be enclosed. He laid it carefully between the door and the doorpost, and then shut the door so that the nut cracked directly. But there was not much kernel to be seen; it was what we should call hollow or worm-eaten, and looked as if it had been filled with tobacco or rich black earth. "It is just what I expected!" exclaimed Ib. "How should there be room in a little nut like this for the best thing of all? Christina will find her two nuts just the same; there will be neither fine clothes or a golden carriage in them."

Winter came; and the new year, and indeed many years passed away; until Ib was old enough to be confirmed, and, therefore, he went during a whole winter to the clergyman of the nearest village to be prepared.

One day, about this time, the boatman paid a visit to Ib's parents, and told them that Christina was going to service, and that she had been remarkably fortunate in obtaining a good place, with most respectable people. "Only think," he said, "she is going to the rich innkeeper's, at the hotel in Herning, many miles west from here. She is to assist the landlady in the housekeeping; and, if afterwards she behaves well and remains to be confirmed, the people will treat her as their own daughter."

So Ib and Christina took leave of each other. People already called them "the betrothed," and at parting the girl showed Ib the two nuts, which she had taken care of ever since the time that they lost themselves in the wood; and she told him also that the little wooden shoes he once carved for her when he was a boy, and gave her as a present, had been carefully kept in a drawer ever since. And so they parted.

After Ib's confirmation, he remained at home with his mother, for he had become a clever shoemaker, and in summer managed the farm for her quite alone. His father had been dead some time, and his mother kept no farm servants. Sometimes, but very seldom, he heard of Christina, through a postillion or eel seller who was passing. But she was well off with the rich innkeeper; and after being confirmed she wrote a letter to her father, in which was a kind message to Ib and his mother. In this letter, she mentioned that her master and mistress had made her a present of a beautiful new dress, and some nice underclothes. This was, of course, pleasant news.

One day, in the following spring, there came a knock at the door of the house where Ib's old mother lived; and when they opened it, lo and behold, in stepped the boatman and Christina. She had come to pay them a visit, and to spend the day. A carriage had to come from the Herning hotel to the next village, and she had taken the opportunity to see her friends once more. She looked as elegant as a real lady, and wore a pretty dress, beautifully made on purpose for her. There she stood, in full dress, while Ib wore only his working clothes. He could not utter a word; he could only seize her hand and hold it fast in his own, but he felt too happy and glad to open his lips. Christina, however, was quite at her ease; she talked and talked, and kissed him in the most friendly manner. Even afterwards, when they were left alone, and she asked, "Did you know me again, Ib?" he still stood holding her hand, and said at last, "You are become quite a grand lady, Christina, and I am only a rough working man; but I have often thought of you and of old times." Then they wandered up the great ridge, and looked across the stream to the heath, where the little hills were covered with the flowering broom. Ib said nothing; but before the time came for them to part, it became quite clear to him that Christina must be his wife: had they not even in childhood been called the betrothed? To him it seemed as if they were really engaged to each other, although not a word had been spoken on the subject. They had only a few more hours to remain together, for Christina was obliged to return that evening to the neighboring village, to be ready for the carriage which was to start the next morning early for Herning. Ib and her father accompanied her to the village. It was a fine moonlight evening; and when they arrived, Ib stood holding Christina's hand in his, as if he could not let her go. His eyes brightened, and the words he uttered came with hesitation from his lips, but from the deepest recesses of his heart: "Christina, if you have not become too grand, and if you can be contented to live in my mother's house as my wife, we will be married someday. But we can wait for a while."

"Oh yes," she replied, "let us wait a little longer, Ib. I can trust you, for I believe that I do love you. But let me think it over." Then he kissed her lips; and so they parted.

On the way home, Ib told the boatman that he and Christina were as good as engaged to each other; and the boatman found out that he had always expected it would be so, and went home with Ib that evening, and remained the night in the farmhouse; but nothing further was said of the engagement. During the next year, two letters passed between Ib and Christina. They were signed, "Faithful till death;" but at the end of that time, one day the boatman came over to see Ib, with a kind greeting from Christina. He had something else to say, which made him hesitate in a strange manner. At last it came out that Christina, who had grown a very pretty girl, was more lucky than ever. She was courted and admired by everyone; but her master's son, who had been home on a visit, was so much pleased with Christina that he wished to marry her. He had a very good situation in an office at Copenhagen, and as she had also taken a liking for him, his parents were not unwilling to consent. But Christina, in her heart, often thought of Ib, and knew how much he thought of her; so she felt inclined to refuse this good fortune, added the boatman. At first Ib said not a word, but he became as white as the wall, and shook his head gently, and then he spoke, "Christina must not refuse this good fortune."

"Then will you write a few words to her?" said the boatman.

Ib sat down to write, but he could not get on at all. The words were not what he wished to say, so he tore up the page. The following morning, however, a letter lay ready to be sent to Christina, and the following is what he wrote:

"The letter written by you to your father I have read, and see from it that you are prosperous in everything, and that still better fortune is in store for you. Ask your own heart, Christina, and think over carefully what awaits you if you take me for your husband, for I possess very little in the world. Do not think of me or of my position; think only of your own welfare. You are bound to me by no promises; and if in your heart you have given me one, I release you from it. May every blessing and happiness be poured out upon you, Christina. Heaven will give me the heart's consolation.

"Ever your sincere friend, Ib."

This letter was sent, and Christina received it in due time. In the course of the following November, her banns were published in the church on the heath, and also in Copenhagen, where the bridegroom lived. She was taken to Copenhagen under the protection of her future mother-in-law, because the bridegroom could not spare time from his numerous occupations for a journey so far into Jutland. On the journey, Christina met her father at one of the villages through which they passed, and here he took leave of her. Very little was said about the matter to Ib, and he did not refer to it; his mother, however, noticed that he had grown very silent and pensive. Thinking as he did of old times, no wonder the three nuts came into his mind which the gypsy woman had given him when a child, and of the two which he had given to Christina. These wishing nuts, after all, had proved true fortune tellers. One had contained a gilded carriage and noble horses, and the other beautiful clothes; all of these Christina would now have in her new home at Copenhagen. Her part had come true. And for him the nut had contained only black earth. The gypsy woman had said it was the best for him. Perhaps it was, and this also would be fulfilled. He understood the gypsy woman's meaning now. The black earth—the dark grave—was the best thing for him now.

Again years passed away; not many, but they seemed long years to Ib. The old innkeeper and his wife died one after the other; and the whole of their property, many thousand dollars, was inherited by their son. Christina could have the golden carriage now, and plenty of fine clothes. During the two long years which followed, no letter came from Christina to her father; and when at last her father received one from her, it did not speak of prosperity or happiness. Poor Christina! Neither she nor her husband understood how to economize or save, and the riches brought no blessing with them, because they had not asked for it.

Years passed; and for many summers the heath was covered with bloom; in winter the snow rested upon it, and the rough winds blew across the ridge under which stood Ib's sheltered home. One spring day the sun shone brightly, and he was guiding the plough across his field. The ploughshare struck against something which he fancied was a firestone, and then he saw glittering in the earth a splinter of shining metal which the plough had cut from something which gleamed brightly in the furrow. He searched, and found a large golden armlet of superior workmanship, and it was evident that the plough had disturbed a Hun's grave. He searched further, and found more valuable treasures, which Ib showed to the clergyman, who explained their value to him. Then he went to the magistrate, who informed the president of the museum of the discovery, and advised Ib to take the treasures himself to the president.

"You have found in the earth the best thing you could find," said the magistrate.

"The best thing," thought Ib; "the very best thing for me—and found in the earth! Well, if it really is so, then the gypsy woman was right in her prophecy."

So Ib went in the ferryboat from Aarhus to Copenhagen. To him who had only sailed once or twice on the river near his own home, this seemed like a voyage on the ocean; and at length he arrived at Copenhagen. The value of the gold he had found was paid to him; it was a large sum—six hundred dollars. Then Ib of the heath went out, and wandered about in the great city.

On the evening before the day he had settled to return with the captain of the passage boat, Ib lost himself in the streets, and took quite a different turning to the one he wished to follow. He wandered on till he found himself in a poor street of the suburb called Christian's Haven. Not a creature could be seen. At last a very little girl came out of one of the wretched-looking houses, and Ib asked her to tell him the way to the street he wanted; she looked up timidly at him, and began to cry bitterly. He asked her what was the matter; but what she said he could not understand. So he went along the street with her; and as they passed under a lamp, the light fell on the little girl's face. A strange sensation came over Ib, as he caught sight of it. The living, breathing embodiment of Little Christina stood before him, just as he remembered her in the days of her childhood. He followed the child to the wretched house, and ascended the narrow, crazy staircase which led to a little garret in the roof. The air in the room was heavy and stifling, no light was burning, and from one corner came sounds of moaning and sighing. It was the mother of the child who lay there on a miserable bed. With the help of a match, Ib struck a light, and approached her.

"Can I be of any service to you?" he asked. "This little girl brought me up here; but I am a stranger in this city. Are there no neighbors or any one whom I can call?"

Then he raised the head of the sick woman, and smoothed her pillow. He started as he did so. It was Christina of the heath! No one had mentioned her name to Ib for years; it would have disturbed his peace

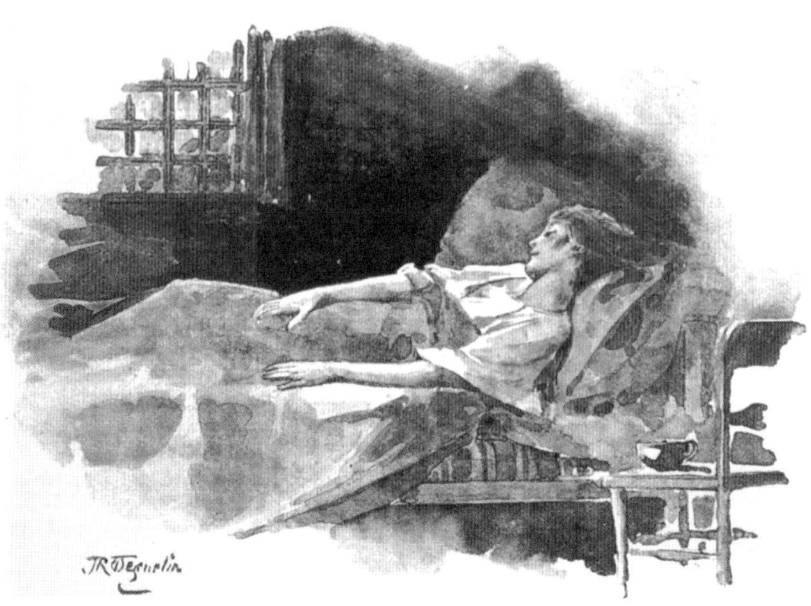

of mind, especially as the reports respecting her were not good. The wealth which her husband had inherited from his parents had made him proud and arrogant. He had given up his certain appointment, and travelled for six months in foreign lands, and, on his return, had lived in great style, and got into terrible debt. For a time he had trembled on the high pedestal on which he had placed himself, till at last he toppled over, and ruin came. His numerous merry companions, and the visitors at his table, said it served him right, for he had kept house like a madman. One morning his corpse was found in the canal. The cold hand of death had already touched the heart of Christina. Her youngest child, looked for in the midst of prosperity, had sunk into the grave when only a few weeks old; and at last Christina herself became sick unto death, and lay, forsaken and dying, in a miserable room, amid poverty she might have borne in her younger days, but which was now more painful to her from the luxuries to which she had lately been accustomed. It was her eldest child, also a Little Christina, whom Ib had followed to her home, where she suffered hunger and poverty with her mother.

"It makes me unhappy to think that I shall die, and leave this poor child," sighed she. "Oh, what will become of her?" She could say no more.

Then Ib brought out another match, and lighted a piece of candle which he found in the room, and it threw a glimmering light over the wretched dwelling. Ib looked at the little girl, and thought of Christina in her young days. For her sake, could he not love this child, who was a stranger to him? As he thus reflected, the dying woman opened her eyes, and gazed at him. Did she recognize him? He never knew; for not another word escaped her lips.

In the forest by the river Gudenau, not far from the heath, and beneath the ridge of land, stood the little farm, newly painted and whitewashed. The air was heavy and dark; there were no blossoms on the heath; the autumn winds whirled the yellow leaves towards the boatman's hut, in which strangers dwelt; but the little farm stood safely sheltered beneath the tall trees and the high ridge. The turf blazed brightly on the hearth, and within was sunlight, the sparkling light from the sunny eyes of a child; the birdlike tones from the rosy lips ringing like the song of a lark in spring. All was life and joy. Little Christina sat on Ib's knee. Ib was to her both father and mother; her own parents had vanished from her memory, as a dream picture vanishes alike from childhood and age. Ib's house was well and prettily furnished; for he was a prosperous man now, while the mother of the little girl rested in the churchyard at Copenhagen, where she had died in poverty. Ib had money now—money which had come to him out of the black earth; and he had Christina for his own, after all.

The Story of the Year

It was near the end of January, and a terrible fall of snow was pelting down, and whirling through the streets and lanes; the windows were plastered with snow on the outside, snow fell in masses from the roofs. Everyone seemed in a great hurry; they ran, they flew, fell into each other's arms, holding fast for a moment as long as they could stand safely. Coaches and horses looked as if they had been frosted with sugar. The footmen stood with their backs against the carriages, so as to turn their faces from the wind. The foot passengers kept within the shelter of the carriages, which could only move slowly on in the deep snow. At last the storm abated, and a narrow path was swept clean in front of the houses; when two persons met in this path they stood still, for neither liked to take the first step on one side into the deep snow to let the other pass him. There they stood silent and motionless, till at last, as if by tacit consent, they each sacrificed a leg and buried it in the deep snow. Towards evening, the weather became calm. The sky, cleared from the snow, looked more lofty and transparent, while the stars shone with new brightness and purity. The frozen snow crackled under foot, and was quite firm enough to bear the sparrows, who hopped upon it in the morning dawn. They searched for food in the path which had been swept, but there was very little for them, and they were terribly cold. "Tweet, tweet," said one to another; "they call this a new year, but I think it is worse than the last. We might just as well have kept the old year; I'm quite unhappy, and I have a right to be so."

"Yes, you have; and yet the people ran about and fired off guns, to usher in the new year," said a little shivering sparrow. "They threw things against the doors, and were quite beside themselves with joy, because the old year had disappeared. I was glad too, for I expected we should have some warm days, but my hopes have come to nothing. It freezes harder than ever; I think mankind have made a mistake in reckoning time."

"That they have," said a third, an old sparrow with a white poll; "they have something they call a calendar; it's an invention of their own, and everything must be arranged according to it, but it won't do. When spring comes, then the year begins. It is the voice of nature, and I reckon by that."

"But when will spring come?" asked the others.

"It will come when the stork returns, but he is very uncertain, and here in the town no one knows anything about it. In the country they have more knowledge; shall we fly away there and wait? We shall be nearer to spring then, certainly."

"That may be all very well," said another sparrow, who had been hopping about for a long time, chirping, but not saying anything of consequence, "but I have found a few comforts here in town which, I'm afraid, I should miss out in the country. Here in this neighborhood, there lives a family of people who have been so sensible as to place three or four flowerpots against the wall in the courtyard, so that the openings are all turned inward, and the bottom of each points outward. In the latter a hole has been cut large enough for me to fly in and out. I and my husband have built a nest in one of these pots, and all our young ones, who have now flown away, were brought up there. The people who live there of course made the whole arrangement that they might have the pleasure of seeing us, or they would not have done it. It pleased them also to strew breadcrumbs for us, and so we have food, and may consider ourselves provided for. So I think my husband and I will stay where we are; although we are not very happy, but we shall stay."

"And we will fly into the country," said the others, "to see if spring is coming." And away they flew.

In the country it was really winter, a few degrees colder than in the town. The sharp winds blew over the snow-covered fields. The farmer, wrapped in warm clothing, sat in his sleigh, and beat his arms across his chest to keep off the cold. The whip lay on his lap. The horses ran till they smoked. The snow crackled, the sparrows hopped about in the wheel-ruts, and shivered, crying, "Tweet, tweet; when will spring come? It is very long in coming."

"Very long indeed," sounded over the field, from the nearest snow-covered hill. It might have been the echo which people heard, or perhaps the words of that wonderful old man, who sat high on a heap of snow, regardless of wind or weather. He was all in white; he had on a peasant's coarse white coat of frieze. He had long white hair, a pale face, and large clear blue eyes. "Who is that old man?" asked the sparrows.

"I know who he is," said an old raven, who sat on the fence, and was condescending enough to acknowledge that we are all equal in the sight of Heaven, even as little birds, and therefore he talked with the sparrows, and gave them the information they wanted. "I know who the old man is," he said. "It is Winter, the old man of last year; he is not dead yet, as the calendar says, but acts as guardian to little Prince Spring who is coming. Winter rules here still. Ugh! the cold makes you shiver, little ones, does it not?"

"There! Did I not tell you so?" said the smallest of the sparrows. "The calendar is only an invention of man, and is not arranged according to nature. They should leave these things to us; we are created so much more clever than they are."

One week passed, and then another. The forest looked dark, the hard frozen lake lay like a sheet of lead. The mountains had disappeared, for over the land hung damp, icy mists. Large black crows flew about in silence; it was as if nature slept. At length a sunbeam glided over the lake, and it shone like burnished silver. But the snow on the fields and the hills did not glitter as before. The white form of Winter sat there still, with his un-wandering gaze fixed on the south. He did not perceive that the snowy carpet seemed to sink as it were into the earth; that here and there a little green patch of grass appeared, and that these patches were covered with sparrows.

"Tee-wit, tee-wit; is spring coming at last?"

Spring! How the cry resounded over field and meadow, and through the dark-brown woods, where the fresh green moss still gleamed on the trunks of the trees, and from the south came the two first storks flying through the air, and on the back of each sat a lovely little child, a boy and a girl. They greeted the earth with a kiss, and wherever they placed their feet white flowers sprung up from beneath the snow. Hand in hand they approached the old iceman, Winter, embraced him, and clung to his breast; and as they did so, in a moment all three were enveloped in a

thick, damp mist, dark and heavy, that closed over them like a veil. The wind arose with mighty rustling tone, and cleared away the mist. Then the sun shone out warmly. Winter had vanished away, and the beautiful children of Spring sat on the throne of the year.

"This is really a new year," cried all the sparrows, "now we shall get our rights, and have some return for what we suffered in winter."

Wherever the two children wandered, green buds burst forth on bush and tree, the grass grew higher, and the cornfields became lovely in delicate green.

The little maiden strewed flowers in her path. She held her apron before her: it was full of flowers; it was as if they sprung into life there, for the more she scattered around her, the more flowers did her apron contain. Eagerly she showered snowy blossoms over apple and peach trees, so that they stood in full beauty before even their green leaves had burst from the bud. Then the boy and the girl clapped their hands, and troops of birds came flying by, no one knew from whence, and they all twittered and chirped, singing "Spring has come!" How beautiful everything was! Many an old dame came forth from her door into the sunshine, and shuffled about with great delight, glancing at the golden flowers which glittered everywhere in the fields, as they used to do in her young days. The world grew young again to her, as she said, "It is a blessed time out here today." The forest already wore its dress of dark-green buds. The thyme blossomed in fresh fragrance. Primroses and anemones sprung forth, and violets bloomed in the shade, while every blade of grass was full of strength and sap. Who could resist sitting down on such a beautiful carpet? and then the young children of Spring seated themselves, holding each other's hands, and sang, and laughed, and grew. A gentle rain fell upon them from the sky, but they did not notice it, for the raindrops were their own tears of joy. They kissed each other, and were betrothed; and in the same moment the buds of the trees unfolded, and when the sun rose, the forest was green. Hand in hand the two wandered beneath the fresh pendant canopy of foliage, while the sun's rays gleamed through the opening of the shade, in changing and varied colors. The delicate young leaves filled the air with refreshing odor. Merrily rippled the clear brooks and rivulets between the green, velvety rushes, and over the many-colored pebbles beneath. All nature spoke of abundance and plenty. The cuckoo sang, and the lark carolled, for it was now beautiful spring. The careful willows had, however, covered their blossoms with woolly gloves; and this carefulness is rather tedious. Days and weeks went by, and the heat increased. Warm air waved the corn as it grew golden in the sun. The white northern lily spread its large green leaves over the glossy mirror of the woodland lake, and the fishes sought the shadows beneath them. In a sheltered part of the wood, the sun shone upon the walls of a farmhouse, brightening the blooming roses, and ripening the black juicy berries, which hung on the loaded cherry trees, with his hot beams. Here sat the lovely wife of Summer, the same whom we have seen as a child and a bride; her eyes were fixed on dark gathering clouds, which in wavy outlines of black and indigo were piling themselves up like mountains, higher and higher. They came from every side, always increasing like a rising, rolling sea. Then they swooped towards the forest, where every sound had been silenced as if by magic, every breath hushed, every bird mute. All nature stood still in grave suspense. But in the lanes and the highways, passengers on foot or in carriages were hurrying to find a place of shelter. Then came a flash of light, as if the sun had rushed forth from the sky, flaming, burning, all-devouring, and darkness returned amid a rolling crash of thunder. The rain poured down in streams—now there was darkness, then blinding light—now thrilling silence, then deafening din. The young brown reeds on the moor waved to and fro in feathery billows; the forest boughs were hidden in a watery mist, and still light and darkness followed each other, still came the silence after the roar, while the corn and the blades of grass lay beaten down and swamped, so that it seemed impossible they could ever raise themselves again. But after a while the rain began to fall gently, the sun's rays pierced the clouds, and the waterdrops glittered like pearls on leaf and stem. The birds sang, the fishes leaped up to the surface of the water, the gnats danced in the sunshine, and yonder, on a rock by the heaving salt sea, sat Summer himself, a strong man with sturdy limbs and long, dripping hair. Strengthened by the cool bath, he sat in the warm sunshine, while all around him renewed nature bloomed strong, luxuriant, and beautiful: it was summer, warm, lovely summer. Sweet and pleasant was the fragrance wafted from the clover-field, where the bees swarmed round the ruined tower, the bramble twined itself over the old altar, which, washed by the rain, glittered in the sunshine; and thither flew the queen bee with her swarm, and prepared wax and honey. But Summer and his bosom-wife saw it with different eyes, to them the altar-table was covered with the offerings of nature. The evening sky shone like gold, no church dome could ever gleam so brightly, and between the golden evening and the blushing morning there was moonlight. It was indeed summer. And days and weeks passed, the bright scythes of the reapers glittered in the cornfields, the branches of the apple trees bent low, heavy with the red and golden fruit. The hop, hanging in clusters, filled the air with sweet fragrance, and beneath the hazel bushes, where the nuts hung in great bunches, rested a man and a woman—Summer and his grave consort.

"See," she exclaimed, "what wealth, what blessings surround us. Everything is home-like and good, and yet, I know not why, I long for rest and peace; I can scarcely express what I feel. They are already ploughing the fields again; more and more the people wish for gain.

See, the storks are flocking together, and following the plough at a short distance. They are the birds from Egypt, who carried us through the air. Do you remember how we came as children to this land of the north; we brought with us flowers and bright sunshine, and green to the forests, but the wind has been rough with them, and they are now become dark and brown, like the trees of the south, but they do not, like them, bear golden fruit."

"Do you wish to see golden fruit?" said the man, "then rejoice," and he lifted his arm. The leaves of the forest put on colors of red and gold, and bright tints covered the woodlands. The rosebushes gleamed with scarlet hips, and the branches of the elder trees hung down with the weight of the full, dark berries. The wild chestnuts fell ripe from their dark, green shells, and in the forests the violets bloomed for the second time. But the queen of the year became more and more silent and pale.

"It blows cold," she said, "and night brings the damp mist; I long for the land of my childhood." Then she saw the storks fly away everyone, and she stretched out her hands towards them. She looked at the empty nests; in one of them grew a long-stalked corn flower, in another the yellow mustard seed, as if the nest had been placed there only for its comfort and protection, and the sparrows were flying round them all.

"Tweet, where has the master of the nest gone?" cried one. "I suppose he could not bear it when the wind blew, and therefore he has left this country. I wish him a pleasant journey."

The forest leaves became more and more yellow, leaf after leaf fell, and the stormy winds of Autumn howled. The year was now far advanced, and upon the fallen, yellow leaves, lay the queen of the year, looking up with mild eyes at a gleaming star, and her husband stood by her. A gust of wind swept through the foliage, and the leaves fell in a shower. The summer queen was gone, but a butterfly, the last of the year, flew through the cold air. Damp fogs came, icy winds blew, and the long, dark nights of winter approached. The ruler of the year appeared with hair white as snow, but he knew it not; he thought snowflakes falling from the sky covered his head, as they decked the green fields with a thin, white covering of snow. And then the church bells rang out for Christmas time.

"The bells are ringing for the newborn year," said the ruler, "soon will a new ruler and his bride be born, and I shall go to rest with my wife in yonder light-giving star."

In the fresh, green fir wood, where the snow lay all around, stood the angel of Christmas, and consecrated the young trees that were to adorn his feast.

"May there be joy in the rooms, and under the green boughs," said the old ruler of the year. In a few weeks he had become a very old man, with hair as white as snow. "My resting time draws near; the young pair of the year will soon claim my crown and sceptre."

"But the night is still thine," said the angel of Christmas, "for power, but not for rest. Let the snow lie warmly upon the tender seed. Learn to endure the thought that another is worshipped whilst thou art still lord. Learn to endure being forgotten while yet thou livest. The hour of thy freedom will come when Spring appears."

"And when will Spring come?" asked Winter.

"It will come when the stork returns."

And with white locks and snowy beard, cold, bent, and hoary, but strong as the wintry storm, and firm as the ice, old Winter sat on the snowdrift-covered hill, looking towards the south, where Winter had sat before, and gazed. The ice glittered, the snow crackled, the skaters skimmed over the polished surface of the lakes; ravens and crows formed a pleasing contrast to the white ground, and not a breath of wind stirred, and in the still air old Winter clenched his fists, and the ice lay fathoms deep between the lands. Then came the sparrows again out of the town, and asked, "Who is that old man?" The raven sat there still, or it might be his son, which is the same thing, and he said to them,

"It is Winter, the old man of the former year; he is not dead, as the calendar says, but he is guardian to the spring, which is coming."

"When will Spring come?" asked the sparrows, "for we shall have better times then, and a better rule. The old times are worth nothing."

And in quiet thought old Winter looked at the leafless forest, where the graceful form and bends of each tree and branch could be seen; and while Winter slept, icy mists came from the clouds, and the ruler dreamt of his youthful days and of his manhood, and in the morning dawn the whole forest glittered with hoar frost, which the sun shook from the branches, and this was the summer dream of Winter.

"When will Spring come?" asked the sparrows. "Spring!" Again the echo sounded from the hills on which the snow lay. The sunshine became warmer, the snow melted, and the birds twittered, "Spring is coming!"

And high in the air flew the first stork, and the second followed; a lovely child sat on the back of each, and they sank down on the open field, kissed the earth, and kissed the quiet old man; and, as the mist from the mountain top, he vanished away and disappeared. And the story of the year was finished.

"This is all very fine, no doubt," said the sparrows, "and it is very beautiful; but it is not according to the calendar, therefore, it must be all wrong."

The Travelling Companion

Poor John was very sad; for his father was so ill, he had no hope of his recovery. John sat alone with the sick man in the little room, and the lamp had nearly burnt out; for it was late in the night.

"You have been a good son, John," said the sick father, "and God will help you on in the world." He looked at him, as he spoke, with mild, earnest eyes, drew a deep sigh, and died; yet it appeared as if he still slept.

John wept bitterly. He had no one in the wide world now; neither father, mother, brother, nor sister. Poor John! he knelt down by the bed, kissed his dead father's hand, and wept many, many bitter tears. But at last his eyes closed, and he fell asleep with his head resting against the hard bedpost. Then he dreamed a strange dream; he thought he saw the sun shining upon him, and his father alive and well, and even heard him laughing as he used to do when he was very happy. A beautiful girl, with a golden crown on her head, and long, shining hair, gave him her hand; and his father said, "See what a bride you have won. She is the loveliest maiden on the whole earth." Then he awoke, and all the beautiful things vanished before his eyes, his father lay dead on the bed, and he was all alone. Poor John!

During the following week the dead man was buried. The son walked behind the coffin which contained his father, whom he so dearly loved, and would never again behold. He heard the earth fall on the coffin-lid, and watched it till only a corner remained in sight, and at last that also disappeared. He felt as if his heart would break with its weight of sorrow, till those who stood round the grave sang a psalm, and the sweet, holy tones brought tears into his eyes, which relieved him. The sun shone brightly down on the green trees, as if it would say, "You must not be so sorrowful, John. Do you see the beautiful blue sky above you? Your father is up there, and he prays to the loving Father of all, that you may do well in the future."

"I will always be good," said John, "and then I shall go to be with my father in heaven. What joy it will be when we see each other again! How much I shall have to relate to him, and how many things he will be able to explain to me of the delights of heaven, and teach me as he once did on earth. Oh, what joy it will be!"

He pictured it all so plainly to himself, that he smiled even while the tears ran down his cheeks.

The little birds in the chestnut trees twittered, "Tweet, tweet;" they were so happy, although they had seen the funeral; but they seemed as if they knew that the dead man was now in heaven, and that he had wings much larger and more beautiful than their own; and he was happy now, because he had been good here on earth, and they were glad of it. John saw them fly away out of the green trees into the wide world, and he longed to fly with them; but first he cut out a large wooden cross, to place on his father's grave; and when he brought it there in the evening, he found the grave decked out with gravel and flowers. Strangers had done this; they who had known the good old father who was now dead, and who had loved him very much.

Early the next morning, John packed up his little bundle of clothes, and placed all his money, which consisted of fifty dollars and a few shillings, in his girdle; with this he determined to try his fortune in the world. But first he went into the churchyard; and, by his father's grave, he offered up a prayer, and said, "Farewell."

As he passed through the fields, all the flowers looked fresh and beautiful in the warm sunshine, and nodded in the wind, as if they wished to say, "Welcome to the green wood, where all is fresh and bright."

Then John turned to have one more look at the old church, in which he had been christened in his infancy, and where his father had taken him every Sunday to hear the service and join in singing the psalms. As he looked at the old tower, he espied the ringer standing at one of the narrow openings, with his little pointed red cap on his head, and shading his eyes from the sun with his bent arm. John nodded farewell to him, and the little ringer waved his red cap, laid his hand on his heart, and kissed his hand to him a great many times, to show that he felt kindly towards him, and wished him a prosperous journey.

John continued his journey, and thought of all the wonderful things he should see in the large, beautiful world, till he found himself farther away from home than ever he had been before. He did not even know the names of the places he passed through, and could scarcely understand the language of the people he met, for he was far away, in a strange land. The first night he slept on a haystack, out in the fields, for there was no other bed for him; but it seemed to him so nice and comfortable that even a king need not wish for a better. The field, the brook, the haystack, with the blue sky above, formed a beautiful sleeping room. The green grass, with the little red and white flowers, was the carpet; the elder bushes and the hedges of wild roses looked like garlands on the walls; and for a bath he could have the clear, fresh water of the brook; while the rushes bowed their heads to him, to wish him good morning and good evening. The moon, like a large lamp, hung high up in the blue ceiling, and he had no fear of its setting fire to his curtains. John slept here quite safely all night; and when he awoke, the sun was up, and all the little birds were singing round him, "Good morning, good morning. Are you not up yet?"

It was Sunday, and the bells were ringing for church. As the people went in, John followed them; he heard God's word, joined in singing the psalms, and listened to the preacher. It seemed to him just as if he were in his own church, where he had been christened, and had sung the psalms with his father. Out in the churchyard were several graves, and on some of them the grass had grown very high. John thought of his father's grave, which he knew at last would look like these, as he was not there to weed and attend to it. Then he set to work, pulled up the high grass, raised the wooden crosses which had fallen down, and replaced the wreaths which had been blown away from their places by the wind, thinking all the time, "Perhaps someone is doing the same for my father's grave, as I am not there to do it."

Outside the church door stood an old beggar, leaning on his crutch. John gave him his silver shillings, and then he continued his journey, feeling lighter and happier than ever. Towards evening, the weather became very stormy, and he hastened on as quickly as he could, to get shelter; but it was quite dark by the time he reached a little lonely church which stood on a hill. "I will go in here," he said, "and sit down in a corner; for I am quite tired, and want rest."

So he went in, and seated himself; then he folded his hands, and offered up his evening prayer, and was soon fast asleep and dreaming, while the thunder rolled and the lightning flashed without. When he awoke, it was still night; but the storm had ceased, and the moon shone in upon him through the windows. Then he saw an open coffin standing in the centre of the church, which contained a dead man, waiting for burial. John was not at all timid; he had a good conscience, and he knew also that the dead can never injure anyone. It is living wicked men who do harm to others. Two such wicked persons stood now by the dead man, who had been brought to the church to be buried. Their evil intentions were to throw the poor dead body outside the church door, and not leave him to rest in his coffin.

"Why do you do this?" asked John, when he saw what they were going to do; "it is very wicked. Leave him to rest in peace, in Christ's name."

"Nonsense," replied the two dreadful men. "He has cheated us; he owed us money which he could not pay, and now he is dead we shall not get a penny; so we mean to have our revenge, and let him lie like a dog outside the church door."

"I have only fifty dollars," said John, "it is all I possess in the world, but I will give it to you if you will promise me faithfully to leave the dead man in peace. I shall be able to get on without the money; I have strong and healthy limbs, and God will always help me."

"Why, of course," said the horrid men, "if you will pay his debt we will both promise not to touch him. You may depend upon that;" and then they took the money he offered them, laughed at him for his good nature, and went their way.

Then he laid the dead body back in the coffin, folded the hands, and took leave of it; and went away contentedly through the great forest. All around him he could see the prettiest little elves dancing in the moonlight, which shone through the trees. They were not disturbed by his appearance, for they knew he was good and harmless among men. They are wicked people only who can never obtain a glimpse of fairies. Some of them were not taller than the breadth of a finger, and they wore golden combs in their long, yellow hair. They were rocking themselves two together on the large dewdrops with which the leaves and the high grass were sprinkled. Sometimes the dewdrops would roll away, and then they fell down between the stems of the long grass, and caused a great deal of laughing and noise among the other little people. It was quite charming to watch them at play. Then they sang songs, and John remembered that he had learnt those pretty songs when he was a little boy. Large speckled spiders, with silver crowns on their heads, were employed to spin suspension bridges and palaces from one hedge to another, and when the tiny drops fell upon them, they glittered in the moonlight like shining glass. This continued till sunrise. Then the little elves crept into the flower buds, and the wind seized the bridges and palaces, and fluttered them in the air like cobwebs.

As John left the wood, a strong man's voice called after him, "Hallo, comrade, where are you travelling?"

"Into the wide world," he replied, "I am only a poor lad, I have neither father nor mother, but God will help me."

"I am going into the wide world also," replied the stranger; "shall we keep each other company?"

"With all my heart," he said, and so they went on together. Soon they began to like each other very much, for they were both good; but John found out that the stranger was much more clever than himself. He had travelled all over the world, and could describe almost everything. The sun was high in the heavens when they seated themselves under a large tree to eat their breakfast, and at the same moment an old woman came towards them. She was very old and almost bent double. She leaned upon a stick and carried on her back a bundle of firewood, which she had collected in the forest; her apron was tied round it, and John saw three great stems of fern and some willow twigs peeping out. Just as she came close up to them, her foot slipped and she fell to the ground screaming loudly; poor old woman, she had broken her leg! John proposed directly that they should carry the old woman home to her cottage; but the stranger opened his knapsack and took out a box, in which he said he had a salve that would quickly make her leg well and strong again, so that she would be able to walk home herself, as if her leg had never been broken. And all that he would ask in return was the three fern stems which she carried in her apron.

"That is rather too high a price," said the old woman, nodding her head quite strangely. She did not seem at all inclined to part with the fern stems. However, it was not very agreeable to lie there with a broken leg, so she gave them to him; and such was the power of the ointment, that no sooner had he rubbed her leg with it than the old mother rose up and walked even better than she had done before. But then this wonderful ointment could not be bought at a chemist's.

"What can you want with those three fern rods?" asked John of his fellow-traveller.

"Oh, they will make capital brooms," said he; "and I like them because I have strange whims sometimes." Then they walked on together for a long distance.

"How dark the sky is becoming," said John; "and look at those thick, heavy clouds."

"Those are not clouds," replied his fellow-traveller; "they are mountains—large lofty mountains—on the tops of which we should be above the clouds, in the pure, free air. Believe me, it is delightful to ascend so high, tomorrow we shall be there." But the mountains were not so near as they appeared; they had to travel a whole day before they reached them, and pass through black forests and piles of rock as large as a town. The journey had been so fatiguing that John and his fellow-traveller stopped to rest at a roadside inn, so that they might gain strength for their journey on the morrow. In the large public room of the inn a great many persons were assembled to see a comedy performed by dolls. The showman had just erected his little theatre, and the people were sitting round the room to witness the performance. Right in front, in the very best place, sat a stout butcher, with a great bulldog by his side who seemed very much inclined to bite. He sat staring with all his eyes, and so indeed did everyone else in the room. And then the play began. It was a pretty piece, with a king and a queen in it, who sat on a beautiful throne, and had gold crowns on their heads. The trains to their dresses were very long, according to the fashion; while the prettiest of wooden dolls, with glass eyes and large mustaches, stood at the doors, and opened and shut them, that the fresh air might come into the room. It was a very pleasant play, not at all mournful; but just as the queen stood up and walked across the stage, the great bulldog, who should have been held back by his master, made a spring forward, and caught the queen in the teeth by the slender wrist, so that it snapped in two. This was a very dreadful disaster. The poor man, who was exhibiting the dolls, was much annoyed, and quite sad about his queen; she was the prettiest doll he had, and the bulldog had broken her head and shoulders off. But after all the people were gone away, the stranger, who came with John, said that he could soon set her to rights. And then he brought out his box and rubbed the doll with some of the salve with which he had cured the old woman when she broke her leg. As soon as this was done the doll's back became quite right again; her head and shoulders were fixed on, and she could even move her limbs herself: there was now no occasion to pull the wires, for the doll acted just like a living creature, excepting that she could not speak. The man to whom the show belonged was quite delighted at having a doll who could dance of herself without being pulled by the wires; none of the other dolls could do this.

During the night, when all the people at the inn were gone to bed, someone was heard to sigh so deeply and painfully, and the sighing continued for so long a time, that everyone got up to see what could be the matter. The showman went at once to his little theatre and found that it proceeded from the dolls, who all lay on the floor sighing piteously, and staring with their glass eyes; they all wanted to be rubbed with the ointment, so that, like the queen, they might be able to move of themselves. The queen threw herself on her knees, took off her beautiful crown, and, holding it in her hand, cried, "Take this from me, but do rub my husband and his courtiers."

The poor man who owned the theatre could scarcely refrain from weeping; he was so sorry that he could not help them. Then he immediately spoke to John's comrade, and promised him all the money he might receive at the next evening's performance, if he would only rub the ointment on four or five of his dolls. But the fellow-traveller said he did not require anything in return, excepting the sword which the showman wore by his side. As soon as he received the sword he anointed six of the dolls with the ointment, and they were able immediately to dance so gracefully that all the living girls in the room could not help joining in the dance. The coachman danced with the cook, and the waiters with the chambermaids, and all the strangers joined; even the tongs and the fire-shovel made an attempt, but they fell down after the first jump. So after all it was a very merry night. The next morning John and his companion left the inn to continue their journey through the great pine forests and over the high mountains. They arrived at last at such a great height that towns and villages lay beneath them, and the church steeples looked like little specks between the green trees. They could see for miles round, far away to places they had never visited, and John saw more of the beautiful world than he had ever known before. The sun shone brightly in the blue firmament above, and through the clear mountain air came the sound of the huntsman's horn, and the soft, sweet notes brought tears into his eyes, and he could not help exclaiming, "How good and loving God is to give us all this beauty and loveliness in the world to make us happy!"

His fellow-traveller stood by with folded hands, gazing on the dark wood and the towns bathed in the warm sunshine. At this moment there sounded over their heads sweet music. They looked up, and discovered a large white swan hovering in the air, and singing as never bird sang before. But the song soon became weaker and weaker, the bird's head drooped, and he sunk slowly down, and lay dead at their feet.

"It is a beautiful bird," said the traveller, "and these large white wings are worth a great deal of money. I will take them with me. You see now that a sword will be very useful."

So he cut off the wings of the dead swan with one blow, and carried them away with him.

They now continued their journey over the mountains for many miles, till they at length reached a large city, containing hundreds of towers, that shone in the sunshine like silver. In the midst of the city stood a splendid marble palace, roofed with pure red gold, in which dwelt the king. John and his companion would not go into the town immediately; so they stopped at an inn outside the town, to change their clothes; for they wished to appear respectable as they walked through the streets. The landlord told them that the king was a very good man, who never injured anyone: but as to his daughter, "Heaven defend us!"

She was indeed a wicked princess. She possessed beauty enough—nobody could be more elegant or prettier than she was; but what of that? for she was a wicked witch; and in consequence of her conduct many noble young princes had lost their lives. Anyone was at liberty to make her an offer; were he a prince or a beggar, it mattered not to her. She would ask him to guess three things which she had just thought of, and if he succeed, he was to marry her, and be king over all the land when her father died; but if he could not guess these three things, then she ordered him to be hanged or to have his head cut off. The old king, her father, was very much grieved at her conduct, but he could not prevent her from being so wicked, because he once said he would have nothing more to do with her lovers; she might do as she pleased. Each prince who came and tried the three guesses, so that he might marry the princess, had been unable to find them out, and had been hanged or beheaded. They had all been warned in time, and might have left her alone, if they would. The old king became at last so distressed at all these dreadful circumstances, that for a whole day every year he and his soldiers knelt and prayed that the princess might become good; but she continued as wicked as ever. The old women who drank brandy would color it quite black before they drank it, to show how they mourned; and what more could they do?

"What a horrible princess!" said John; "she ought to be well flogged. If I were the old king, I would have her punished in some way."

Just then they heard the people outside shouting, "Hurrah!" and, looking out, they saw the princess passing by; and she was really so beautiful that everybody forgot her wickedness, and shouted "Hurrah!"

Twelve lovely maidens in white silk dresses, holding golden tulips in their hands, rode by her side on coal-black horses. The princess herself had a snow-white steed, decked with diamonds and rubies. Her dress was of cloth of gold, and the whip she held in her hand looked like a sunbeam. The golden crown on her head glittered like the stars of heaven, and her mantle was formed of thousands of butterflies' wings sewn together. Yet she herself was more beautiful than all.

When John saw her, his face became as red as a drop of blood, and he could scarcely utter a word. The princess looked exactly like the beautiful lady with the golden crown, of whom he had dreamed on the night his father died. She appeared to him so lovely that he could not help loving her.

"It could not be true," he thought, "that she was really a wicked witch, who ordered people to be hanged or beheaded, if they could not guess her thoughts. Everyone has permission to go and ask her hand, even the poorest beggar. I shall pay a visit to the palace," he said; "I must go, for I cannot help myself."

Then they all advised him not to attempt it; for he would be sure to share the same fate as the rest. His fellow-traveller also tried to persuade him against it; but John seemed quite sure of success. He brushed his shoes and his coat, washed his face and his hands, combed his soft flaxen hair, and then went out alone into the town, and walked to the palace.

"Come in," said the king, as John knocked at the door. John opened it, and the old king, in a dressing gown and embroidered slippers, came towards him. He had the crown on his head, carried his sceptre in one hand, and the orb in the other. "Wait a bit," said he, and he placed the orb under his arm, so that he could offer the other hand to John; but when he found that John was another suitor, he began to weep so violently, that both the sceptre and the orb fell to the floor, and he was obliged to wipe his eyes with his dressing gown. Poor old king! "Let her alone," he said; "you will fare as badly as all the others. Come, I will show you." Then he led him out into the princess's pleasure gardens, and there he saw a frightful sight. On every tree hung three or four king's sons who had wooed the princess, but had not been able to guess the riddles she gave them. Their skeletons rattled in every breeze, so that the terrified birds never dared to venture into the garden. All the flowers were supported by human bones instead of sticks, and human skulls in the flowerpots grinned horribly. It was really a doleful garden for a princess. "Do you see all this?" said the old king; "your fate will be the same as those who are here, therefore do not attempt it. You really make me very unhappy. I take these things to heart so very much."

John kissed the good old king's hand, and said he was sure it would be all right, for he was quite enchanted with the beautiful princess. Then the princess herself came riding into the palace yard with all her ladies, and he wished her "Good morning." She looked wonderfully fair and lovely when she offered her hand to John, and he loved her more than ever. How could she be a wicked witch, as all the people asserted? He accompanied her into the hall, and the little pages offered them gingerbread nuts and sweetmeats, but the old king was so unhappy he could eat nothing, and besides, gingerbread nuts were too hard for him. It was decided that John should come to the palace the next day, when the judges and the whole of the counsellors would be present, to try if he could guess the first riddle. If he succeeded, he would have to come a second time; but if not, he would lose his life, and no one had ever been able to guess even one. However, John was not at all anxious about the result of his trial; on the contrary, he was very merry. He thought only of the beautiful princess, and believed that in some way he should have help, but how he knew not, and did not like to think about it; so he danced along the high-road as he went back to the inn, where he had left his fellow-traveller waiting for him. John could not refrain from telling him how gracious the princess had been, and how beautiful she looked. He longed for the next day so much, that he might go to the palace and try his luck at guessing the riddles. But his comrade shook his head, and looked very mournful. "I do so wish you to do well," said he; "we might have continued together much longer, and now I am likely to lose you; you poor dear John! I could shed tears, but I will not make you unhappy on the last night we may be together. We will be merry, really merry this evening; tomorrow, after you are gone, shall be able to weep undisturbed."

It was very quickly known among the inhabitants of the town that another suitor had arrived for the princess, and there was great sorrow in consequence. The theatre remained closed, the women who sold sweetmeats tied crape round the sugar sticks, and the king and the priests were on their knees in the church. There was a great lamentation, for no one expected John to succeed better than those who had been suitors before.

In the evening John's comrade prepared a large bowl of punch, and said, "Now let us be merry, and drink to the health of the princess." But after drinking two glasses, John became so sleepy, that he could not keep his eyes open, and fell fast asleep. Then his fellow-traveller lifted him gently out of his chair, and laid him on the bed; and as soon as it was quite dark, he took the two large wings which he had cut from the

dead swan, and tied them firmly to his own shoulders. Then he put into his pocket the largest of the three rods which he had obtained from the old woman who had fallen and broken her leg. After this he opened the window, and flew away over the town, straight towards the palace, and seated himself in a corner, under the window which looked into the bedroom of the princess.

The town was perfectly still when the clocks struck a quarter to twelve. Presently the window opened, and the princess, who had large black wings to her shoulders, and a long white mantle, flew away over the city towards a high mountain. The fellow-traveller, who had made himself invisible, so that she could not possibly see him, flew after her through the air, and whipped the princess with his rod, so that the blood came whenever he struck her. Ah, it was a strange flight through the air! The wind caught her mantle, so that it spread out on all sides, like the large sail of a ship, and the moon shone through it. "How it hails, to be sure!" said the princess, at each blow she received from the rod; and it served her right to be whipped.

At last she reached the side of the mountain, and knocked. The mountain opened with a noise like the roll of thunder, and the princess went in. The traveller followed her; no one could see him, as he had made himself invisible. They went through a long, wide passage. A thousand gleaming spiders ran here and there on the walls, causing them to glitter as if they were illuminated with fire. They next entered a large hall built of silver and gold. Large red and blue flowers shone on the walls, looking like sunflowers in size, but no one could dare to pluck them, for the stems were hideous poisonous snakes, and the flowers were flames of fire, darting out of their jaws. Shining glow-worms covered the ceiling, and sky-blue bats flapped their transparent wings. Altogether the place had a frightful appearance. In the middle of the floor stood a throne supported by four skeleton horses, whose harness had been made by fiery-red spiders. The throne itself was made of milk-white glass, and the cushions were little black mice, each biting the other's tail. Over it hung a canopy of rose-colored spider's webs, spotted with the prettiest little green flies, which sparkled like precious stones. On the throne sat an old magician with a crown on his ugly head, and a sceptre in his hand. He kissed the princess on the forehead, seated her by his side on the splendid throne, and then the music commenced. Great black grasshoppers played the mouth organ, and the owl struck herself on the body instead of a drum. It was altogether a ridiculous concert. Little black goblins with false lights in their caps danced about the hall; but no one could see the traveller, and he had placed himself just behind the throne where he could see and hear everything. The courtiers who came in afterwards looked noble and grand; but any one with common sense could see what they really were, only broomsticks, with cabbages for heads. The magician had given them life, and dressed them in embroidered robes. It answered very well, as they were only wanted for show. After there had been a little dancing, the princess told the magician that she had a new suitor, and asked him what she could think of for the suitor to guess when he came to the castle the next morning.

"Listen to what I say," said the magician, "you must choose something very easy, he is less likely to guess it then. Think of one of your shoes, he will never imagine it is that. Then cut his head off; and mind you do not forget to bring his eyes with you tomorrow night, that I may eat them."

The princess curtsied low, and said she would not forget the eyes.

The magician then opened the mountain and she flew home again, but the traveller followed and flogged her so much with the rod, that she sighed quite deeply about the heavy hailstorm, and made as much haste as she could to get back to her bedroom through the window. The traveller then returned to the inn where John still slept, took off his wings, and laid down on the bed, for he was very tired. Early in the morning John awoke, and when his fellow-traveller got up, he said that he had a very wonderful dream about the princess and her shoe, he therefore advised John to ask her if she had not thought of her shoe. Of course the traveller knew this from what the magician in the mountain had said.

"I may as well say that as anything," said John. "Perhaps your dream may come true; still I will say farewell, for if I guess wrong I shall never see you again."

Then they embraced each other, and John went into the town and walked to the palace. The great hall was full of people, and the judges sat in armchairs, with eiderdown cushions to rest their heads upon, because they had so much to think of. The old king stood near, wiping his eyes with his white pocket handkerchief. When the princess entered, she looked even more beautiful than she had appeared the day before, and greeted every one present most gracefully; but to John she gave her hand, and said, "Good morning to you."

Now came the time for John to guess what she was thinking of; and oh, how kindly she looked at him as she spoke. But when he uttered the single word shoe, she turned as pale as a ghost; all her wisdom could not help her, for he had guessed rightly. Oh, how pleased the old king was! It was quite amusing to see how he capered about. All the people clapped their hands, both on his account and John's, who had guessed rightly the first time. His fellow-traveller was glad also, when he heard how successful John had been. But John folded his hands, and thanked God, who, he felt quite sure, would help him again; and he knew he had to guess twice more. The evening passed pleasantly like the one preceding. While John slept, his companion flew behind the princess to the mountain, and flogged her even harder than before; this time he had taken two rods with him. No one saw him go in with her, and he heard all that was said. The princess this time was to think of a glove, and he told John as if he had again heard it in a dream. The next day, therefore, he was able to guess correctly the second time, and it caused great rejoicing at the palace. The whole court jumped about as they had seen the king do the day before, but the princess lay on the sofa, and would not say a single word. All now depended upon John. If he only guessed rightly the third time, he would marry the princess, and reign over the kingdom after the death of the old king: but if he failed, he would lose his life, and the magician would have his beautiful blue eyes. That evening John said his prayers and went to bed very early, and soon fell asleep calmly. But his companion tied on his wings to his shoulders, took three rods, and, with his sword at his side, flew to the palace. It was a very dark night, and so stormy that the tiles flew from the roofs of the houses, and the trees in the garden upon which the skeletons hung bent themselves like reeds before the wind. The lightning flashed, and the thunder rolled in one long-continued peal all night. The window of the castle opened, and the princess flew out. She was pale as death, but she laughed at the storm as if it were not bad enough. Her white mantle fluttered in the wind like a large sail, and the traveller flogged her with the three rods till the blood trickled down, and at last she could scarcely fly; she contrived, however, to reach the mountain. "What a hailstorm!" she said, as she entered; "I have never been out in such weather as this."

"Yes, there may be too much of a good thing sometimes," said the magician.

Then the princess told him that John had guessed rightly the second time, and if he succeeded the next morning, he would win, and she could never come to the mountain again, or practice magic as she had done, and therefore she was quite unhappy. "I will find out something for you to think of which he will never guess, unless he is a greater conjuror than myself. But now let us be merry."

Then he took the princess by both hands, and they danced with all the little goblins and Jack-o'-lanterns in the room. The red spiders sprang here and there on the walls quite as merrily, and the flowers of fire appeared as if they were throwing out sparks. The owl beat the drum, the crickets whistled and the grasshoppers played the mouth organ. It was a very ridiculous ball. After they had danced enough, the princess was obliged to go home, for fear she should be missed at the palace. The magician offered to go with her, that they might be company to each other on the way. Then they flew away through the bad weather, and the traveller followed them, and broke his three rods across their shoulders. The magician had never been out in such a hailstorm as this. Just by the palace the magician stopped to wish the princess farewell, and to whisper in her ear, "Tomorrow think of my head."

But the traveller heard it, and just as the princess slipped through the window into her bedroom, and the magician turned round to fly back to the mountain, he seized him by the long black beard, and with his sabre cut off the wicked conjuror's head just behind the shoulders, so that he could not even see who it was. He threw the body into the sea to the fishes, and after dipping the head into the water, he tied it up in a silk handkerchief, took it with him to the inn, and then went to bed. The next morning he gave John the handkerchief, and told him not to untie it till the princess asked him what she was thinking of. There were so many people in the great hall of the palace that they stood as thick as radishes tied together in a bundle. The council sat in their armchairs with the white cushions. The old king wore new robes, and the golden crown and sceptre had been polished up so that he looked quite smart. But the princess was very pale, and wore a black dress as if she were going to a funeral.

"What have I thought of?" asked the princess, of John. He immediately untied the handkerchief, and was himself quite frightened when he saw the head of the ugly magician. Everyone shuddered, for it was terrible to look at; but the princess sat like a statue, and could not utter a single word. At length she rose and gave John her hand, for he had guessed rightly.

She looked at no one, but sighed deeply, and said, "You are my master now; this evening our marriage must take place."

"I am very pleased to hear it," said the old king. "It is just what I wish."

Then all the people shouted "Hurrah." The band played music in the streets, the bells rang, and the cake-women took the black crape off the sugar-sticks. There was universal joy. Three oxen, stuffed with ducks and chickens, were roasted whole in the marketplace, where everyone might help himself to a slice. The fountains spouted forth the most delicious wine, and whoever bought a penny loaf at the baker's received six large buns, full of raisins, as a present. In the evening the whole town was illuminated. The soldiers fired off cannons, and the boys let off crackers. There was eating and drinking, dancing and jumping everywhere. In the palace, the high-born gentlemen and beautiful ladies danced with each other, and they could be heard at a great distance singing the following song:

Here are maidens, young and fair,
Dancing in the summer air;
Like two spinning-wheels at play,
Pretty maidens dance away—
Dance the spring and summer through
Till the sole falls from your shoe.

But the princess was still a witch, and she could not love John. His fellow-traveller had thought of that, so he gave John three feathers out of the swan's wings, and a little bottle with a few drops in it. He told him to place a large bath full of water by the princess's bed, and put the feathers and the drops into it. Then, at the moment she was about to get into bed, he must give her a little push, so that she might fall into the water, and then dip her three times. This would destroy the power of the magician, and she would love him very much. John did all that his companion told him to do. The princess shrieked aloud when he dipped her under the water the first time, and struggled under his hands in the form of a great black swan with fiery eyes. As she rose the second time from the water, the swan had become white, with a black ring round its neck. John allowed the water to close once more over the bird, and at the same time it changed into a most beautiful princess. She was more lovely even than before, and thanked him, while her eyes sparkled with tears, for having broken the spell of the magician. The next day, the king came with the whole court to offer their congratulations, and stayed till quite late. Last of all came the travelling companion; he had his staff in his hand and his knapsack on his back. John kissed him many times and told him he must not go, he must remain with him, for he was the cause of all his good fortune. But the traveller shook his head, and said gently and kindly, "No: my time is up now; I have only paid my debt to you. Do you remember the dead man whom the bad people wished to throw out of his coffin? You gave all you possessed that he might rest in his grave; I am that man." As he said this, he vanished.

The wedding festivities lasted a whole month. John and his princess loved each other dearly, and the old king lived to see many a happy day, when he took their little children on his knees and let them play with his sceptre. And John became king over the whole country.

The Elderbush

Once upon a time there was a little boy who had taken cold. He had gone out and got his feet wet; though nobody could imagine how it had happened, for it was quite dry weather. So his mother undressed him, put him to bed, and had the teapot brought in, to make him a good cup of Elderflower tea. Just at that moment the merry old man came in who lived up atop of the house all alone; for he had neither wife nor children—but he liked children very much, and knew so many fairy tales, that it was quite delightful.

"Now drink your tea," said the boy's mother; "then, perhaps, you may hear a fairy tale."

"If I had but something new to tell," said the old man. "But how did the child get his feet wet?"

"That is the very thing that nobody can make out," said his mother.

"Am I to hear a fairy tale?" asked the little boy.

"Yes, if you can tell me exactly—for I must know that first—how deep the gutter is in the little street opposite, that you pass through in going to school."

"Just up to the middle of my boot," said the child; "but then I must go into the deep hole."

"Ah, ah! That's where the wet feet came from," said the old man. "I ought now to tell you a story; but I don't know any more."

"You can make one in a moment," said the little boy. "My mother says that all you look at can be turned into a fairy tale: and that you can find a story in everything."

"Yes, but such tales and stories are good for nothing. The right sort come of themselves; they tap at my forehead and say, 'Here we are.'"

"Won't there be a tap soon?" asked the little boy. And his mother laughed, put some Elder flowers in the teapot, and poured boiling water upon them.

"Do tell me something! Pray do!"

"Yes, if a fairy tale would come of its own accord; but they are proud and haughty, and come only when they choose. Stop!" said he, all on a sudden. "I have it! Pay attention! There is one in the teapot!"

And the little boy looked at the teapot. The cover rose more and more; and the Elderflowers came forth so fresh and white, and shot up long branches. Out of the spout even did they spread themselves on all sides, and grew larger and larger; it was a splendid Elderbush, a whole tree; and it reached into the very bed, and pushed the curtains aside. How it bloomed! And what an odour! In the middle of the bush sat a friendly looking old woman in a most strange dress. It was quite green, like the leaves of the elder, and was trimmed with large white Elderflowers; so that at first one could not tell whether it was a stuff, or natural green and real flowers.

"What's that woman's name?" asked the little boy.

"The Greeks and Romans," said the old man, "called her a Dryad; but that we do not understand. The people who live in the New Booths have a much better name for her; they call her 'old Granny'—and she it is to whom you are to pay attention. Now listen, and look at the beautiful Elderbush.

"Just such another large blooming Elder Tree stands near the New Booths. It grew there in the corner of a little miserable courtyard; and under it sat, of an afternoon, in the most splendid sunshine, two old people; an old, old seaman, and his old, old wife. They had great-grandchildren, and were soon to celebrate the fiftieth anniversary of their marriage; but they could not exactly recollect the date: and old Granny sat in the tree, and looked as pleased as now. 'I know the date,' said she; but those below did not hear her, for they were talking about old times.

"'Yes, can't you remember when we were very little,' said the old seaman, 'and ran and played about? It was the very same courtyard where we now are, and we stuck slips in the ground, and made a garden.'

"'I remember it well,' said the old woman; 'I remember it quite well. We watered the slips, and one of them was an Elderbush. It took root, put forth green shoots, and grew up to be the large tree under which we old folks are now sitting.'

"'To be sure,' said he. 'And there in the corner stood a waterpail, where I used to swim my boats.'

"'True; but first we went to school to learn somewhat,' said she; 'and then we were confirmed. We both cried; but in the afternoon we went up the Round Tower, and looked down on Copenhagen, and far, far away over the water; then we went to Friedericksberg, where the King and the Queen were sailing about in their splendid barges.'

"'But I had a different sort of sailing to that, later; and that, too, for many a year; a long way off, on great voyages.'

"'Yes, many a time have I wept for your sake,' said she. 'I thought you were dead and gone, and lying down in the deep waters. Many a night have I got up to see if the wind had not changed: and changed it had, sure enough; but you never came. I remember so well one day, when the rain was pouring down in torrents, the scavengers were before the house where I was in service, and I had come up with the dust, and remained standing at the door—it was dreadful weather—when just as I was there, the postman came and gave me a letter. It was from you! What a tour that letter had made! I opened it instantly and read: I laughed and wept. I was so happy. In it I read that you were in warm lands where the coffee-tree grows. What a blessed land that must be! You related so much, and I saw it all the while the rain was pouring down, and I standing there with the dust-box. At the same moment came someone who embraced me.'

"'Yes; but you gave him a good box on his ear that made it tingle!'

"'But I did not know it was you. You arrived as soon as your letter, and you were so handsome—that you still are—and had a long yellow silk handkerchief round your neck, and a brand-new hat on; oh, you were so dashing! Good heavens! What weather it was, and what a state the street was in!'

"'And then we married,' said he. 'Don't you remember? And then we had our first little boy, and then Mary, and Nicholas, and Peter, and Christian.'

"'Yes, and how they all grew up to be honest people, and were beloved by everybody.'

"'And their children also have children,' said the old sailor; "yes, those are our grandchildren, full of strength and vigor. It was, methinks, about this season that we had our wedding."

"'Yes, this very day is the fiftieth anniversary of the marriage,' said old Granny, sticking her head between the two old people; who thought it was their neighbor who nodded to them. They looked at each other and held one another by the hand. Soon after came their children, and their grandchildren; for they knew well enough that it was the day of the fiftieth anniversary, and had come with their gratulations that very morning; but the old people had forgotten it, although they were able to remember all that had happened many years ago. And the Elderbush sent forth a strong odour in the sun, that was just about to set, and shone right in the old people's faces. They both looked so rosy-cheeked; and the youngest of the grandchildren danced around them, and called out quite delighted, that there was to be something very splendid that evening—they were all to have hot potatoes. And old Nanny nodded in the bush, and shouted 'hurrah!' with the rest."

"But that is no fairy tale," said the little boy, who was listening to the story.

"The thing is, you must understand it," said the narrator; "let us ask old Nanny."

"That was no fairy tale, 'tis true," said old Nanny; "but now it's coming. The most wonderful fairy tales grow out of that which is reality; were that not the case, you know, my magnificent Elderbush could not have grown out of the teapot." And then she took the little boy out of bed, laid him on her bosom, and the branches of the Elder Tree, full of flowers, closed around her. They sat in an aerial dwelling, and it flew with them through the air. Oh, it was wondrous beautiful! Old Nanny had grown all of a sudden a young and pretty maiden; but her robe was still the same green stuff with white flowers, which she had worn before. On her bosom she had a real Elderflower, and in her yellow waving hair a wreath of the flowers; her eyes were so large and blue that it was a pleasure to look at them; she kissed the boy, and now they were of the same age and felt alike.

Hand in hand they went out of the bower, and they were standing in the beautiful garden of their home. Near the green lawn papa's walking-stick was tied, and for the little ones it seemed to be endowed with life; for as soon as they got astride it, the round polished knob was turned into a magnificent neighing head, a long black mane fluttered in the breeze, and four slender yet strong legs shot out. The animal was strong and handsome, and away they went at full gallop round the lawn.

"Huzza! Now we are riding miles off," said the boy. "We are riding away to the castle where we were last year!"

And on they rode round the grassplot; and the little maiden, who, we know, was no one else but old Nanny, kept on crying out, "Now we are in the country! Don't you see the farmhouse yonder? And there is an Elder Tree standing beside it; and the cock is scraping away the earth for the hens, look, how he struts! And now we are close to the church. It lies high upon the hill, between the large oak trees, one of which is half decayed. And now we are by the smithy, where the fire is blazing, and where the half-naked men are banging with their hammers till the sparks fly about. Away! away! To the beautiful countryseat!"

And all that the little maiden, who sat behind on the stick, spoke of, flew by in reality. The boy saw it all, and yet they were only going round the grassplot. Then they played in a side avenue, and marked out a little garden on the earth; and they took Elder blossoms from their hair, planted them, and they grew just like those the old people planted when they were children, as related before. They went hand in hand, as the old people had done when they were children; but not to the Round Tower, or to Fredericksburg; no, the little damsel wound her arms round the boy, and then they flew far away through all Denmark. And spring came, and summer; and then it was autumn, and then winter; and a thousand pictures were reflected in the eye and in the heart of the boy; and the little girl always sang to him, "This you will never forget." And during their whole flight the Elder Tree smelt so sweet and odorous; he remarked on the roses and the fresh beeches, but the Elder Tree had a more wondrous fragrance, for its flowers hung on the breast of the little maiden; and there, too, did he often lay his head during the flight.

"It is lovely here in spring!" said the young maiden. And they stood in a beech wood that had just put on its first green, where the woodroof at their feet sent forth its fragrance, and the pale-red anemone looked so pretty among the verdure. "Oh, would it were always spring in the sweetly smelling Danish beech forests!"

"It is lovely here in summer!" said she. And she flew past old castles of bygone days of chivalry, where the red walls and the embattled gables were mirrored in the canal, where the swans were swimming, and peered up into the old cool avenues. In the fields the corn was waving like the sea; in the ditches red and yellow flowers were growing; while wild-drone flowers, and blooming convolvuluses were creeping in the hedges; and towards evening the moon rose round and large, and the haycocks in the meadows smelt so sweetly. "This one never forgets!"

"It is lovely here in autumn!" said the little maiden. And suddenly the atmosphere grew as blue again as before; the forest grew red, and green, and yellow colored. The dogs came leaping along, and whole flocks of wild fowl flew over the cairn, where blackberry bushes were hanging round the old stones. The sea was dark blue, covered with ships full of white sails; and in the barn old women, maidens, and children were sitting picking hops into a large cask; the young sang songs, but the old told fairy tales of mountain-sprites and soothsayers. Nothing could be more charming.

"It is delightful here in winter!" said the little maiden. And all the trees were covered with hoar frost; they looked like white corals; the snow crackled under foot, as if one had new boots on; and one falling star after the other was seen in the sky. The Christmas tree was lighted in the room; presents were there, and good humor reigned. In the country the violin sounded in the room of the peasant; the newly baked cakes were attacked; even the poorest child said, "It is really delightful here in winter!"

Yes, it was delightful; and the little maiden showed the boy everything; and the Elder Tree still was fragrant, and the red flag, with the white cross, was still waving: the flag under which the old seaman in the New Booths had sailed. And the boy grew up to be a lad, and was to go forth in the wide world, far, far away to warm lands, where the coffee-tree grows; but at his departure the little maiden took an Elder blossom from her bosom, and gave it him to keep; and it was placed between the leaves of his Prayer Book; and when in foreign lands he opened the book, it was always at the place where the keepsake-flower lay; and the more he looked at it, the fresher it became; he felt, as it were, the fragrance of the Danish groves; and from among the leaves of the flowers he could distinctly see the little maiden, peeping forth with her bright blue eyes—and then she whispered, "It is delightful here in Spring, Summer, Autumn, and Winter;" and a hundred visions glided before his mind.

Thus passed many years, and he was now an old man, and sat with his old wife under the blooming tree. They held each other by the hand, as the old grandfather and grandmother yonder in the New Booths did, and they talked exactly like them of old times, and of the fiftieth anniversary of their wedding. The little maiden, with the blue eyes, and with Elder blossoms in her hair, sat in the tree, nodded to both of them, and said, "Today is the fiftieth anniversary!" And then she took two flowers out of her hair, and kissed them. First, they shone like silver, then like gold; and when they laid them on the heads of the old people, each flower became a golden crown. So there they both sat, like a king and a queen, under the fragrant tree, that looked exactly like an elder: the old man told his wife the story of "Old Nanny," as it had been told him when a boy. And it seemed to both of them it contained much that resembled their own history; and those parts that were like it pleased them best.

"Thus it is," said the little maiden in the tree, "some call me 'Old Nanny,' others a 'Dryad,' but, in reality, my name is 'Remembrance'; 'tis I who sit in the tree that grows and grows! I can remember; I can tell things! Let me see if you have my flower still?"

And the old man opened his Prayer Book. There lay the Elder blossom, as fresh as if it had been placed there but a short time before; and Remembrance nodded, and the old people, decked with crowns of gold, sat in the flush of the evening sun. They closed their eyes, and—and—! Yes, that's the end of the story!

The little boy lay in his bed; he did not know if he had dreamed or not, or if he had been listening while someone told him the story. The teapot was standing on the table, but no Elder Tree was growing out of it! And the old man, who had been talking, was just on the point of going out at the door, and he did go.

"How splendid that was!" said the little boy. "Mother, I have been to warm countries."

"So I should think," said his mother. "When one has drunk two good cupfuls of Elder flower tea, 'tis likely enough one goes into warm climates;" and she tucked him up nicely, least he should take cold. "You have had a good sleep while I have been sitting here, and arguing with him whether it was a story or a fairy tale."

"And where is old Nanny?" asked the little boy.

"In the teapot," said his mother; "and there she may remain."

The Bell

People said, "The Evening Bell is sounding, the sun is setting." For a strange wondrous tone was heard in the narrow streets of a large town. It was like the sound of a church bell: but it was only heard for a moment, for the rolling of the carriages and the voices of the multitude made too great a noise.

Those persons who were walking outside the town, where the houses were farther apart, with gardens or little fields between them, could see the evening sky still better, and heard the sound of the bell much more distinctly. It was as if the tones came from a church in the still forest; people looked thitherward, and felt their minds attuned most solemnly.

A long time passed, and people said to each other, "I wonder if there is a church out in the wood? The bell has a tone that is wondrous sweet; let us stroll thither, and examine the matter nearer." And the rich people drove out, and the poor walked, but the way seemed strangely long to them; and when they came to a clump of willows which grew on the skirts of the forest, they sat down, and looked up at the long branches, and fancied they were now in the depth of the green wood. The confectioner of the town came out, and set up his booth there; and soon after came another confectioner, who hung a bell over his stand, as a sign or ornament, but it had no clapper, and it was tarred over to preserve it from the rain. When all the people returned home, they said it had been very romantic, and that it was quite a different sort of thing to a picnic or tea party. There were three persons who asserted they had penetrated to the end of the forest, and that they had always heard the wonderful sounds of the bell, but it had seemed to them as if it had come from the town. One wrote a whole poem about it, and said the bell sounded like the voice of a mother to a good dear child, and that no melody was sweeter than the tones of the bell. The king of the country was also observant of it, and vowed that he who could discover whence the sounds proceeded, should have the title of "Universal Bellringer," even if it were not really a bell.

Many persons now went to the wood, for the sake of getting the place, but one only returned with a sort of explanation; for nobody went far enough, that one not further than the others. However, he said that the sound proceeded from a very large owl, in a hollow tree; a sort of learned owl, that continually knocked its head against the branches. But whether the sound came from his head or from the hollow tree, that no one could say with certainty. So now he got the place of "Universal Bellringer," and wrote yearly a short treatise "On the Owl;" but everybody was just as wise as before.

It was the day of confirmation. The clergyman had spoken so touchingly, the children who were confirmed had been greatly moved; it was an eventful day for them; from children they become all at once grown-up-persons; it was as if their infant souls were now to fly all at once into persons with more understanding. The sun was shining gloriously; the children that had been confirmed went out of the town; and from the wood was borne towards them the sounds of the unknown bell with wonderful distinctness. They all immediately felt a wish to go thither; all except three. One of them had to go home to try on a ball-dress; for it was just the dress and the ball which had caused her to be confirmed this time, for otherwise she would not have come; the other was a poor boy, who had borrowed his coat and boots to be confirmed in from the innkeeper's son, and he was to give them back by a certain hour; the third said that he never went to a strange place if his parents were not with him—that he had always been a good boy hitherto, and would still be so now that he was confirmed, and that one ought not to laugh at him for it: the others, however, did make fun of him, after all.

There were three, therefore, that did not go; the others hastened on. The sun shone, the birds sang, and the children sang too, and each held the other by the hand; for as yet they had none of them any high office, and were all of equal rank in the eye of God.

But two of the youngest soon grew tired, and both returned to town; two little girls sat down, and twined garlands, so they did not go either; and when the others reached the willow tree, where the confectioner was, they said, "Now we are there! In reality the bell does not exist; it is only a fancy that people have taken into their heads!"

At the same moment the bell sounded deep in the wood, so clear and solemnly that five or six determined to penetrate somewhat further. It was so thick, and the foliage so dense, that it was quite fatiguing to proceed. Woodroof and anemones grew almost too high; blooming convolvuluses and blackberry bushes hung in long garlands from tree to tree, where the nightingale sang and the sunbeams were playing: it was very beautiful, but it was no place for girls to go; their clothes would get so torn. Large blocks of stone lay there, overgrown with moss of every color; the fresh spring bubbled forth, and made a strange gurgling sound.

"That surely cannot be the bell," said one of the children, lying down and listening. "This must be looked to." So he remained, and let the others go on without him.

They afterwards came to a little house, made of branches and the bark of trees; a large wild apple tree bent over it, as if it would shower down all its blessings on the roof, where roses were blooming. The long stems twined round the gable, on which there hung a small bell.

Was it that which people had heard? Yes, everybody was unanimous on the subject, except one, who said that the bell was too small and too fine to be heard at so great a distance, and besides it was very different tones to those that could move a human heart in such a manner. It was a king's son who spoke; whereon the others said, "Such people always want to be wiser than everybody else."

They now let him go on alone; and as he went, his breast was filled more and more with the forest solitude; but he still heard the little bell with which the others were so satisfied, and now and then, when the wind blew, he could also hear the people singing who were sitting at tea where the confectioner had his tent; but the deep sound of the bell rose louder; it was almost as if an organ were accompanying it, and the tones came from the left hand, the side where the heart is placed. A rustling was heard in the bushes, and a little boy stood before the King's Son, a boy in wooden shoes, and with so short a jacket that one could see what long wrists he had. Both knew each other: the boy was that one among the children who could not come because he had to go home and return his jacket and boots to the innkeeper's son. This he had done, and was now going on in wooden shoes and in his humble dress, for the bell sounded with so deep a tone, and with such strange power, that proceed he must.

"Why, then, we can go together," said the King's Son. But the poor child that had been confirmed was quite ashamed; he looked at his wooden shoes, pulled at the short sleeves of his jacket, and said that he was afraid he could not walk so fast; besides, he thought that the bell must be looked for to the right; for that was the place where all sorts of beautiful things were to be found.

"But there we shall not meet," said the King's Son, nodding at the same time to the poor boy, who went into the darkest, thickest part of the wood, where thorns tore his humble dress, and scratched his face and hands and feet till they bled. The King's Son got some scratches too; but the sun shone on his path, and it is him that we will follow, for he was an excellent and resolute youth.

"I must and will find the bell," said he, "even if I am obliged to go to the end of the world."

The ugly apes sat upon the trees, and grinned. "Shall we thrash him?" said they. "Shall we thrash him? He is the son of a king!"

But on he went, without being disheartened, deeper and deeper into the wood, where the most wonderful flowers were growing. There stood white lilies with blood-red stamina, sky blue tulips, which shone as they waved in the winds, and apple trees, the apples of which looked exactly like large soap bubbles: so only think how the trees must have sparkled in the sunshine! Around the nicest green meads, where the deer were playing in the grass, grew magnificent oaks and beeches; and if the bark of one of the trees was cracked, there grass and long creeping plants grew in the crevices. And there were large calm lakes there too, in which white swans were swimming, and beat the air with their wings. The King's Son often stood still and listened. He thought the bell sounded from the depths of these still lakes; but then he remarked again that the tone proceeded not from there, but farther off, from out the depths of the forest.

The sun now set: the atmosphere glowed like fire. It was still in the woods, so very still; and he fell on his knees, sung his evening hymn, and said: "I cannot find what I seek; the sun is going down, and night is coming—the dark, dark night. Yet perhaps I may be able once more to see the round red sun before he entirely disappears. I will climb up yonder rock."

And he seized hold of the creeping plants, and the roots of trees—climbed up the moist stones where the water snakes were writhing and the toads were croaking—and he gained the summit before the sun had quite gone down. How magnificent was the sight from this height! The sea—the great, the glorious sea, that dashed its long waves against the coast—was stretched out before him. And yonder, where sea and sky meet, stood the sun, like a large shining altar, all melted together in the most glowing colors. And the wood and the sea sang a song of rejoicing, and his heart sang with the rest: all nature was a vast holy church, in which the trees and the buoyant clouds were the pillars, flowers and grass the velvet carpeting, and heaven itself the large cupola. The red colors above faded away as the sun vanished, but a million stars were lighted, a million lamps shone; and the King's Son spread out his arms towards heaven, and wood, and sea; when at the same moment, coming by a path to the right, appeared, in his wooden shoes and jacket, the poor boy who had been confirmed with him. He had followed his own path, and had reached the spot just as soon as the son of the king had done. They ran towards each other, and stood together hand in hand in the vast church of nature and of poetry, while over them sounded the invisible holy bell: blessed spirits floated around them, and lifted up their voices in a rejoicing hallelujah!

The Old House

In the street, up there, was an old, a very old house—it was almost three hundred years old, for that might be known by reading the great beam on which the date of the year was carved: together with tulips and hop-binds there were whole verses spelled as in former times, and over every window was a distorted face cut out in the beam. The one story stood forward a great way over the other; and directly under the eaves was a leaden spout with a dragon's head; the rainwater should have run out of the mouth, but it ran out of the belly, for there was a hole in the spout.

All the other houses in the street were so new and so neat, with large windowpanes and smooth walls, one could easily see that they would have nothing to do with the old house: they certainly thought, "How long is that old, decayed thing to stand here as a spectacle in the street? And then the projecting windows stand so far out, that no one can see from our windows what happens in that direction! The steps are as broad as those of a palace, and as high as to a church tower. The iron railings look just like the door to an old family vault, and then they have brass tops—that's so stupid!"

On the other side of the street were also new and neat houses, and they thought just as the others did; but at the window opposite the old house there sat a little boy with fresh rosy cheeks and bright beaming eyes: he certainly liked the old house best, and that both in sunshine and moonshine. And when he looked across at the wall where the mortar had fallen out, he could sit and find out there the strangest figures imaginable; exactly as the street had appeared before, with steps, projecting windows, and pointed gables; he could see soldiers with halberds, and spouts where the water ran, like dragons and serpents. That was a house to look at; and there lived an old man, who wore plush breeches; and he had a coat with large brass buttons, and a wig that one could see was a real wig. Every morning there came an old fellow to him who put his rooms in order, and went on errands; otherwise, the old man in the plush breeches was quite alone in the old house. Now and then he came to the window and looked out, and the little boy nodded to him, and the old man nodded again, and so they became acquaintances, and then they were friends, although they had never spoken to each other—but that made no difference. The little boy heard his parents say, "The old man opposite is very well off, but he is so very, very lonely!"

The Sunday following, the little boy took something, and wrapped it up in a piece of paper, went downstairs, and stood in the doorway; and when the man who went on errands came past, he said to him, "I say, master! will you give this to the old man over the way from me? I have two pewter soldiers—this is one of them, and he shall have it, for I know he is so very, very lonely."

And the old errand man looked quite pleased, nodded, and took the pewter soldier over to the old house. Afterwards there came a message; it was to ask if the little boy himself had not a wish to come over and pay a visit; and so he got permission of his parents, and then went over to the old house.

And the brass balls on the iron railings shone much brighter than ever; one would have thought they were polished on account of the visit; and it was as if the carved-out trumpeters—for there were trumpeters, who stood in tulips, carved out on the door—blew with all their might, their cheeks appeared so much rounder than before. Yes, they blew—"Trateratra! The little boy comes! Trateratra!"—and then the door opened.

The whole passage was hung with portraits of knights in armor, and ladies in silken gowns; and the armor rattled, and the silken gowns rustled! And then there was a flight of stairs which went a good way upwards, and a little way downwards, and then one came on a balcony which was in a very dilapidated state, sure enough, with large holes and long crevices, but grass grew there and leaves out of them altogether, for the whole balcony outside, the yard, and the walls, were overgrown with so much green stuff, that it looked like a garden; only a balcony. Here stood old flowerpots with faces, and the flowers grew just as they liked. One of the pots was quite overrun on all sides with pinks, that is to say, with the green part; shoot stood by shoot, and it said quite distinctly, "The air has cherished me, the sun has kissed me, and promised me a little flower on Sunday! a little flower on Sunday!"

And then they entered a chamber where the walls were covered with hog's leather, and printed with gold flowers.

"The gilding decays, but hog's leather stays!" said the walls.

And there stood easy chairs, with such high backs, and so carved out, and with arms on both sides. "Sit down! sit down!" said they. "Ugh! how I creak; now I shall certainly get the gout, like the old clothespress, ugh!"

And then the little boy came into the room where the projecting windows were, and where the old man sat.

"I thank you for the pewter soldier, my little friend!" said the old man. "And I thank you because you come over to me."

"Thankee! thankee!" or "cranky! cranky!" sounded from all the furniture; there was so much of it, that each article stood in the other's way, to get a look at the little boy.

In the middle of the wall hung a picture representing a beautiful lady, so young, so glad, but dressed quite as in former times, with clothes that stood quite stiff, and with powder in her hair; she neither said "thankee, thankee!" nor "cranky, cranky!" but looked with her mild eyes at the little boy, who directly asked the old man, "Where did you get her?"

"Yonder, at the broker's," said the old man, "where there are so many pictures hanging. No one knows or cares about them, for they are all of them buried; but I knew her in bygone days, and now she has been dead and gone these fifty years!"

Under the picture, in a glazed frame, there hung a bouquet of withered flowers; they were almost fifty years old; they looked so very old!

The pendulum of the great clock went to and fro, and the hands turned, and everything in the room became still older; but they did not observe it.

"They say at home," said the little boy, "that you are so very, very lonely!"

"Oh!" said he. "The old thoughts, with what they may bring with them, come and visit me, and now you also come! I am very well off!"

Then he took a book with pictures in it down from the shelf; there were whole long processions and pageants, with the strangest characters, which one never sees now-a-days; soldiers like the knave of clubs, and citizens with waving flags: the tailors had theirs, with a pair of shears held by two lions—and the shoemakers theirs, without boots, but with an eagle that had two heads, for the shoemakers must have everything so that they can say, it is a pair! Yes, that was a picture book!

The old man now went into the other room to fetch preserves, apples, and nuts—yes, it was delightful over there in the old house.

"I cannot bear it any longer!" said the pewter soldier, who sat on the drawers. "It is so lonely and melancholy here! But when one has been in a family circle one cannot accustom oneself to this life! I cannot bear it any longer! The whole day is so long, and the evenings are still longer! Here it is not at all as it is over the way at your home, where your father and mother spoke so pleasantly, and where you and all your sweet children made such a delightful noise. Nay, how lonely the old man is—do you think that he gets kisses? Do you think he gets mild eyes, or a Christmas tree? He will get nothing but a grave! I can bear it no longer!"

"You must not let it grieve you so much," said the little boy. "I find it so very delightful here, and then all the old thoughts, with what they may bring with them, they come and visit here."

"Yes, it's all very well, but I see nothing of them, and I don't know them!" said the pewter soldier. "I cannot bear it!"

"But you must!" said the little boy.

Then in came the old man with the most pleased and happy face, the most delicious preserves, apples, and nuts, and so the little boy thought no more about the pewter soldier.

The little boy returned home happy and pleased, and weeks and days passed away, and nods were made to the old house, and from the old house, and then the little boy went over there again.

The carved trumpeters blew, "Trateratra! There is the little boy! Trateratra!" and the swords and armor on the knights' portraits rattled, and the silk gowns rustled; the hog's leather spoke, and the old chairs had the gout in their legs and rheumatism in their backs: Ugh! it was exactly like the first time, for over there one day and hour was just like another.

"I cannot bear it!" said the pewter soldier. "I have shed pewter tears! It is too melancholy! Rather let me go to the wars and lose arms and legs! It would at least be a change. I cannot bear it longer! Now, I know what it is to have a visit from one's old thoughts, with what they may bring with them! I have had a visit from mine, and you may be sure it is no pleasant thing in the end; I was at last about to jump down from the drawers.

"I saw you all over there at home so distinctly, as if you really were here; it was again that Sunday morning; all you children stood before the table and sung your Psalms, as you do every morning. You stood devoutly with folded hands; and father and mother were just as pious; and then the door was opened, and little sister Mary, who is not two years old yet, and who always dances when she hears music or singing, of whatever kind it may be, was put into the room—though she ought not to have been there—and then she began to dance, but could not keep time, because the tones were so long; and then she stood, first on the one leg, and bent her head forwards, and then on the other leg, and bent her head forwards—but all would not do. You stood very seriously all together, although it was difficult enough; but I laughed to myself, and then I fell off the table, and got a bump, which I have still—for it was not right of me to laugh. But the whole now passes before me again in thought, and everything that I have lived to see; and these are the old thoughts, with what they may bring with them.

"Tell me if you still sing on Sundays? Tell me something about little Mary! And how my comrade, the other pewter soldier, lives! Yes, he is happy enough, that's sure! I cannot bear it any longer!"

"You are given away as a present!" said the little boy. "You must remain. Can you not understand that?"

The old man now came with a drawer, in which there was much to be seen, both "tin boxes" and "balsam boxes," old cards, so large and so gilded, such as one never sees them now. And several drawers were opened, and the piano was opened; it had landscapes on the inside of the lid, and it was so hoarse when the old man played on it! and then he hummed a song.

"Yes, she could sing that!" said he, and nodded to the portrait, which he had bought at the broker's, and the old man's eyes shone so bright!

"I will go to the wars! I will go to the wars!" shouted the pewter soldier as loud as he could, and threw himself off the drawers right down on the floor. What became of him? The old man sought, and the little boy sought; he was away, and he stayed away.

"I shall find him!" said the old man; but he never found him. The floor was too open—the pewter soldier had fallen through a crevice, and there he lay as in an open tomb.

That day passed, and the little boy went home, and that week passed, and several weeks too. The windows were quite frozen, the little boy was obliged to sit and breathe on them to get a peep hole over to the old house, and there the snow had been blown into all the carved work and inscriptions; it lay quite up over the steps, just as if there was no one at home—nor was there any one at home—the old man was dead!

In the evening there was a hearse seen before the door, and he was borne into it in his coffin: he was now to go out into the country, to lie in his grave. He was driven out there, but no one followed; all his friends were dead, and the little boy kissed his hand to the coffin as it was driven away.

Some days afterwards there was an auction at the old house, and the little boy saw from his window how they carried the old knights and the old ladies away, the flowerpots with the long ears, the old chairs, and the old clothespresses. Something came here, and something came there; the portrait of her who had been found at the broker's came to the broker's again; and there it hung, for no one knew her more—no one cared about the old picture.

In the spring they pulled the house down, for, as people said, it was a ruin. One could see from the street right into the room with the hog's-leather hanging, which was slashed and torn; and the green grass and leaves about the balcony hung quite wild about the falling beams. And then it was put to rights.

"That was a relief," said the neighboring houses.

A fine house was built there, with large windows, and smooth white walls; but before it, where the old house had in fact stood, was a little garden laid out, and a wild grapevine ran up the wall of the neighboring house. Before the garden there was a large iron railing with an iron door, it looked quite splendid, and people stood still and peeped in, and the sparrows hung by scores in the vine, and chattered away at each other as well as they could, but it was not about the old house, for they could not remember it, so many years had passed—so many that the little boy had grown up to a whole man, yes, a clever man, and a pleasure to his parents; and he had just been married, and, together with his little wife, had come to live in the house here, where the garden was; and he stood by her there whilst she planted a field-flower that she found so pretty; she planted it with her little hand, and pressed the earth around it with her fingers. Oh! what was that? She had stuck herself. There sat something pointed, straight out of the soft mould.

It was—yes, guess! It was the pewter soldier, he that was lost up at the old man's, and had tumbled and turned about amongst the timber and the rubbish, and had at last laid for many years in the ground.

The young wife wiped the dirt off the soldier, first with a green leaf, and then with her fine handkerchief—it had such a delightful smell, that it was to the pewter soldier just as if he had awaked from a trance.

"Let me see him," said the young man. He laughed, and then shook his head. "Nay, it cannot be he; but he reminds me of a story about a pewter soldier which I had when I was a little boy!" And then he told his wife about the old house, and the old man, and about the pewter soldier that he sent over to him because he was so very, very lonely; and he told it as correctly as it had really been, so that the tears came into the eyes of his young wife, on account of the old house and the old man.

"It may possibly be, however, that it is the same pewter soldier!" said she. "I will take care of it, and remember all that you have told me; but you must show me the old man's grave!"

"But I do not know it," said he, "and no one knows it! All his friends were dead, no one took care of it, and I was then a little boy!"

"How very, very lonely he must have been!" said she.

"Very, very lonely!" said the pewter soldier. "But it is delightful not to be forgotten!"

"Delightful!" shouted something close by; but no one, except the pewter soldier, saw that it was a piece of the hog's-leather hangings; it had lost all its gilding, it looked like a piece of wet clay, but it had an opinion, and it gave it: "The gilding decays, but hog's leather stays!"

This the pewter soldier did not believe.

The Happy Family

Really, the largest green leaf in this country is a dock-leaf; if one holds it before one, it is like a whole apron, and if one holds it over one's head in rainy weather, it is almost as good as an umbrella, for it is so immensely large. The burdock never grows alone, but where there grows one there always grow several: it is a great delight, and all this delightfulness is snails' food. The great white snails which persons of quality in former times made fricassees of, ate, and said, "Hem, hem! how delicious!" for they thought it tasted so delicate—lived on dock-leaves, and therefore burdock seeds were sown.

Now, there was an old manor house, where they no longer ate snails, they were quite extinct; but the burdocks were not extinct, they grew and grew all over the walks and all the beds; they could not get the mastery over them—it was a whole forest of burdocks. Here and there stood an apple and a plum tree, or else one never would have thought that it was a garden; all was burdocks, and there lived the two last venerable old snails.

They themselves knew not how old they were, but they could remember very well that there had been many more; that they were of a family from foreign lands, and that for them and theirs the whole forest was planted. They had never been outside it, but they knew that there was still something more in the world, which was called the manor house, and that there they were boiled, and then they became black, and were then placed on a silver dish; but what happened further they knew not; or, in fact, what it was to be boiled, and to lie on a silver dish, they could not possibly imagine; but it was said to be delightful, and particularly genteel. Neither the chafers, the toads, nor the earthworms, whom they asked about it, could give them any information—none of them had been boiled or laid on a silver dish.

The old white snails were the first persons of distinction in the world, that they knew; the forest was planted for their sake, and the manor house was there that they might be boiled and laid on a silver dish.

Now they lived a very lonely and happy life; and as they had no children themselves, they had adopted a little common snail, which they brought up as their own; but the little one would not grow, for he was of a common family; but the old ones, especially Dame Mother Snail, thought they could observe how he increased in size, and she begged father, if he could not see it, that he would at least feel the little snail's shell; and then he felt it, and found the good dame was right.

One day there was a heavy storm of rain.

"Hear how it beats like a drum on the dock-leaves!" said Father Snail.

"There are also raindrops!" said Mother Snail. "And now the rain pours right down the stalk! You will see that it will be wet here! I am very happy to think that we have our good house, and the little one has his also! There is more done for us than for all other creatures, sure enough; but can you not see that we are folks of quality in the world? We are provided with a house from our birth, and the burdock forest is planted for our sakes! I should like to know how far it extends, and what there is outside!"

"There is nothing at all," said Father Snail. "No place can be better than ours, and I have nothing to wish for!"

"Yes," said the dame. "I would willingly go to the manorhouse, be boiled, and laid on a silver dish; all our forefathers have been treated so; there is something extraordinary in it, you may be sure!"

"The manor house has most likely fallen to ruin!" said Father Snail. "Or the burdocks have grown up over it, so that they cannot come out. There need not, however, be any haste about that; but you are always in such a tremendous hurry, and the little one is beginning to be the same. Has he not been creeping up that stalk these three days? It gives me a headache when I look up to him!"

"You must not scold him," said Mother Snail. "He creeps so carefully; he will afford us much pleasure—and we have nothing but him to live for! But have you not thought of it? Where shall we get a wife for him? Do you not think that there are some of our species at a great distance in the interior of the burdock forest?"

"Black snails, I dare say, there are enough of," said the old one. "Black snails without a house—but they are so common, and so conceited. But we might give the ants a commission to look out for us; they run to and fro as if they had something to do, and they certainly know of a wife for our little snail!"

"I know one, sure enough—the most charming one!" said one of the ants. "But I am afraid we shall hardly succeed, for she is a queen!"

"That is nothing!" said the old folks. "Has she a house?"

"She has a palace!" said the ant. "The finest ant's palace, with seven hundred passages!"

"I thank you!" said Mother Snail. "Our son shall not go into an anthill; if you know nothing better than that, we shall give the commission to the white gnats. They fly far and wide, in rain and sunshine; they know the whole forest here, both within and without."

"We have a wife for him," said the gnats. "At a hundred human paces from here there sits a little snail in her house, on a gooseberry bush; she is quite lonely, and old enough to be married. It is only a hundred human paces!"

"Well, then, let her come to him!" said the old ones. "He has a whole forest of burdocks, she has only a bush!"

And so they went and fetched little Miss Snail. It was a whole week before she arrived; but therein was just the very best of it, for one could thus see that she was of the same species.

And then the marriage was celebrated. Six earthworms shone as well as they could. In other respects the whole went off very quietly, for the old folks could not bear noise and merriment; but old Dame Snail made a brilliant speech. Father Snail could not speak, he was too much affected; and so they gave them as a dowry and inheritance, the whole forest of burdocks, and said—what they had always said—that it was the best in the world; and if they lived honestly and decently, and increased and multiplied, they and their children would once in the course of time come to the manor house, be boiled black, and laid on silver dishes. After this speech was made, the old ones crept into their shells, and never more came out. They slept; the young couple governed in the forest, and had a numerous progeny, but they were never boiled, and never came on the silver dishes; so from this they concluded that the manor house had fallen to ruins, and that all the men in the world were extinct; and as no one contradicted them, so, of course it was so. And the rain beat on the dock-leaves to make drum music for their sake, and the sun shone in order to give the burdock forest a color for their sakes; and they were very happy, and the whole family was happy; for they, indeed, were so.

The Garden of Paradise

There was once a king's son who had a larger and more beautiful collection of books than anyone else in the world, and full of splendid copperplate engravings. He could read and obtain information respecting every people of every land; but not a word could he find to explain the situation of the garden of paradise, and this was just what he most wished to know. His grandmother had told him when he was quite a little boy, just old enough to go to school, that each flower in the garden of paradise was a sweet cake, that the pistils were full of rich wine, that on one flower history was written, on another geography or tables; so those who wished to learn their lessons had only to eat some of the cakes, and the more they ate, the more history, geography, or tables they knew. He believed it all then; but as he grew older, and learnt more and more, he became wise enough to understand that the splendor of the garden of paradise must be very different to all this. "Oh, why did Eve pluck the fruit from the tree of knowledge? why did Adam eat the forbidden fruit?" thought the king's son: "if I had been there it would never have happened, and there would have been no sin in the world." The garden of paradise occupied all his thoughts till he reached his seventeenth year.

One day he was walking alone in the wood, which was his greatest pleasure, when evening came on. The clouds gathered, and the rain poured down as if the sky had been a waterspout; and it was as dark as the bottom of a well at midnight; sometimes he slipped over the smooth grass, or fell over stones that projected out of the rocky ground. Everything was dripping with moisture, and the poor prince had not a dry thread about him. He was obliged at last to climb over great blocks of stone, with water spurting from the thick moss. He began to feel quite faint, when he heard a most singular rushing noise, and saw before him a large cave, from which came a blaze of light. In the middle of the cave an immense fire was burning, and a noble stag, with its branching horns, was placed on a spit between the trunks of two pine trees. It was turning slowly before the fire, and an elderly woman, as large and strong as if she had been a man in disguise, sat by, throwing one piece of wood after another into the flames.

"Come in," she said to the prince; "sit down by the fire and dry yourself."

"There is a great draught here," said the prince, as he seated himself on the ground.

"It will be worse when my sons come home," replied the woman; "you are now in the cavern of the Winds, and my sons are the four Winds of heaven: can you understand that?"

"Where are your sons?" asked the prince.

"It is difficult to answer stupid questions," said the woman. "My sons have plenty of business on hand; they are playing at shuttlecock with the clouds up yonder in the king's hall," and she pointed upwards.

"Oh, indeed," said the prince; "but you speak more roughly and harshly and are not so gentle as the women I am used to."

"Yes, that is because they have nothing else to do; but I am obliged to be harsh, to keep my boys in order, and I can do it, although they are so headstrong. Do you see those four sacks hanging on the wall? Well, they are just as much afraid of those sacks, as you used to be of the rat behind the looking glass. I can bend the boys together, and put them in the sacks without any resistance on their parts, I can tell you. There they stay, and dare not attempt to come out until I allow them to do so. And here comes one of them."

It was the North Wind who came in, bringing with him a cold, piercing blast; large hailstones rattled on the floor, and snowflakes were scattered around in all directions. He wore a bearskin dress and cloak. His sealskin cap was drawn over his ears, long icicles hung from his beard, and one hailstone after another rolled from the collar of his jacket.

"Don't go too near the fire," said the prince, "or your hands and face will be frostbitten."

"Frostbitten!" said the North Wind, with a loud laugh; "why frost is my greatest delight. What sort of a little snip are you, and how did you find your way to the cavern of the Winds?"

"He is my guest," said the old woman, "and if you are not satisfied with that explanation you can go into the sack. Do you understand me?"

That settled the matter. So the North Wind began to relate his adventures, whence he came, and where he had been for a whole month. "I come from the polar seas," he said; "I have been on the Bear's Island with the Russian walrus-hunters. I sat and slept at the helm of their ship, as they sailed away from North Cape. Sometimes when I woke, the storm-birds would fly about my legs. They are curious birds; they give one flap with their wings, and then on their outstretched pinions soar far away."

"Don't make such a long story of it," said the mother of the winds; "what sort of a place is Bear's Island?"

"A very beautiful place, with a floor for dancing as smooth and flat as a plate. Half-melted snow, partly covered with moss, sharp stones, and skeletons of walruses and polar bears, lie all about, their gigantic limbs in a state of green decay. It would seem as if the sun never shone there. I blew gently, to clear away the mist, and then I saw a little hut, which had been built from the wood of a wreck, and was covered with the skins of the walrus, the fleshy side outwards; it looked green and red, and on the roof sat a growling bear. Then I went to the seashore, to look after birds' nests, and saw the unfledged nestlings opening their mouths and screaming for food. I blew into the thousand little throats, and quickly stopped their screaming. Farther on were the walruses with pig's heads, and teeth a yard long, rolling about like great worms."

"You relate your adventures very well, my son," said the mother, "it makes my mouth water to hear you."

"After that," continued the North Wind, "the hunting commenced. The harpoon was flung into the breast of the walrus, so that a smoking stream of blood spurted forth like a fountain, and besprinkled the ice. Then I thought of my own game; I began to blow, and set my own ships, the great icebergs sailing, so that they might crush the boats. Oh, how the sailors howled and cried out! but I howled louder than they. They were obliged to unload their cargo, and throw their chests and the dead walruses on the ice. Then I sprinkled snow over them, and left them in their crushed boats to drift southward, and to taste salt water. They will never return to Bear's Island."

"So you have done mischief," said the mother of the Winds.

"I shall leave others to tell the good I have done," he replied. "But here comes my brother from the West; I like him best of all, for he has the smell of the sea about him, and brings in a cold, fresh air as he enters."

"Is that the little Zephyr?" asked the prince.

"Yes, it is the little Zephyr," said the old woman; "but he is not little now. In years gone by he was a beautiful boy; now that is all past."

He came in, looking like a wild man, and he wore a slouched hat to protect his head from injury. In his hand he carried a club, cut from a mahogany tree in the American forests, not a trifle to carry.

"Whence do you come?" asked the mother.

"I come from the wilds of the forests, where the thorny brambles form thick hedges between the trees; where the water snake lies in the wet grass, and mankind seem to be unknown."

"What were you doing there?"

"I looked into the deep river, and saw it rushing down from the rocks. The water drops mounted to the clouds and glittered in the rainbow. I saw the wild buffalo swimming in the river, but the strong tide carried him away amidst a flock of wild ducks, which flew into the air as the waters dashed onwards, leaving the buffalo to be hurled over the waterfall. This pleased me; so I raised a storm, which rooted up old trees, and sent them floating down the river."

"And what else have you done?" asked the old woman.

"I have rushed wildly across the savannahs; I have stroked the wild horses, and shaken the coconuts from the trees. Yes, I have many stories to relate; but I need not tell everything I know. You know it all very well, don't you, old lady?" And he kissed his mother so roughly, that she nearly fell backwards. Oh, he was, indeed, a wild fellow.

Now in came the South Wind, with a turban and a flowing Bedouin cloak.

"How cold it is here!" said he, throwing more wood on the fire. "It is easy to feel that the North Wind has arrived here before me."

"Why it is hot enough here to roast a bear," said the North Wind.

"You are a bear yourself," said the other.

"Do you want to be put in the sack, both of you?" said the old woman. "Sit down, now, on that stone, yonder, and tell me where you have been."

"In Africa, mother. I went out with the Hottentots, who were lion hunting in the Kaffir land, where the plains are covered with grass the color of a green olive; and here I ran races with the ostrich, but I soon outstripped him in swiftness. At last I came to the desert, in which lie the golden sands, looking like the bottom of the sea. Here I met a caravan, and the travellers had just killed their last camel, to obtain water; there was very little for them, and they continued their painful journey beneath the burning sun, and over the hot sands, which stretched before them a vast, boundless desert. Then I rolled myself

in the loose sand, and whirled it in burning columns over their heads. The dromedarys stood still in terror, while the merchants drew their caftans over their heads, and threw themselves on the ground before me, as they do before Allah, their god. Then I buried them beneath a pyramid of sand, which covers them all. When I blow that away on my next visit, the sun will bleach their bones, and travellers will see that others have been there before them; otherwise, in such a wild desert, they might not believe it possible."

"So you have done nothing but evil," said the mother. "Into the sack with you;" and, before he was aware, she had seized the South Wind round the body, and popped him into the bag. He rolled about on the floor, till she sat herself upon him to keep him still.

"These boys of yours are very lively," said the prince.

"Yes," she replied, "but I know how to correct them, when necessary; and here comes the fourth." In came the East Wind, dressed like someone from China.

"Oh, you come from that quarter, do you?" said she; "I thought you had been to the garden of paradise."

"I am going there tomorrow," he replied, "I have not been there for a hundred years. I have just come from China, where I danced round the porcelain tower till all the bells jingled again. In the streets an official flogging was taking place, and bamboo canes were being broken on the shoulders of men of every high position, from the first to the ninth grade. They cried, 'Many thanks, my fatherly benefactor;' but I am sure the words did not come from their hearts, so I rang the bells till they sounded, 'ding, ding-dong.'"

"You are a wild boy," said the old woman; "it is well for you that you are going tomorrow to the garden of paradise; you always get improved in your education there. Drink deeply from the fountain of wisdom while you are there, and bring home a bottleful for me."

"That I will," said the East Wind; "but why have you put my brother South in a bag? Let him out; for I want him to tell me about the phoenix bird. The princess always wants to hear of this bird when I pay her my visit every hundred years. If you will open the sack, sweetest mother, I will give you two pocketfuls of tea, green and fresh as when I gathered it from the spot where it grew."

"Well, for the sake of the tea, and because you are my own boy, I will open the bag."

She did so, and the South Wind crept out, looking quite cast down, because the prince had seen his disgrace.

"There is a palm leaf for the princess," he said. "The old phoenix, the only one in the world, gave it to me himself. He has scratched on it with his beak the whole of his history during the hundred years he has lived. She can there read how the old phoenix set fire to his own nest, and sat upon it while it was burning, like a Hindu widow. The dry twigs around the nest crackled and smoked till the flames burst forth and consumed the phoenix to ashes. Amidst the fire lay an egg, red hot, which presently burst with a loud report, and out flew a young bird. He is the only phoenix in the world, and the king over all the other birds. He has bitten a hole in the leaf which I give you, and that is his greeting to the princess."

"Now let us have something to eat," said the mother of the Winds. So they all sat down to feast on the roasted stag; and as the prince sat by the side of the East Wind, they soon became good friends.

"Pray tell me," said the prince, "who is that princess of whom you have been talking! and where lies the garden of paradise?"

"Ho! ho!" said the East Wind, "would you like to go there? Well, you can fly off with me tomorrow; but I must tell you one thing—no human being has been there since the time of Adam and Eve. I suppose you have read of them in your Bible."

"Of course I have," said the prince.

"Well," continued the East Wind, "when they were driven out of the garden of paradise, it sunk into the earth; but it retained its warm sunshine, its balmy air, and all its splendor. The fairy queen lives there, in the island of happiness, where death never comes, and all is beautiful. I can manage to take you there tomorrow, if you will sit on my back. But now don't talk anymore, for I want to go to sleep;" and then they all slept.

When the prince awoke in the early morning, he was not a little surprised at finding himself high up above the clouds. He was seated on the back of the East Wind, who held him faithfully; and they were so high in the air that woods and fields, rivers and lakes, as they lay beneath them, looked like a painted map.

"Good morning," said the East Wind. "You might have slept on a while; for there is very little to see in the flat country over which we are passing unless you like to count the churches; they look like spots of chalk on a green board." The green board was the name he gave to the green fields and meadows.

"It was very rude of me not to say goodbye to your mother and your brothers," said the prince.

"They will excuse you, as you were asleep," said the East Wind; and then they flew on faster than ever.

The leaves and branches of the trees rustled as they passed. When they flew over seas and lakes, the waves rose higher, and the large ships dipped into the water like diving swans. As darkness came on, towards evening, the great towns looked charming; lights were sparkling, now seen, now hidden, just as the sparks go out one after another on a piece of burnt paper. The prince clapped his hands with pleasure; but the East Wind advised him not to express his admiration in that manner, or he might fall down, and find himself hanging on a church steeple. The eagle in the dark forests flies swiftly; but faster than he flew the East Wind. The Cossack, on his small horse, rides lightly o'er the plains; but lighter still passed the prince on the wings of the wind.

"There are the Himalayas, the highest mountains in Asia," said the East Wind. "We shall soon reach the garden of paradise now."

Then, they turned southward, and the air became fragrant with the perfume of spices and flowers. Here figs and pomegranates grew wild, and the vines were covered with clusters of blue and purple grapes. Here they both descended to the earth, and stretched themselves on the soft grass, while the flowers bowed to the breath of the wind as if to welcome it. "Are we now in the garden of paradise?" asked the prince.

"No, indeed," replied the East Wind; "but we shall be there very soon. Do you see that wall of rocks, and the cavern beneath it, over which the grape vines hang like a green curtain? Through that cavern we must pass. Wrap your cloak round you; for while the sun scorches you here, a few steps farther it will be icy cold. The bird flying past the entrance to the cavern feels as if one wing were in the region of summer, and the other in the depths of winter."

"So this then is the way to the garden of paradise?" asked the prince, as they entered the cavern. It was indeed cold; but the cold soon passed, for the East Wind spread his wings, and they gleamed like the brightest fire. As they passed on through this wonderful cave, the prince could see great blocks of stone, from which water trickled, hanging over their heads in fantastic shapes. Sometimes it was so narrow that they had to creep on their hands and knees, while at other times it was lofty and wide, like the free air. It had the appearance of a chapel for the dead, with petrified organs and silent pipes. "We seem to be passing through the valley of death to the garden of paradise," said the prince.

But the East Wind answered not a word, only pointed forwards to a lovely blue light which gleamed in the distance. The blocks of stone assumed a misty appearance, till at last they looked like white clouds in moonlight. The air was fresh and balmy, like a breeze from the mountains perfumed with flowers from a valley of roses. A river, clear as the air itself, sparkled at their feet, while in its clear depths could be seen gold and silver fish sporting in the bright water, and purple eels emitting sparks of fire at every moment, while the broad leaves of the waterlilies, that floated on its surface, flickered with all the colors of the rainbow. The flower in its color of flame seemed to receive its nourishment from the water, as a lamp is sustained by oil. A marble bridge, of such exquisite workmanship that it appeared as if formed of lace and pearls, led to the island of happiness, in which bloomed the garden of paradise. The East Wind took the prince in his arms, and carried him over, while the flowers and the leaves sang the sweet songs of his childhood in tones so full and soft that no human voice could venture to imitate. Within the garden grew large trees, full of sap; but whether they were palm trees or gigantic water plants, the prince knew not. The climbing plants hung in garlands of green and gold, like the illuminations on the margins of old missals or twined among the initial letters. Birds, flowers, and festoons appeared intermingled in seeming confusion. Close by, on the grass, stood a group of peacocks, with radiant tails outspread to the sun. The prince touched them, and found, to his surprise, that they were not really birds, but the leaves of the burdock tree, which shone with the colors of a peacock's tail. The lion and the tiger, gentle and tame, were springing about like playful cats among the green bushes, whose perfume was like the fragrant blossom of the olive. The plumage of the woodpigeon glistened like pearls as it struck the lion's mane with its wings; while the antelope, usually so shy, stood near, nodding its head as if it wished to join in the frolic. The fairy of paradise next made her appearance. Her raiment shone like the sun, and her serene countenance beamed with happiness like that of a mother rejoicing over her child. She was young and beautiful, and a train of lovely maidens followed her, each wearing a bright star in her hair. The East Wind gave her the palm leaf, on which was written the history of the phoenix; and her eyes sparkled with joy. She then took the prince by the hand, and led him into her palace, the walls of which were richly colored, like a tulip leaf when it is turned to the sun. The roof had the appearance of an inverted flower, and the colors grew deeper and brighter to the gazer. The prince walked to a window, and saw what appeared to be the tree of knowledge of good and evil, with Adam and Eve standing by, and the serpent near them. "I thought they were banished from paradise," he said.

The princess smiled, and told him that time had engraved each event on a windowpane in the form of a picture; but, unlike other pictures, all that it represented lived and moved—the leaves rustled, and the persons went and came, as in a looking glass. He looked through another pane, and saw the ladder in Jacob's dream, on which the angels were ascending and descending with outspread wings. All that had ever happened in the world here lived and moved on the panes of glass, in pictures such as

time alone could produce. The fairy now led the prince into a large, lofty room with transparent walls, through which the light shone. Here were portraits, each one appearing more beautiful than the other—millions of happy beings, whose laughter and song mingled in one sweet melody: some of these were in such an elevated position that they appeared smaller than the smallest rosebud, or like pencil dots on paper. In the centre of the hall stood a tree, with drooping branches, from which hung golden apples, both great and small, looking like oranges amid the green leaves. It was the tree of knowledge of good and evil, from which Adam and Eve had plucked and eaten the forbidden fruit, and from each leaf trickled a bright red dewdrop, as if the tree were weeping tears of blood for their sin. "Let us now take the boat," said the fairy: "a sail on the cool waters will refresh us. But we shall not move from the spot, although the boat may rock on the swelling water; the countries of the world will glide before us, but we shall remain still."

It was indeed wonderful to behold. First came the lofty Alps, snow-clad, and covered with clouds and dark pines. The horn resounded, and the shepherds sang merrily in the valleys. The banana trees bent their drooping branches over the boat, black swans floated on the water, and singular animals and flowers appeared on the distant shore. New Holland, the fifth division of the world, now glided by, with mountains in the background, looking blue in the distance. They heard the song of the priests, and saw the wild dance of the savage to the sound of the drums and trumpets of bone; the pyramids of Egypt rising to the clouds; columns and sphinxes, overthrown and buried in the sand, followed in their turn; while the northern lights flashed out over the extinguished volcanoes of the north, in fireworks none could imitate.

The prince was delighted, and yet he saw hundreds of other wonderful things more than can be described. "Can I stay here forever?" asked he.

"That depends upon yourself," replied the fairy. "If you do not, like Adam, long for what is forbidden, you can remain here always."

"I should not touch the fruit on the tree of knowledge," said the prince; "there is abundance of fruit equally beautiful."

"Examine your own heart," said the princess, "and if you do not feel sure of its strength, return with the East Wind who brought you. He is about to fly back, and will not return here for a hundred years. The time will not seem to you more than a hundred hours, yet even that is a long time for temptation and resistance. Every evening, when I leave you, I shall be obliged to say, 'Come with me,' and to beckon to you with my hand. But you must not listen, nor move from your place to follow me; for with every step you will find your power to resist weaker. If once you attempted to follow me, you would soon find yourself in the hall, where grows the tree of knowledge, for I sleep beneath its perfumed branches. If you stooped over me, I should be forced to smile. If you then kissed my lips, the garden of paradise would sink into the earth, and to you it would be lost. A keen wind from the desert would howl around you; cold rain fall on your head, and sorrow and woe be your future lot."

"I will remain," said the prince.

So the East Wind kissed him on the forehead, and said, "Be firm; then shall we meet again when a hundred years have passed. Farewell, farewell." Then the East Wind spread his broad pinions, which shone like the lightning in harvest, or as the northern lights in a cold winter.

"Farewell, farewell," echoed the trees and the flowers.

Storks and pelicans flew after him in feathery bands, to accompany him to the boundaries of the garden.

"Now we will commence dancing," said the fairy; "and when it is nearly over at sunset, while I am dancing with you, I shall make a sign, and ask you to follow me: but do not obey. I shall be obliged to repeat the same thing for a hundred years; and each time, when the trial is past, if you resist, you will gain strength, till resistance becomes easy, and at last the temptation will be quite overcome. This evening, as it will be the first time, I have warned you."

After this the fairy led him into a large hall, filled with transparent lilies. The yellow stamina of each flower formed a tiny golden harp, from which came forth strains of music like the mingled tones of flute and lyre. Beautiful maidens, slender and graceful in form, and robed in transparent gauze, floated through the dance, and sang of the happy life in the garden of paradise, where death never entered, and where all would bloom forever in immortal youth. As the sun went down, the whole heavens became crimson and gold, and tinted the lilies with the hue of roses. Then the beautiful maidens offered to the prince sparkling wine; and when he had drank, he felt happiness greater than he had ever known before. Presently the background of the hall opened and the tree of knowledge appeared, surrounded by a halo of glory that almost blinded him. Voices, soft and lovely as his mother's, sounded in his ears, as if she were singing to him, "My child, my beloved child." Then the fairy beckoned to him, and said in sweet accents, "Come with me, come with me." Forgetting his promise, forgetting it even on the very first evening, he rushed towards her, while she continued to beckon to him and to smile. The fragrance around him overpowered his senses, the music from the harps sounded more entrancing, while around the tree appeared millions of smiling faces, nodding and singing. "Man should know everything; man is the lord of the earth." The tree of knowledge no longer wept tears of blood, for the dewdrops shone like glittering stars.

"Come, come," continued that thrilling voice, and the prince followed the call. At every step his cheeks glowed, and the blood rushed wildly through his veins. "I must follow," he cried; "it is not a sin, it cannot be, to follow beauty and joy. I only want to see her sleep, and nothing will happen unless I kiss her, and that I will not do, for I have strength to resist, and a determined will."

The fairy threw off her dazzling attire, bent back the boughs, and in another moment was hidden among them.

"I have not sinned yet," said the prince, "and I will not;" and then he pushed aside the boughs to follow the princess. She was lying already asleep, beautiful as only a fairy in the garden of paradise could be. She smiled as he bent over her, and he saw tears trembling out of her beautiful eyelashes. "Do you weep for me?" he whispered. "Oh weep not, thou loveliest of women. Now do I begin to understand the happiness of paradise; I feel it to my inmost soul, in every thought. A new life is born within me. One moment of such happiness is worth an eternity of darkness and woe." He stooped and kissed the tears from her eyes, and touched her lips with his.

A clap of thunder, loud and awful, resounded through the trembling air. All around him fell into ruin. The lovely fairy, the beautiful garden, sunk deeper and deeper. The prince saw it sinking down in the dark night till it shone only like a star in the distance beneath him. Then he felt a coldness, like death, creeping over him; his eyes closed, and he became insensible.

When he recovered, a chilling rain was beating upon him, and a sharp wind blew on his head. "Alas! what have I done?" he sighed; "I have sinned like Adam, and the garden of paradise has sunk into the earth." He opened his eyes, and saw the star in the distance, but it was the morning star in heaven which glittered in the darkness.

Presently he stood up and found himself in the depths of the forest, close to the cavern of the Winds, and the mother of the Winds sat by his side. She looked angry, and raised her arm in the air as she spoke. "The very first evening!" she said. "Well, I expected it! If you were my son, you should go into the sack."

"And there he will have to go at last," said a strong old man, with large black wings, and a scythe in his hand, whose name was Death. "He shall be laid in his coffin, but not yet. I will allow him to wander about the world for a while, to atone for his sin, and to give him time to become better. But I shall return when he least expects me. I shall lay him in a black coffin, place it on my head, and fly away with it beyond the stars. There also blooms a garden of paradise, and if he is good and pious he will be admitted; but if his thoughts are bad, and his heart is full of sin, he will sink with his coffin deeper than the garden of paradise has sunk. Once in every thousand years I shall go and fetch him, when he will either be condemned to sink still deeper, or be raised to a happier life in the world beyond the stars."